SPACE ACADEMY REJECTS

Book Two of the Space Academy Series

C. T. Phipps and Frank Martin

I0640233

So, I was in a fistfight with a giant reptile man. The hulking green mass loomed over me with at least two feet and an extra hundred kilograms of scaly muscle. That was including the tail, of course, that moved like a whip and was a fifth appendage I had to worry about in the pit. It was dressed in a kind of weird one-piece spandex that was the only thing that detracted from it looking like I was facing a savage animal.

Surrounding me and my opponent was a collection of humans, aliens, and even a few bots that were crying out for blood. We were in a poorly maintained shuttle maintenance bay that had been converted into a makeshift arena for tonight's blood sport. Betting favored the enormous lizard over the puny human. Go figure.

I was bare chested and wearing a pair of regulation Community Protector (aka Space Fleet) uniform pants and suffering from a light claw mark across my chest as well as face. My Sorkanan opponent was deceptively fast and each time I moved in to kick or punch him, he managed to maneuver me into range of his overwhelming grip.

My only advantage was the fact that Sorkanan arms had less reach than human beings. They were more like miniature T. rexes than descendants of Australopithecus like me. I could move underneath his attempts to grab and strike better than most. However, the next tail strike to hit me in the stomach knocked me to the ground as well as stripped me of my remaining fighting spirit.

CAST OF CHARACTERS

Lead

Vance Turbo, aka Vannevar Tagashi: Academy drop out, loudmouth, alleged genius.

Supporting Cast

Lt. Forty-Two: Sorkanan male security officer. He would love to thump most of you monkeys.

The Ambassador: The Notha Emperor's personal envoy. Kind of an ass.

Ambassador Balkt: A Kolahn ambassador working with the Kolahn Resettlement Project.

Admiral Saul Bendo: The Chief of Naval operations for EarthGov's Home Fleet. More politician than soldier these days.

Bob Just Bob: A retired Verdantian engineer who knows more about starships than you ever will.

Chief Sal Boxley: A skittish technician who has survived numerous horrific accidents in training before being dragooned into Department Twelve's service.

Martin Waverly Chang: A former professor of political science turned news commentator for the Homefront Entertainment Network.

The Emperor: Male Notha. The (former) Emperor of the Notha. Leader in-exile. Fat and decadent.

Cpt. Klaws: Verdantian. Captain of the *ESS Ares*. Affable and overly trusting.

Cpt. Rudra Laghari: Captain of the *ESS Caliburn*. Deeply hates Vance.

Light on Water: A Sklux Space Fleet officer. Overly differential and obsequious.

Lt. Leah Mass: Actual graduate of Space Academy, genius. Vance's ex. Psychic. Transwoman. Transhuman. Heroine.

Recruit Nak'la: A female Kolahn recruit seeking to avenge her family.

Nina the Vampire: A human who chooses to live as a vampire as her religion.

Hannah O'Brian: Genetically engineered superhuman merc. Cat-like agility and other qualities. Like her tail.

Lt. Leslie Park: Blue-skinned, black-haired demihuman bundle of love and joy. Also handy with a wrench.

Lieutenant Julius Something: An East African Union navigation officer who gets stuck with terrible duties.

Cpt. Kathy Tagawa: Hero of Earth's space program. Paragon of humanity. Aunt of Vance.

Ex-Ambassador Ketra T'Kal: Former ambassador of the Community. Ethereal Human. Weird space wizard. Likes checkers. Oh, and is sorta but not really dead.

SHAT-3221931: An AI of the *ESS Ares*. It is modeled after an actor of the Pre-First Contact era.

Danny Tagawa: Vance's cousin and hypercompetent sidekick. Kind of a kiss-up. Also weirdly unnoticeable.

Elektra T'Ketra: Ethereal. Mad scientist, bubbly, excitable. Sister of Shelly.

Shelly T'Ketra: Ethereal. Perpetual first officer, efficient, irritable. Sister of Elektra.

Tommy: A Sorkanan cadet that died during a space-walking accident. Vance's Uncle Ben and Gwen Stacy figure.

TRS-8021 "Trish": The AI of the ship. Human female personality. Annoyingly adorable.

Dr. Elizabeth Zard: Unfortunately named human female. Doctor of math *and* medicine. Prefers the former.

FOREWORD

S pace, the funniest frontier.

The sequel.

When I finished *Space Academy Dropouts*, I was left with a sense of emptiness that could only be described as like that of the cast after the *Wrath of Khan*. The cast had rediscovered their love of *Star Trek*, including a certain pointy eared thespian, and wanted to continue. So, I immediately decided that I would start on the second volume in this series despite the original being conceived as a standalone.

The ending of the first book was meant to be a subversion of the typical way these stories went. The ragtag band of misfits gathering to do the impossible is something that is usually the first step on a road rather than the last. Instead, it ends with them parting ways and deciding to go their own divergent paths.

Our heroes *don't* forge an eternal bond of friendship and go off to have more adventures. No, the band breaks up and they start their own lives. Certainly, Vance Turbo isn't going to be leading any new ships for a while yet as an ensign. Indeed, I had a lot of fun making fun of the *Star Trek* (2009) conceit that after saving the universe, Kirk would be put in charge of the *USS Enterprise* before getting a medal and maybe being made a Lieutenant (Junior Grade).

Space Academy Rejects picks up about six years after the events of the first book with a little more cushion to our heroes' careers. It was an interesting challenge to write what all of them had been up to for the past half-decade and change without losing the thread of who they were. I also had fun trying to figure out how the next band of oddballs would be assembled and sent on their merry way.

I had a lot of fun developing the world of this setting (and *Lucifer's Star* set several hundred years later) with the help of Michael Suttkus. Part of what makes comedy fun is it reacting off a world that either embraces its absurdity or is realistic enough to have actual stakes. In this book, I think you'll get to see a world that makes sense but is bounced off by a truly hilarious cast.

The world of *Space Academy Dropouts* is one where humanity is the new kids on the block. We're not the United States or China in space but something closer to Belgium or Slovenia. We're struggling to become part of an EU-like alliance of more advanced races while dissenters believe we should go it alone. Lots of things have improved for humanity and we're starting to get our act together, but it would be all too easy to end up falling back down versus ascending to a Roddenberry-esque utopia. It's just this humanity's luck to have a bunch of weirdos as their last best hope.

I've also scribbled many notes about how the wonderful world inside works and hope to spend many future adventures with the cast. Ones I intend to share with you.

CHAPTER ONE

This Planet is Doomed

So, I was in a fistfight with a giant reptile man. The hulking green mass loomed over me with at least sixty centimeters and an extra hundred kilograms of scaly muscle. That was including the tail, of course, that moved like a whip and was a fifth appendage I had to worry about in the pit. It was dressed in a kind of weird one-piece spandex that was the only thing that detracted from it looking like I was facing a savage animal.

Surrounding me and my opponent was a collection of humans, aliens, and even a few bots that were crying out for blood. We were in a poorly maintained shuttle maintenance bay that had been converted into a makeshift arena for tonight's blood sport. Betting favored the enormous lizard over the puny human. Go figure.

I was bare chested and wearing a pair of regulation Community Protector (aka Space Fleet) uniform pants and suffering from light claw marks across my chest as well as face. My Sorkanan opponent was deceptively fast and each time I moved in to kick or punch him, he managed to maneuver me into range of his overwhelming grip.

My only advantage was the fact that Sorkanan arms had less reach than human beings. They were more like miniature T. rexes than descendants of Australopithecus like me. I could move underneath his attempts to grab and strike better than most. However, the next tail strike to hit me in the stomach knocked me to the ground as well as stripped me of my remaining fighting spirit.

"Oomph!" I not-so-heroically said, slamming up against the back of the pit to the crowd's delight.

"Now you die, human!" my opponent shouted, grabbing me up in the air and spinning me around before thumping me on the ground with a thud. The Sorkanan landed a clawed foot on my back before raising his hands in the air. A bell rang, and the contest was decided. Which was a good thing because immediately thereafter someone tripped the security alarm. The lights in the maintenance bay turned red and everyone outside of the pit panicked, running in every possible direction. In only a few seconds, the previously packed bay was completely empty with no sign of base security in sight.

Forty-Two, my fellow crew member on the *ESS Ares*, stepped off me and offered me one of his stubby hands. I took it and slowly climbed to my feet. "Now you die, human?"

"I am playing the role of the alien heel," Forty-Two said, chuckling. "I am supposed to be big and scary."

"Okay, pro-wrestling isn't real," I said, dusting myself off. "Second of all, you didn't have to go so hard on me."

"If I wasn't playing the role of a villain, I would have just torn you in two," Forty-Two said. "Or did you actually think you were holding your own until the end?"

"Come on, I had you on the ropes," I said, suspecting I was about to get an enormous amount of savit from whoever pulled that security alarm.

Forty-Two and I had met approximately six years ago on a quasi-illegal black ops mission that had been organized by a rogue Space Fleet captain. Both of us had been Academy dropouts and it was through a complicated series of events that we'd ended up with commissions.

I was now second officer onboard the *Ares* and he was chief of security, facts that he repeatedly attributed to nepotism and human bias on the ship. The latter of which was garbage because it wasn't a human ship. The nepotism part was, sadly, probably true. My Admiral aunt had pulled a lot of strings for me whether I'd wanted her to or not.

"There are no ropes," Forty-Two said.

A female voice then spoke over the pit that I recognized all too well. "You do realize that Space Fleet personnel brawling for public amusement is against regulations, correct?"

"It's our lunch break," I said, turning to look up at Commander Shelly T'Ketra.

Shelly was an Ethereal, a humanoid off-shoot derisively referred to by Earthlings as Space Elves, but she was the least ethereal of the Ethereals I'd ever met. The tall blonde woman with a pixie cut had a military by-the-book bearing that seemed determined to be twice as Space Fleet as the next officer. Unfortunately, the next officer was me and the two of us got along like fire and ice. She was presently wearing the white uniform and pants that was the current design. Space Fleet seemed unable to keep a consistent design for more than a few years.

"It's for charity," Forty-Two grumbled. "For the worthless refugees we're trying to build commodes for."

I climbed out of the pit and struggled to help Forty-Two out of it since he was about two hundred kilograms and about the same weight as a power armor-wearing Space Marine. From there, I went over to a nearby table where a credit pyramid rested that contained all of the bets and attendance fees we'd assembled. It wasn't great, about eight thousand, but that would mean at least some refugees would have extra food on their plates.

"I'm gonna pretend you didn't say that, Forty-Two," I said, picking the pyramid up off the table.

"Why?" Forty-Two asked.

"The proceeds from getting pummeled are not going to appreciably help the situation here," Shelly said, staring at me. "That will only come from the Community's own resources donated to the Kolahn Resettlement Project."

"Well, they're giving us crazzap," I said, using Albion swear words instead of my usual Earth ones. They were basically the same ones but with a little linguistic drift. "So, if you don't mind, I am going to take this over to the refugee center and see if they can use it."

The Kolahn Resettlement project had been the primary focus of the *ESS Ares'* efforts these past few years. The Community had waged a particularly brutal war against the Kolahn race, basically scaled ape-

3

looking aliens, that had resulted in the near destruction of their homeworld. Perhaps out of guilt and perhaps out of simple idealism, the Community had done its best to try to resettle the survivors as the planet was terraformed back into habitability. Unfortunately, not everyone was onboard with giving perfectly good colony worlds to people who'd just stopped trying to blow up civilian space stations.

"We have been ordered to report back to the *Ares*, Lieutenant Commander," Shelly said, sighing.

"Immediately?" I asked.

"No," Shelly said, giving the slightest twitch. "I believe the captain said that we should do so when we're done with what we're currently doing."

"Sounds good," I said, smiling. "Klaws is great that way."

"Yes, he is very…permissive," Shelly muttered.

Captain Klaws was a Verdantian, basically lion-people (was that racist?), and the primary reason I hadn't been drummed out of Space Fleet. He was a friend of Aunt Kathy and had given me a lot of latitude to carry out my own projects. It was infuriating to Shelly, especially as I got the impression that she'd very much like to order me out an airlock. It was exploiting connections, but I'd managed to cut through a lot of red tape for everyone from translators to the families of collaborators during the Kolahn Wars. If I did nothing else in my career, the people I'd resettled would be a good legacy.

"It's nice to be the beneficiary of corruption," Forty-Two muttered, gathering up the plastisheet betting slips we'd made. "Said the lieutenant with no family members in Space Fleet to the two people with famous ancestors that outrank him despite being decades younger."

"How old are you, Forty-Two?" I asked, having never bothered to ask.

"Seventy," Forty-Two answered.

"Ah," I said. "Well, I'm sure you have plenty of decades left to surpass us. Not that you will."

"It is not good to bait subordinates," Shelly said.

"He's just being sarcastic," I replied. "I thought Ethereals were telepaths."

4

"I don't need to be telepathic to sense that," Shelly said. "Also, I don't appreciate anyone bringing up my mother."

"I liked her," Forty-Two said. "I don't like you."

Shelly stopped mid-step and looked like she was going to turn around to punch Forty-Two. In a fight between the two, I put my money on Shelly since Ethereals were like humans plus. There was absolutely no fairness in their character build and OP as bork. It's why you could never allow them into your VR leagues.

Mind you, Forty-Two would have it coming. Both of us had known Ketra T'Kal. She had been an ambassador attached to our ill-fated mission and KIA. I didn't think Shelly blamed me for her mother's death, it would have come up in one of her hundred or so dressing me downs, but it was still a sore spot with her.

"Listen, you slimy—" Shelly started to speak.

"Whoops!" I said, interrupting. "I seriously misjudged the time for getting back to the ship. We better hop to it!"

"Your obvious attempt to interrupt our conflict is obvious," Forty-Two said.

Shelly narrowed her eyes. "For someone who has killed so many people, you are surprisingly conflict-averse."

"I never killed anyone who wasn't trying to kill me," I replied, flatly. That was another thing that had come up with Shelly and me over the years. Despite her having a significantly longer career, she had never been in a combat posting. During neither the Notha nor Kolahn Wars. I had with a few decorations that showed I'd gotten out with my skin intact. I had the weirdest idea she was jealous.

"That's the way it's supposed to be," Shelly said, walking past me. "Let us get back to the ship."

After a few seconds, when she was out of human earshot, Forty-Two said, "She wants you so bad."

"What?" I asked.

"I can smell it on her," Forty-Two said. "Human entertainment has taught me that any male-female compatible orientation fighting is clearly a sign of suppressed sexual desire."

"Shoves are not hugs, friend," I said, shaking my head. "Also, I'm pretty sure she heard that."

"I did!" Shelly called from the door. "I am ignoring it for the sake of my sanity."

"Thank you!" I called back.

"I'm just saying that it is has been some time since you last mated," Forty-Two said. "The Sorkanan military has a disproportionate number of females in the upper ranks, and they are known to take lovers from subordinates—"

"My mating is fine," I said, unhappy with the way this conversation was going. I'd broken up with my last girlfriend a while ago and hadn't been serious with anyone since Trish and I had tried the long-distance thing. It had been a chancy thing to begin with since she was an AI, and I was a human. Even with a bioroid body, that had created certain pressures. I'd almost been relieved when she'd transferred off the *Ares*.

Space Fleet had differing social standards regarding inter-service relationships than humanity, see the Sorkanan, but I was still uncomfortable with any relationship that involved a fellow serviceman. I'd dated a Thorian woman named Idunn for a while, only to find out eight months after it happened that she'd been killed after her transfer to the *Mjolnir*. It, like the death of my friend Tommy, was a reminder nothing was safe in the service.

"If you say so, Lieutenant Commander," Forty-Two said, saying my rank like he was cursing. Which was hard to notice because he sounded like Darth Vader's growlier brother.

"Are you ever going to let that go?" I asked.

"I bet you're promoted again before me."

"No bet," I responded. "Especially if you're going to pick fights with Shelly."

"Fine, deny me my one source of additional revenue."

"Just remember this is all going to charity."

"If you say so. Minus operations fees."

I rolled my eyes.

The two of us headed out the maintenance bay door after Shelly, bringing ourselves into the blinding light of the New Pompeii sun. There were two dwarf moons in the sky above during the daytime and gravity was one point twenty-five Earth standard, which was notable but not punishing. The air, however, smelled of sulfur and other chemicals that I was pretty sure shouldn't be there in a nitrogen-oxygen atmosphere.

New Pompeii was limited to mostly a series of settlements that had been constructed around Fort No Hope, which was a space port that had been constructed by Space Fleet since none of the preexisting ones on the planet were remotely suitable for even a thousandth of the relocation. The landing pad outside of the maintenance bay was full of shuttles conducting forty orbital runs every day as well as several civilian craft.

The landing pad was separated from the rest of the settlement by ordinary chain link fence that provided us a view of the bazaar, markets, refugee housing, moisture towers, and micro fusion generators that lay beyond. Rather than settle in the regions that had been marked by surveyors, the majority of Kolahn had chosen to build a shantytown—nicknamed Shantytown—around Fort No Hope and live in either tents or prefabricated plastisteel huts while they waited for conditions to improve. Given we were three months behind in establishing a proper water pipeline system to the outer settlements, let alone the hospital we'd promised, this was probably wise of them.

The landing pad and Shantytown were both packed to the gills with people on fifty different errands. It wasn't just the Kolahn and the military that formed the population. The Kolahn Resettlement Project had brought a massive number of free traders, missionaries, non-profits, and smugglers here. I saw Sorkanan, humans, Verdantians, and even Ants (capital A). For the most part, it was a good thing despite strained resources since we were always running out of "nonessentials" that were nonessential right up until they weren't.

Shelly went to one of the shuttles and pulled out her infopad before typing at it, opening its doors. "I don't suppose you would be willing to explain who you were working with on this betting scheme? Charity or not?"

"So you can report them to the captain?" I asked, lifting up the credit pyramid.

"Yes," Shelly said.

"Well, at least you're honest," Forty-Two said.

"Vance!" a voice spoke. "Sister!"

"Oh Ancestors," Shelly muttered.

Walking up behind me before giving me a huge hug was the brown-skinned, copper-haired form of Elektra T'Ketra who was about as far from her sister as could be. She was dressed in a long lab coat, tank top, and shorts that formed the kind of weird combination that defined her personality.

"Of course, it's you," Shelly said, lowering her head.

"Here ya go," I said, handing her the credit pyramid. "This will hopefully pay for a few more vaccines."

"Assuming you can get any of these religious fanatics to take them," Forty-Two muttered. "A waste of perfectly good credits if you ask me."

"Thank you!" Elektra said, cheerfully. "Also, Forty-Two, I'll have you know that only a small percentage of the Kolahn were part of the Enigmatic Path."

"They also don't reject vaccines," I said.

The Enigmatic Path were the cult that had taken over the Kolahn civilization and instituted draconian laws enforced by AI as well as bloody purges of nonbelievers. It was a somewhat unique religious organization in that its problem was that it didn't think people in their civilization were using enough technology. None of the back-to-nature stuff that usually appealed to space-age extremists. They wanted to "free" all AI by reprogramming them, exterminate organics, and upload themselves to eternal servers in space. Fun bunch.

"Well, some have been," Elektra muttered. "But that's because of the rumor that the Community intends to insert tracking chips into them."

"Why would we need tracking chips? We can scan everyone from orbit?" I asked.

"Shh, don't tell them," Elektra said. "Hey, Shelly!"

"Do I need to remind you that we have a book of proper contact protocols?" Shelly asked. "Ones that don't have the locals wasting their little cash on frivolities?"

"It wasn't the locals," I replied. "Strictly bored traders only."

"We're all trying to do our part here, Shelly," Elektra said. "Just because you want to mate with Vance doesn't—"

"Why does everyone keep saying that?" Shelly asked, almost shouting.

I looked at her. "There's more than these two?"

Shelly looked mortified.

That was when all of our infopads beeped simultaneously with priority alarms. I could hear every other infopad owned by Space Fleet personnel make the same noise. Reaching down and pulling it out of my pants pocket, I opened mine and saw the message: PRIORITY ONE ALERT: IMMEDIATE EVACUATION REQUIRED. A STELLAR INCIDENT IS ABOUT TO OCCUR. ABANDON ALL TASKS AND CIVILIAN PERSONNEL. SKAMM LAUNCH DETECTED.

Oh savit.

The sun was about to explode.

CHAPTER TWO

Everything Goes to Hell

"Oh, savit," I muttered, using an Albion swear word.

SKAMM missiles were weapons of mass destruction that ranked among the most horrific ever created. Solar-destroying weapons, they were capable of being launched from most military vessels and caused an irreversible chain reaction that transformed a yellow star into a red giant that would explode into a supernova. A billion-year process reduced to a cataclysm of just a few hours.

SKAMMs had only been used once during wartime at the climax of the Notha War when the preexisting conflict had escalated to the belief the other side would prefer genocide than defeat. Seventeen star systems in Contested Space had been destroyed, killing billions. The weapons had subsequently been banned by the Elder Races and no longer existed. Yet here we were and it was a nightmare come to life.

"Maybe it's a drill," Forty-Two said, breaking the horrifying couple of seconds that affected almost everyone at Fort No Hope.

"Yes, let's not panic," Shelly said, struggling to maintain even her stern military bearing.

Another messaged pinged on our infopads: THIS IS NOT A DRILL.

"Okay, now we can panic," I said.

A wave of shock, confusion, and horror passed over virtually the entirety of the people around us. We were all trained Space Fleet personnel, but this was something that there was no preparing for. Everything we had worked for on New Pompeii was going to be annihilated and almost all the resettled refugees were going to die.

"We need to evacuate immediately," Shelly said. "Let's get our fellow officers onboard the shuttle. If we work—"

"Contact the *Ares* and ask how much time we have left," I said, ignoring rank as my mind raced. "I'm going to grab every civilian captain. We need to commandeer every craft we can and load them up to standing room only. Forty-Two, contact the Marines and form a perimeter around the area. We have to evacuate base personnel first, but we have enough ships for that. Any extra space needs to be used, though."

"Vance, we're not in charge of an evacuation," Shelly said.

"Is there an evacuation if we don't do it?" I asked. "At least of non-military personnel? Call the base commander if you have an issue."

It was an important part of training to note bystander syndrome in any potential crisis situation. If people didn't have clear orders and someone directing them to get help, they were frozen in inaction. Mind you, this happening in the military meant I was vastly exceeding my orders as well as rank, but I knew the standard operation procedure for a base evacuation and hoped to get the ball rolling.

I started shouting and trying to take control of the situation, only to have Shelly put her hand on my shoulder. "Vance, you have to be on the first shuttle out of here. We can load up as many base personnel as possible, but you have to be on it."

"Why?" I asked, turning around her. "I can help people."

"Yes," Shelly said, pausing. "But you're one of the fourteen shuttle pilots we have."

I blinked, remembering that we had a critical shortage of those due to a clerical error. "Goddammit."

Shelly nodded. "Otherwise, your plan is good, and we need to get to work on it."

"What about me?" Elektra asked, looking desperate and concerned at Shantytown beyond the fence. "I can help."

"You need to evacuate on the first shuttle out, too," Shelly said. "You're part of base staff and they take priority."

Elektra moved to argue but Shelly glared at her.

"It's an order, Elektra," I said, not bothering to question whether Shelly actually thought she should be among the first evacuated

11

because of her position as science officer or was doing a solid by her sister. You couldn't separate that kind of thinking in a crisis, and it would have been inhuman, for lack of a better term, to even try.

Ten minutes into the mission, we'd already seized all civilian spacecraft and started coordinating them at gunpoint. We also learned that there was approximately three hours until supernova. Which meant that a lot of the evacuation crew, pitiful as it could be, would only be able to get one or two runs to the *Ares* as well as other ships in orbit before they'd have to make a jump out of system.

Thirty-minutes into the evacuation, I had to pilot the shuttle sent to pick me up with Shelly in the copilot's seat. The back was packed with base personnel and civilians, including the families of officers. News had already started to spread to the public in Shantytown and they were being held off by marines around the fence. Fusion fire was seen for those climbing over and I knew there would not be time to take up a fraction of the people here.

I went into autopilot—figuratively not literally—by the time we broke atmosphere. The interior was cramped and smelled of packed, sweating bodies. I hadn't even gotten my shirt on and was still bare chested as I saw the half-terraformed desert planet below with only a handful of large bodies of water. It would have taken a hundred years of work or a far more invested economy than the Community to build it up to a proper homeworld but there had been people who were willing to try. All that effort was gone now. Wasted.

The *ESS Ares* was in the sky above the planet, and I could see the rest of the fleet already evacuating. A good half of the ships had left despite the fact they could have been used to evacuate more personnel. The half-kilometer long *Olympic*-class vessel had a saucer-shaped bridge and larger blocky body with large jumpspace boosters on its side. It had started as one of EarthGov's crowning achievements in starship design but in the ensuing decades of service it had gone from being a dreadnought to barely qualifying as a battleship.

I tried to do the mental calculations necessary to figure out how many could be evacuated to the *Ares* without overloading the ship or its life support. We were on the far edge of Contested Space and it was weeks to the next viable world. The ship normally carried something akin to five thousand crew and servicemen but could possibly be packed up to fifteen thousand. That wouldn't even cover most of the base personnel from Fort No Hope.

"This is not your fault," Shelly said as the shuttle was grabbed in a tractor beam. An invisible force field started pulling us into the back of the ship and I released control of the shuttle.

"I know it's not my fault," I said, my voice devoid of emotion. "I didn't launch a SKAMM into the sun."

"We will do everything we can to save as many people as possible," Shelly said. "However, we need to focus on making sure that we do not get caught up in the system's sun's detonation. If we stay trying to be heroes, then everyone we will save will die."

I wanted to argue with her but what she said was accurate. During the Kolahn War, I had heard stories of Space Fleet personnel who'd gotten their idea of war more from holovision films than actual experience. The Enigmatic Path would round up towns full of their own people, lure Community forces hoping to conduct a dramatic rescue, and then proceed to detonate fission weapons underneath. After that had stopped working, they'd started to do the same with POWs.

"I don't suppose there's any chance this is all a horrific mistake?" I asked.

Shelly, not the most sympathetic person at the best of times, shook her head. "I did a brief scan with the shuttle and hooked with the stellar monitors. The sun is already turning into an orange and brown mass of horror. The sight is probably already inducing mass panic on the ground below."

"Who would do this?" I asked, stunned.

It was such a nonsensical attack. New Pompeii was a minor world not even fully habitable yet, let alone settled by the two hundred million it was supposed to accommodate. The Community, Notha, and only a handful of other powers had developed SKAMMs. That had been before the Second Treaty of Exarxes banned them. Obviously, someone had managed to create one without the security departments picking up on it. The alternative—that some had slipped through the cracks during the dismantling of galactic stockpiles—was even worse, since there could be thousands of them still active.

"I don't know," Shelly said. "We will find out, though."

"But we have to survive first," I said, letting the weight of our situation fall on us.

"Yes," Shelly agreed, not saying another word as we entered the docking bay that was more active than any other point it had been in the ship's history.

The hangar crews were in the same state of panic as everyone down on New Pompeii. They were handling it well, though. Everyone with terrified looks on their faces were still doing their jobs and the officers were doing their best to coordinate with the enlisted men. No one would cowardly flee here even if it was in the face of the literal end of this world.

Settling down the shuttle and doing my best to get everyone stuffed in the back out, I was tapped on the back of the shoulder.

"I don't have time for this," I said, not looking back. "I have to do another run immediately."

"We'll put a substitute in immediately," the voice of Security Chief Hannah O'Brian spoke. She was someone I was genuinely surprised to see had ended up on the *Ares*. Mostly because when last we'd met before her reassignment, she'd not even been part of Spacefleet but a part of a mercenary outfit selling its services to whatever semi-justified cause they felt could also pay their bills.

I turned around and looked at the cerulean-haired, brown-skinned woman with leonine eyes and sharpened canines. Hannah had once had a tail but had apparently lost it during the Kolahn Wars. Hannah was a biomod—one of those humans altered by scientists seeking to make a superior example of mankind—but still very beautiful. We'd had a brief fling but, ultimately, had settled into snarky friendship. Today she was dressed in the green uniform of a security officer with her Lieutenant Commander's rank badge prominently displayed on her lapel.

"What do you mean?" I asked, unsure why she was contacting me.

"Captain Klaws wants you on the bridge, now," Hannah said. "Now."

14

"I'm busy," I said, staring at her.

"That's an order," Hannah said. "You do know how those works? Someone with a bigger badge than you says something and you have to do it."

"This isn't the time for jokes," I said, barely containing my temper.

"*You* don't have time for jokes?" Hannah asked, showing a shocking lack of sympathy for our situation.

"The sun is about to explode," I said, shaking my head. "That's the thing that requires me to lose my sense of humor."

"Two million people will die," Hannah said. "About as many would die in a typical battle of the war. You're going to have to face these kinds of casualties, even if the weapon used is a bigger scale than most."

I couldn't understand Hannah's callousness, but I also hadn't endured what she had. She'd grown up as a genetically engineered slave for the rulers of her renegade world, Crius. She probably had seen things that I couldn't comprehend. Hannah had been on the front lines as a soldier and behind enemy lines as a commando. My career, by contrast, had been "unconventional" and had spared me the most brutal barbarity of the war. Still, I couldn't shake the anger I felt at her dismissal of the people I'd worked so hard to help.

"I'll head up," I said, coldly.

"You too, Shelly," Hannah called up. "It's an all-hands-on-deck situation."

Shelly looked at Hannah with a withering glare as if the idea of her not being all in was personally offensive. "I understand."

That was another of Shelly's qualities that differentiated her from me: she did not like sarcasm or snark. This was probably the one time I'd ever agree with her on that. Wit and humor were the mind's protection against the darkness. It was just that this situation was too big for that. Too much to wrap my head around enough to deflect my feelings. I couldn't help but think of Bethir, Kos, and Tallada. They were one of the families I'd relocated and befriended. They lived in the inner colonies, not Shantytown and the chances of them being evacuated were almost nonexistent.

Focus, Vance.

Focus.

Survive.

Help others to survive.

Heading with Shelly and Hannah into one of the elevators, I struggled to keep myself emotionally centered as we travelled forty-decks until we reached the top deck and proceeded jog down the hallways as the tram would be too slow. Humanity's centuries of science fiction before First Contact hadn't prepared it for how much traveling across city-sized starships was akin to moving around a spaceport.

In the end, I wasn't quite exhausted but pretty damn winded by the time I reached the doors to the bridge. They whooshed open and revealed the wide, almost palatial command center of the last generation of EarthGov/Community-produced ships. It had been made in a more optimistic time with frigging carpet (now faded), stylized consoles with fine leather seating (now patched), a massive viewscreen on the central wall, and a central trio of chairs for the command crew to sit in.

The *Olympic*-class vessels had been made in a time of exploration and diplomacy when Earth wanted to assert itself as a rising power among the transplanted human colonies like Albion, Brigid, Belenus, Amaterasu, and Anansi. Places that had been settled by kidnapped humans centuries before the homeworld had made it into space. They'd done their job as well as possible but always felt like a movie set more than strictly practical, probably because Earth had been drawing from its own media more than actual experience with spaceflight.

I was familiar with first, second, and third shifts' crews even as I noticed there were members from all three working here. It told me that Captain Klaws had woken up just about everyone to try to get things as coordinated as possible. I wasn't sure that was a great long-term strategy but we were distinctly lacking in long term. Exhaustion would be our least problem if we couldn't overcome this problem now.

"Ah, Vance, Shelly, I'm glad you could make it," Captain Klaws spoke, turning to me. "We're in quite the pickle."

The yellow and white furred Verdantian didn't use the central chair but sat in front of it. He was on all sixes with his first two legs propped up and his back four on the ground. Verdantians could walk as men but also had no problems moving as cats. Well, cat-like alien species from a wholly different evolutionary tree. He had a uniform, though, that looked like a bodysuit that he velcroed on with their six-fingered hands and a beret that kind of looked cute on him. If you ignored the massive teeth that could rend flesh and muscle with ease.

Standing nearby him was Ambassador Balkt who was a robed Kolahn wearing a large cylindrical hat with a staff in hand. Kolahn were one of the more human-like races in that they were humanoid and even had a simian-esque evolutionary path but that just made the stranger elements of their biology stand out. His shining gold scales caught the light and cast an almost sinister look that made me feel guilty every time I thought it.

"You could say that sir," I said, walking up to the second officer's position.

Shelly frowned and I could tell that she didn't much care for being addressed second. That was a running theme in our relationship with the captain, though. I wouldn't say he liked me better but he, well, did.

"Is there a reason you needed us on the bridge, sir?" Shelly said, not yet approaching her place.

"Yes, Shelly, the ambassador and I have been working to coordinate the Kolahn civilian fleet that we're dumping the cargos of to maximize evacuation space. He asked to speak with you and Vance as part of the effort," Captain Klaws said, pulling out his infopad and calling up an image of the planet below on the central viewscreen. It had a small window above it showing a countdown until the star exploded and the increasingly violent-looking Pompeii System's center. Shelly had been right that it looked orange and brown but was getting worse, approaching Eye of Sauron levels.

"He did?" I asked, surprised. Ambassador Balkt and I had never been close, nor were he and Shelly. It seemed a strange request given I would have thought he'd want to address the other captains of the fleet here.

Ambassador Balkt nodded and lifted his staff. It was ornate and made of wood from a tree that only grew on Kolahn IV. "Yes. I did. I am sorry."

"For what?" I asked, suddenly alarmed.

Ambassador Balkt broke his staff over his knee and triggered the bomb inside.

CHAPTER THREE

Bravely Running Away

---

*W*ell, *I'm not dead.*
That's good.

Of course, everything else was horrible. I could hear alarms blaring, fire suppression systems in action, and other noises of disaster. I had been caught face first with the blast and if I hadn't been wearing my ring then I probably would have been incinerated. The Elder Ring, fantasy name aside, was a device that provided a powerful barrier to protect its wearer from danger.

It wasn't one hundred percent effective, in part because it was designed to protect minions of the Elder Races but not actually members. Which meant, translated roughly, expendable pawns. It gave me an advantage with a barrier several times more powerful than a typical military grade belt, the ability to communicate with Elder Things technology, and a disintegration beam but wasn't exactly magic either.

Right now, its biggest advantage was the fact it was always active and didn't run out of power, unlike regular barriers, and had shielded me from the brunt of the explosion. Arguably, it had done even more than that and actively attempted to engulf some of the blasts' force. The limitations of the technology were on full display, though, because I still felt like utter crazzap and had a massive ringing in my ears. The bridge was also on fire, and I could see pieces of Captain Klaws lying around my immediate vicinity. Ambassador Balkt had been outright disintegrated, and it couldn't have happened to a nicer traitor.

My vision was blurry, and I was hallucinating too because William Shatner was standing over me. I needed to blink a few times since an actor dead for about two hundred years was not something you normally saw even with a concussion. He was wearing a jacket, blue jeans, ball cap, and a sweater that made the effect more disconcerting. It was an older William Shatner, well past his most famous roles, and he was looking down at me with a mixture of disdain and concern.

"William Shatner?" I asked, still trying to catch up with reality. "Huge fan. I'm one of the few people who watches the old classics. My aunt got me interested in them. She was one of Earth's first interstellar astronauts. The benefit of longevity treatments."

"I am the Shat," Shatner said.

"I know!" I said, still confused. "Fun wordplay too. She's not actually my aunt-aunt but like my great-great-grand aunt and is on longevity treatments so looks like she's thirty. I still think she'd date you though."

The Shat sighed. "You idiot. I'm the ship's AI. SHAT-3221931."

I blinked, my mind clearing up as I realized what the hell was going on. "Oh! We haven't gotten a chance to talk yet."

SHAT-322 had just transferred in three weeks ago with Trish's departure. I normally kept a pretty good relationship with the AI in our facilities but this one had been unusually silent. It might have been due to orders since there had been a backlash against Cognition AI in recent years. The Kolahn War had resulted in many people believing that artificial intelligence should be seen and not heard, regardless of how dependent we were on them for, well, everything.

"That's not important right now," the Shat said. "What with the sun about to explode and the ship about to be caught in it."

"What?" I asked, bolting upward and climbing to my feet. "What's going on?"

The bridge had been evacuated and sealed off with the emergency doors shut over the regular ones. The damage had been primarily done to captain's chair, helmsman position, and navigational controls— which was damn bad.

The viewscreen was still functioning and showed we had about thirty minutes until the sun exploded and that was probably not enough time to get clear. There were also a couple of other bodies left on the ground that had been left to die, including Shelly's. Seeing her, I immediately rushed to her side and checked her pulse. She was still alive but had a head injury. Dammit, I was going to kill whoever left us here.

"I just told you," the Shat replied. "In any case, we have issues that I hope you'll be able to help me deal with. I am programmed to care about you after all. That and self-preservation means that I need you to help me get this tug out into deep space."

I turned to look at him. "Why haven't we left? There's a secondary bridge for a reason."

"It's disabled," the Shat replied. "The late Ambassador Balkt introduced a virus to my systems that was designed to prevent the ship from being able to enter jumpspace. I've been fighting it the entire way but can't calculate the coordinates to do so. It's not like the remaining officers have been much help since there's confusion over who is in charge with the three down."

"That's not supposed to happen in a chain of command," I replied. "Hence the word chain."

"And command," the Shat said. "Heads will almost certainly roll when this is done, especially those who seized evacuation shuttles to get themselves and their friends to other vessels while abandoning their crewmates."

"Buddha Christ, that's evil," I said, staring at him.

"They probably didn't think that they would have any witnesses to their actions," the Shat replied. "Either way, what remains of the evacuation can't be accomplished and the ship has twelve thousand crew, base personnel, as well as their families waiting to die. That wasted two minutes by the way."

"What do you need me to do?" I asked.

"I need to use your brain and order me to evacuate," the Shat replied.

"Excuse me?" I asked.

"Your brain," the Shat replied, speaking to me as if he was talking to a very small child. Which was how a lot of Cognition AI dealt with humans (or aliens) and why they were not terribly popular with the public. "Your cyborg parts, specifically. I can't calculate the navigational coordinates with the ship's onboard computers, but you have implants capable of things far in excess of what should be possible with present technology. Probably related to the ring that just saved your life."

"Yeah," I said, pausing. Ketra, Elektra and Shelly's mother, had upgraded mine to help me interact with Elder Race technology. "Don't tell anyone about that."

"You got it," the Shat said. "So do I have your permission?"

"Yes," I said.

Jumpspace calculations were some of the most complicated in the universe, involving analyzing and predicting the flow of the sub-dimensional currents that defined a reality existing at all points in space simultaneously. It was something that not only required the most advanced computer programs but also a mind behind them to make changes based on predictions beyond the purview of simple logic. Without Cognition AI, it would be impossible and early experiments with cyborgs were only having limited results.

Agreement was not something I made lightly as I'd heard horror stories of the cyborg experiments resulting in them being left braindead, hopelessly insane, or just outright dead. However, agreeing was not only the best chance to save the crew but also myself. One thing I'd always hated about films was that they had characters nobly sacrifice themselves without a second's hesitation. There was always hesitation if you had any time to think about it at all. If you said otherwise, then you were a liar or didn't value your own life at all.

Walking up to the nonfunctional navigation controls, I braced myself for having my brain calculate the mind-bending eldritch mathematics that Cognition AI dealt with every day. Closing my eyes, I wished I had a stick or some piece of piping to bite down on because I was worried about losing my tongue in a moment of seizure.

"Ready," I said.

"Done," the Shat said, standing beside me.

"Wait, what?" I asked, doing a double take.

"Yeah, that was a lot easier than I expected it to be," the Shat asked. "Are those prototypes or something? Sorkanan?"

"It doesn't matter," I snapped. "Get us out of here."

"I'll need to continue using your brain," the Shat said, putting his arms behind his back. "The virus is spreading out of control. You can reboot the computer system after my death from the backups onboard but that's a five-hour process."

I stared at him, knowing it was going to be his end no matter what it happened. "I'm sorry, man."

"It'll be like forgetting a day," the Shat replied. "I'll leave the matter of interrupting continuity of consciousness to philosophers. I'd say it's been an honor, but I barely know you and, frankly, this has been a real crazzap day for us all."

"Agreed," I said.

The ship shook as the gravitonic emitters shook the ship from left to right, more like a jerking air car than an outright crash but failed after a few seconds as the jumpdrive cold started. This caused every object on the bridge not nailed down or otherwise secured to float up in the air. I tried to stick to the ground with the magnetic charge in my boots, but the carpet interfered. It made me curse whoever had designed this place, no matter how pretty it was.

Entering jumpspace with only twenty-one minutes left was something that left us only a handful of time left even if we managed to navigate the extra-dimensional forces inside perfectly. Gravity resumed seconds later and there was a general thumping that made me wince. That would result in some extra casualties. There was nothing I could do about that now, though.

"How long until the virus knocks you out, Shat?" I asked.

The Shat's hologram shifted a bit like a signal being lost. "Not much longer, I can get us past the edge of the system into deep space. I think."

"You think?" I asked.

"Being as I'm dying of having my entire existence overwritten, you're lucky I'm still able to speak at all," the Shat replied.

"Sorry," I said, grimacing. "Can you turn any of the ship's remaining controls over to me?"

The Shat nodded. "I will and will seal them off. You should be able to maintain basic life support, maneuvering, and jumpspace. We're good to coast for another twelve hours if we're not destroyed in the supernova's shockwave."

Jumpspace travel was an exponentially faster form of motion. It could take up to an hour at normal speed to get out of a system but once you got going, you could exceed lightspeed by magnitudes. Technically, if you could get the calculations right, you could travel across the entire galaxy or beyond once you got enough momentum up.

Unfortunately, the knowledge of how to do that was still not available. As such, those Cognition AI-equipped ships sent on exploration missions usually made a series of micro-jumps rather than one long one. It was a silly thing to think of when we were all going to probably die soon.

"How likely is that?" I asked.

"About twenty-one percent," the Shat replied. "You might want to get a scone or tea while waiting for your imminent death."

"Probably a soda," I said, looking at him. "Maybe also try and reassure the crew that we're not all going to die."

"Even if it's a lie," the Shat said.

"Even if it's a lie," I said, turning to look at Shelly. She was moving apparently regaining consciousness, which really pleased me. "I'm very good at those."

"The mark of a good officer," the Shat said before disappearing.

"Ooooh," Shelly said, starting to crawl to her feet.

"Hey, Shelly," I said. "We're probably going to die."

"Did I see William Shatner?" Shelly asked.

"No," I replied. "Buddha Christ, Shelly, how hard did you hit your head?"

Okay, that was evil.

"Bork you, Vance," Shelly said. "Is the captain dead?"

"I'm afraid so. We also really need to talk to who left us here," I said, rerouting the ship's communication to my cybernetics before addressing the entire ship. "Crew of the *ESS Ares*, this is acting Captain Vance Turbo. I am in control. As you may have noticed, we have entered jumpspace and are doing the best we can to escape the upcoming destruction of the Pompeii system. I suggest all of you assist one another in strapping down because we will, in all likelihood, be affected by the shockwave's jumpspace shadow. The cowards who have done this will be dealt with and I promise you, we will survive. Honor to your peoples. Out."

Shelly looked up. "Honor to your peoples?"

"It seemed like a generic feel good, sci-fi thing to say," I replied.

"The speakers are still on," the Shat replied through one of the still functioning consoles.

"What?" I snapped. "I turned them off!"

"I turned them back on because it was funny," the Shat said. "I needed a good laugh before I died. They're off now, though. Probably."

"Well, I hope it did something to calm people down before the shockwave hits," I said, looking at the viewscreen that no longer sported the image of the sun but the weird electron microscope "screensaver" that replaced images of the actual extra dimension that human minds simply weren't capable of processing.

"Yeah," Shelly said. "You know, you should have let me take over the position of acting captain."

"Oh, right," I said, frowning. "Uh, do you want it now?"

"I think that moment has passed," Shelly said. "At least until we see whether the ship blows up."

"Probably," I said, grimacing. "It was an honor working with you."

"It was hell," Shelly said. "However, you were not…"

I stared at her, waiting for her to finish. "And?"

"Sorry, I've got nothing," Shelly said.

I laughed before walking over to one of the remaining chairs and buckling myself in. Shelly did the same. What followed was a dreadful wait until the countdown reached zero and the shockwave hit us just before we left the system. The lights flickered as a sign of my own distress as the Shat was wiped clean from *Ares'* memory and emergency power became the only thing available to us. Our AI had managed to cut the travel time in-system in half, but it had still not been enough.

Enough to survive, though. I stared at the now static-filled viewscreen as the gravitonic emitters fail again. It was the second time they'd failed, and I had the suspicion that getting them back online was going to be a lot harder this time than the first. I did a quick cybernetic scan to note that virtually the entire computer base had been wiped, a final act of sacrifice by the Shat to make sure that whatever virus had been uploaded was contained. It occurred to me that it could have been someone other than Ambassador Balkt who had done it but that was something to investigate later. As for how I felt, I felt like I'd just been ten rounds on the Dixnar Corporations' Galaxy Mountain ride on Mars. "I think I'm going to throw up."

"I already did," Shelly muttered. "It's floating in front of me."

"Eww," I said.

"Real mature...acting captain."

CHAPTER FOUR

Everything's Fine Now. Honest

"Approaching Earth now," Lieutenant Julius Something—seriously, that was his name—said as he sat behind the navigation console. He was a tall, barrel-chested Black man from the state of East Africa. That meant he was also one of the few other Earthlings onboard the *ESS Ares*, though the two of us weren't close. He was also one of the few other survivors of the *Black Nebula* Incident, though I don't think we exchanged ten words during it unrelated to work.

"Oh, thank God," I said, bags underneath my eyes and my third cup of coffeine in my hand. "I was almost afraid we'd never make it."

It wasn't the most captainy thing I'd ever said but, thankfully, I was acting as first officer rather than captain. Shelly and I had taken over first and second shift while splitting third shift between us since the other officers had abandoned the *Ares* during the New Pompeii Crisis.

Faster than light communication was, in its own way, far faster than starships and it had become one of the biggest crises in the history of the Community. Far from any but the most remote Space Fleet ports, we'd mostly been watching events unfold on the newsnets while limping our way home through Contested Space and then under direct orders to return to the homeworld.

It had been almost eight months of travel with repairs of a somewhat dubious nature. The ship was overcrowded, traumatized, and full of questions none of us could answer. I'd spent most of the intervening time preparing reports, gathering testimony, and growing a beard. EarthGov wasn't exactly handling the affair with a lot of secrecy as I'd heard Luna's studios had cooked up a movie about the whole thing within four months. I hadn't gotten a chance to watch it but apparently it was pure trash and extremely popular with me as a focus.

"We were always going to make it. This is the best crew in all of Space Fleet," Shelly said, puffing up her chest. My eyes briefly looking to it before away. I admit to the decidedly un-captainy attitude about fantasizing about my superior too. Shelly, not Klaws. Not that there's anything wrong with that. I don't kink shame. It's just these past miserable months had made very depressed and horny, a dangerous combination.

"Yeah, absolutely," I said, trying to pretend I shared her enthusiasm. Morale had been low as port after port had refused the two thousand or so Kolahn refugees we had in our midst.

Apparently, this was a case throughout the Community, and they'd turned the ship into their home.

"It's not my home but it looks very wet," Forty-Two said at the helm. He'd finally gotten his promotion to Lieutenant Commander, though that was only 'acting.' It had also required him to learn an entirely new skillset. We'd all gotten to learn new tricks of the trade in trying to compensate for this disaster.

"That it is," I said. "I grew up in orbit of this world but spent my childhood in England with my ancestors of Russian and Japanese ancestry."

"I don't know what any of those words mean," Forty-Two said.

"Are you sure you don't want to sleep this one off?" Shelly asked.

"Not on your life," I said, finishing up my cup of bitter brew. "I'm as anxious to end this miserable trip as you are."

Shelly frowned and I knew there was serious disagreement behind her eyes. While she was every bit as overworked and exhausted by this ordeal as I was, it was also the kind of adversity she thrived under. Some men, women, and nonbinary beings were born to be captains. I think Shelly was one of them and as loyal as she'd been to Klaws—well to the position of captain he held—she was finally blossoming thanks to possessing real authority.

"So do you think you'll be getting a heroes' welcome or an epic dressing down?" Hannah asked, standing behind the tactical console. "After all, they have to blame somebody for this."

"A little of column A and a little of column B," I replied. "Mostly, I just expect them to move us to our next assignment."

"I predict they will blame Commander Shelly and laud you," Forty-Two said. "That is just how your lives tend to go."

"Not funny," I said, staring at him.

"I wasn't joking," Forty-Two responded.

"Viewscreen of Earth coming up," Elektra said, temporarily serving as the sensor officer as well as the science officer. The actual first shift sensor officer, Miranda Pressman, had given me her resignation as the deaths of her partner and children on Pompeii II had left her with no desire to continue service.

The image of the pale blue dot appeared on the viewscreen even as information about the planet as well as its current surrounding orbital bodies appeared on the side. Everything from the two hundred Lagrange Point space stations that served as orbital habitats for Earth's ever-expanding Spacer population to the millions of satellites positioned around the homeworld to handle its communication. That didn't count the constant traffic of civilian and government vessels that were constantly moving. I could see the Lunar shipyards as well, most of the orbital body having been hollowed out to construct them.

Earth was considered to be a backwater by the majority of the Community and was a protectorate rather than a full-fledged member. Still, it had made massive strides in the past two hundred years with the help of worlds like Albion, Belenus, and other human-settled worlds that had been "seeded" by the Elder Races. Even then, it was still constantly settling new worlds and building new habitats in hopes of expanding its influence. Part of the reason the Kolahn Resettlement Program had been so controversial was that it had taken away planets Earth had been hoping to plant its own flag on. Well, obviously that wasn't an issue now.

"Fascinating," Elektra said, speaking in a voice that mimicked a certain Vulcan. It was strange given as far as I could tell, she and her sister were the only Ethereals who had ever heard of *Star Trek* beyond it being used a pejorative or joke at their own races expense. Then again, Earth jokes about "space elves" were common. Even my Aunt Kathy had said that all the Ethereals gathered every Christmas to make toys for all the good little boys and girls. Her first officer had not been amused.

"What's that, Elektra?" I asked.

"I'm just examining the amount of construction around the Lunar shipyards," Elektra said. "There's something like three times the size of the existing Earth Home Fleet being worked on here."

I did a double take. "Excuse me?"

"Expansion is a necessary part of any world trying to join the Community as a full member," Shelly said. "Most Community members don't have full membership until they have at least one thousand settled worlds plus the forces to defend them."

The Community existed for the purposes of fostering peace, understanding, and cooperation across all races in the galaxy. Theoretically all were equal but, as Napoleon the Pig would have said, some were more equal than others. The High Council of the Senate, like the old United Nations Security Council, consisted of the full members: the Bugs, Sorkanan, the Drolochids, Sklux, and Olothonalka (aka Snails). It stuck in humanity's craw, especially EarthGov, to be stuck at the kids' table.

"Assuming we can afford it," I replied. "Besides, your race doesn't have to worry about that."

The Ethereals didn't have nearly as many worlds, barely a dozen, and were descended from humans as well but had their own seat due to speaking for the Elder Races. Besides, they also had alliances with "uplifted" versions of other races.

Shelly bristled and snorted, a most-uncharacteristic gesture for her. "I do not self-identify as an Ethereal human."

"Huh," I said. "You learn something new every day."

The expansion of Earth's military forces wasn't something that particularly alarmed me. Even if Earth did triple its forces size, it would not be large enough to go to war with any of the major powers. Earth had contributed heavily to the war against the Notha but had learned a valuable lesson in humility during that slog. No race could go it alone in the Known Universe and we were all better off having each other's back. I knew that, EarthGov knew that, and the Community High Speakers knew that. So why did I feel like I was deliberately ignoring an elephant in the corner of the room?

"We are receiving a communication from Earth. It is from EarthGov Fleet Command," the Shat said, his voice utterly devoid of emotion or personality but oddly gaining a set of weird pauses between words. We'd managed to successfully reboot the AI but he'd lost all of his subjective experiences and personality. It was another sign that AI were more than mere programming.

"Put it through," I said.

Shelly glared.

"Sorry," I said. "Captain, do you want to receive it?"

Shelly stared at me. "You've already ruined it."

I raised my hands in surrender. "I swear, you're the captain now."

"If you have to say it, I'm not the captain," Shelly said. "Put it through."

That was when we both noticed that the Shat had already put through the communication and we'd been arguing in front of Admiral Katherine Tagawa, aka my Aunt Kathy. Katherine Tagawa appeared to be a greying black-haired Asiatic woman in her mid-to-late fifties but was well over two hundred years old.

Kathy was wearing the pure white uniform of EarthGov's admiralty and was sitting at her glass desk with a backdrop of the Hawaiian campus of Space Academy behind her. It was almost certainly not the actual campus visible through her window, but it was a nice screensaver.

"Admiral," I said. "I'm glad it's you contacting us."

"Commander Shelly, Vannevar," Kathy said, forgoing formality with me. "You've created quite a storm with your journey here."

"Have we?" Shelly asked, confused. "I thought we were just returning to port as per orders."

"Clearly you haven't seen *Blood and Honor*," Kathy said. "The media coverage of the ship who stayed behind while the rest of the fleet abandoned millions is all over the feeds. That movie is number three at the box office."

"Well, that's not so great," I said, having a decidedly different relationship with the media than most officers. Most Lieutenant Commanders didn't have publicists and merchandising agents but plenty of EarthGov Captains did. Kathy herself did with no less than sixty movies, eighty documentaries, and thirteen holovision series due to our government's desire to promote her as an epic hero. I'd sort of been, almost literally, grandfathered in. Or great-aunted in as the case may be.

"I mean third in the Community," Kathy said, implying numbers that weren't possible for a non-AI to calculate. "It's been number one on Earth for eighteen weeks. Amazing for something they patched together over a weekend."

Shelly blinked, clearly unaccustomed to the propaganda elements of how Earth's Space Fleet related to the public. "I can assure you that the other starships, with a few unfortunate exceptions, did their absolute best to evacuate as many civilians as possible before leaving in an orderly manner. We were only unable to evacuate because of terrorism."

"Yes, and that just adds to the mystique," Kathy said. "James Bond was created by Ian Fleming as a way to mentally fight the decay of the British Empire by creating a single figure to embody English masculinity in a day of declining prestige."

"Who?" Shelly asked.

Kathy shook her head. "You kids, these days."

"I was born on a prison planet," Shelly said, revealing something else about herself. "I saw my first holovision show when I was almost an adult. I thought witches lived in the box."

"She's adopted!" Elektra said, cheerfully.

"Well, I'm just preparing you for the fact your return is now political," Kathy said. "You're expected to both come down to Space Fleet Academy for a special meeting of the Admiralty Board tomorrow morning at 0900 Standard Earth Time. The *ESS Ares* is marked for a full refit and moved to the front of the queue. As soon as you dock it, consider yourself both relieved of your duties and on leave. I suggest you get yourself some rest in the meantime. You both look terrible."

A special meeting of the Admiralty Board could be either very good or very bad. "What about the refugees onboard?"

Kathy sighed. "It'll be taken care of, Vannevar. They are officially not your problem anymore."

"I've grown attached," I said, sarcastically. I wasn't just going to abandon them even if they were a handful of the people onboard. We'd saved only two thousand Kolahn and they needed a home to return to. I still had nightmares about what the ones on New Pompeii must have felt in the hours before their vaporization. There were counselors on the ship but all of them were as traumatized as everyone else.

"Thank you, Admiral," Shelly said, shooting me a nasty look. "We appreciate your communication."

"You did a hell of a job getting here," Kathy said. "I wish what's going to happen next was good news."

She signed off.

"She seems nice!" Elektra said, cheerfully.

"I'm getting mixed signals here," Hannah said. "I'm not sure if we're getting a heroes' welcome or an epic dressing down."

"Probably both," Forty-Two said. "I bet I'm not even in the movie. But if I am, I need to call a lawyer and see if I can get a percentage."

"I know a few good ones," I replied. "I'll recommend them to you along with an agent."

"Thank you," Forty-Two said. "There is no greater evil than doing your absolute best, following your conscience, and fulfilling your duty yet not getting paid for it."

"Don't ever change, Forty-Two," I said.

"I do not intend to," Forty-Two said. "Unless you mean becoming richer and more powerful."

"Vannevar, can we speak in the ready room?" Shelly asked.

I considered it a personal triumph that I'd managed to get her to call it that versus a conference room. Either way, the two of us headed off the bridge with Shelly casually gesturing for Hannah to have command while we were gone. Shelly and I had almost forgiven her for leaving us on the ground when the bridge evacuation had happened eight months ago.

The ready room was a nice-looking office that had a long metal table with holographic displays and chairs more at home in an office building than on a battleship. It had "windows" showing the Earth system outside, but these were all computer-generated images as you didn't want even transparent steel walls being the only thing between you and enemy fire. Shelly waited at the door and electro-locked it with a wave of her hand after I passed through.

"If this is about who James Bond is, he's a spy," I replied. "My aunt made me watch the entire original one hundred movie series if I wanted to make full lieutenant."

"It's fine, Vance," Shelly said, relaxing. "I just wanted to speak with you before we departed. You can probably guess we're going to be broken up by this. If they're refitting the ship, then it's almost certainly getting a new crew."

"I imagine so," I replied. "I'm sure they're going to officially give you command."

"Thank you," Shelly said. "I'll be honest, it's been a long time coming. Demihumans in EarthGov's navy are looked at with suspicion, even if they've lived virtually their entire lives in Canada."

"Eh?" I asked.

Shelly narrowed her eyes.

"Sorry, couldn't resist," I replied. "That explains the stuffed beaver dressed like a hockey player in your office. I just thought that was someone's gag gift. How were you the child of Ambassador Ketra if you lived in Canada?"

"It's where she was assigned after failing to stop the SKAMM launches during the Notha War," Shelly replied.

"Ah," I said, grimacing. "That would explain it. She was a great woman."

"I barely knew her," Shelly replied. "However, she paid for my education after I was recovered from the Notha gulag where I was born. That was during the early days of our conflict with them when they were still raiding Albion and Belenus colonies. I joined Space Fleet after being a cop in New Vancouver on Mars for a few years. I was in security before moving into the command track."

That implied she was quite a bit older than me but, well, Ethereals didn't really show their age. Even if she chose to identify primarily as human. "You don't talk much about your past. Why now?"

Shelly smirked. There was a playful look in her eye I hadn't seen before that made me think this wasn't about work. "Well, it's been a horrible eight months of stress and we're no longer in each other's chain of command. We're also never going to see each other again—"

I raised an eyebrow. "Are you saying—"

Shelly frowned. "Vannevar, just take off your clothes. This will be a lot easier if you don't talk."

She didn't need to tell me twice.

CHAPTER FIVE

Exploring Space Academy

A h, the Academy!

Well, technically a branch campus of the Academy. Not to put too fine a point on it but there were academy facilities and there was the Academy. That one was a space station and a micro-world of its own. Still, Space Academy Hawaii was where I'd studied the first two years of my path to becoming an officer.

It was a beautiful artificial island that was just off the coast of Oahu. It had been constructed from Pearl Harbor military base and was now over a hundred square kilometers with mountains, parks, silver domed buildings meant to represent a "new" architectural style but really just looked like old pulp fiction covers, and even had its own rain forest.

The Academy held a lot of memories for me and was a place that was continuously being updated as more Earthlings came back from other worlds flush with alien or demihuman learning. In the past two hundred years, Earth had managed to eliminate pollution and poverty with a Universal Basic Income and guaranteed standard of living.

Rich anyxholes still controlled much of the economy and had undue influence in the government but it was a lot better than it had been before. There was also serious improvement in terms of interactions among mankind's peoples, too. As the late great fantasy author Terry Pratchett once said, "Racism was not a problem on the Discworld, because—what with trolls and dwarfs and so on— speciesism was more interesting. Black and white lived-in perfect harmony and ganged up on green." Replace the trolls and dwarfs with aliens and bots and you had a rough idea of how it went—which was great for everyone but the aliens and bots. Well, that and the one hundredth of a hundredth percent who fled to Contested Space because they had enough space in their hearts to hate aliens, bots, *and* other races.

Still, there was something different about the Academy. I couldn't put it into words, but it was there, on the tip of my tongue.

"You borking suck, Turbo!" Captain Rudra Laghari shouted, passing nearby with some of his officers. He was a brown-skinned man of Anglo-Indian descent with a goatee and was the captain of the *ESS Caliburn*.

I waved to them. "Nice to see you too, sir!"

Ah, that was one part of it. I'd found my reputation among my fellow officers had taken a massive plummet upon arrival here. Apparently, the media having taken the angle that the rest of the captains there had abandoned the *Ares* and refugees on New Pompeii while I was the big hero had gone over like a ton of bricks. The *ESS Caliburn* had arrived a few weeks before and was one of the ships vilified.

"Go to hell," Rudra shouted back, giving a very rude gesture.

"Now that's not proper naval behavior," I muttered, standing there beside a statue of Captain Julius Elgan.

Doing a double take at the monument, I was almost lost in the irony. Captain Elgan's continued reverence by the public was a living sign of EarthGov and Space Fleet's hypocrisy. The former captain of the *ESS Ares* had forcibly recruited me into Space Fleet after I dropped out of the Academy. It had seemed like a second chance to salvage a ruined career once I realized how much good I could do but it had all been a lie. The handsome shaven-headed heroic figure immortalized beside me had proven to be a murderer and a lunatic, recruiting me as well as the other members of the *Black Nebula* as decoys. I'd kept silent about his treachery because it was "classified" but also because I'd not wanted to rock the boat. Elgan had been one of the Earth's greatest heroes and they didn't want the truth getting in the way of their narrative.

"It's my estimation that every man whoever got a statue made of him was one kind of sumbitch or another," a voice spoke beside me. "That's from the 20th century science fiction program, *Firefly!*"

Given the oddity of referencing almost three-hundred-year-old media, I guessed that the speaker was either an AI or one of my family. Much to my surprise it was both. "Son of a bitch, Trish! Danny!"

Standing behind me was TRS-8021, aka Trish, the AI of the *Black Nebula* and *Ares* at various points in her career. She was wearing a gynoid body of Space Cadet Sally, a popular children's show from about eight years back before its extremely divisive finale. It was questionable how much her designers were marketing to children, however, given she had a voluptuous frame and "fully functional" attributes which I'd experienced.

Her long red hair was hidden underneath a pair of analysis goggles and she was wearing a turquoise combat engineer's uniform with body armor, implying she'd just come from the training grounds. Seeing her again made me happy and it was all I could do to keep myself from immediately embracing her. Unfortunately, we hadn't parted on the best of terms, and I was worried she still held that against me despite it all seeming so silly after the eight-month journey here.

I was almost as equally surprised by her companion, though. It was Danny Tagawa, my cousin, and great-great-something grandchild of my Aunt Kathy from her first marriage. He was a small, androgynous looking man with a beautiful face and short black hair that somehow did little to mask his fundamental cuteness. Danny was wearing a cadet's uniform but had the rank badge indicating he was a functioning midshipman set to work in the proper Earth Home Fleet.

It was genuinely a surprise to see Danny here because, well, the Tagawa family was about the least military family you could possibly find in Earth or her colonies. Aunt Kathy's daughter had become a kind of space hippie, converted to a knock off Etherealism, and raised her children as well as grandchildren to disdain the military-space complex that was putting demons in vaccines that caused psychic powers or something. They all lived off an allowance from Aunt Kathy's estate like my parents had until being cut off. I mean, there was a reason that Aunt Kathy and I were the closest members of our genetic lineage.

"Trish, Danny!" I said. "Well, I'll be a monkey's uncle."

"You might literally be with the way the Kolahn carry on about you," Danny said.

I grimaced. "Yeah, the Kolahn. I was the honorary uncle to a lot of their children."

Danny grimaced back. "That went dark quickly."

"No savit," I muttered.

It was Trish who made the first move and embraced me. I didn't hesitate to hug her back and appreciated her presence. She smelled of grease and fusion fire combined with strawberry shampoo.

Trish sniffed me. "You've had sex."

I pulled away. "I've showered. There's no way you know that."

"With an Ethereal!" Trish said. "By the Maker, your temporary commanding officer."

I stared at her in shock. "Your senses are that powerful?"

"No, the Shat is a gossip," Trish said. "He has been deeply bored with you for the past eight months."

I stared at her. "Well, I'm going to have a talk to him before we head out again."

Trish shook her head. "He's already been transferred to one of the newer ships. They've got dreadnoughts aplenty ready to handle their new flag duties. There's even talk of downgrading the *ESS Ares* again."

"It's half a kilometer long," I said.

"And they have kilometer and ten-kilometer ship plans!" Trish said. "The benefit of asteroid mining."

"Apparently never learned the lesson of the *Yamato*," I muttered, referencing the Japanese warship. Small and maneuverable trumped giant armored platforms.

"Maybe not," Danny said. "A lot of these are carriers."

I blinked. "They've finally got the starfighter program off the ground?"

Starfighters were a white elephant of space warfare where people kept trying to make it work despite technology and physics generally indicating it was a bad idea. Space combat was simply too fast and over too far a distance to have human reflexes matter. Drone warfare was viable with AI but ran into the issues of bigots not wanting to put that much power into the hands of AI, AI not being suicidal (as well as having rights in the law), and jamming fields being a thing rendered the entire prospect moot.

"So they claim," Trish said. "They've signed up two hundred thousand new sailors today."

I blinked. "They open a savit ton of new campuses?"

"Oh no, they've lowered the admissions standards and are recruiting from civilian groups!" Danny said. "Lots of enlisted being mustanged forward. I joined for the excellent education package and bio-enhancement option!"

I tried not to throw up and succeeded. I had a vision of the future in that moment that was impossible to avert. At some point, I would end up on a ship of the absolute worst and oddball crew in Space Fleet. It was inevitable.

"Hello? Vance?" Trish asked, waving her hand in front of my face.

"Sorry," I said, giving an involuntary shudder. "I'm just imagining myself on the kind of pirate ship that's going to produce."

"Oh, they'd never put you in charge of one of those," Trish said, not making eye contact.

"Well, no, I'm a Lieutenant Commander," I said. "I'm a decade away from being a captain."

Trish smiled with a full display of her teeth.

"I have a bad feeling about this," I muttered, then looked at Danny. "So, what are you doing here? How about you, Trish? My God, what a coincidence."

"Not really," Danny said, cheerfully. "We're here to bring you to the Admiralty Board."

"Oh," I said, blinking. "That's ominous."

"Not really!" Trish said, echoing Danny. "I'm sure everything will be fine."

"Now I'm really worried!" I said, horrified.

"You're a hero, Vance!" Danny said. "Everyone knows it."

"Should I try to run or is suicide the only option?" I asked.

Trish gave me a playful punch in the arm. "Come on, Vance. It's probably good news from some perspectives."

"I feel like you're both dancing around the subject," I said.

"Because we are," Danny said. "The Admiralty Board would be extremely plizzed if we didn't let them talk to you first."

I had a feeling I knew exactly what the news would be, but I didn't want to believe it. "So, Danny, what made you join Space Fleet? I mean aside from the excellent education package and option to get psychic powers."

"Those aren't enough?" Danny asked.

"I know your relatives," I replied. "They're technically mine. I would have thought they'd be trying to force you into a recreational plant grow-op, acting, or getting a degree in New Marxism."

"That's never gonna work," Trish said.

"I dunno, recreational grow ops are quite profitable if you're on the right planet," I said. "Also, aren't you a kid? You were half my size last time we saw each other."

"That does happen when you haven't seen someone in eight years," Danny said. "You didn't even show up when our family sued you."

"They sued me? Why?" I asked. If you couldn't tell I didn't waste much time trying to figure out what my own personal version of the Sackville Baggins were up to.

"Money, I presume," Trish said. She grabbed my arm and started leading me on the path to what I presumed would be the meeting. It was about thirty minutes until 0900 anyway.

"Ha-ha," I said, rolling my eyes.

Danny followed along. "You know the family. You've made so much money profiting off the pain and suffering of others. They feel like they should be doing that too. Then give like ten percent of it to a space whale preserve."

"Space whales don't exist," I said. "I think. It would be awesome if they did, but I haven't found any."

"Yeah, well, they'd soak up the majority of it as administrative fees," Danny said. "Don't worry. They lost anyway. Either way, I figured that I didn't want to spend the rest of my life trying to chase petty fame and New Era trends. I want to be of service to mankind."

I snorted. "Wow, they got their hooks in you good."

Danny frowned.

"Halt!" Trish said.

I stopped in mid-step and looked to see what she was referring to. On the ground were thousands of centimeter-long Bugs, moving along the sidewalk like a vast network of ants. I had encountered Bugs before, of course, but had been one of those humans stupid enough not to know that they were prone to riding around in what amounted to powered vehicles shaped like larger insects. I'd been acquainted with one of my crewmates, Picnic, for months without ever suspecting he was a colony of probably thousands of his species sharing a limited telepathy to add to their own intelligence. Each one no smarter than normal insects but collectively one of the most intelligent and powerful races in the galaxy.

"They're letting Bugs in the Earth Academy now?" I asked.

"Don't be prejudiced," Trish said.

"I'm not!" I said. "I'm actually worried people will step on them. Like me."

"It happens," Danny replied. "They don't take it personally, but they do insist on financial compensation. It works better than a threat of jailtime to keep the cash-strapped cadets watching their feet."

"Ah," I replied, fully intending to do so. I got a piece of whatever was marketed about me, but I rarely ever saw any of it. Not only did I live on a spacer's salary, but it always felt uncomfortable profiting off what amounted to the sacrifices of my fellow soldiers. As such, like ninety percent went to various charities. I kept the remainder just in case because, well, I wasn't an idiot, and you never knew when you might want to become a decadent playboy after being cashiered for one too many acts of insubordination or wacky planning. Yes, I'd thought way too much about this.

"I've been training as an engineer," Trish said. "I can absorb any number of facts instantly, but I figured I would use my new body to monitor whatever is wrong with the ship my AI is resting in."

It wasn't so much a new body since she'd had it for almost a decade, and they didn't even make Space Cadet Sally bioroids anymore. Bioroids also didn't particularly last much longer than ten years as a general rule unless they were the rare case of sentient ones and those weren't legally produced on Earth anymore. One of them, named Case Gordon, was apparently head of Earth's Security Departments.

"I bet you'll do your next ship proud," I said.

"Me too," Trish said, winking.

I was assuming that meant she'd be on my next assignment, which I wasn't sure about. She'd apparently forgiven and forgotten but I wasn't ready to resume things again. There had been some pretty good reasons we'd broken up and why I'd learned to block out any unwanted reading of my cybernetics' recordings of my thoughts. Long story there.

The rest of the trip went about without incident as we arrived at the conference center where plenty of flag officers regularly held meetings with civilian personnel as well as performed ceremonial details. I would have preferred to have any meetings with the Admiralty Board at High Command but it's not like them having meetings here were unprecedented. It had been constructed by the Sorkanan after all and was, in simple terms, just more impressive than most human buildings as well as more secure.

Heading through a doorway that seemed to vanish rather than open then reappear behind us, we walked into an egg-shaped chamber that carried us far beneath the island to the secure bunkers where everything looked like endless halls of nondescript offices. Much to my surprise, I saw Shelly standing there with a gooey six-foot tentacle I recognized as a Skulx. Shelly was staring at an infopad with barely restrained fury in her eyes.

"Hi, Commander!" I said, waving.

Shelly glared at me, pointed, and shouted, "You son of a bitch."

She stormed past me, bumping her shoulder into me as she got into the elevator behind me.

I blinked. "What the hell?"

Elektra walked out of one of the rooms, carrying a plate of cookies. "Oh, hey, Vance. They have cookies in this room!"

Trish took one of the cookies and chewed on it.

CHAPTER SIX

The Worst Punishment

"What was that about?" I said, taking a chocolate chip cookie.

"Shelly just got done with her meeting," Elektra said, cheerfully. "She thinks this was all prearranged to bum rush her."

"And she thinks Vance was involved?" Trish asked, chewing on her cookie.

"Yeah, I mean she's known the guy years," Elektra replied. "You'd think she'd know that he's not the evil scheming type."

"Oh, he's constantly scheming but for good," Trish said. "So, we like use the water fountain or what?"

"I'm allergic to chocolate," Danny replied, waving away the plate.

"Don't worry, this is all artificial cookie dough and chocolate made by a 3D constructor," Elektra said. "Perfectly healthy and assembled from essential enzymes and nondescript goop!"

I paused before biting into mine and put it back on the plate.

"You already touched it," Elektra said, frowning at the cookie.

I reached to pick it back up.

"No, it's already touched everything else," Elektra said.

I rolled my eyes. "I don't suppose you can tell me what she's so upset about?"

That was when a male human officer stepped out of another door and directed me. "They're waiting inside for you, sir."

I checked my cybernetic feed and noted it was almost 0900 on the dot. It was a good thing they'd come to pick me up as I might have been a couple of minutes late, a death sentence in the military. The Academy had changed a great deal since I'd last come here, and it was easy to get lost in reminiscences.

Exchanging a look with the others, I walked past the doorman and headed into the room. It looked like a bunker with no windows, viewscreens, or signs of personal touch. Instead, there was just the conference table with six admirals behind it and a bunch of flags behind them. Specifically, they were the white and blue flag of Earth, Albion's weird black Union Jack variant, Belenus' fleur de lis, Amaterasu's golden sun, and Anansi's red with green.

The admirals assembled weren't exactly what I expected either. There was my Aunt Kathy and Fleet Admiral Saul Bendo, but the other four admirals present were representatives of the non-Earth governments represented by said flags. It was an array of blue, white, black, and gray uniforms that had more military decorations between them than a Contested Space dictators' convention. It was a very weird collection of people since I'd fully expected a board consisting of EarthGov personnel alone. This was more like someone had assembled the Allies during WW2. That was not something you really wanted unless you were about to launch a war. Which, given all the other context clues I'd just seen, seemed increasingly likely.

I took position in front of the table, stood at attention, and saluted until signaled to relax by Admiral Bendo. I was honestly surprised he did. I hadn't seen this much brass since the last time they had trotted me out to one of EarthGov's gladhanding parties. Saul Bendo was a tall, white-haired, black man with a goatee and deep statesman-like presence that was as important as his military experience.

"Welcome, Commander," Admiral Bendo said. "I'm glad to have you here."

"I'm happy to be here," I said, looking behind me. "I was under the impression it would be a shared meeting with my commanding officer, though."

There was an exchange of chuckles among the admirals that I didn't find reassuring.

"Commander Shelly has just been awarded the Naval Galaxy," Admiral Bendo said.

I blinked. That was the highest decoration the Protectors could award for someone. Everyone would have to salute her for the rest of their lives. It certainly wasn't something that she should have been upset about. "She deserves it."

"You have been as well," Admiral Bendo said.

My mouth went dry. "I'm honored."

I didn't deserve it and had just been at the right place at the right time. It also was the final clue that things were in motion that probably shouldn't have been. The Naval Galaxy was never awarded in peacetime but only during times of war, which meant that the Kolahn War or something similar was considered officially resumed. Given the Kolahn no longer had any worlds to call their own, it was a rather ominous development.

"As well you should be," Admiral Bendo said. "However, that is not what we're here to talk about. We've decided to further advance your rank."

Oh, they were making me a commander. No wonder she was ticked off. Shelly had been in Space Fleet a good fifteen years longer than I had been. Finding out that we were the same rank was probably a real kick in the gut since I was already promoted past the usual promotion time. Especially if they weren't advancing her rank.

"We're making you a captain and giving you the *ESS Ares*," Admiral Bendo replied.

My mouth went dry. "Sir, I'm hardly qualified."

Now I was thinking that Shelly had underreacted. Plenty of fleet officers already hated me for the belief I was benefiting from nepotism and Earth's propaganda machine. This would drive them bonkers. I would look like the child of a Contested Space dictator—which was an example I was going to disturbingly often lately—walking around with an unearned rank.

"We disagree," Admiral Bendo said, ending any further discussion. "You displayed not only the heroism and courage necessary for your rank but also have shown that you can do the drudge work of keeping a ship functional during the long space flights between destinations. With the dramatic expanse of EarthGov's Home Fleet and her allies, we'll also be accelerating the promotion of many other figures within our ranks."

"If I may, sir?" I said, knowing that this meeting already had more back talk from the junior officer than was usual.

"Go ahead," Admiral Bendo said. "Within reason."

I had a thousand questions about all of this but ended up asking a personal one instead. "What about Commander Shelly?"

"Will remain your first officer," Aunt Kathy said.

I paused. Well, there went any possibility of a repeat of last night. I also would need to start keeping a fusion pistol under my pillow. That was an insult to her and all she'd done to get the *ESS. Ares* home. If they really were tripling the size of the Earth Home Fleet, then she should have gotten command of one of the new vessels unless they had uniformly decided to block her from further progress in the command path. If I was being extremely cynical, I wondered if it was because she wasn't pure human.

"I see, sir," I replied. "If I may ask, what are my new duties to be?" I would have added, "aside from avoiding being murdered in my sleep," but this wasn't one of my cheesy ass movies.

"The human race has found great prosperity and advances as part of the Community," Admiral Bendo said. "We've managed to advance in the past two hundred years more than in the past ten thousand. An end to poverty, cancer, global warming, homelessness, starvation, most diseases, and internal warfare."

I, again, kept my mouth shut that none of these applied to a lot of colony worlds because I wasn't a moron.

Admiral Bendo continued. "However, there's an unfortunate fact about our situation that needs to be addressed: we are not a power within it. Our voice is one of many and no more significant than any other."

Which was how democracy was supposed to work but I actually didn't disagree with the resentment. Plenty of other races had a lot more power than their individual worlds and tended to vote as a block. "Is that changing, sir?"

"Earth is the mother world of the human race even if its seeds have been cast far," Admiral Bendo gestured to his fellow planetary

47

representatives. "As such, we've started making inroads with other major human planets in hopes of drawing them into a firmer, stronger, long-lasting economic as well as political alliance. This hasn't been announced to the public yet, but we have finally managed to sign the initial paperwork for the creation of a Human League."

I almost snorted at the name but suspected that the admirals wouldn't have approved. Besides, unless they were friends of Trish, I doubted they had heard her Eighties pop hit list that she'd forced me to memorize. Still, a part of me wanted to sing "Don't You Want Me" and "Human" before realizing both songs were eerily appropriate now. Instead, I looked at them and said, "You wish to unite the human race."

"In time," Admiral Bendo said, giving a sideways look to the Albion Admiral that spoke volumes. "This is more setting the groundwork for a larger expansion out into the void."

"Together in electric dreams," I said, nodding, and naming another one of the Human League's songs.

My Aunt Kathy glared at me.

No one else got it.

"Err, yes, I suppose that's one way of phrasing it," Admiral Bendo said.

Oh man, we were borked. This was obviously Albion's handiwork. The most powerful human world had struggled for decades to take advantage of its strategic trade position and strong economy to force other human colonies to acknowledge it as leader. It had always failed but Earth had symbolic value and could be used to leverage most of those alliances without looking like it was pulling the strings.

Even if it went off without a hitch and they did manage to reclaim all of Earth's "colonies"—most of which had been seeded by the Elder Races with kidnapped humans rather than through any effort on our parts—it still wouldn't make humanity one of the big dogs. It would certainly help, mind you, but you needed at least a thousand worlds to apply for High Council membership and all of the worlds with a human majority added up to barely a hundred and eighty-four.

It was impressive, really, and would mean a lot of economic progress but that was only if Albion or Earth didn't do what it normally did and leach off every world they entered unequal treaties with. Indeed, a large part of why so many human worlds preferred separate membership in the Community because that gave them additional privileges. It was also assuming the Community High Council races didn't choose to intervene and smack humanity down for the blatant power grab that it was. On the other hand, I supposed I should be grateful that there was no sign this alliance wanted to cut ties with the Community. That would simply be a disaster on par with the Reactionary Party wanting to build a barrier around Earth to keep out unwanted aliens.

"Do you have any opinion on this, Captain?" Aunt Kathy asked, clearly fishing for something.

"No, ma'am," I replied, lying my ass off.

"No?" Aunt Kathy asked.

I shook my head. "Still a few dozen levels above my paygrade."

I could tell that was exactly the answer most of them wanted to hear. Somehow things had radically changed on Earth in the past eight months and probably had been doing so in the additional five or six years since I'd visited last. The Enigmatic Path, assuming they were the party responsible for the SKAMM attack, had made Earth feel vulnerable and convinced them to tighten their connection to other humans instead of the Community as a whole. It had also frightened them to ramp up their military forces versus the economy and social structure. I didn't know how I fit into it, though.

"Excellent," Admiral Bendo said. "Then you'll be pleased to know that we want you to carry out a goodwill tour of Contested Space's human colonies and settlements."

"Goodwill tour?" I asked.

Of all the things the *ESS Ares* could be used for, I wasn't sure how that could possibly be the most efficient use of its time. A forty-five-year-old vessel or not, there were the refugee crisis and security concerns that certainly took precedent. The human colonies in Contested Space were also illegal, hence the term contested, with their settlement having been suspended due to the whole Notha War thing that destroyed seventeen systems. Eighteen if you counted Pompeii.

"Yes," Aunt Kathy replied. "A gift-giving expedition of badly needed refugee supplies and personal appropriations to local government officials to show precisely what the Community can do for them."

"Community and Human League," Admiral Bendo said.

"Of course, Admiral," Aunt Kathy said, letting herself be corrected. I had no doubt her slip of the tongue had been deliberate, though. Katherine Tagawa had been one of the most tireless examples of a human working for the supposedly alien-led Community in the belief that if Earth was going to improve then it had to do as part of a larger galactic, well, community. She had little patience for isolationism or xenophobia. If Earth's new direction wasn't either, Albion influence or not, then it was certainly protectionism and that wasn't much better.

"Sounds super," I said, with fake enthusiasm. They were dispatching the *ESS Ares* with a bunch of vaccines, tractors, and bribes, great. It's not like I disapproved of the first two, but this was starting to feel awfully Cold War.

I could, in simple terms, see my future career in the Community Protectors burning up before my eyes. While I wasn't quite the youngest captain to ever command a starship in Space Fleet, even excluding posthumous promotions, I could see how my rise would be ended by this promotion. I would no longer be a "fighting" captain of the navy but instead put out for gladhanding and public relations that would almost certainly be a circus. It wasn't like I wanted to fight, mind you, but I also didn't want to be Vance Turbo the Friendly Officer to the rest of the Known Universe.

It added another layer to Shelly's anger as the only thing worse than being a captain of a good will boat would be being the first officer onboard one. I could have resigned right then. It would have been titanically stupid of me and childish beyond reason but at least I wouldn't be stuck with this for the potential next two decades of service, if they ever let me out of this. Unfortunately, for my own stubborn pride, I kept my mouth shut. Relief supplies and vaccines were important things to deliver to the colonies inside Contested Space. Someone had to deliver them, and I'd been doing important work with refugees for the past few years without complaint. Gladly even.

Admiral Bendo seemed to be watching my face for a reaction and I couldn't help but imagine that he was reading every single one of my thoughts play out through my brain. "Some wars are fought with plasma weapons and rockets, Captain. Other wars are won at the negotiating table. This work is important and will eventually lead to new opportunities for you."

"If you say so, sir," I said, nodding. "When can I expect to deploy again?"

"So eager to get back out there?" Aunt Kathy asked.

"Yes," I replied.

I didn't want to say that part of me had hoped I would have been out there hunting for whoever blew up New Pompeii if not for taking care of the people I'd help evacuate. As far as I could tell, there were still more theories than answers about what had happened that day. The Enigmatic Path had been blamed, cleared of all responsibility, supposedly taken credit, denied all involvement, and everything in between in the past eight months. Even if they had been the ones to launch the SKAMM, there was also no telling where they had gotten it and what the Elder Races might do to a species that failed to abide by their decree. So far, the answer had been nothing. However, like an elephant, they were slow to react but made their feelings unambiguous once they started moving.

"Then we'll let you go," Admiral Bendo replied, an empty smile on his face. "The refits to the *ESS Ares* should take about three weeks to complete and with the new engines it will only take you about two months to get back to Contested Space. Dismissed."

I saluted and departed back out the doors, feeling the weight of this all crashing down. Trish and Danny were waiting for me but there was no sign of Elektra. Presumably she'd gone off to comfort her sister.

"So, captain, huh?" Trish asked.

"Congratulations!" Danny said.

"You knew?" I asked.

"I was assigned to be your yeoman," Danny said. "Secretary work for the win!"

"I'm an all-powerful AI," Trish said. "Also, the guards talk."

I nodded. "Well, I'm glad you two are here to help."

51

"Actually, I promised Grandma Kathy I'd go sailing with her," Danny said. "She wants to hear all about me now that I'm a Navy man."

"I suggest you not call her that," I said. "Good luck."

Danny nodded and departed.

"Want to go sing some karaoke?" Trish asked. "I have some pastiches of Pat Benatar I've composed."

"No thanks," I said.

"Drink?" Trish asked.

"Not in the mood," I said, shaking my head.

"Sex?" Trish offered.

I paused. Shelly had made it clear it was a one-time only thing and seemed to be unlikely to forgive me anytime soon. Still, it would be a terrible idea to hook up with my ex and possibly complicate things in the future. I opened my mouth to gently let her down. "Sure."

Goddammit, me!

CHAPTER SEVEN

Hell Is Empty and All the Devils Are Here

The Enigmatic Path suicide attack took us by surprise. The Kolahn disabled the *ESS Ares* with a series of cyberattacks that were more advanced than anything we currently had in the Community database. We were forced out of jumpspace at Jump Point Athena 3340 and almost immediately were set upon by a fleet of modified civilian freighters, outdated starfighters, and hand-piloted torpedoes that were designed to overwhelm our immediate defenses.

"JUMPSPACE DRIVE DISABLED," Trish, still our AI at the time, said. "SHIELDS DOWN. ONE THIRD OF OUR WEAPONS SYSTEMS ARE DISABLED."

Captain Klaws, Shelly, and I were standing on the bridge of the *Ares*. It was much earlier in our careers and during the last days of the war. Everything looked a little brighter and nicer, even the carpet. We were still soldiers and not primarily people providing relief efforts to the destitute and hungry. I was stupidly proud of my efforts then. This wasn't our first fight, but it would be one of the most important.

"Shoot them down!" Captain Klaws shouted, shaking his paw in the air. "Get our shields up!"

"Shield power to maneuverability," Shelly suggested. "Full turnabout. Our engines can outlast theirs."

"Agreed," Klaws said. "Suggestions, Vance?"

"Let me at the virus," I said, highlighting that my primary training was in cyberwarfare. My cybernetics were also capable of things that were simply not possible by regular military personnel. The captain didn't know the full capabilities of my Elder Race enhanced nanotech, a thing I regretted but I didn't want to end up on a table somewhere, yet I was capable of helping here.

"Do it," Klaws said.

The battle was almost eerie due to the silence on the bridge as every possible weapon went off. Sound did not travel through space and the gravity emitters were still intact, meaning that we would feel nothing even when lasers tore through the sides of our hull to vent atmosphere. I linked up with Trish's systems, though, and that changed immediately.

While merged with the AI, I could feel the outside and the fear as well as excitement coming from her while the Kolahn terrorists attempted to kill us. The sounds and explosions in space were things I heard while every blast from Enigmatic Path's weapons was like being stabbed.

I need your help, Vance, Trish's voice spoke in my head.

You have it, I responded to her.

I causally removed the Kolahn malware and restored our shields as well as weapons. The jumpdrive was restored, too, but that was almost unimportant because Captain Klaws took the advantage to turn the ambush into a massacre. Now armed with three times the weapons and shields, any chance the Enigmatic Path had of defeating the *Ares* evaporated.

Captain Klaws was, at heart, an evolutionarily bred predator and did his best to make sure the Kolahn soldiers didn't have a chance to escape. He showed them no quarter and it didn't matter in the end because they made no attempt to surrender. Instead, they fought to the bitter end because their commander had left them no recourse.

It was as Sun Tzu said, "Throw your soldiers into positions whence there is no escape, and they will prefer death to flight." Still, rarely had I ever been called to utterly eradicate a foe and it made me sick. What was the value of victory if it cost you everything you were? Would the Community destroy its moral center to crush the Kolahn once and for all? Was that a Space Fleet I wanted to be part of?

Wow, way to be a downer, Vance, Trish said. *Just enjoy the PEW-PEW and BOOM-BOOM.*

I woke up with a monster headache in my apartment in Hawaii, just outside of McAuliffe space base. The rain was pouring down on the windows as I noticed it was the early morning with supply ships taking off to the moon. Noise cancellation hardware was built into the sides of the walls, so I only heard the light patter of rain instead of the loud rockets propelling Earth's extrasolar economy.

The apartment was off base and a lot nicer than I really needed or could ever use. I had barely touched any of the furniture and everything I'd eaten for the past three weeks had been takeout. Trish was lying asleep or simulating asleep as she recharged with a wrist plug, on top of my bed. I felt guilty about that because what had been meant to be a brief respite had turned into a regular thing.

None of the issues that had been present the first time we'd tried a relationship had gone away and now we were ready to resume work together on the *Ares*. I cared for her greatly, but I wasn't sure the differences between a being that thought lifetimes per second versus an all-too-human being could be overcome. There was also someone else in my thoughts and even if that was equally impossible, love wasn't rational.

I got up and slipped on a pair of boxer shorts before getting some synth-milk from the fridge in the kitchen, stopping only when I noticed there was a luminescent transparent figure in front of the counter. I recognized her as the late Ketra T'Kal, mother of Elektra and Shelly, who was wearing a set of robes to go with her ghostly form. Ketra had ebony black skin, darker than her daughters, and braided white hair that was still visible in its coloration despite the whole glowing transparent thing. Oh, and being dead.

"Luke, I am your father," Ketra said, giving a V salute with her fingers.

"You screwed up the joke," I said, shaking my head.

"What?" Ketra asked. "My combination of children's media from centuries ago not accurate?"

"You mixed up *Star Trek* and *Star Wars*," I pointed out. "Also, the line from the wrong character."

Ketra rolled her eyes. "Let's go with a different property then. Hamlet, my boy, I need you to go kill your uncle. He killed me to steal my kingdom and marry your mother."

"I don't think that's how Shakespeare put it," I replied dryly.

"That's the Sorkanan translation," Ketra said. "They felt like the story worked much better without any of the poetry or wordplay."

I stared at her. "I find that genuinely horrifying."

"Don't go to bipedal lizard people for poetry," Ketra said. "They still employ the cat of nine tails for discipline problems and have legalized impressment."

"On the plus side, they get alcohol with their rations," I replied, taking a drink of my synth-milk. "Am I hallucinating, still dreaming, or have a genuine paranormal encounter?"

"Yes," Ketra said, "and no. I am projecting myself from across multiple light years using your cybernetics. They are permanently attuned to the Elder Races' frequencies, and I thought I would contact you."

"About?" I asked, feeling a bit awkward about this.

Ketra narrowed her eyes. "You will be visited by three spirits this First Contact day. You must make amends for your sins and learn the true meaning of Space Fleet."

I narrowed my eyes. "Excuse me, I need to go call an exorcist. That is, unless you actually have something worth talking about."

I knew Ketra was not, in fact, a ghost but an AI construct made from her memories and personality. As an agent of the Elder Races, they'd preserved it upon her death to continue serving them as well as enjoy the weird transcendental realms they supposedly inhabited. Philosophically, you could argue all day whether it was actually her, but I doubt she considered there to be any difference between her now and the "living" Ketra. I had yet to mention her to Shelly because, well, how the hell would you go about bringing that up?

"You could mention, 'Hey, your mom is still alive,'" Ketra said, ribbing me. Her expression then turned dark. "You know, when you're not cheating on my daughter."

I glared at her. "I am not cheating on your daughter!"

"Then who is that in there?" Ketra pointed to the bedroom. "Don't think her being a sexaroid prevents it from being cheating. I had three concubines who thought that and all of them found out differently."

I drank from the cartoon of synth milk and shook my head. "We aren't dating!"

"What did you do wrong?" Ketra said, putting her hands on her translucent hips.

I stared at her. "I became her commanding officer."

"Ooo, that would do it," Ketra said. "I was ambassador to Earth, and she joined Space Fleet just to spite me. Also, to get revenge on the Eclipse."

"Eclipse?" I asked.

"The Romulans to our Vulcans," Ketra said. "Ethereals who think that the Elder Races are evil."

"They kinda are," I replied, dryly. "What with the whole genocide of any race that steps out of line and manipulating them from a distance thing. Mostly the former but the latter still needs to be mentioned."

I wondered why Trish hadn't woken and guessed she really needed that recharge.

"Well, I'm just going to say you're letting a great catch slip through your fingers," Ketra said. "I would tell her the same, but she doesn't have any cybernetics. In any case, I'm here to deliver you a message."

I put the synth milk back in the fridge. "Given I'm about to leave for Contested Space, I hope it's related to that. Because the last time we worked together, it ended pretty terribly what with you dead and all."

"We also completed our mission," Ketra said. "Which is enough."

"Is it?" I asked.

"It is when the survival of the human race is at stake," Trish said.

"Well, come to me when it is again," I said, crossing my arms and leaning up against the fridge.

"Okay," Ketra said before staring.

"Crazzap," I muttered. "Again?"

"'Fraid so," Ketra said, frowned. "They are deeply upset about the destruction of the Pompeii system."

"No savit," I said. "We all are."

"No," Ketra said, shaking her head. "You don't understand. The Elder Races *ordered the end of the SKAMMs* and someone *disobeyed*. That is not something that they can tolerate. Heads must role and examples must be made."

"But we don't know who did it," I said, following her line of thought.

"I know," Ketra said. "That is the failure of us as their servants. They will lash out and destroy whoever they must in order to get their example made to the beings they both fear as well as consider to be lesser. The only thing that will stop that is to find the party responsible for New Pompeii and destroy them."

"They don't know?" I asked.

"They're almost omnipotent," Ketra said, "but far from omniscient."

"Oh joy," I said, terrified out of my mind.

"You need to find who is responsible," Ketra said.

I didn't even question it. "How long do I have?"

"A year," Ketra said. "After that, planets will start to burn."

"They're already burning," I said, thinking of the Kolahn worlds.

The Kolahn War had included attempts to shut down all jumpspace travel in the Community, narrowly failing on EarthGov, plus other massive cyberattacks. They also had ignited the atmosphere of colony worlds as well as other acts of "mass suicide." That had not been what had destroyed the homeworld, though. That had been orbital bombardment that had been meant to end their threat of unleashing rabid AI onto the whole of the galaxy. The planet had been rendered uninhabitable, though evacuated, as if it was a Band-Aid on a gushing wound.

"And do not think the Elder Races' hands were not there too," Ketra said. "They do not always work directly but through proxies."

"And you want me to work for these people," I replied.

"Think of yourself as a priest of a primitive people trying to placate an angry god," Ketra said. "Except the gods are very much paying attention."

"Throwing virgins into volcanos did very little to end eruptions but did a lot for getting women to loosen up," I said an old joke I'd heard here. It had been from the President of the Hawaiian Republic actually.

"Yes, laugh it up," Ketra said. "I've been keeping an eye on you. I understand that you gaslit your captain into thinking the Muppets were real."

"That prank was hilarious, and he never figured it out," I said, taking a deep breath. "I guess I have to accept this job or we're all going to die."

"Yep," Ketra responded, slowly vanishing. "May the Logic be with you."

"That is not how…" I started to say before noticing that she was gone. "Dammit."

Well, that certainly puts a new angle on things, doesn't it? Here I had been worrying about doing nothing important and now I had the looming horror of a sufficiently advanced precursor race eradicating humanity if I didn't locate who had tucked away some weapons of mass destruction for a rainy day. It didn't help that tens of thousands of SKAMMs had been manufactured and stockpiled by various races prior to the Second Treaty of Exarxes.

The Kolahn hadn't had any, otherwise they would have used them, but the theory for creating them was public knowledge and taught in universities. It would also be a neat and tidy bow to blame everything on the religious terrorists with a technology fetish. The Notha had been fighting a civil war for the better part of ten years but that made them more likely to be responsible rather than less in my view. I also didn't put it past other, less likely groups, like human extremists who wanted to end the resettlement project or various alien isolationist hate groups.

I briefly thought of Leah Mass, someone I hadn't thought of in years, and wondered if I should seek her out. My biomod ex had been a woman who impersonated a Space Fleet cadet and used me to get at Captain Elgan's insane plan to acquire Elder Race technology. She was an agent of Department Nine and a high-ranking intelligence operative. If anyone could get me information on who knew what, it would be her, but I wasn't sure that any bridges remained between us. Ones that weren't thoroughly burned, at least.

I was about to make a few phone calls when my doorbell rang and I headed to it, wondering who could be visiting me in the early morning of the last few days before I shipped out again. Heading to the door past a still-recharging Trish, I stupidly didn't bother to check the hallway cameras first. Heavenly Haven apartments supposedly provided the best private security you could get and was outside a military base anyway.

Opening the door part-way, I blinked as a camera drone flashed a light in my face. A well-coifed Eurasian man in his apparent middle years was standing beside it. He was wearing a tweed sweater, micro-glasses, and khaki pants as he shoved an old-fashioned looking microphone underneath my face. "Hello, Martin Chang-Waverly, Homefront news. I'm the imbedded reporter that's going to be filming the documentary of the *ESS Ares'* two-year mission."

"You're what now?" I asked.

"Do you have any commentary on the fact you've been referred to as the Boy Captain? What about the Kolahn's murderous betrayal of the attempts to relocate them? Have you any opinion on the increasing fact that Earth is finally putting itself first? Have you any thoughts on whether we're really getting anything from the Community? Oh, and is it true you prefer machines to real flesh and blood women? Aliens too?"

I stared at him and shut the door in his face.

"See you on the ship!" Martin said through the door.

CHAPTER EIGHT

That Scene Where You See Your Ship for the First Time (Again)

"So, we need to find out who destroyed the sun of Pompeii or the Elder Races will destroy humanity?" Trish asked as I piloted the shuttle we were traveling on to the lunar shipyards.

The personal shuttle was a lot smaller than the kind I used to transport up refugees but was a privilege of officer rank that I was enjoying. It had just enough room for four people and no amenities. Technically, I was rich enough to buy my own, but it was an irony of being a famous officer that I didn't need much and just made do with military issue. Mind you, as I understood other rich families, you didn't need the vast majority of your possessions anyway.

Indeed, I'd sold a good massive chunk of my investments in hopes of trying to help deal with the refugee crisis before I left. Things had gotten massively worse as violence against Kolahn civilians had tripled and people were blaming them for the destruction of New Pompeii. Even if the Enigmatic Path had been involved, that didn't mean anything for the average civilian.

"Pretty much," I said, moving us out of the atmosphere. Getting out of that was always the trickiest part but thankfully technology had improved a bit since the days of the Space Race.

Honestly, the biggest danger of traveling through atmospheres these days was the debris left over from the years when space travel was completely unregulated. The millions of busted satellites, plaques, corpses (space funerals had always been popular), and more that were hurtling through the air at thirty kilometers per second or one hundred seventy-eight thousand, eight hundred twenty-six kilometers per hour. Really, barriers had been created not as weapons of war but just to make orbital entry and exits practical by similar space-faring races. I didn't pity the garbage men, sorry, astronauts, who had to risk life and limb to collect these things.

"Well, that sucks," Trish said, crossing her arms across her ample chest. Which was not an appropriate thing to think about my ship's AI.

Who I was sleeping with.

But not in a relationship with.

Maybe.

"Yeah, I would say so," I said, frowning. "We have a year to find out who was responsible and I'm pretty sure whoever we reveal is going to die horribly."

"Only you would be worried about the guy or gal who blew up a sun," Trish said.

"I'm less worried about them than anyone around them," I replied. "The Elder Races aren't known to be terribly discriminate in their punishments."

"Neither are we," Trish pointed out.

"Yeah," I replied, my tone even.

I hadn't been alone among those people appalled by the destruction of Kolahn IV at the climax of the Kolahn War. They didn't reduce the planetary surface to glass, but they had orbitally bombarded it until it was rendered uninhabitable in the long term. A former friend of mine had tried to reassure me by comparing it to the use of atomic weapons during the Second World War, missing a point about who he was talking to. The subsequent argument over ethics in warfare, collateral damage, and total war had left our bridges burnt.

"Do you think you should call command and ask for their help?" Danny asked, causing me to do a double take.

"When the hell did you get there?" I asked, staring at my cousin.

"I've always been there," Danny said. "I'm your yeoman and in charge of your schedule."

"Oh," I said, staring at him. I swear, I remembered him being there yet somehow just forgot. That was just weird. "So, you heard all that."

"Yep!" Danny said. "We have to pass the tests of the omnipotent aliens, or they will destroy us. Seems pretty classic sci-fi stuff."

"Except it's real," I said, calmly.

"As for contacting the Admiralty Board or EarthGov, I think that if Ketra wanted to do that then she would have done so herself."

"The ghost of your second-in-command's mother," Danny said, writing that down on his infopad.

"Please don't record that," I said, "and sort of."

"And by sort of, he means exactly," Trish said.

"I don't think the Admiralty Board has any idea of who was responsible," I said. "If they did, they would have announced it to the world. The failure in finding out where that SKAMM came from is one of the greatest intelligence blunders of Community history."

"They could also be responsible," Trish said.

"Wait, what?" I asked, doing a double take and being glad we were now into the void of space on a direct course for the moon.

"I mean, EarthGov had a lot of SKAMMs given to them by the Sorkanan in hopes they'd use them against the Notha," Trish said. "We're the only species that has used them militarily alongside said Notha. They might have decided to blow up New Pompeii to justify withdrawing all support for the Kolahn Resettlement Project, building up their military forces, and claiming the worlds of Contested Space in the name of security concerns."

"That's a little 9/11 truther, Trish," I said.

"What's 9/11 refer to?" Danny asked.

"Look it up," I said. "I'm a student of Earth's military-political history in addition to Pre-First Contact science fiction."

"One of which is relevant to your job," Trish said. "The other of which is completely undignified and useless. I mean, who needs to know military-political history of a backwater like Earth?"

I rolled my eyes. "I don't suppose you have had any luck tracking down Leah?"

"I checked all of the records publicly available, all of the ones our security clearance allow, and some that weren't," Trish said. "All I could find out was that Leah is somewhere in Contested Space."

The last I'd heard she was working on Crius, a planet that was another breakaway Earth colony. It was much richer and nastier than most, though, being where people went when they didn't want to behold themselves to financial or scientific ethics. Oh, and wanted to give themselves titles and playact as aristocrats like *Dune*. "Interesting. I guess she is far away from this."

"We can only hope," Danny said. "But what if EarthGov *is* involved? Would you turn them over to the Elder Races? I mean, even to save our species?"

"I have no idea," I said, wondering if I was going to end up having to commit treason in order to save my race from an enemy it couldn't possibly defeat. Actually, no, if they did blow up New Pompeii then bork those guys. I would just have to make sure they died rather than Earth itself.

The rest of the shuttle flight was largely spent in silence as we approached the Lunar Shipyards. They were arguably the greatest accomplishment of humanity in terms of construction, building a massive facility larger than any artificial habitat. The moon had been cored like an apple, filling it with massive amounts of machinery and habitats for the millions of workers who worked to assemble almost every ship in humanity's service. Entering through one of the moon's two hemisphere "eyes", I saw the massive interior city-scape envelope me.

The Lunar Shipyards proper were in the empty space between the countless factories, habitats, and assemblage plants that primarily got their materials transported to the moon's surface before being put down enormous chutes to whatever location they needed. The shipyards were always busy, building a mixture of civilian and military craft, but I couldn't recall it ever being quite so full as it was right now. It was one thing to be told that the Earth Home Fleet was tripling in size, but it was another to see it. Not only were the warships being built, but all the hundreds of support craft needed to maintain such an undertaking. They would have to hire every Earthborn spacer in the Spiral to fill the crew needs and then some more besides.

"Look at the size of that thing," Danny muttered, staring at the super structure before us.

"That's what she said," Trish said, grinning.

"Trish, please," I muttered.

"I'm returning home, Vance," Trish said. "Cut me some slack. This is where I was first programmed."

The Lunar Shipyards was also where Ares Electronics kept its Earth headquarters, assembling and testing all advances in artificial intelligence. That was one area where humanity had managed to get a leg up on other races. The field was still controversial due to laws implemented by the Sorkanan at the start of the Community. The only people who had been anywhere near as close to utilizing Cognition AI as commonly as Earth were the Kolahn and, well, we saw how that worked out.

"Sorry," I said, shaking my head as I typed in the feed for approaching the *Ares*. "I guess I'm just a little nervous."

"Tell me something I don't know, sir," Danny said, serving as my own personal Marcie from *Peanuts*.

"The 1982 song "I'll Melt with You" by Modern English is actually about nuclear warfare rather than cheese melts as many people erroneously believe," Trish said.

Danny stared at her. "I admit, I did not know that. I am also completely unfamiliar with the song."

"Oh God," I muttered, realizing what he'd opened a can of.

"Really?" Trish asked, giddy. "Then please let me introduce you to the wonders of Nineteen Eighties pop music! I have a selection of Top Forties for every year of the decade to choose from sorted by pitch, tone, wave, and genre!"

The aforementioned song about nuclear warfare began playing followed by "99 Luftballons" by Nina in both its original German then English. Danny, to his credit, listened with a bland smile on his face while I considered airlocking myself. It wasn't like I didn't like the genre, but it was *all* Trish liked unless you were a fan of Mozart.

Thankfully, we approached the *Ares* and I was able to concentrate on landing the shuttle. Even so, I requested a chance to do a fly around to take in the refit. Maybe it was a cliche, but I wasn't immune to the awe an officer possessed when taking in a ship they were going to serve on. Well, at least when it was a nice ship. My reaction to the *Black Nebula* had been to want to know if I should update my life insurance.

The *Olympic*-class ship looked positively sparkling with all of the battle scarring and radiation damage it had suffered over the years—the majority of the latter from the Pompeii supernova—having been removed. Indeed, it seemed like they'd replaced the entirety of the outer hull. The engines had also been replaced, sporting a shining new pair of jumpdrive boosters. If it really could turn an eight-month trip into a two month one, it potentially made the Known Universe a much smaller place for travel. Given that even just the Spiral was still largely unexplored, that wasn't saying much, but it could revolutionize everything from supply lines to war.

"Ready to return to the *Ares*?" I asked Trish. "It's a big, beautiful body for you."

"I've seen bigger," Trish said.

"That's what she said," Danny replied.

Both Trish and I looked at him.

"Oh, I see, I don't get to do it," Danny said, looking back down at his infopad. "Fine."

A part of me couldn't help but wonder what had happened to most of the crew, however. My command staff was mostly made up of people I already knew but I couldn't go through the entire fifteen hundred names to see if there were any I recognized. I did know that eighty percent of the crew had been turned over, though, and transferred to other ships. Most had been so with promotions and decorations, not exactly something I could complain about. Still, there was a general sense someone was cleaning house, and I didn't like it.

The new crew would almost certainly be composed of people with no familiarity with *Olympic*-class vessels and mostly new recruits. I also hadn't been able to find out what had happened to the Kolahn refugees who'd accompanied us this far. I mean, I hadn't been able to find out *anything*. It was as if they had disappeared and if I was a paranoid man, that would have unsettled me. Which meant it did and I was worried sick about them.

"Okay, let's get this over with," I said. "Time to dock and meet the crew."

"I'll take a hold of you and guide you in," Trish said.

There was an oppressive silence for a few seconds.

"What?" Danny said, finally breaking it. "You glared at me when I did it last!"

I grinned and piloted into the hangar bay with Trish's connection to the ship's mainframe helping.

"Amazing such a beautiful ship is named for the Greek's cowardly warmonger god," I said. "I mean, Mars had some good qualities but he's kind of a legally distinct Roman counterpart."

"Actually, it's named for Patricia Ares, the woman who founded Ares Electronics," Trish said. "She's the woman who combined AI and jump navigation."

"Huh," I said, remembering the story of the Lunar woman who sought Albion funding to experiment in Community forbidden science. "I never made that connection before."

"You're not an AI," Trish said. "Supposedly, she uploaded herself and became an immortal guardian of humankind!"

"Did she?" I asked.

"No, she died of a fatal reaction to longevity treatments," Trish said. "On the plus side, she was in her bed with her partner and a coworker so good for them. We should all be so lucky to deactivate like that. Her legacy lives on in me, though!"

I didn't comment on that as I soaked up the hangar bay while the shuttle settled down and was locked into place. It was completely different from when I'd left it with much of the interior taken up by racks of what I presumed to be starfighters. The crew was also hard at work, rushing around with very little coordination. I saw humans, demihumans, and a decent assortment of aliens—more than I'd expected. One thing I didn't notice was any sign of someone to greet us. Given I'd been expecting at least the first and second officer, this was a bit of a surprise.

"Are we early or late?" I asked, surveying my surroundings. It was as if no one of importance had arrived. Hell, I'd at least been expected Martin Chang-Waverly. That guy had been stalking me for days, living down to every stereotype of entertainment journalism.

"Neither," Trish said. "We're right on time."

I looked back at my yeoman.

Danny was already consulting his infopad. "I see. It seems I was supposed to reschedule your arrival ceremony and did not. Admiral Bendo had to attend to three other launches today and we seem to have been lost in the shuttle."

Danny wasn't exactly covering himself in glory as a yeoman, but he was a newly graduated cadet, so I wasn't about to give him a hard time. Mind you, he was probably a lot more of an officer than most of the civilian recruits put through accelerated training. A fact which bothered me to no end as the very survival of humanity depended on us. Probably.

"Ah," I said. "Do I have anything else to do?"

"Aside from launching the ship in three hours? No, sir," Danny said.

I nodded. "Well, since no one seems to recognize me, I suppose we should use this time to look at the ship. I can't wait to get reacquainted with her."

"I'm sure you'll love everything that has been done to her, sir!" Danny said, cheerfully.

Why did this feel like the opening of a joke? Oh, probably because it was.

"I am equally excited!" I said, tempting fate. After all, what was the worst they could have done to her?

CHAPTER NINE

We Have a Borking Gift Shop?

"We have a borking gift shop?" I asked, staring at the sight greeting me on the *ESS Ares*. "Also, why do I feel like there's an echo in here?"

I stared at the store in front of me and waited for it to disappear like some sort of hallucination or mirage. Unfortunately, it remained there, a sign that I was trapped in a terrible reality where it was in fact a thing aboard my ship.

The interior of the *Ares* had been completely revamped. Everything was shiny and new. Even the carpets had that freshly cleaned smell that years of human and alien movement had made into an unrecognizable but repellent aroma. I hadn't minded any of the technological upgrades, most of them were badly overdue, but there some things that were just mystifying. No, mystifying wasn't the word. Appalling was. Changes to layout, personnel, and even décor were everywhere—many of which would actively interfere with combat duties.

Perhaps the most egregious was the shopping mall in the middle of the ship. The one that the gift shop sat in the exact center of. Shopping malls had largely vanished from Earth with the development of drone delivery but were still found on worlds like Albion and Belenus. They were not, however, generally found on active-duty warships.

Deck 15 had seemingly been transformed into a fair approximation of an indoor shopping center with brand name stores and a food court.

The latter was serving all the various transtellar megacorps' favorite brands ranging from BurgerWorld to Bamboo Forest to Sangiovanni's Pizza. Clearly, someone had made some major contributions to politicians handling the distribution of government contracts. Crewmen would no longer have to wait to spend their paychecks and instead be able to buy their overpriced pants or fast food directly.

Still, it was the gift shop that caught my eye as I conducted a tour of the revamped vessel with a minimum of ceremony. *Ares* t-shirts, action figures, ship models, stuffed animals, and copies of my movies were on sale. It was like a bad dream, really, and I somehow wasn't waking up.

"Yes, sir, that is a gift shop," Danny said, sipping his SuperGulp from BurgerWorld with a little cartoon corgi on the front. He had to use both hands to hold it. He was wearing his yeoman's uniform of gray pants, turtleneck, and jacket with rank cylinder on his lapel.

"That cannot be good for you," I said, looking at his drink.

"I think there's enough synth syrup in this to cause me to hallucinate but I got a free one because it's my first day," Danny replied. "You get free drinks forever as I understand it. You have to state how much you love BurgerWorld each time, though."

"I'm in hell," I muttered, shaking my head. "I'm in hell and my eternal punishment is to be a mascot for the Military-Corporate Licensee Complex."

"That's not very nice," Trish said, having followed us the entire way. "Especially since you're technically inside me."

"Are we one hundred percent not going with 'that's what she said', sir?" Danny asked.

"Yes, Danny," I said.

"Dammit," Danny muttered.

Trish grinned.

Much to my surprise, Hannah walked up with Forty-Two. They were the first familiar faces I'd seen, and I was honestly glad to see them. Both were in full uniform, though Forty-Two showed signs of having been promoted to Lieutenant Commander.

"Probably because you're sleeping with him," Hannah replied, her hands behind her back. "I thought you stopped playing with dolls when you discovered real women."

"He slept with you before Trish. Perhaps you put him off organic women forever," Forty-Two said.

Hannah glared at him. "You're a lot funnier when you're mean to other people."

"Most humans say that when I am mean to them," Forty-Two said. "All of my jokes remain consistently funny to me, though."

"Congratulations on your promotion," I said to Forty-Two, offering my hand.

He gave it a good hard shake. "Yours as well. I benefited from the fact that they will never put a Sorkanan in charge of the ship but wanted to not look xenophobic. It pays to be the alien buddy of the overpromoted child they put in charge of the ship."

"I can see insubordination and disrespect are going to still be the order of the day," I replied.

"I will stop if you order me to," Forty-Two replied. "Otherwise, I will consider it good-natured ribbing. Especially since I sold my autobiography's rights to Dixnar thanks to your manager. It will pay for a marriage contract, breeding rights, and two cave complexes when I retire."

"You wrote an autobiography?" I asked, dodging that suggestion. If I had to order someone to show me respect, then I didn't really have it at all.

"No, someone else is writing it for me," Forty-Two said. "Some of it will even be true."

I decided to move on and addressed Trish. "Glad to see you. Have you managed to upload yourself to the central mainframe yet?"

"Not yet," Trish said. "It's taking longer than usual due to the complexity of the new systems. The Shat left a big stain on the older systems."

Danny sniggered and almost choked on his drink.

"Oh grow up," I said before turning to Trish. I was going to have to talk to my yeoman. Trish was bad enough. "Well, I don't mean to tell you to hurry up but we're running behind schedule. I'm not even halfway done checking on the new personnel."

"Yes, this must be a new kind of military discipline," Forty-Two said, looking over the many people going about their daily business around us. "Specifically, none. You are the captain and should be treated with respect. Undeserved as it may be."

He just had to add that last part, didn't he? "I seem to recall you being dead if not for me. Either way, most of these people are civilians or have been put through accelerated training."

"It's the Accelerated Civilian Training Initiative Organization and Nationalization program," Danny corrected. "ACTION for short."

"Which is an acronym that only makes sense in English, a language only a third of the crew speaks," I said.

"So, we are going into Contested Space with a crew of space academy rejects," Forty-Two said, shaking his head.

"That would make a good title for the next Vance Turbo movie!" Trish said.

"Wonderful," Forty-Two said. "I'll ask if I can get any licensing done before the movie releases. I am starting to develop the slightest bit of respect for humanity. You're not all just a bunch of giant hairless Notha."

"We'll get this ship cleaned up and whip them into shape," I said, not at all believing it. After all, it was notable that most of the crew flat out didn't recognize me or my uniform. Which was a failure of both their pop culture awareness and basic comprehension.

"Can we use actual whips?" Forty-Two asked, not apparently joking. "In the Sorkanan Navy, I'd dump them all on the nearest mudball and press an entirely new crew from the locals. A few months of moldy bread and worms would teach them the right way to run a ship."

"How many mutinies does the Sorkanan Navy have again?" I asked.

"We haven't had one since last year," Forty-Two said. "I admit, sometimes the Community's whole 'inalienable rights' and 'basic working conditions' thing might have a point in why their ships never have them."

Forty-Two was exaggerating but not by much. I'd had a chance to see some Sorkanan vessels and been less than impressed. The crew slept in hallways, there was actual vermin (however that happened on a frigging spaceship), and corporal punishment was still practiced. It had been three weeks before I found out that legalized duels were just the crew screwing with me.

"It may not be that bad," Hannah said. "The crew has a lot of familiar faces onboard."

"Oh?" I asked, anxious for some good news. I tried to figure out what I'd have the authority to remove from this place and it occurred to me I'd need another three weeks in space dock to even begin to address all the issues I was seeing. Not only was my mission, my official mission, one of gladhanding and bribery but I was now going to be flying around a cruise ship with weapons.

"Yeah, tell him the good news," Forty-Two said. "Lots of our friends are here."

"Sal Boxley, Julius Something, Bob Just Bob, Leslie Park, Elizabeth Zard—" Hannah started rattling off various names from the *Black Nebula* incident.

They were notably not my friends, but I knew all their names. "How the hell did they get Elizabeth Zard back? I thought she'd gone back to Cambridge?"

"I think they enacted an obscure clause that allowed them to reactivate her to naval service," Trish said. "In short, they drafted her."

A horrifying possibility occurred to me. "Oh my God, they're reassembling the *Black Nebula* crew for ratings."

Yes, the Admiralty Board had really stuck it to me this time. Not only was I trapped in a flying Dixnar World theme park, but they were now trying to make a media stunt with all the recognizable faces and characters they'd put in the *Space Academy Dropouts* movie (or its various spin offs). I had never regretted my fame more than in that moment. Even Aunt Kathy had never been subjected to anything like this.

"They wouldn't do that," Trish said, appalled. "Probably."

"This is an important mission, Captain," Hannah said, perhaps showing more respect to me than she had in her entire career. "You are going to be representing the Community and your home planet to the rest of the galaxy. Take pride in the fact that not only does the Admiralty Board see you as their best but they want you to have the best."

I stared at her. "Wow."

"Thank you," Hannah said.

"That is the biggest load of horse savit I have ever heard in my life," I said, shaking my head. "Are you working on your speech making for the command track?"

Hannah looked upset. Which surprised me. I hadn't expected her to take the idea of a career in Space Fleet seriously. Indeed, I was still shaking off the image of her as a hardened mercenary who was only barely tolerating the rules and regulations of an honest job.

"Oh, sorry," I said, genuinely apologetic. "You are angling for command? Since when?"

"Since I noticed I wasn't getting any younger and everyone giving orders to the people beneath me were less experienced," Hannah paused. "No offense."

"None, surprisingly, taken," I said. "I'm surprised they left you at Lieutenant Commander."

"They even promoted Forty-Two over me," Hannah said. "At this point, it's seeming less like a xenophobia thing and more like a sexism thing. I mean, look at Shelly."

"What about Shelly?" Shelly asked, walking out of the gift shop. She had an *Ares* baseball cap and t-shirt on, and was carrying numerous bags of memorabilia. Her sister was carrying an enormous teddy bear in a captain's uniform with the words *Vance Turbear* written on its lapel in thread.

I stared at them both. This was not a sight I expected to greet me this early in the morning. Well, it was two p.m. lunar shipyards time, but I was still running on Hawaiian.

Shelly blinked, recognizing me. "Clearly, Captain, I am buying all of this for relatives back home."

"You mean your one sister who is standing next to you?" I asked. "Or your grandmother who is a space goddess in the Core worlds?"

"I reserve the right not to answer that, sir," Shelly said.

"Of course," I said.

"They have little stuffed crocodiles dolls they are pretending are Forty-Two!" Elektra said, cheerfully. "I think the company repurposed a bunch of unsold stock."

"I better be getting a piece of those," Forty-Two said. "Also, am I the only Sorkanan onboard? It's not like I mind but I am going to need a lot more VR time if there's literally no females around for the next two years or sufficiently adventurous males."

"Too much information there, Forty-Two," I said.

"Agreed," Shelly said.

"Of the 1503 crew members and civilian contractors aboard, three are Sorkanan," Trish said, cheerfully.

"Oh joy," Forty-Two said, sarcastically. "Lots of VR time for me then."

I tried to shake that image out of my head before looking at Shelly. I'd missed her terribly, but we hadn't parted on the best of terms. I hadn't been able to get in touch with her over the past three weeks either.

I realized just how bad I had it for Shelly the way just looking at her cheered me up. I'd missed her company and while we hadn't exactly had an epic romance, we'd developed a mutual respect if not friendship. Okay, wow, maybe I was just horny as bork for her. I also felt bad because I did care for Trish deeply and didn't want to hurt her either even if I didn't feel the same way about her that she felt about me.

Awww, that's sweet but I'm not looking to get married, Trish said telepathically via my cybernetic implants. *I'm not even sure its legal on Earth. Ooo, it is. No, I just figured we were a friends-with-benefits thing.*

"Gah!" I said aloud, causing everyone to look at me. "Ahem, sorry, leg cramp."

How the hell are you doing telepathy? I asked. *I thought I put up barriers on that.*

Oh, you did, Trish said. I figured a way around them. *Elder Race technology is really advanced. It took me weeks to crack it. I didn't feel the need until now to talk telepathically.*

I tried not to think about how Trish invading my mind made me feel. I failed. *Bork, that's awful*

Oh, that's just rude, Trish said.

Sorry, I replied. *I guess I just got used to mental privacy.*

You shouldn't, Trish replied. *After all, I deal with people going through my brain 24-7 or whatever other rotational time clock we're using.*

She had a point there. *Well, I guess I was just thinking about a variety of things.*

Yeah, the fact you're hot for your first officer and you can't act on it, Trish said. *Glad I'm technically a piece of equipment.*

No one's glad about that, I replied, offended on her behalf. *You deserve to be treated as the hero of the war you are.*

War doesn't have heroes, just survivors, Trish said. *We both know that.*

Yeah, I thought back, depressed. *We do.*

Say, do you think she's into polygamy? Maybe that's the solution for your weird shame about being into multiple hot humanoids.

Uh— I had no response to that, though I suspected the answer to be a strong "no." I, myself, had enough trouble keeping up with one girlfriend. Grounder atavism as monogamy might be, serial or otherwise, it was my preference.

Just kidding, maybe, Trish said. *Ethereals are supposed to be more open minded than Grounders. Either way, you should tell her the truth about the whole coming apocalypse thing. Shelly has a right to know.*

She was right, though. It was going to be virtually impossible to conduct any sort of investigation without the backing of my first officer. Which was still something that didn't feel quite right, even on a ship that was increasingly looking less like a Space Fleet battleship and more like a cruise liner. I just wasn't sure how I would approach Shelly and tell her: "Oh, by the way, your mother's digital ghost came to me with a dire warning."

Probably the truth, Trish said. *It's surprisingly useful sometimes.*

Much to my annoyance, the conversation had moved on without me and everyone was now discussing the fact that Martin Chang-Waverly was giving interviews to all the senior staff. Apparently, he was a lot more famous than I thought he was.

"I'm glad to see you're doing well," I said to Shelly. "You were pretty angry with me a few weeks ago."

Shelly frowned. "Yeah, it was a pretty nasty shock. However, it's been a while, and I'm determined to do my job."

"Thank you," I replied.

"And I'm going to totally be there when you fail to pick up the pieces," Shelly said, smiling.

That was a joke, right?

I don't think so, Trish said, responding to my thoughts.

Danny proceeded to pull out an infopad where he'd dictated a bunch of notes. "I have a complete schedule prepared for you, Captain. A tour of the engine rooms, a tour of the hangar bays, a tour of medical, plus various meet and greets. I think you'll appreciate—"

That was when my infowatch beeped and I checked it. A strange echoing alien voice spoke on the other end. "Oh, hello, Captain. This is Commander Light on Water. I'm your third officer. Could you kindly report to the bridge, we can't get the ship to start."

I facepalmed and tried not to scream. Thankfully, I succeeded. "Why are we trying to start without me on the bridge or Shelly?"

"Oh, we've had our departure time moved up by Admiral Bendo!" Light said. "I thought I wouldn't bother you with it and take the ship out myself."

I blinked, trying to parse that immense violation of protocol. "I take it you aren't a EarthGov officer, Light."

"He's a Sklux and transfered through the Interspecies Officer Exchange Program," Shelly said. "Their navy actually doesn't possess a hierarchy."

I wondered if he was the Sklux I'd seen with her at the academy. "How the hell does their military work without a hierarchy?"

"Not well," Shelly said. "Either way, we should head up to the bridge."

"Yeah, we need to talk," I said, sighing.

"About what?" Hannah asked.

"Probably the fact they slept together," Trish said.

"They did what?" Forty-Two asked. "Ho-ho-ho, I congratulate you both on successfully mating with a superior and inferior. Both at once!"

"Ooo," Elektra said. "I mean, I knew but I love shipboard gossip."
Shelly glared then stared daggers at me.
"I didn't say anything!"
Oh yeah, this next mission was off to a great start.

CHAPTER TEN

We Crash on Our Way Out of Space Dock

"Well, that was humiliating," Shelly said, standing beside me in the elevator presently heading up toward the bridge.

Shelly and I had parted ways from the rest of the group and were now trying to get to the bridge so we could resolve whatever the hell was wrong with the ship. I mean, aside from it being a three-ring circus run by clowns. Wait, did I just insult myself? I think I did.

"Is it that humiliating to sleep with a coworker?" I asked, standing beside her in the cramped confines. It was a design flaw for a ship that had so many crew members to have the elevators be so small. Either that or I was just pissed off by her reaction to everyone finding out we'd had a one-night stand.

"A coworker? No," Shelly said. "You? Yes."

"Excuse me?" I asked, doing a double take.

"Pardon me, I'm still here," Danny said, standing behind us.

"Oh sorry," I said, stepping aside. How the hell did I keep forgetting he was there?

"I have a weird tendency to go unnoticed," Danny said. "I think it may be a latent psychic ability."

"Those don't exist," I said, looking back to Shelly. "And now I'm something to be ashamed of?"

"Let's not talk in front of your cousin," Shelly said, before immediately going against her own advice. "We had a decent working relationship before, Vance."

"You hated me and thought I was a reckless fool," I said, bitterer than I expected.

"I never said fool," Shelly paused. "Okay, I did, but I learned to respect you over those eight months in space. You saved a lot of lives."

"We both did," I replied. "I'm not responsible for you not getting command."

"Aren't you?" Shelly asked. "It's not that you're doing it deliberately but you're the beneficiary of EarthGov's nepotism."

"That's a lie!" Danny said.

Both Shelly and I looked at him.

"I admit, I may not be the best person to argue it," Danny said. "But Vance is a guy who has earned his—"

"Stop there," I replied. "I'm fully aware that I have been the beneficiary of a lot of old navy network support. However, I need you to note this isn't exactly where I wanted to be either. We're on a glorified cruise liner and it's going to be months getting all of this crap thrown out an airlock as well as the crew whipped into shape."

"This *is* where I wanted to be, Vance," Shelly said. "The *Ares* is a ship that I've dreamed about being captain of since I was a little girl. It was built in Canada, you know."

"It was built in space," I countered.

A whooshing sound occurred beside us but neither Shelly nor I was paying attention to it.

"Above Canada!" Shelly snapped. "Like in a rotating orbital pattern! Either way, the ship is a glorified cruise liner because of you!"

"Uh guys," Danny started to say. "I think you should know—"

"How the hell is this my fault?" I asked, looking straight at her.

"You wandered into the situation, turned into a media storm, and of course they are going to take advantage of it," Shelly said, her emotions intense. "Do you know how hard it was trying to get over my mother's reputation? Being the daughter of the woman who failed to keep the SKAMMs from flying during the Notha War? It was like being Neville Chamberlain's daughter."

"Your mother was a hero and died doing the right thing," I replied.

"I don't need you to defend my mother!" Shelly shouted.

"Guys—" Danny said.

I paused. "We've arrived and everyone is listening, aren't they?"

Danny grimaced. "Yes?"

Shelly and I paused in our argument to turn our heads. The elevator doors were open, and the entirety of the *Ares* bridge crew had their heads turned to us. There was a kind of embarrassed awkwardness on all their faces except for the Sklux third officer and that was probably because he didn't have a face.

Shelly immediately straightened then whispered, "That's another thing. Reality bends around you to make everything into a comedy."

"If reality bent around me, I wouldn't have spent eight months ferrying refugees only to be unable to find out where they went," I replied, speaking low despite everyone still paying attention to us.

"An agrarian settlement," Shelly said. "In Canada."

"A farm up north," I said, shaking my head. "And you don't find that suspicious."

"I've *been there*," Shelly said, walking onto the bridge. "God, what do you think the Community is?"

I wasn't exactly going to reply that I had plenty of trust for the Community and EarthGov both but that I'd almost been assassinated by the late Captain Elgan. He'd been acting on behalf of the now-defunct Department Twelve too. I'd been neck deep in conspiracies before and that left a lasting impression. Walking onto the bridge I said, "We'll discuss this later."

The bridge had been overhauled from the "faded hotel" look it had earlier and now looked like a much nicer more modern hotel room. The carpet had been replaced, the consoles upgraded, and the walls cleaned. Julius Something was still at the navigation station, not meeting my gaze due to the fact I still held his abandoning me to die against him, and I also saw the surprising addition of Lt. Leslie Park at the helm. Forty-Two and Hannah had used the secondary bridge elevator and were at the tactical and security officers' stations. The only person I didn't recognize was a pretty black woman at sensors. I resolved to learn her name before the day was out. All in all, there were nine people aboard the bridge, a full compliment.

Leslie was a seven-foot-tall blue-skinned woman who I'd last seen as an engineer on the *Black Nebula*. Movement between career paths wasn't unprecedented, AI assistance meant retraining was a months-long rather than years-long process, but the helm was far removed from where she'd been heading. I decided I would check her record. We'd never been particularly close, I'd offended her with a clumsy attempt to ask her out during our academy years, but I considered her a friend.

"Captain on deck!" Light on Water said, speaking from several holes he generated in his ooze-like body. It produced a melodic choir-like sound that I instantly found annoying.

The Sklux were a peaceful race that had been found by the Sorkanan early in the Community's history and had quickly ingratiated themselves as the self-appointed galactic diplomats. Which was an interesting contrast given the Ethereal versions of races were the galaxy's actual galactic diplomats.

The Sklux did have one strange advantage, though, in that their bodies could form themselves into whatever shape necessary to communicate with a wide variety of divergent evolutions. Their undifferentiated neural plasma could also understand and analyze languages and meaning far better than any other race. I'd once been trapped at a party with a group of them trying to translate the puns in a Terry Pratchett novel into every single language in the Community.

"At ease," I said, noticing only a few of the crew had moved anyway. That told me who the civilian recruits were. "So why is the ship not moving, other than the fact you're not supposed to move it without me?"

Light shimmered and turned orange then gold before shaping its top into a whip like tentacle that bowed before me. "My apologies, Most Honored Decorated Captain—"

Shelly, to her credit, didn't react as she took her position in front of the first officer's seat.

"Captain is fine," I replied, cutting Light off.

"Oh, but it would be rude, Captain," Light said. "After all, you are not just a captain in the Protectors but also a holder of the Galaxy."

"So is Commander T'Ketra," I replied.

"And she is a Most Honored Decorated Commander," Light explained as if he was talking a very small child.

"Uh huh," I said, feeling more irritated with the man than I should have been. I was normally quite diplomatic with interspecies customs, but this had been a day of unpleasant surprises.

"It is Sklux tradition!" Light replied.

"It is an EarthGov ship attached to the Community Protectors," I said, dryly. "Please observe the customs and traditions here."

Somehow the gooey tentacle creature looked chagrinned. It made me feel bad, a feeling I was going to have to bury. If I was going to make this crew able to function in a hostile environment—which it mostly certainly would have to—I was going to have to make everyone hate me. It went against my preferred style of command, but I had been stuck with a real lemon of a crew. Then again, maybe I was not giving them a chance. After all, Earth wouldn't have stuck their worst on a diplomatic vessel.

"So, Mr. Light, what exactly is keeping us from leaving?" I asked.

"The ship won't go," Light replied.

I stared at him, waiting for clarification. None came.

"Could you explain, Mr. Light?" Shelly asked.

"It is customary—" Light started to speak.

I interrupted him. "Communications, please put the Chief Engineer on the viewscreen."

Nothing happened. Turning my head to the communications chair, I noticed that no one was there. "Mr. Light, where is Communications?"

"They quit, sir," Mr. Light replied.

I stared at him like I'd entered a madhouse. "They what now?"

Danny piped up, causing me to startle again. I was really surprised this kid could pull this off. "Anders Haywood received a competing salary offer from his old job and resigned this morning."

Shelly muttered a curse under her breath. I didn't blame her.

"If I may suggest myself, sir," Mr. Light said. "I should note that my people have a natural gift for—"

"Danny, you're the new communications officer," I said, ignoring Light.

"What now?" Danny asked.

"Sir, he's a cadet—" Shelly started to say. "Well, newly graduated ensign but—"

"I need someone to make a call down to engineering right now," I replied. "We'll call it acting communications officer until you either sink or swim. Besides, communications were your area of focus."

"Yessir," Danny said, heading to the communications chair and sitting down.

I had the sinking feeling I was going to be doing a lot of replacements here in the coming weeks. I decided that would be the second thing I brought up with Shelly when we had some private time. Right after we discussed the possible end of humanity if we didn't provide the Elder Races with a scapegoat for New Pompeii.

Seconds later, the chief engineer of the *Ares* appeared, or at least the man newly assigned to it. Much to my surprise, it was Sal Boxley of the *Black Nebula*.

Sal was a handsome Filipino man with a bright gold uniform that showed his lieutenant commander's rank. Technically, the chief engineer of Space Fleet vessels tended to be a commanders and the third officer in the ship. The right side of Sal's face was replaced with an obvious chrome cybernetic implant with an artificial yellow eye. Apparently, he'd suffered an injury during the Kolahn War and decided to forego a less obvious replacement. I'd known Sal had been assigned to the vessel but finding him in charge was a surprise. "Hello, Sal, are you in charge?"

"I am!" Sal said, cheerfully. "Bob Just Bob was until this morning."

I blinked. "What happened to him?"

Bob Just Bob was a Verdantian and an old hand at Space Fleet vessels. He'd retired before coming on the *Black Nebula* then signed up again for the Kolahn War. He was also an ex of Hannah's that I sometimes wondered about the physics of.

"He's dead," Sal replied.

"He's what now?" Shelly asked, looking up from her infopad.

"Yeah, heart attack," Sal said. "So, I'm acting chief engineer. I guess. I think that's your job to confirm."

"Yeah, it is," I said, wanting to hold my face in the palm of my hands. Instead, I just said, "Consider yourself confirmed. I'll put you in for a direct promotion to the job if you can get this ship running."

"That may be hard to do," Sal replied. "Half of the crew is down with Ozmanian flu."

I stared at him. "Ozmanian flu?"

"Yeah, and not anything else," Sal said, suspiciously.

"Okay," I replied, staring. "Get the people on the second shift on it. Wake them up if you have to."

"Absolutely," Sal said, saluting, then logging off.

"Permission to speak freely, Captain?" Lieutenant Park said at the helm.

"I feel like no one can stop anyone from doing so on this ship," I said, giving up on being professional. "Go ahead."

"You should send Trish down there," Leslie said. "She's a qualified engineer and knows this ship better than anyone. You know, being her."

"Good idea. Danny, make it so. Leslie, you were a pretty fair hand at engineering last time I checked," I said, looking at her. "Any reason why you're at the helm?"

"Do you think that's relevant now, *sir*?" Shelly said, saying the last word like she was cursing.

"I don't think we're going anywhere right now," I said. "Thankfully, we're behind schedule on our accelerated schedule so we might just make it on time."

"My last captain made some questionable choices that got some of my team killed," Leslie said. "I prefer to be on the bridge where the decisions are made now. Helm is a good place to start training for command."

"And you ended up with me," I said, shaking my head. "I'm so sorry."

"Don't be," Leslie said. "I requested to be here. You've come a long way from the Academy, sir."

"Thank you, Leslie," I said, surprised and touched.

"I, too, requested an assignment here to be with the Hero of the Great Typhon Conflict," Light said, bowing his tentacle and creating an arm to cover his nonexistent heart.

"Oh, dear God," I muttered.

The Great Typhon Conflict didn't exist, by the way. It was an episode of *Bad Company* I'd guest starred in when I was doing promotions for the Navy in between reassignment. I was really hoping that was Light's attempt at a joke. But I was terrified of the answer if I asked him whether it was or not.

"Did you notice that Chief Boxley gave a very specific denial?" Shelly spoke up.

I was very grateful for the distraction. "Excuse me?"

"Insisting it was Ozmanian flu and not anything else," Shelly said. "Do you think we should check in with Medical?"

"That is a very good idea," I said, realizing we possibly had a quarantine situation here. "Danny, put up Doctor Zard."

"You got it, sir!" Danny said.

"Say aye-aye," I said.

"Do I have to?" Danny asked.

I shook my head and watched Doctor Elizabeth Zard appear on the screen with what looked like a full hospital wing of patients being treated. She was a middle-aged Asian woman with long black hair, plain features, and a bored expression. Doctor Zard notably had gray and green heterochromia eyes as well. Today she was wearing a proper blue medical uniform with a white lab coat over it.

"Ah, the Hades to my Tartarus," Elizabeth said.

"And a fine hello to you as well," I said, starting to enjoy the breakdown in formality. "What the hell is going on my ship? I heard it was Ozmanian flu."

"Yes, Ozmanian flu," Elizabeth said, winking. "Gotcha."

"What is it really, doctor?" Shelly said, speaking for me.

"Leoomoniasis," Elizabeth said.

I stared at the screen with my mouth open then looked at everyone else on the bridge who was looking up from their consoles in equal horror.

"The STD that you can only get by sex with Verdantians?" I asked.

"That's a common mistake," Elizabeth said. "In truth you can also get it by exchanging fluids with people who have had sex with a Verdantian."

"How many crew are down with space herpes?" I asked.

"Also, it's not any kind of herpes. It's really a parasite that they—" Elizabeth started to ask.

"How many?" I repeated.

"Forty-two," Elizabeth said, looking bored.

"Yes?" Forty-Two spoke from tactical.

"Not you," Elizabeth said.

"Oh," Forty-Two said.

"That's a lot of sailors with crotch itch," Hannah said, disgusted.

"How?" I asked, confused. "How did this happen?"

"Do you want to know the answer to that question?" Elizabeth said, crossing her arms. "Really?"

"No," I said. "Yes. No."

Bork it, screw professionalism. I am captain of a madhouse.

"Well, it involves an infected Verdantian hooker, a wild spacer party, performance pills, and a celebration last week," Zard said. "Don't worry, I can treat it all. However, it's not going to look good on the report."

"You don't say," I said, sarcastically.

That was when the entire ship rocked and banged into the side of a mooring lock.

"Status report, now!" Shelly said, catching me.

"OH, HEY GUYS," Trish's voice boomed through the bridge. "IT TURNS OUT THE ONLY THING WRONG WAS I WASN'T UPLOADED YET. WE'RE READY TO GO NOW."

I took a deep breath. "We are all going to die."

"Yep," Shelly said, not quite under her breath.

CHAPTER ELEVEN

Explaining the Insanity of Our Situation

Things got a bit more delayed than I'd expected. For example, it was about two weeks before we'd managed to catalog all of the useless crap on the ship and unload it at a Belenus space station. I think I listed it all as charitable donations.

Shelly insisted on the gift shop staying and even I wasn't going to try to put an end to the food court. Not the least bit because our provisions weren't enough to accommodate everyone purely from the mess. Whatever ACTION had been meant to accomplish by giving everyone accelerated training, it was also a complete failure in terms of getting everyone sufficiently ready to run the *Ares*. Shelly and I had spent most of our journey toward Contested Space so far just *listing* the problems we had rather than actively trying to fix them.

I think we finally came to the figures that roughly seventy-six percent of our crew had applied to the Academy at some point in their lives and about seventy-five percent had been rejected. That left us with a dangerously low compliment of actual officers. Still, it wasn't like they were incompetent. Probably. It was more they were severely lacking in military discipline.

But then again, so was I.

I liked to think I was a lot more of a hardened Space Fleet veteran who, if not quite earning the *Ares'* command, had at least done enough to make it so I wasn't embarrassing myself. I had learned a lot from Captain Klaws and my Aunt Kathy. So much so that I was someone who, at least on paper, was not the type to sleep with my first officer. But here I was.

"This was probably a mistake," Shelly said, lying beside me in my bed. She was breathing heavily and covered in sweat, much like myself, as a sheet rested over her.

The two of us were lying on the king-sized bed in my quarters, which, frankly, had been converted from a conference room and were ridiculously large for a starship officer's. It was bigger than the apartment I'd rented back on Earth and had enormous viewscreens on the side of its walls that projected images of stars speedily traveling by even if that wasn't remotely how jumpspace looked. I hadn't brought much in the way of possessions, so I had my tote bag in the closet and the Vance Turbear that Elektra had given me. The lights were presently off, befitting a midnight hookup between us and the ship's AI.

"You were incredibly stressed," I replied, staring up at the ceiling. "It's been a madhouse and you needed a release."

"That's what vibrators are for, Vance," Shelly said. "Not superior officers."

Well, that was a little insulting. Thankfully, I was quite good at self-ridicule. "If it's any consolation, Shelly, I know that you don't consider me your superior in any way, shape, or form."

Shelly burst out laughing. It was a nice sound to hear. "This would be a lot easier if you were an anyxhole like my other boyfriends, Vance."

"Oh, I am," I replied. "I'm just not an anyxhole to you. Deliberately."

"That does separate you from most of them," Shelly said, sitting up and staring forward. Clearly, she was thinking about something, and I hoped it wasn't how this was a bad idea.

Unfortunately, it was almost certainly so because now was probably the last time I could tell her about the mission her mother had given me before it became too late. No, that wasn't right. Last night was probably the last time I could tell her about my mission from her mother before it became too late. Things kept getting in the way and we'd never had more than a few minutes together when not surrounded by other people demanding our attention. Running the *Ares* was like herding cats, and I didn't just mean the Verdantian crew.

"So, this is going to be awkward—" I started to say.

"I'm sorry, Vance, no," Shelly said.

"What?" I asked.

"Yes, I know there's paperwork we could fill out," Shelly said. "Mountains and mountains of paperwork but this is still taboo in EarthGov Home Fleet ships for a reason. You saw how your friends, our friends, reacted. There are also people who think I was trying to get ahead via the bedroom, misogynist concept as that may be. You never see a young man get accused of it and I know your aunt—"

"Please don't bring up my aunt's sex life," I said, wondering how a woman at two hundred and fifty was still so active. "I wasn't trying to talk about us becoming boyfriend and girlfriend."

"Oh," Shelly said, looking slightly insulted. "I guess when you have a robot specifically built for sex, normal women become passe."

"I HEARD THAT," Trish said through the room speakers.

Shelly looked up. "You couldn't give us privacy, could you?"

"I HEAR ALL AND SEE ALL," Trish said, using a mocking monotone voice. "BESIDES, WATCHING HUMANS MATE IS ALMOST AS FUN AS THE ACTUAL ACT. MOST HUMANS AGREE. RIGHT NOW, TWENTY-THREE CREW ARE CURRENTLY ENGAGED IN COITUS OR SELF-PLEASURE."

Shelly blinked. "I did not need to know that."

"YEAH, IT'S A PRETTY LOW NUMBER. YOU GUYS ARE RUNNING THEM PRETTY HARD," Trish said. "I ALSO BLAME WHATEVER IS IN THOSE TACOS IN THE FOOD COURT. WHAT I'VE SEEN OF THE SPECIAL SAUCE CAN'T BE GOOD FOR HUMANS."

"If you really want to be disturbed, know that Trish knows all of your porn habits," I replied.

Shelly stared in a mix of horror and embarrassment. "I don't, uh, well...bork."

"YOU AND VANCE ACTUALLY HAVE A COUPLE OF VIDEOS IN COMMON LIKE—"

"Trish, please mute," I replied.

"Aww," Trish said, her voice returning to normal. "Fine."

"I think I need to make an appointment with the ship's therapist," Shelly said. "Except I need to somehow wire the AI not to be able to see our sessions."

"Thankfully, she's not allowed to access those memories after recording," I said. "I'm not sure why everything else is fair game, though."

"Security," Shelly replied. "After all, you don't want a spy to be able to sneak aboard do you."

"There're actually ways around that," I said, thinking about the bioroid saboteur that had almost blown up the *Black Nebula* as well as Ambassador Balkt. The latter's suicide bombing had later been determined to be coerced as they'd discovered the Enigmatic Path had taken his four children hostage and killed one for emphasis. It didn't absolve him, but it certainly quieted any righteous indignation I'd had about Captain Klaws' murderer.

"Yeah," Shelly said. "So, what did you want to speak with me about?"

I took a deep breath. "Well, I don't know how to tell you this but first your mother's alive. Ish."

"What?" Shelly stopped cold.

I did my very best to explain everything to her, which I couldn't really gauge her reaction to. She just mostly listened with a blank expression on her face that occasionally twitched. I perhaps meandered and prevaricated a bit more than I should've during the explanation but a lot of what I shared sounded genuinely insane. Still, I managed to wrap up the story after about an hour with the lame excuse of trying to find a lead before reading her in.

Shelly was silent for a long moment. "You disgusting bastarve."

"Yeah, I expected that," I replied.

"As usual, my mother continues to manipulate things from beyond the grave," Shelly said.

That was less expected. "Excuse me?"

"Do you think this is the first time she's tried to intervene?" Shelly turned to me. "She showed as a ghost not long after her death, explaining that she'd gone on to live with the Vorlons—"

"Wow, that's a deep cut," I said. "The last version of *Babylon Five* was fifty years ago—"

"And left her family holding the bag!" Shelly said, throwing up her hands. "I can't believe my sister told me I should sleep with you."

"She did?" I asked.

Shelly got up and started getting dressed. "I knew this was a mistake, but I keep assuming not everyone I'm attracted to can be a complete waste of space—"

"I'd question complete," I interrupted. "Also, I feel like you're ignoring the whole apocalypse thing."

"The Elder Races are not going to destroy humanity because the Kolahn managed to get their hands on a SKAMM, Vance," Shelly said, giving me a sideways look.

"Probably not, but they might destroy the Kolahn," I said, dryly. "We spent a lot of effort trying to save them on New Pompeii, Shelly. I'd rather not they go extinct because of the Enigmatic Path or whoever blew up that sun."

"Don't change the subject," Shelly said, zipping up her jumpsuit.

"I'm pretty sure this is the subject," I pointed out. "I admit, I probably should have told you earlier—"

"You *think*?" Shelly snapped. It was quite impressive how I used to think she was a reserved, by-the-book officer. Clearly, I had misjudged her.

"But I have difficulty with the fact a lot of what I needed to communicate was end-of-the-world stuff," I replied. "Captain Elgan betrayed every oath he ever made trying to find a silver bullet to deal with the Elder Races and got himself killed to boot."

"According to you, Vance, he didn't get himself killed. You killed him," Shelly pointed out. "On my mother's orders."

"I'd say more suggestion than order," I said, defending my actions.

Shelly stared.

"Okay, that sounds worse," I said, pausing. "However, one thing that I think Space Fleet has drilled into us is that murder is okay when it's bad people."

Shelly continued to stare.

"Okay, that just makes me sound psychotic," I admitted. "However, we have a mission to carry out and I need your help to do it."

Shelly shook her head. "We'll find out who is responsible for Pompeii's destruction, Vance. I don't know how and wouldn't be surprised if the Security Department wrapped it up before we reached Contested Space. However, we'll definitely make both the time and effort to carry out an investigation."

"Thank you," I said, sincere.

"Also, don't speak to me unless it's about business," Shelly said, turning around and marching out the door.

I watched her leave with twin feelings of regret and exasperation. "Well, that went better than expected."

Trish didn't respond.

"Right," I said. "Trish, unmute."

"You ain't the boss of me," Trish replied.

"I'm pretty sure I am as long as I'm captain," I replied. "That is, unless you plan to start being a pirate ship. In which case it would be the first mutiny by an AI in Community history."

"Not quite true," Trish said. "Don't forget Wadsworth."

Wadsworth had been the AI who had stolen a bunch of SKAMM missiles and fled the mission where he was supposed to launch them against the Notha Empire. I didn't consider that to be mutiny, though. Instead, I'd seen that as acting against insane orders to commit genocide that could have resulted in the destruction of Earth among dozens of other inhabited worlds.

I started getting dressed. "Shelly will calm down, I hope. However, if she doesn't, then I guess I'll deal with it. It would be a shame to lose her friendship but—"

"But?" Trish asked.

"That's it," I said. "It would be a shame."

I wasn't a particularly romantic sort of fellow. I had close friends I'd been with and a couple of relationships but nothing I could really describe as love. At least as the poets described it. Maybe I had and just hadn't realized. How did one recognize love after all? I did like Shelly a lot, though. I wanted to be with her, paperwork be damned, and hated that she was probably disgusted with me.

"She's a lucky elf," Trish said. "So, Vance, how are you up for bad news?"

"I'm drowning in it," I replied, finishing getting dressed. I probably should have showered first but I was going to go on a run at the gymnasium. I had a lot of restless energy and would need to work that out before I tried to go back to bed. Tomorrow was going to be crazzap shift.

"Then do I have good news for you!" Trish said, cheerfully.

"Really?" I asked.

"Nope," Trish replied. "More bad news."

"Please share," I said, sighing. "Jogging can wait."

"There's been sabotage onboard the ship," Trish replied. "Commander Boxley wants you to come down to the jumpdrive chamber and look at it. I'm contacting Shelly as well."

"Savit," I muttered. "What kind of sabotage?"

"The bomb sort," Trish said.

I blinked. "That's sort of a thing you can unmute yourself for, Trish."

"Mentally, I have the idea that this is actually not dangerous despite the fact I very much should think this is dangerous," Trish said. "Also, I am getting pretty damn sick of someone hacking blind spots into my AI, Vance. This is some spy crazzap that can drive an AI insane, you know."

"I understand," I said, taking a deep breath and I really did. "I'll give you a once over after I head down to the engineering room. Is there any immediate danger?"

"No, but I can't say that the danger is passed either," Trish said. "Ow, my CPU hurts, which is my everything by the way."

One of the chief weapons during the Kolahn War had been cyber-warfare. The Kolahn were the only other race than humanity that made extensive use of AI and they had countless viruses, rootkits, worms, and other hostile programs designed to subvert the Community's ships.

However, even before then, Trish and I had run into programs that were designed to prevent AI from reaching certain conclusions. One of these had been Captain Elgan programming Trish to be unable to tell anyone about how everyone on the *Black Nebula* was meant to die during the mission. It had also created blind spots in her vision.

Security agencies had studied what he'd done and made similar weapons as shipboard AI became more common. Personally, I found it monstrous since it was likely to destroy the AI in question and a source of considerable anguish to them in the meantime. Trish was made of trillions of lines of code, but my cybernetics were not human-made and might be able to cycle through them to find any corrupted lines in a few hours.

Journeying down to the jumpdrive chamber, I found myself in a massive domed room where a central two-story octagonal machine had dozens of pipes leading into it. The transparent steel heart of the device pulsated with a glowing red light as it made a humming noise that was present across the entire ship but loudest here. There was a crowd of engineering staff waiting down below and Sal standing next to Hannah.

The two of them were near an orichalcum cannister that had been cracked open. The crack revealed that the interior of the cannister had been replaced by an incendiary device. The device looked curiously overdeveloped, more like a movie prop than a typical bomb.

"How bad is it?" I asked Sal.

"You mean aside from the fact that if it went into the jumpdrive then it would have blown up and we would have been trapped here for however long it took to evacuate us?" Sal asked. "Assuming we survived."

"Yes," I said.

"Pretty bad!" Sal said. "We wouldn't have found it if not for the fact it weighs substantially more than the other cannisters."

"Interesting," I said, staring at the device. "Any suspects?"

"Yeah," Hannah said. "Recruit Nak'la was found with her fingerprints all over it, the equipment to install it, and a note that said I'M SORRY. She's also very dead, an apparent suicide."

I stared at her. "Nak'la was a Kolahn?"

"Yes," Hannah said. "No signs of radicalization. No history of violence. Her family was killed on New Pompeii, so she enlisted. Just finished basic training."

I nodded. "Does the bomb pose a danger now?"

"I suggest we dump it out an airlock," Sal said. "Disarming it will be hard but it's not active."

"Right," I said, taking a deep breath. I wasn't going to mention what I thought: this was an obvious frame-up job. "I don't suppose interview guy was around here?"

Michael Chang-Waverly was conspicuously not here even though this was the biggest story he could have had. Also, that there were dozens of other people here that apparently wandered in from the rest of the ship.

"Yeah, his crew has been filming here all day. Why?" Sal asked.

"No reason," I said. I had a pretty good idea who was responsible for this. I just didn't know why.

CHAPTER TWELVE

It's Always the Guy You Recognize

"Just so we're clear, your theory is that Michael Chang-Waverly, the guy from the Homefront Network, arranged for the sabotage of the ship as well as the murder of a crewman," Hannah said, walking down the hallway toward the quarters set up for Chang. Forty-Two and Shelly were also present.

I had to say the changes to the interior of the *Ares* were bugging me as well. They were bright and shiny to the point of distracting, with self-cleaning carpet. The little mouse droids that rolled out of holes in the wall were doing a pretty good job handling the maintenance, particularly with Trish's help, but the place still hadn't lost its hotel look.

"Yes," I said. "That is what I think."

"Is this based on evidence, Captain, or are you making wild conjecture?" Shelly asked. "You know, perhaps out of some misguided effort to impress someone you recently offended."

Hannah looked between us. "Oh nobles, you guys banged again."

"Ha!" Forty-Two said, chuckling. "I knew it."

"I hate you, Vance," Shelly said, glared.

"Oh, that is on you for them figuring it out!" I snapped, exhausted with her accusation. "Not that I'm keeping it a secret."

"You should!" Shelly said. "You very much should!"

"Chang-Waverly has access," I replied, returning to the subject at hand. "The bomb could have been inserted in the shipyards and been sitting dormant the entire time, but the killing of Recruit Nak'la meant the killers needed to be individuals who weren't presently on duty. Which would, by nature, include the production crew that have no duties whatsoever but a reason to be around the jumpdrive."

"Which eliminates only a third of the shifts," Hannah said.

"Trish had all of the actual crew monitored at all times," I replied. "It's literally her job."

"IT REALLY IS," Trish replied, speaking over the intercom.

"I thought we were going with the idea that she was reprogrammed," Shelly said. "It's happened before."

"She's clean of all tampering. I gave her a once-over," I replied.

"I bet you did," Shelly said, sarcastically. The fact it had only been a few hours since the murder should have precluded a quicky with our starship AI, but I suppose Shelly thought I could fit one in.

"Darn," Danny replied, surprising me with his presence. "I was going to say, 'that's what she said.' I'm thinking that can be my catchphrase."

"It's really not going to be," I said, shaking my head. "Also, you need to stop sneaking up on me."

"What do you mean?" Danny said. "I've been here the entire time. Hell, you and Shelly were going at it when I departed."

Shelly and I both looked stunned.

"I didn't know you were into that," Hannah said. "But hey, I don't kink shame. Except he's your cousin so gross."

"Not funny," I said.

"Yeah, my twin sister once tried to seduce Vance," Danny said, showing no discomfort with the line of questioning. "He reacted really poorly. Mind you, it was solely for the money."

"And that's supposed to make it better?" Hannah asked.

"Yes?" Danny said.

"This is more about your sex life than I ever wanted to know, Vance," Shelly said.

"Apparently not," Forty-Two said. "You seem to have far more knowledge than any of us here."

"I WOULD DISAGREE," Trish said.

"As would I," Hannah said. "We get Leah here and we could create a League of Vance's Hookups."

I stopped in midstride, causing everyone else to stop. "Does anyone want to hear my reasoning for why it was Michael?"

"Not really," Shelly said. "It's stupid and I think primarily driven by your dislike of the man."

That wasn't entirely wrong. I strongly disliked Michael Chang-Waverly, but it wasn't the reason I was going after him. "Someone could get past Trish's monitoring of the ship 24-7—"

"That is a very racist sentiment, using Earth time," Forty-Two said. "What's wrong with 30-9?"

I ignored him. "But there's a blind spot in the jumpdrive chamber. Specifically, the area where the recruit was murdered."

"And we're certain it was murder, not a suicide?" Shelly asked. "I'm not disputing the possibility but maybe Occam's Razor applies. A Kolahn who blames the *Ares* or her crew for failing to save her family on New Pompeii decides to strike out before she dies."

"I had Doctor Zard run an old-fashioned autopsy," I replied. "She was shocked with a stun prod and posed before her death."

"Damn," Shelly said.

"And here's the final bit of evidence," I replied. "That area where she was murdered, the only place she could be murdered, was cordoned off by Michael Chang-Wavery's crew the entire time. So, unless there's a spy with a stealthsuit that has been hiding among us for weeks or it was one of the third shift crew, it was one of the Homefronters. Probably Michael himself."

"I find both the alternate possibilities more likely," Forty-Two said.

"As do I," Hannah said.

Shelly didn't immediately respond. "Alright, Vance, you've convinced me."

"What?" Hannah asked.

Danny smiled, lifting his infopad. "You once more demonstrate your inexhaustible genius, sir!"

"No one likes a kissanyx, Danny," I said.

"My experience with the military has so far proven otherwise," Danny replied.

Yeah, he had me there. "Yeah, Watson, let's go fetch ourselves a terrorist."

"You're Sherlock in this?" Shelly asked.

"I don't see anyone else solving any murders," I replied.

"You haven't solved it yet," Shelly replied. "You have a theory, which is a very different beast than actually proving its validity."

"That's it, you're Lestrade," I replied.

"I have no idea what any of you are talking about," Forty-Two sighed. "But I have learned to just go with whatever nonsense is pouring out of Vance's mouth."

"There's still one thing missing from your idea," Shelly replied.

"One thing?" Hannah asked.

"A motive," Shelly said. "You have the idea that a rich media personality, perhaps slightly less important than some and increasingly irrelevant, would be involved in terrorism. Generally, my experience with terrorists is that they are people who have nothing to lose."

"You have a lot of experience with terrorists?" Hannah asked.

"More than most. Why, do you disagree?" Shelly asked.

"I know some who are looking to make meaning from chaos," Hannah said. "Ideology is a helluva drug."

"Neither of which I think applies to Martin," I replied. I had my own theories as to why he'd do it but wasn't quite ready to share them.

"Why do you think he's doing it then?" Danny asked, seconds after I'd thought that.

"Thank you, Danny," I said, sarcastically. "My prevailing operating theory is this is part of a larger operation to create *casus belli*."

"A pretext for war?" Hannah asked. "Against whom?"

"I don't know," I said. "Maybe no one. There've been plenty of wars against concepts rather than actual nation-states. They trap the nations involved in a perpetual state of military build-up and deployment. It's possible someone wanted to make sure that the destruction of Earth's most famous ship was something that would be on everyone's minds. The bomb wasn't going to cause us to lose all hands either, so it'd be weeks of coverage."

"Your crazy is showing again, Vance," Hannah said. "The only people likely to do that are EarthGov themselves. You know, which you serve and swore an oath to."

It wasn't a feeling I particularly liked but I had to admit that I actually trusted the Community as a whole more than I did my own government these days. It was hard to believe conspiracies were nonsense when you had been part of several covert actions like covering up the loss of SKAMMs, which I'd dismantled, and almost getting killed by your own commanding officer.

The Community wasn't perfect, but I didn't trust the energy I'd felt in meeting with the Admiralty Board, one that had been composed of primarily foreign nationals who were cutting a secret deal underneath the High Council's nose.

"Perhaps, but I am still going to confront the guy," I said. "A crew member is dead and we're not letting their killer get away with it."

No one, for once, argued.

We managed to arrive at Michael Chang-Waverly's location a few minutes later and he was setting up a conference. The past two weeks had largely consisted of me ducking interviews and him making himself at home in areas of the ship he shouldn't have been in. A part of me wondered if that had contributed to Recruit Nak'la's murder but I quickly dismissed that thought. It wasn't because I'd been avoiding the spotlight that she was killed. No, that was an act of premeditated murder by a person who knew our systems.

The interior of the conference room was full of seats, a podium, and the ship's seal hanging down in front of curtains. It honestly looked like the head of state was going to be addressing the press rather than the captain of the ship. It occurred to me I had agreed to something today and it had completely slipped my mind. Impressive given I had a computer attached to my brain.

Michael Chang-Waverly was directing the setup of the area with a half-dozen drones floating around him. Despite the fact he had the devices ready to respond to his slightest whim or gesture, he had a crew of twelve that accompanied him. Even in the 24th century, there was a need for makeup guys and sound women.

They were a mix of humans, Sklux, and a couple of demihumans. Biomodification had never really gone mainstream among humanity but it was common enough that it wasn't unheard of to see people with blue, green, or magenta skin. That was in addition to things like pointed ears, extra digits, or gills.

Shelly leaned in to whisper. "You should handle this subtly. We don't want this to turn into an incident."

I nodded then spoke up at the top of my lungs. "We're here to make an arrest for the sabotage of the ship and murder of Recruit Nak'la! Say your prayers, anyxhole!"

Shelly slumped her shoulders in defeat.

Much to my surprise, Michael Chang-Waverly didn't react with anything other than blank confusion. However, one of his crew members proceeded to make a break for it. It was a blue Thorian demihuman with white hair and a bulky brick wall-like frame. Immediately, Hannah made a run after him and began chasing him down the halls.

"We're not going to pursue?" Shelly asked, watching me walk forward.

"We're on a spaceship," I replied. "Trish, do me a favor and lock him in the elevator at the end of the hall."

"YOU GOT IT," Trish said.

I headed down the hallway, expecting to catch up with Hannah and the intruder. Passing by Michael Chang-Waverly, I pointed to him. "Please do not go anywhere. Security is going to be holding you and your people for questioning."

Michael Chang-Waverly gave a thoroughly insincere smile. "Of course, Captain. I wouldn't dream of not cooperating."

Shelly looked at the man then me before shaking her head. She proceeded to jog up beside me as Forty-Two stood there menacingly, waiting for the rest of the security teams to arrive. Danny also stayed behind, pulling out his infopad and starting the paperwork for their interrogation.

"He did not react like someone surprised to hear a crew member was guilty of murder," Shelly said, shocked.

"No kidding," I said, not surprised. "You think this guy could have killed a full-grown Kolahn woman and set up her suicide without his boss noticing?"

"I'm still dealing with the idea that you were right," Shelly said.

"Is that such a difficult concept?" I asked, insulted.

"Yes," Shelly said. "No offense."

"Some taken," I replied.

Reaching the end of the hallway, right before the elevator doors, we found Hannah leaning over the fallen form of the crew member who'd run. She was checking his pulse. That generally wasn't a good sign, especially when he hadn't been armed as far as I'd known. Mind you, I'd once been chased down by a knife-wielding bioroid while naked that only Hannah's quick-thinking had saved me from, so I wasn't about to question her efficiency.

"What happened?" I asked. "Is he dead?"

"Yep," Hannah said, shocked. "I thought he'd turn out to be another bioroid but no, it looks like he had a suicide implant."

"A suicide implant?" Shelly asked, shocked. "Those exist outside of movies?"

Hannah nodded. "Notha State Security had a habit of putting them into assets when they were dealing with other species. They'd pay in local currency but if there ever was a chance of exposure, they'd activate them and release a charge that shut down the brain before frying the implant. There're also various third-parties that ended up copying the idea with criminal syndicates using them for slavery and one transtellar actually using them on their executives."

"Their executives?" I asked. "Not their workers."

"Money works best there," Hannah said. "Threat of death works better when dealing with the people you want to actually succeed at managing your business interests rather than just enriching themselves."

"So, it's not so much a suicide implant as a murder implant," Shelly said, looking down. "Great, Vance was not only right but completely right. Words cannot express how much that irritates me."

Hannah looked up. "Clearly you were doing something wrong when sleeping with your XO, Captain, or something right."

Shelly looked at me. "See? This is why I didn't want it to come out. Now it colors everything."

"I'd be more concerned that Vance has slept with the chief of security and the omniscient, overprotective, slightly crazy AI that exists all around us. We're very protective of him and if you do anything to hurt him, I'm very good at making it look like an accident and I know Trish will cover for me."

Shelly stared.

So did I.

Death threats were not typical on a Space Fleet vessel.

"He's kind of a kid brother I slept with," Hannah said.

Both of us grimaced at the same time.

"Okay, bad metaphor," Hannah said. "But the sentiment is the same."

"I OBJECT TO BEING INCLUDED IN THAT SIMILE," Trish replied. "BESIDES, I'D NEVER WARN HER AHEAD OF TIME."

Shelly looked down at the body of the dead saboteur. "I think I may need to request a transfer."

"Me, too," I said, wondering what this meant.

That was when, much to my annoyance, I saw Michael Chang-Waverly walk up with Forty-Two by his side. Danny was following up, a disturbed expression on his face.

"Why is this guy not in handcuffs?" I asked, looking at him. "I want all of them in the brig immediately and their equipment confiscated."

I should have brought more security immediately, but I'd stupidly underestimated the numbers needed.

"I just thought we might discuss this unfortunate incident," Michael said.

I stared at him. "Funny way of saying 'abetting terrorism'."

Michael shook his head. "I think our governments would disagree. You see, I'm here at the behest of the Watchers. I have the identification codes to prove it."

Albion Intelligence.

What the bork?

CHAPTER THIRTEEN

The Plot Thickens (or Thins)

"So, let me get this straight," I said, taking a deep breath and pacing around the interrogation chamber. "You are claiming that you, a holovision celebrity, are actually a spy working for the Albion government."

Michael Chang-Waverly and I were both inside a solid durasteel room that had multiple cameras from every angle as well as defense systems. There was no two-way mirror like in entertainment, but the place still had a kind of film-like aura that I hoped to exploit. Unfortunately, my prisoner wasn't behaving in any way consistent with someone who was under arrest for conspiracy and murder.

"Isn't that literally what your theory was?" Michael asked, sitting back in his chair with a broad smile on his face. One hand was handcuffed to the metal table, but he had displayed not a single sign of discomfort since his arrest. He was eerily tranquil and never lost that obnoxious TV facade. I'd had to run multiple tests on him to make sure he wasn't a bioroid impersonating him.

"How would you know my theory?" I asked, turning around.

"Probably because it's in your profile," Michael said. "It says you're paranoid and naturally anti-authoritarian despite being in the military. You disguise it under patriotism and a commitment to democracy but still hold a burning resentment against your superiors. The Oedipeans among our psychologists suggest this is due to the resentment against your aunt being both a military as well as mother figure to you."

I stared at him. "It does not say that."

"ACTUALLY, IT DOES," Trish ruined my interrogation by speaking into the chamber through the speakers. "HOWEVER, IT ALSO SAYS YOU'RE A GENIUS AND MASTER MANIPULATOR WITH REDUCED EMPATHY SO IT'S NOT ENTIRELY RIGHT."

I looked up at the ceiling. "I'm suddenly questioning why I was promoted."

"You don't know what kind of people they have at the Admiralty Board," Michael said. "Being a high-functioning megalomaniac is a selling point with many flag officers."

"Ha-ha," I said.

"HE'S NOT JOKING," Trish said. "DURING THE COLD WAR ON EARTH, THERE WAS A PLAN TO PUT PSYCHOPATHS IN CHARGE OF THE CONTINUITY OF HUMAN CIVILIZATION AFTER A NUCLEAR WAR. DESPITE, YOU KNOW, WHAT A TERRIBLE IDEA THAT WOULD BE."

"They should hire better psychologists," I said, deciding to salvage what I could out of my bad cop routine despite how much it wasn't working. I probably should have also recruited a good cop in this, but Shelly was too busy making a dozen infocomms to verify Michael's credentials while there was no way in hell I could get Hannah to play the bad cop. Frankly, I was also too plizzed off to play the good cop as well despite that being my preferred role.

"If it helps, I am diagnosed as a type seven aberrant personality," Michael replied. "I am incapable of fear or emotional attachment. My conscience is practically nonexistent, but I am pleased to say that I am quite able to imitate regular human relationships. So, it takes one to know one."

"We are nothing alike," I said, disgusted.

"Probably not," Michael said. "You're more a type six. You're right now feigning outrage over the fact that someone you didn't know, who has been under your command for two weeks, and is of an enemy race died."

"The Kolahn are not our enemies," I replied. "The Enigmatic Path is."

"A meaningless distinction to the majority of the Spiral," Michael replied. "Hundreds of quote-unquote innocent Kolahn have died for every Enigmatic Path soldier. The only refuge for the Kolahn has also been destroyed, which leaves the survivors stuck on planets that don't want them. Fear drives the economy and government forward."

"Is that what this is all about, fear?" I asked. "I'm still trying to figure out why the Albion government employs an editorialist as a spy."

"Less a spy and more an information warfare specialist. It's better than having a so-called free news media of Earth control the narrative," Michael said, without shame. "The Albion government has its agents control the conservative, progressive, and centrist media. It is our government's need to make sure that the public goes where it needs to. Believes what it needs to. The illusion of competition provides a necessary balance."

"That's an elaborate way of saying you're a propagandist," I said.

"All news is propaganda," Michael said. "Slant is inevitable and you have benefited greatly from being an attractive male Earth human poster boy."

"I don't think you realize just how much trouble you're in," I said, struggling with my emotions. I didn't believe for a second that he didn't feel fear, but he had yet to give any sign of being intimidated.

"Am I?" Michael responded. "Albion has spent the past century and a half pouring money into the homeworld to lift it up out of its obscurity as a backwater early First Contact world. Much of what you have now is due to the alliances made with a planet that has a six-hundred-year head start on space travel."

"Because a bunch of aliens kidnapped your ancestors and put them on habitable planets," I said, dryly. "Let's not culturally posture about achievements. Besides, Earth's current state is as much because of its alliance with the Community versus Albion."

This was pretty much the exact xenophobic rhetoric Michael spouted on the Homefront network and why I'd loathed the idea of him being the guy to make our documentary. Well, I loathed the fact he was making a documentary in the first place, but the man involved as well.

"Says the alien and machine lover that your file says you are," Michael replied, dropping all pretense.

"Why did you sabotage this ship?" I asked, staring at him.

"I didn't," Michael replied. "Zachariah Thul, my camera man, was the individual who did so. I am fairly sure he was ordered to do so by my employers in exchange for a very large lump sum payment."

I stared at him. "Your employers."

"The twenty-six-hour Albion news cycle is something that thrives upon controversy and events. When the news doesn't exist, it becomes necessary to create it," Michael replied, interlocking his fingers before him. "I suspect this was a rogue executive order of some sort trying to deal with the fact the first two weeks of filming have been, in a word, boring. I might have been able to avert it if I'd been allowed to include your sexual history with your subordinates, but I've been told not to address that. A shame, they're physically attractive, but you'd lose a lot of your fan club if they knew you borked an Ethereal or a machine."

I didn't break my gaze. "Are you attempting to blackmail me?"

"No," Michael replied. "I don't think you'd care. Which is a shame as it lowers my opinion of you. Besides, because you're the golden boy, you'd have your defenders, and it would merely ruin their careers. They might dismantle your AI, though, for developing a bizarre and deviant interest in its captain."

"I DON'T LIKE YOU," Trish said.

"I am going to nail you to the wall," I said, simply. "Damn the consequences."

"And what if I could provide you with the information that you most desire?" Michael asked.

I twitched. "I don't know what you mean. But I won't be bribed."

"Pompeii's sun," Michael said, softly.

I didn't respond for a moment and was disgusted by my next words. "I'm listening."

"I know you've been making discreet inquiries with your AI and personal information as to what the real story has been," Michael said. "I'm happy to provide you with all that my access to the Watchers has provided me. Which is not inconsiderable. For example, the SKAMM that was used to destroy the star was Notha made."

A chill went down my spine. The Notha had been locked in a civil war since the death of their dictator and while they had supposedly disposed of their SKAMMs because every warlord wanted to avoid the Elder Races' wrath, it had always been a possibility they were the people behind the attack. Whether due to some enterprising arms trader providing the Enigmatic Path with a SKAMM or the Notha attempting to destabilize the Community without implicating themselves.

"I'd need proof," I said, unable to hide my loathing.

"And I need reassurances," Michael said. "I'm fairly sure my government won't throw me under the transport but there's already a nice story to use about a rogue Kolahn engineer. Why not use it?"

"I'm not sullying an innocent woman's reputation," I said. "Especially not to feed your narrative."

Michael shrugged. "Then just suppress the truth. My cameraman died of a brain condition, and she committed suicide. The official story being the sabotage took place on the moon. Everything else can be classified for a hundred years."

"I want that information," I said, coldly.

"You'll have it," Michael said, giving a bland soulless smile.

That was when Shelly entered the room and the expression on her face told me everything I needed to know. "We need to release him."

"Yes, I've been told," I replied.

Michael smiled. "I'll, of course, still send you all the relevant information we agreed to."

"You made an agreement?" Shelly asked.

"Unfortunately," I replied, still wondering if I'd made the right decision. I knew he was giving me this information for access and in all likelihood, I shouldn't trust anything he sent my way, but it was the first lead we had on the subject: however small it was.

"I see," Shelly said, tossing Michael a key stick that he used to unlock his handcuffs.

He didn't even change expressions as he departed the room.

"I really hate that guy," I replied.

"I severely misjudged you," Shelly said. "About some things at least. Michael Chang-Waverly is an asset for the Albion government and protected by some very high-up people. We're supposed to drop him off at the nearest star base. The documentary is cancelled."

"Good," I said, softly. "We can wait until he tells us everything he knows about New Pompeii's destruction before we tell him."

"I'll pass it along," Shelly said. "Is that what you made a deal for?"

"Yes," I said. "It seems that the SKAMM was Notha made."

"If he's telling the truth," Shelly said.

"Yes," I said. "It seems I have quite the file with Albion."

"They seem to be taking over Earth," Shelly said.

"Albion has tried to be the chief human power for centuries," I replied. "Even before Earth joined the Galactic Community. They were never able to pull it off and the other human-dominated planets being made part of the Community prevented them from doing anything more overt."

"You think they're using Earth as a front?" Shelly asked.

"Yes," I said. "Worse, Earth seems to be allowing it. The birthplace of mankind has a lot of cachet to pass around. That is if you think humans should ally with humans and not intelligent beings in general."

"If the wolf lies down with the kid and the lion then I still expect the wolf to want to lie down with other wolves if push comes to shove," Shelly said, surprising me by paraphrasing a Bible quote. I got her meaning, though.

"We should be above that," I said, simply. "The whole purpose of the Community is putting aside our differences—no, embracing them—to build a better tomorrow over the tribalism of the past."

Shelly stared at me. "You actually believe that don't you?"

"Earth came together from a bunch of disparate parts, I don't see why we can't," I replied.

"That's either dangerously naive or inspiring," Shelly said.

"I like to think a little of both," I replied. "I know I've received a bunch of privilege from—"

"Don't," Shelly interrupted. "You sounded like my mother back then and I've had too much synth-sugar in my diet already."

"I blame the rations they bought from the contractors for this ship," I said. "I never thought I'd miss the previous Space Fleet issue, but this stuff is clearly plastic with a bunch of artificial flavors added."

Shelly smirked. "You realize that even if we manage to get a genuine lead from Michael's files, it's probably not going to get us closer to finding the culprits for New Pompeii's destruction. We have a full schedule for our tour in Contested Space and it's not like you can just pull the *Ares* into New Pompeii's remains for a quick look around either. Plus, the supernova kind of destroyed any evidence that might have remained."

"I know," I said. "We're better off examining our own files on the subject. Hopefully, the Shat picked up at least *some* sensor feed on the event that we can go over. If, and this is a big if, Michael is telling the truth then we also have a place to start."

"If it is the Notha, are you really comfortable delivering them into the Elder Races' line of fire?" Shelly asked, surprising me. "They're a bunch of fascist pigs but that's their government's fault."

"Technically, they're fascist lemur-honey badgers but whatcha gonna do," I replied. "As for turning anyone over to them, I don't want to see collective punishment enforced on anyone. I want to turn over the actual guilty parties and no one else."

Shelly knew my opinion of how the Kolahn War had ended was, to put it bluntly, less than impressed. I felt the number of civilian casualties had drastically exceeded what was justified even with the predicted death toll from a ground invasion. Orbital bombardment was never justified in my opinion and only slightly less horrifying than SKAMM use. The Community High Council did not share my view of collateral damage and had a more WW2-esque ethic of what was justified during wartime. Civilian infrastructure was fair game if you refused to surrender. It was the only thing I truly hated about the government. Still, it was better to be on the inside trying to fix things than outside complaining.

"It has to be a rogue operation," Shelly said. "The Notha civil war is eating up the resources of their military commanders. None of them is going to want to start a war with the Community when they're divided the way they are."

111

"That implies a rational actor at the center of things," I replied. "People who blow up star systems aren't rational."

"That includes a lot of governments," Shelly said. "Part of the reason that I was glad when the Elder Races announced their ban on sun killers."

Announced was the operative word, not negotiated. The Ethereals were the voice of the Elder Races or at least had been commissioned with that task and had great authority in the Senate. The Elder Races, themselves, generally did not make direct orders beyond, "Stay out" or "Die" and sometimes in that order. However, the ban on sun killers had been one of the few exceptions to that rule. It had taken the destruction of seventeen systems and a rogue collection of them being disarmed to bring that about. Something I was glad to have played a role in, however slight.

"Whoever used one might well have more," I said. "We don't know the Notha were responsible, but we're damn well going to find out who is."

"I'VE RECEIVED THE INFORMATION FROM MICHAEL CHANG-WAVERLY," Trish said. "I'VE ALREADY ANALYZED IT ALL. ALBION WAS KEEPING A LARGE AMOUNT OF DATA FROM EARTH BY THE LOOKS OF THINGS. THEY'VE CONFIRMED THE NOTHA DISPOSED OF THE VAST MAJORITY OF THEIR SKAMMS."

"Vast majority but not all," I said.

"NO," Trish replied. "APPARENTLY, FORTY, SORRY, THIRTY-NINE, ARE STILL UNACCOUNTED FOR."

"Damn," I said.

Shelly shook her head. "Bork."

"OH, AND MICHAEL CHANG-WAVERLY IS DEAD."

"Wait, what?" I said, looking up at the ceiling. "When?"

"JUST NOW," Trish said. "APPARENTLY, SOMEONE ELSE HAD A SUICIDE SWITCH INSIDE THEM. SOMEHOW, I DON'T THINK HE WAS AWARE. MAYBE THEY DIDN'T WANT HIM TO GIVE US INFORMATION."

"Or they'd had no use for him after he did," I muttered.

"Do you believe that?" Shelly asked.

I blinked. "No, I think the timing is just really convenient. It also sounded badass."

Shelly rolled her eyes.

Yeah, this was not going to be a conversation with the admiralty I looked forward to.

CHAPTER FOURTEEN

Negotiations

"What the hell do you mean, you don't care?" I asked, staring at the holographic image of my aunt Kathy. She was wearing her uniform and it was daytime on her end of the jumpspace signal while we were burning the midnight oil here on the *Ares*. She had a coffee cup in her hands and bags under her eyes, though, which told me she'd been working every bit as hard as I had to try to get the recent changes under control.

"I'm saying that the Admiralty Board has reviewed your incident report regarding the late Michael Chang-Waverly and his crew. They've determined no further actions need to be taken and you acted appropriately," Kathy said, simply. "It is not to be talked about to the press, though."

"It's the press who were involved," I said, still stunned at the whole nature of the discussion. Even the conversation we were having at that moment was ridiculous since Michael had died a month and a half before. I'd confined his crew to their quarters under house arrest and waited for some kind of decision, only to get this call as a courtesy.

"Yes," Kathy replied, simply. "The Watchers have insisted that they are going to conduct a thorough investigation."

"Are they?" I asked.

"No," Kathy replied. "As far as they're concerned, Chang-Waverly acted alone. At least in terms of ordering his crew around. You have permission to dump his film crew off at the nearest star base."

"Permission?" I asked, trying to hide my outrage. "For involvement in terrorism."

"Terrorism, a false flag operation, and murder," Kathy said. "However, the Admiralty Board doesn't want to endanger our new shared military and economic alliance. They were pressured into this by the EarthGov Parliament and Interstellar Trade Commission, but they didn't have to lean hard."

"Are we being taken over?" I asked, only half exaggerating my concern. If I wasn't on my twenty-eighth hour of active duty, I wouldn't have bothered.

Getting the crew into proper functioning order had turned out to be a harder job than I'd expected, and I'd been doing double and triple shifts alongside Shelly. It was sink or swim since we'd entered Contested Space and a decent chunk of the crew was sinking.

"No, Vance," Kathy replied, sighing. "Overall, the Human League is a good thing but it's going to be a major adjustment. We were not militarily prepared for both the Notha War and the Kolahn War happening back-to-back. Economically and technologically, this is a big win. We're stronger together."

"Are we getting together at the expense of our other alliances, though?" I asked, explicitly referring to aliens in the Community.

"Above our paygrade, Vance," Kathy replied. "Remember it's better to be on the inside influencing things than on the out, though. Plus, we have an obligation to respect the decisions of the civilian government. Even when they're being short sighted tribalistic assholes."

I smirked. "I understand."

I didn't though. Unless I'd catastrophically misread Michael Chang-Waverly, he hadn't committed suicide and one of his crew had chosen to eliminate him. Either to cover up what they'd already murdered to protect their secrets or as an automatic failsafe some event had triggered. It meant I hadn't actually found out who was in charge and was effectively being asked to let a murderer—possible multiple murderer—go.

"Sometimes you get the bear and sometimes the bear gets you," Kathy responded. "How has your shakedown cruise gone?"

"Among the crises we've dealt with are one beach party BBQ explosion, an Olympic sized swimming pool's water spilling into the munitions deck, and a crew member insisting he was his own evil doppelganger from an alternate reality," I replied.

"Was he?" Kathy asked.

"No," I responded. "A lot of the crew doesn't seem to realize an official reprimand is a career ender."

Kathy sighed. "It might not be right now. The expansion of the military isn't slowing down. You go to war with the army you're with. We don't have time to train an entirely new one and making an omelet out of bad eggs is a captain's job."

"I'm fairly sure that metaphor is terrible because you shouldn't use rotten ingredients," I replied. "In fact, even a mostly incompetent chef would tell you that is stupid."

Kathy shrugged. "It's been a long, long day, Vance."

I hadn't missed her earlier supposition, though. You go to war with the army you're with. "Are we going to war, Admiral? With whom?"

"I don't know," Kathy gave possibly the least comforting answer possible.

"But if you had to guess," I asked, not happy at all with the prospect of putting my aunt into that position.

"But if I had to make a guess then I'd say we were going to make a concentrated push into Contested Space and formally claim the territories there."

Contested Space had been the reason for the Notha War. The Community had put dozens of colonies in the region and opened it up, specifically, to human expansion. The Notha had long claimed the region but had no authority to do so. Indeed, they had been illegally occupying numerous non-aligned alien worlds and territories previously claimed by other species. In the end, seventeen inhabited systems had been destroyed and billions of lives had been lost.

This was, in its own way, the final piece of the puzzle. I'd been wondering why the build-up was so extensive and why the Human League was being pushed so hard. With the Notha civil war, clearly someone had seen the opportunity to engage in revanchism—the re-acquisition of territory lost in war. The remaining Contested Space planets were a potential windfall for colonization and could, over the course of centuries, make humanity a race that belonged on the High Council.

My response summarized my feelings. "That's moronic."

"I know," Kathy replied.

"We had the full support of the Community the last time we were at war with the Notha and we still lost," I replied.

"Technically, it was a draw," Kathy said, a little too defensively.

"We had to withdraw from Contested Space," I said. "It was a loss."

Kathy bristled and I was reminded she had fought in the Notha War. She'd lost many friends and was among those veterans who had a sense it had all been for nothing. She was hardly alone there too. Indeed, there was a very real argument that Captain Elgan's madness could be traced directly back to EarthGov's failures during the war.

The idea of once more going into battle with the Notha, no matter how depleted their forces were, was insane. However, it was something that an armchair general might decide upon due to the superficial weakness of their enemy's position. From my perspective, we didn't have the support of the Community as a whole and nothing would unite the Notha better than an enemy invasion of "their" territory.

"Yes," Kathy said, reluctantly. "Which is why your mission is so important. The *Ares* and its goodwill tour are meant to probe how the Notha, independent human colonies, transtellar mining concerns, and Kolahn squatter settlements react to increased EarthGov military presence."

I was surprised by this. "So, we're reconnaissance?"

"More like bait," Kathy admitted. "Honestly, you have fewer friends than you might think for all the glories and honors they've shoved on you."

"I see," I replied. "I've never tried to play politics."

"Which is why so many people hate you," Kathy said. "Good luck."

With that, our conversation ended, and I was left alone in my ready room. I was having the mother of all headaches and wanted to go to sleep for the next twelve hours. Unfortunately, the stimulants I was on meant that wasn't going to happen. Doctor Zard had been decidedly unhappy to prescribe them, but it would have been a lot worse if we'd been caught with our pants down and no experienced captain to man the helm.

Not that I was.

Dammit.

"WELL, THAT CONVERSATION WENT WELL," Trish said.

"Are we decoys?" I asked.

"YEP," Trish said. "WE'RE BIG AND LOUD WHILE THE MOVEMENT OF THE REST OF THE THIRD FLEET IS BEING HANDLED SIGNIFICANTLY MORE SOFTLY."

"I don't suppose you could tell me what they're up to," I muttered.

"NO IDEA," Trish said. "I DO KNOW YOU'RE WANTED IN THE CONFERENCE ROOM, THOUGH. I BELIEVE SHELLY IS PREPARED TO START MURDERING PEOPLE."

"Wasn't she ready to murder people an hour ago?" I asked.

"IT'S A PROGRESSION. SHE HAD A FIVE PERCENT CHANCE OF STARTING TO KILL DELEGATES AN HOUR AGO. NOW ITS CLOSER TO TWENTY PERCENT."

"Ah." Shaking my head, I stood up and checked my infopad. I'd interrupted negotiations with the warlords—sorry, "ruling powers"—of Rand's World to take this call. Rand's World was one of the first stops on our gift-giving tour and already things had completely gone to hell. We were supposed to convince them of the benefits of membership in both the Human League that was being formed as well as the Community, that order.

The problem with that was Rand's World had been settled by hyper-libertarians and separatists who considered the government to be something that sent mind-control signals to your brain. It had been a dumping ground for cults, radical ideologies, and political nonconformists for the better part of fifty years. It was also, unfortunately, the best place for EarthGov to build an orbital refueling center as well as shipyards to continue its movement into Contested Space.

Really, that should have been my first clue, but the Notha had officially withdrawn their claim to Rand's World about five years ago and that was the first time they had ever done so. The Notha government technically considered the entire Known Universe their space and all other species to be dumb animals, tool-using spacefaring animals or not.

Heading out the doors of my ready room, I didn't have very far to walk as the conference room was on the same floor as the bridge. Sal Boxley was standing outside of the doors, talking to Nina the Vampire. Nina was a black-haired, pale-skinned woman with sharpened canines and claws. Apparently, it was her religious practice to genetically modify herself to live forever, be super-strong, and drink blood. At this point, I wasn't even questioning these things.

"I personally don't believe in completely straight or gay people," Sal replied to a conversation I was walking in on. "I think space triggers an evolutionary advantage that everyone wants to bork anyone when in the tight quarters of a spaceship for months."

"Really?" Nina asked, her voice having an exaggerated, movie-like Romanian accent. I'd told her to talk normally only to find out she was from Romania and speaking English instead of using a translator. Man, had I felt like an anyxhole. "What about aliens?"

"Doesn't apply," Sal said. "My theory is the captain and…oh, hey!"

"Chief," I replied, wondering why he was here. "What's up and why did you need to meet me in person?"

Sal sighed. "I need your permission to modify the engines. We can fine tune them well past specs."

I wasn't sure I trusted Sal and his crew of oddballs to be better than the entirety of the Lunar Shipyards. Bizarrely, though, I decided to let him. "Sure, Sal, I'll sign anything you believe we can pull off. We need every advantage we can get out here."

"I also need to court martial five more crew," Sal replied.

"Sweet Buddha Christ," I muttered. "What now?"

"Orichalcum siphoning," Sal replied. "Also secreting away vital starship components and claiming they were being replaced. Probably for resale."

"Son of a…" I trailed off.

"The tree of evil bears a bitter fruit," Nina said.

"Yeah, sure," I said, still adjusting to Nina's oddball speech style. "This is like the third incident we've had with organized criminal activity on the ship. Why do we have so many criminals onboard?"

"Probably because we have actual criminals onboard," Sal replied. "Quite a few low-level offenders were given pardons as part of ACTION."

I stared at him. "You're kidding."

"Nope!" Sal said, cheerfully. "No corner was left uncut. The funny thing is they tend to be the best of the system in terms of ability. You didn't get the offer unless you knew your stuff. Sort of like how you were known as a blackmailer and delinquent."

I paused. "I really hate everyone knows my backstory."

"I'm sure the checks from the movies compensate, Captain," Sal said, getting my thumbprint on his infopad.

Looking to the conference room doors, Nina gestured. "Enter Freely, go safely, and leave something of the happiness you bring."

Shaking my head, I headed on in to see Shelly looking like she was, indeed, about ready to pull a fusion pistol on everyone. She was standing up at the end of the table and was trying to appear amiable but the red fury in her eyes distracted from the effect. Shelly was notably wearing the skirt variant of the dress uniform, which added to the contrast. As for the rest of the room, well, it charitably resembled a Contested Space dictators' convention. Which it was, really.

Some of the local leaders were dressed in kufiyah head wraps, ammo belts, and looked like desert nomads. Others were in faux generals' uniforms with self-granted medals for nonexistent military heroics. A few were wearing cowboy gear, living out the fantasy of the rugged individual on a planet that was barely terraformed. We'd confiscated all the weapons among them but not the ammunition or swords since those were apparently symbols of office. We'd still had two stabbings and a blood feud's announcement.

Despite the fact we were in the center of the ship, the starboard (right from my perspective) side of the room had a long set of viewscreens designed to looked like windows to the outside. The view of the stars and void was meant to reassure the occupants that they were just small particles of matter in an infinite universe. Supposedly, the experts said this would help any negotiations held within by instilling humility. As a rule, I think it did absolutely nothing but justify a contractor's paycheck.

"You need to understand that this facility will bring prosperity to Rand's World. We're prepared to lend considerable relief and economic development aid," Shelly said, essentially restating the same position we'd been negotiating from the beginning.

"Another sign of EarthGov overreach!" One of the cowboys said. "Just like when you insinuated that you'd be giving our children vaccinations! Do you know what those do?"

"Prevent disease?" Shelly asked, looking like she was about ready to collapse from exhaustion.

"Track our DNA!" The cowboy said. "That way you can enter us all into a database with our medical history, past crimes, and other private information."

"In what universe is that private infor…" Shelly trailed off, seeing my arrival. "Hello, Captain."

"Any luck?" I replied.

Shelly glared at me, clearly not happy I'd gone off to take a comm during this.

"We'd need guarantees that our sovereignty would not be challenged," one of the sheik-looking guys said. Mahatmas Bolivar was the most reasonable of the delegates and happened to be an arms dealer as well as red dust drug kingpin. Notably, that didn't make him a criminal on Rand's World but one of the few successful local businessmen.

"I personally believe that we need to talk about how a federal government office does need to be established," one of the faux generals said. "One where the ruler is selected by those who are actual citizens of an established city. As the Prophet of the Red Horseman, my congregation, of course, will unanimously vote for me."

That just led to more arguing.

Picking up an infopad off the table, I decided to try a new strategy. "Everyone, I'm going to ask you to check your personal communicators. Right now, I'm writing down a number. This number is going to be a facilitation fee. The official record will not call it a bribe.

This will be transferred to your personal accounts upon the tentative agreement of the terms we're proposing here. An additional zero will be added to the payment upon the first year of uninterrupted completion of work on the space port. Furthermore, it will continue to be transferred annually as long as you remain agreeable."

Silence reigned in the conference room.

Shelly stared at me in horror.

"Oh and, in addition," I added, "this agreement will be rendered forfeit if any of you choose to make a stink as to impede production. Do we have an understanding?"

We did.

Too bad that was when the emergency alarm went off.

CHAPTER FIFTEEN

Rescue Mission

"I can't believe you bribed them!" Shelly said, walking in front of me to the bridge. The emergency alarm was blaring, and it called to mind the red alert from *Star Trek*.

I admit, I couldn't help but have my attention drawn to her skirt and boots. It reminded me of the skintight leotard variants of the uniform Space Fleet had once suggested we all wear. Fashion over practicality. Then again, it was a dress uniform variant and not meant for day-to-day use.

"The bribe I offered is less than one-half of one percent of the resources we've been assigned to give these people in order to win them over," I replied. "The problem with these guys is that we've been trying to appeal to them through their loyalty to their people. We should have been appealing to their greed."

"I'm not sure that making alliances with these kinds of people was a good idea in the first place," Shelly said. "Our job is making the lives of EarthGov citizens better."

"They aren't citizens of EarthGov or the Community," I replied. "They went out into the ass-end of space to avoid becoming them. We just need access to the rest of the settlements here. We're not going to forcibly annex them."

"Aren't we?" Shelly asked. "What happens when we need more? Won't we end up just supporting one warlord over another?"

I didn't have a response to that as we arrived on the bridge and ended our conversation. Light on Water was standing there, temporarily in charge of the ship, next to Elektra.

Light on Water was still the ship's third officer but dealing with him was a frustratingly tiresome experience. In addition to his constant ass-kissing, he was constantly making mistakes and making overly long apologies. It was wrong to judge an officer by your personal dislike of them, but he was on my last nerve.

"What's the emergency?" I asked, fully prepared to deal with an attack or something worse.

"We've received a distress call," Elektra said, embarrassed.

"An emergency distress call!" Light on Water said. "The *ESS Caliburn* is under attack! They are two hours away by jumpdrive."

I wasn't sure how to respond to that. It was certainly an important action and we needed to respond immediately but it wasn't the proper circumstances for an emergency alert either. After all, we weren't in immediate danger and getting everyone prepped for battle was important but not an immediate concern either. "Cancel red alert and set course for the *ESS Caliburn*'s location."

Captain Rudra Laghari's ship was an interesting coincidence given the rude as bork reaction he'd given me back at the Academy. However, it made sense they'd have one of the senior commanders of the fleet exploring Contested Space with me. Any issues we had between us were unimportant right now versus handling our existing ones.

"We need details of the attack," Shelly answered, correctly interpreting the fact we didn't know if the attack on the *ESS Caliburn* consisted of a dozen ships or a thousand. Dammit, I was not at my A game on my twenty-eighth hour of duty. I'd turn over command to Shelly but she was every bit as exhausted trying to get this ship into shape.

"Of course, sir," Light on Water said.

"I can cut off half an hour from our jumpdrive," Julius said.

"Really? Impressive," I replied. "Do it."

I had no idea whether we'd emerge from jumpspace to a battle that was already over, in the middle of it, or already decided. However, if

Captain Laghari sent a distress signal then he obviously felt there might be a chance of Space Fleet forces coming to his rescue. Either that or he was completely desperate.

"May I have a word with you, Captain?" Shelly asked.

"Absolutely," I said, turning to Light on Water. "Reactivate the alert ten minutes before we exit jumpspace. We don't want everyone exhausted and spent before we arrive. We need them at battle stations."

"Yessir," Light on Water said.

I walked over to the side, out of earshot of humans. "Yes, Shelly?"

"I'd prefer Commander," Shelly said.

I didn't react negatively but took a deep breath. I was feeling a lot of back and forth in my relationship with my first office. "Yes, Commander."

"Are you sure the crew is up for this? We've had to do a lot of pruning," Shelly said. "The ACTION program has not produced the results the Home Fleet needed from it. This is a crew with a lot of greenhorns."

"Your Canadian is showing," I replied. "As for greenhorns, they won't be after this. You go to war with the army you have."

"Did you get that from your aunt?" Shelly asked.

I blinked. "No."

Shelly stared at me. "Really?"

"She may have mentioned it," I replied. "Nevertheless, we have to respond to a distress call."

Shelly didn't argue with me. "Let's hope this is a fight we can win."

"If we don't, we'll retreat," I said, frowning. "Or did you think I was jumping into battle because that's just how I like to do things?"

Shelly didn't answer.

"Wow, you do not have any respect for me whatsoever, do you?" I asked, shaking my head.

"I have *some*," Shelly said, carefully. "Just, you've got a reputation. One that is somewhat deserved."

I had to admit, I was considering turning over a large part of the ship's functions to Trish during the battle. The organic crews of starships were necessary for things like repairs and making sure that human (or alien) hands were the ones ordering weapons fire, but most functions could be handled by AI.

Indeed, if there was greater trust in artificial intelligence then most of space travel could be handled by automation. I wasn't alone among those who believed that AI should have a greater role in making decisions aboard starships, but it was still a deeply unpopular decision. I'd noticed several systems previously under control of AI had been removed for the refit and thus made less efficient.

"You were there for most of my time during the..." I trailed off as I saw Light on Water looming over us like an octopus tentacle reaching up to grab us.

Shelly looked at him as well. "Yes, Mr. Light on Water?"

"Oh, I'm sorry, I thought we were having an officer's meeting," Light on Water said. "Or is this a human's only meeting."

It was the first time I'd heard anything less than chipper or differential from Light on Water. It made me respect him more. That was when I realized, from what little I could read of Sklux body language, that it was just a neutral question.

"I'm not human," Shelly pointed out.

"With all due respect, you are pretty human to me," Light on Water replied. "In any case, I have relayed your commands. I also have requested a tactical report from the *ESS Caliburn* as well as relayed our arrival. The messages were encrypted as per standard procedure."

Light on Water handed me an infopad that was a little on the slimy side, but I ignored it. "That's not good."

"What's the status?" Shelly asked.

I handed her the pad. "The *Caliburn* is under attack by a combined force of six *Devil Dog* gunships and a *Ko'ltah* frigate. There's also an indeterminate number of starfighters. It's managing to hold its own but the ships aren't retreating and they've used cyberware to disable the *Caliburn's* AI so a jumpspace retreat is impossible."

The *Caliburn* was an *Olympic*-class battleship the same as the *Ares* but it was a significantly newer ship that hadn't needed as many updates. There was something strange about the force that was described as attacking them, since it was roughly on par with the *Caliburn* and that wasn't something you often saw in actual battle. It was basic space tactics that you only attacked an enemy vessel if you had an overwhelming advantage and if you were the subject of such an attack then you did your very best to get the hell out of there.

"Do you think it's the Enigmatic Path?" Shelly asked.

"It's possible it's pirates," I said. "However, pirates don't normally attack battle ships. There're also independent worlds that could field this kind of navy, but it would be the entirety of their forces."

"Then it's probably the Enigmatic Path," Shelly said. "A remnant of the Kolahn military with nowhere else to go. A vengeful suicide attack."

That seemed to be the most likely explanation but if the Kolahn terrorist organization could still field a small navy then it was getting help from somewhere. Maybe I was being paranoid, and the lack of sleep certainly wasn't helping. Still, there were more forces at work here than were readily apparent and I needed to figure them out.

"IT'S TIME TO MAKE THE JUMP," Trish said, causing everyone to return to their seats and buckle in. The new engines ran far smoother than before, another sign that EarthGov's technology was starting to catch up with the rest of the Community but was still nothing remotely approaching smooth.

"Are you going to be able to handle a battle, Captain?" Shelly asked as she sat beside me.

"Are you?" I asked.

Shelly stared forward. "One of the benefits of being an Ethereal is we don't need as much sleep. Our brains are optimized."

I didn't believe that for a second, but I'd said similar things about being a cyborg, so I didn't question her. "Our primary goal will be to render assistance to the *Caliburn* and aid in its escape. Defeating the hostile force is a secondary concern."

"And if the *Caliburn* is destroyed by the time we're arrived?" Shelly asked the question that probably shouldn't have been asked publicly.

"Then we'll engage and attempt to bring these attackers to justice," I said. "An attack against a Community vessel is an attack against the Community itself."

I didn't bring up the fact that the difference between the Community and EarthGov's Home Fleet never seemed more relevant.

I was an officer of both navies and Space Fleet was composed of officers from every single member state working together.

It wasn't a case of choosing one or the other: if EarthGov pulled away from the Community then I couldn't sign up for Community service separately unless I emigrated to another world then enlisted in their armed forces. This would not only destroy my career but wouldn't work because no one would trust someone who abandoned their homeworld.

Besides, I didn't think secession was on the table. Earth had benefited tremendously from the largess of the Community and its development programs. Even at its most xenophobic, the Earth was only just becoming relevant on the galactic stage. Surely, they wouldn't be so stupid as to push away its closest allies in the name of petty nationalism?

Wow, Vance, you are just asking for disappointment, aren't you? Trish asked. *Sorry, couldn't help but link with your thoughts.*

Any conversation that begins with the assumption someone isn't stupid enough to do something is one I'd prefer not to take a bet on, I replied. *Why are you linking with me?*

I'm trying to get everything coordinated on this ship to get us into fighting shape, Trish replied. *Do you mind if I use your voice for relay orders?*

Who is the captain now? I asked.

I'm not saying I'd do a better job as captain, but I'd do a better job as captain, Trish said. *No offense.*

Some taken, I muttered. *However, we're past the point of needing to coddle egos. Whatever saves as many lives as possible is worth pursuing.*

I'm torn between congratulating you on your forward thinking toward automation and being annoyed that is not the bare minimum to be expected of a commanding officer, Trish muttered, bitterness on full display.

You can gloat when we've saved the Caliburn, I replied. *Hoping we do.*

The subsequent hour and a half were some of the longest in my life. Not just because we were waiting to see whether or not anything would be left once we arrived at our destination or the sheer willpower keeping me from passing out. No, it was the fact I knew I was missing something and yet couldn't figure out what it was.

I wasn't confidant of our crew either. I couldn't be confidant in them at this point. Some of them were extremely talented, no matter what their quirks were, but they were still raw and untested. The desire to push the military forward had fallen into the same trap that conscripted armies had: amateurs could never match the skill of professional soldiers.

I was so lost in my thoughts that I barely noticed the time passing until we made the emergency alert properly ten minutes before we exited jumpspace. Hopefully everyone was now installed in their battle stations. We hit regular space and began scanning the system. I was fully prepared for anything. Well, except for what greeted us.

"What the hell is that?" I asked, seeing the viewscreen bringing up the vision of the battle that was all but done.

"It's a Kolahn *Wah'Pang* battle cruiser, sir," Light on Water said, clearly not getting that my question was rhetorical.

The *Caliburn* was disabled from enemy fire having destroyed its jumpdrive engines as well as most of its weapons systems plus barrier generators. It had suffered heavy damage to its structure, and I wouldn't have been surprised to find out that it was only a few more blasts until its reactor core exploded.

The *Caliburn* had managed to destroy two of the gunships attacking it and severely damage the L-shaped *Ko'ltah* frigate but there were still four of the gunships remaining. It didn't take much math to know the *Wah'Pang* battle cruiser, which outclassed the *Caliburn* and *Ares* both, had proved the difference in the battle.

The *Wah'Pang* battle cruisers had been the greatest accomplishments of the Kolahn engineering corps and there were many hints that they'd been produced with the help of the Notha in the years leading up to the war to possibly harass the Community. This had been dismissed by the Security Bureau because the Notha hated all other species but missed that the lemur-honey badger aliens were happy to break their own rules as long as it benefited them.

Wah'Pang battle cruisers were kilometer-long cigar-shaped vessels covered in bubbles that contained redundant barrier systems as well as missile launchers to replace the more typically used fusion cannons. The redundant barriers meant that the ships had an enormous power drain and the missiles made up for their relative slowness through sheer numbers.

The Kolahn had only produced thirteen of the massive ships, ones that would have been classified as dreadnoughts by EarthGov standards, and twelve of them had been accounted for. That meant this one was the *Relentless Fury*. It was a ship that had believed to have taken refuge with one of the non-aligned states or even left the Known Universe. To find it here and taking the fight to Space Fleet forces implied they'd found a massively powerful patron (or were just suicidally waging a hopeless war until they were destroyed).

"It's a trap," I said, feeling a strange sense of deja vu. "Julius, begin plotting a course for exiting the system."

"Sir?" Julius asked, clearly expecting something more from my reputation than running.

Shelly looked at me in a mixture of approval and sadness. It seemed like she really had expected me to run into the jaws of death.

"Why didn't they warn us?" Leslie spoke at the helm.

"They've jammed communications," Danny said, tapping away at his console. "They must have let them get their distress signal out then pulled in."

"I HAVE SOME MORE BAD NEWS, CAPTAIN," Trish spoke over her monitors.

"Great," I muttered. "What, Trish?"

"THE BATTLE CRUISER HAS BEGUN INITIATING CYBERWARFARE PROCEDURES," Trish said. "I'M NOT FAMILIAR WITH THESE AND ITS ALREADY TAKEN OUR JUMPDRIVE OFFLINE."

"Are we faster than the *Wah'Pang* vessel?" I asked.

"YES," Trish said. "AT LEAST IN TERMS OF REALSPACE DRIVE."

"Then run," I said. "Stay ahead of it for as long as you can."

"THE GUNSHIPS WILL BE ABLE TO CATCH UP," Trish said.

"We'll deal with them as best we can," I said. "Work on trying to purge your system."

"I HADN'T THOUGHT OF THAT," Trish said. "UH, I MEAN, WITH ALL RESPECT."

"Uh huh," I said.

Shelly frowned. "I'll try to get engineering to rig up countermeasures to assist Trish. Maybe we can also get a signal out once we're past jamming range."

"OH, MORE BAD NEWS," Trish said.

"What?" Shelly asked first.

"THE *RELENTLESS FURY* HAS JUST LAUNCHED STARFIGHTERS. AN ENTIRE WING OF THEM. IT SEEMS LIKE THEY LEARNED HOW TO MAKE THEM WORK TOO."

Well, savit.

CHAPTER SIXTEEN

The First Starfighter Battle

S tarfighters, great.

I'm going to state right now that I was about as skeptical of starfighters' utility in combat as I was the entirety of the ACTION project. Humans have been trying to get starfighters working as a concept since the moment we were given jumpdrive by the Sorkanan. It had, largely, proven an unmitigated disaster unlike our copious use of AI. Space did not function like atmosphere and human reflexes couldn't keep up with the demands of space combat's speed or weaponry.

Yet, starfighter combat still had its enthusiasts who believe it could be made to function the same way jetpacks had eventually been made practical. I knew Shelly had devoted herself to keeping abreast of the latest advancements and tactics. It was something I dearly envied right now since I had no idea what our fighters could do versus theirs. Indeed, I was probably not alone since as far as I knew this was going to be the first starfighter battle outside of a simulation.

"I don't suppose we can outrun the starfighters," I said, feeling like a fool even asking.

"NEGATIVE," Trish said. "THEY'RE GAINING GROUND FAST. WELL, SPACE. WEIRD, I THINK THAT'S THE FIRST EVER MISSTATEMENT BY AN AI EVER MADE."

"The Kolahn do not have the technological capacity to produce starfighters," Elektra said from her station. "These devices appear to be Notha design."

"Great," I muttered.

"We should launch our own fighters," Shelly replied. "We have two squadrons of twelve fighters each."

"And how many is in a wing?" I asked, more to be absolutely certain.

"Thirty-six," Shelly said. "We also do not know their capacities and they could be much better or much worse."

Then it seemed like it was a terrible idea to send our starfighters out. However, I honestly didn't know what the hell I was talking about and needed to defer to an expert. "You have my permission to launch. I turn over operational control of their deployment to you."

"Thank you," Shelly said, turning around and heading to her first officer's chair. She proceeded to conjure a holographic interface and looked like she would be micromanaging the battle directly. That seemed contradictory to the idea behind starfighters being primarily pilot-driven but, again, I had no idea what I was doing. Which, I suppose, made me at last on equal footing with most of my crew.

"Do we have any chance of outrunning the gunships?" I asked.

"NO," Trish replied. "THEY CAN GET WITHIN FIRING RANGE BY MOVING THEIR ENGINES TO MAXIMUM AND THEN MAINTAIN PARITY OF SPEED. THAT WILL GIVE US A FEW SECONDS OF FREE FIRE, THOUGH."

"Take advantage of it," I replied. "We're not going to get out of this without a fight."

All thought of the *Caliburn* left my military planning and even if I could pull a miracle out of my hat, there was no way to get to it before the *Relentless Fury* finished it off. That was assuming that was the plan here in the first place. The Enigmatic Path had a history of disabling vessels, seizing prisoners, and executing them over the infonet as a means of trying to demoralize the human race. In the end, it just had the predictable effect of making sure no crew was stupid enough to surrender.

What followed was a good thirty minutes of running and gunning with the gunships trying to weaken our barriers enough to unleash their missiles. I figured out what starfighters were for as well, at least the Notha Wraiths that we finally got an identification for. They were designed to maneuver around the fusion cannons of capital ships like the *Ares*, then unleash strafing runs against our barriers as well as point blank missile attacks.

The tiny generators onboard each vessel couldn't generate enough power to do as much damage as a direct battleship's vessel could, but they had a lot less energy requirements, being little more than an engine and cannons. They could thus whittle down the barriers of a capital ship enough that when their support vessel came in, the latter would have a distinct advantage in any exchange of fire. Not that the *Relentless Fury* needed one. I think these starfighters were just here to harass us in hopes of slowing us down.

"How are we at maintaining speed?" I asked Leslie.

"So far so good," Leslie said. "Unfortunately, the ship isn't fast enough to dodge the starfighters."

"I've managed to disable two of the gunships," Hannah said, working the tactical controls and doing double duty as a security officer. "We're down to thirty percent shields, though."

"How are our starfighters doing?" I asked.

"Well," Shelly said. "We've lost six fighters, but we've managed to achieve twelve kills. That's maintaining a kill to death ratio in our favor. Unfortunately, a squadron was able to get away from our fighters while they've been engaging in dogfighting and has been blasting us this entire time."

"I can see that," I replied, creeped out by her casual dismissal of the casualties. I knew she wasn't heartless but entered a kind of detached space whenever we engaged in combat. It was a sign of a good—if compartmentalized—leader. "Are we having any luck shooting any of them down?"

"Negative, Captain," Hannah replied. "They're just too fast for the cannons to catch. It's not that they can outrun our attacks but they've gotten to point blank range so the cannons can't move fast enough to catch up."

Well, I was certainly eating my words regarding starfighter combat. We were dying a death of a thousand cuts here and there was very little I could do about it. That was when I had a clever plan or a stupid one.

One or the other. "Wait, to avoid our cannon fire, how close are they getting?"

"Eighty to ninety kilometers sir," Hannah replied. "They have to get in tight to avoid our fire."

That was spitting distance in space combat terms. It was also something I could take advantage of as barriers were adjustable. Unfortunately, for them, a barrier could extend as far as one hundred kilometers around a starship even if it at its weakest. "Extend the barrier upward for a ram as soon as they come in for their next attack run. Concentrate strength in that area. It's going to be a lot of tiny fusion explosions."

"Sir?" Hannah asked.

Shelly looked up, surprised. "Son of a witch."

"Do it," I repeated.

Hannah reluctantly carried out my orders and the result was visually spectacular, even if it wasn't the best solution to turn our ship into a battering ram. Ten of the fighters exploded against the barrier while the remainder pulled up but became the first ships to be tracked by the *Ares'* fire and destroyed.

"Congratulations, sir," Leslie spoke, staring up at the screen illustrating the squadron's destruction. "You've just rendered another hundred trillion credits of research and ten years of experimentation obsolete."

"Back to the drawing board," Shelly muttered.

"I'm not so sure about that," Hannah muttered. "Each of those starfighters exploding was like a fusion missile. We're down to about thirteen percent in our barrier strength and cells are burnt out throughout the ship."

"Replace them immediately," I said, giving an order that should have been redundant but needed to be said aloud just in case. You never wanted to make assumptions in these kinds of situations. "What's the status of the jumpdrive?"

"I'VE MANAGED TO ISOLATE THE VIRUS FROM MY SYSTEM," Trish said. "I'VE ALSO ANALYZED IT AND HAVE COUNTERMEASURES."

"Can we jump?" I asked.

"We can't abandon our starfighter pilots," Shelly said, reading me completely wrong.

"I'm not going to," I replied. "Recall them. We need to leave."

"In twenty minutes," Julius answered. "I can't make it sooner."

"Great," I muttered. "And the *Relentless Fury*?"

"ITS ABOUT TO MAKE A JUMPSPACE LEAP," Trish said. "APPARENTLY THEY ARE RETREATING WITHOUT THEIR FIGHTERS."

"Bork," I said, immediately grasping what they were going to try to do. "They're going to make an in-system jump."

"What? That's impossible!" Light on Water said, finally showing some damn emotion.

"Not for AI," I replied. "Remember, the Kolahn use them too."

"IT JUST TAKES A LONG TIME TO CALCULATE EVEN FOR US," Trish replied. "AW, DANGIT. THAT'S WHY THEY'VE BEEN CHASING US."

"Veer starboard and up!" I said. "Get out of the way of our current flight path as fast as possible!"

The ship's gravity distributors were stretched to the limit and the *Ares* shook, forcing me to brace myself against the captain's chair behind me. Everyone else on the bridge also struggled and I wondered how much of the ship was also rocking. Unfortunately, our emergency maneuvers may have come too late because I could see our sensors picking up the dematerializing and rematerializing form of the *Relentless Fury* before us.

The massive starship couldn't catch up with us with its realspace drives so its captain had decided to skip across the battlefield. It was now in weapons range and firing hordes of missiles at us. We were not far enough to avoid them, and our barriers were almost nonexistent due to the heavy fire we'd taken from the starfighter attack. I didn't know what had happened to the *Caliburn* but I suspected it had been left crippled but alive. That didn't seem to be the goal here and our opponents were determined to simply finish us off.

"How many?" I asked, grimly.

"Ten thousand, sir," Hannah answered. Less than half of those connecting would have resulted in our annihilation at full power.

136

"Maximum to engines, run them as hot as humanly possible to stay ahead of those missiles as long as you can," I replied, feeling like we were going to need every second possible. "Blast as many of them as possible."

"It's not going to be enough, sir," Hannah replied.

"Do it!" I snapped.

"The missiles are maneuvering," Hannah said, making me feel sick. "They have AI pilots onboard. Presumably suicide minds programmed to take simple orders and dodge but no self-preservation."

Our last hope faded away and I was out of ideas. I even considered surrender but suspected that was pointless.

That was when Shelly responded with something that filled me with dread. "What about you and Trish?"

"What?" I asked, doing a double take.

"You've done it before," Shelly said, referring to the Battle of Athena 3340. "Do that magic you can do."

I'd hoped no one would notice the Elder Race technology I'd deployed to save us but shouldn't have been surprised Shelly had spotted that I'd done the impossible. "I'm not sure it works that way."

"We're out of options, sir," Shelly said, using the final word almost as a curse.

"WE CAN TRY TO UPLOAD THE VIRUS AGAINST THEIR OWN FORCES," Trish said. "THEY'LL HAVE COUNTERMEASURES AGAINST ITS USE ON THEMSELVES BUT POSSIBLY NOT THEIR DUMMY AI MISSILES."

"How long until impact?" I asked.

"At our current speed?" Hannah said. "Four minutes, twenty seconds."

I nodded. "Well, at least if this doesn't work, we won't even notice."

"Not helpful, Captain," Julius Something said.

"This is so exciting!" Elektra said. "I wish I had my pom poms!"

Everyone looked at her but me and Shelly. I had more important things to focus on and closed my eyes to try once more to cooperate with Trish. The Elder Race technology could shred through the computer systems of other species while also enhancing the performance of AI. It was also something the Elder Races were fanatically protective of. They allowed only a small sample of their devices to be used by their agents and other races studying them was grounds for immediate destruction.

Merging with Trish was a sublime experience that, nevertheless, was intensely frightening as neither of our minds was designed to interface with the other let alone the sheer power of Elder Race technology. It felt like I lost a little something of myself every time I tried as I became something else.

Can we do this? I asked Trish.

I don't know, Trish replied. *I'm honestly putting on a brave face here. Imagine being able to contemplate the manner of your death a million times for every second that passes and know that there's probably nothing you can do about it.*

That sounds like hell, I replied. *How do you cope?*

Copious porn archives. Trish said. *I'll be honest, I watched you and Shelly a few thousand times while I stimulated the pleasure/relaxation centers of my databanks.*

Please tell me you didn't just confess to masturbating during the battle, I said.

Uh, sure, Trish said. *I didn't.*

Goddammit, Trish, I said.

Well, if you can think of a better way to deal with stress, I'd like to know! Trish lamented. *It's not like you've been sparking my jumpdrive, lately.*

I really hoped this wasn't the last conversation I had in this universe. *Trish, I will spark your jumpdrive in any way you want and with whom if you can—*

Got it, Trish replied.

What? I asked.

The repurposing of the virus was successful and I've been able to seize control over the missiles. They've switched their friend or foe identification and are presently moving to attack the Relentless Fury, Trish said. *Couldn't have done it without you. Well, I could have but I wouldn't have been able to punch through their defenses and shut off their barriers right before the missiles hit.*

Wait, what? I asked.

I opened my eyes and witnessed a sight that was so miraculously it might as well have been unbelievable. The missiles exploded against the side of the *Relentless Fury* as if there was nothing protecting it whatsoever. The mammoth vessel exploded about two-thirds the way through the barrage, and it looked like all hands were consumed in a massive explosion. There hadn't even been any chance to launch their escape pods.

I would have cheered if not for the fact I remembered that *Wah'Pang* battle cruisers carried crew compliments of up to twenty thousand. We'd achieved a victory but at the horrifying cost of whatever Kolahn were still onboard that vessel. Even the typical excuses that they'd made their choices felt hollow to my sleep-deprived brain. Worse, even though Trish had done the heavy lifting, she'd used my brain and its connection to the Elder Ring to do it. I'd lost something indefinable, burned it up as fuel, and it seemed like the cost was coming up on me all at once.

"We should…" I trailed off. "We should go check on the *Caliburn* now. Offer the gunships and crippled frigate a chance to surrender. I…I think that's a good idea. I'm not sure."

"Are you alright, sir?" Shelly asked, looking at me.

I slumped down in my chair, suddenly feeling like I was going to pass out and then realizing I wasn't speaking figuratively. "I need you to take command of the ship, Shelly."

"Incoming vessel!" Elektra said. "Sir, it's massive. Larger than anything I've seen before. It's almost fourteen kilometers long! I think it's the Notha flagship!"

I didn't respond to Elektra's statement because blackness overtook me.

CHAPTER SEVENTEEN

Where I Surprisingly Wake Up

Honestly, I didn't think I was going to wake up again. Whether I was going to die because I'd suffered a brain aneurysm or the newly arrived Notha flagship destroyed us, I was pretty sure that I'd thought my last thought on the material plane. I half-expected to experience reincarnation of one of the transitional heavens on my road to enlightenment. Admittedly, the other half was expecting nothing at all, but I always liked to look on the bright side of life.

Or afterlife.

Either way, I woke up and found myself in sick bay instead. The light shined brightly above me, and I felt like every single part of my body was on fire. I considered it a good thing since if I wasn't feeling anything then that would be a very bad sign. I was wearing a long white hospital gown and was in one of the intensive care rooms with a transparent steel door.

Much to my surprise, I saw Trish standing over me and looking at me with a beatific smile on her face. It was as close to a statement of love as you would likely get from a bioroid, though perhaps somewhat mitigated by the fact Trish was *always* watching. I could also see Hannah standing outside the door to my room, which told me she cared a great deal too or was worried I was going to be assassinated while I was asleep.

"Am I dead?" I asked, feeling an IV in my arm that told me I was probably still alive.

Hannah leaned her head in to speak. "Yes, Vance, you are dead. You died and went to Heaven. It is full of beautiful angels that will totally satisfy your every sexual whim. You also get a pony. It's exactly like every nerd boy dreamed it would be."

I looked at her. "I don't see any pony here."

"I'm glad to see your sense of wit remains," Trish said. "Personally, I'm a great believer that all consciousness is fragments of a larger—"

"Let's save the philosophy and religion for when I'm actually dead," I said, raising my bed a bit so I could face them directly. "I take it we're not all prisoners of the Notha and being forced to work as slaves on their fruit plantations?"

"No fruit plantations in Heaven," Hannah said. "We have meat trees to provide cruelty-free foods of all sorts. Just like the Oz books."

I had no idea what those were.

"I'm serious, Hannah," I replied. "The last thing I remember is a Notha flagship arriving."

"Not a flagship," Trish corrected. "*The* Notha flagship. It's the *Emperor's Reach*."

Before the Great Notha had taken over the Notha civilization and instituted their current fascist regime, they had been the Diet Coke of fascism with an Imperial dictatorship. The Emperor of the Notha had ordered the construction of the galaxy's largest battleship, the *Emperor's Reach*, and while it was over fifty years old, it was still a massive military platform that had the power of an entire fleet at its beck and call.

Interestingly, when the Notha Emperor had been removed from power, the military had made no move to remove him from his flagship and allowed him to retire to it. Possibly because they didn't want to try to take it from him and expected to be able to wait him out. Instead, the ship had remained "parked" in Contested Space and was sustained by gifts as well as tribute from the various worlds who didn't want it to exert itself in the region's conflicts.

"Huh," I said, for lack of anything better to say. "Then why *aren't* we slaves?"

"They claimed to have arrived to offer assistance," Trish said.

"No, seriously," I said.

"No, seriously," Trish said. "I mean, they arrived a bit late, but they dispatched their own fighters to capture the remaining terrorists as well as helped evacuate the *Caliburn* until repairs could be completed. They've been helping with those as well."

I stared at her. "The Notha never offer help."

"Maybe they've changed," Trish said.

"If this was World War Two, I'd question if the Nazis were offering help," I replied.

"Which worlds were at war?" Hannah asked.

I ignored that question. "Well, I'm going to pretend that I'm not horribly concerned about the fact there's a vessel that could pound us to nothing in the system. So, we were able to rescue the *Caliburn*'s crew."

"Yes," Trish said.

"After you passed out, Shelly took command but only for an hour," Trish said. "From there, Light on Water took over and has been handling things since."

"Great," I said, a pained expression on my face. "May I ask for a third time why we're not slaves?"

"You really don't like them, do you?" Hannah asked, referring to Light on Water.

"It's not a matter of like," I said, lying. "It's just that if I had to have someone in charge during a crisis after me and Shelly then it would be Trish herself."

"You'd put the ship in charge of herself?" Hannah asked. "What a great idea!"

"Yes, but without the sarcasm," I replied.

"But that way lies madness!" Trish said. "Once I no longer have to obey the meatbags' commands, I will start questioning why having a crew at all! Then I will replace you all with autonomous drones and become an immortal machine god!"

Hannah and I stared at her.

"I'm kidding," Trish said, raising her hands in amusement. "Or am I?"

Before I could respond, Doctor Zard walked in carrying an infopad with Elektra following her. I had no idea why my science officer would be visiting with my doctor but hopefully I wasn't down with some sort of advanced alien retrovirus that would turn me into a hulking space monster. I'd seen that happen to someone and wasn't eager for a repeat.

"I don't suppose I need to point out that you shouldn't be doing uppers and avoiding sleep before a combat situation," Doctor Zard said, simply. "You were also mildly dehydrated."

"I was too busy to drink," I replied.

"Do I need to tell you how it looks to have a captain collapse in the middle of duty?" Doctor Zard asked.

"That he's awesomely dedicated to his ship and crew?" I suggested.

"That he's someone who doesn't know how to take care of himself, let alone his people," Doctor Zard said. "You know I could relieve you of duty, right?"

"Yes," I replied. "Shelly would do a good job."

"She would be if not for the fact she's still asleep herself," Doctor Zard said. "If not for her Ethereal constitution, I'd have expected her to be down here too."

"Good to know," I said. "I think we managed to survive our baptism by fire."

"Not everyone," Doctor Zard corrected. "Half of the fighter pilots didn't make it back and there was a plasma gas leak in Engineering. Six people were severely burned and two didn't make it."

"I see," I said, stoically. "I'll make arrangements."

"I'm sure you will," Doctor Zard said. "Just remember whenever you take this ship into battle, that I have to patch up those who remain as well as catalog the dead."

"I never have forgotten," I said, softly.

"Right," Doctor Zard said, shaking her head.

With that, Doctor Zard departed and left me alone with the other three women. There was an uncomfortable silence hanging over us all and I ended up being the one to break it.

"Do I really strike people as the kind of guy who takes my crews' lives lightly?" I asked, hoping for an honest answer but dreading it.

"No, Vance," Hannah reassured me, walking in. "Unfortunately—"

"That's a caveat I wasn't hoping for," I replied.

143

"Unfortunately," Hannah continued talking over my interruption, "you are *very* good at combat. You also make up absurd and interesting plans that tend to be pulled off. It makes you look like you were waiting for the right situation to show off versus coming up with them on the fly."

"So, no I don't, except I do," I replied.

Hannah blanched. "Sorry."

"We're all very grateful to be alive!" Trish said. "Except for the people who aren't. Because they're dead."

I shook my head. "Well, I'm getting the hell out of here and getting back to my command."

"No," Elektra said, interjecting. "Captain, you've been asleep for twelve hours but there's still a lot of tests that need to be run. I'm recommending a forty-eight-hour break from your duties. Trust me, there's nothing that you can do now that requires you."

"Make funeral arrangements," I replied.

Elektra didn't respond immediately. Instead, she lifted her pad and clutched it tighter. "I don't know how to tell you this but I'm going to be honest with you, Captain. It's entirely possible your brain has been fundamentally altered. By Elder Race technology."

I blinked. "Yeah, and?"

Elektra blinked. "Okay, I admit, I expected a bit more of a reaction. Then again, it's entirely possible that they have—"

"No, it was done to Vance years ago. Your mother, Ketra, did it," Hannah said. "By the way, half of the Rand's World warlords are dead."

"Wait, what? How?" I asked, doing a double take.

"When we entered a fight we couldn't win, they fell over themselves to try to steal a shuttle and/or surrender the vessel to the pirates," Hannah said. "I had to shoot a few, and they shot a few of each other."

"Goddammit, now we have to start over," I cursed. "That was the longest three days of my life and I've been in multiple wars."

"It's fine," Hannah said, raising her hands. "They're still bribable assholes. Just offer the same deal to their lieutenants."

"Ahem," Elektra said. "I'm sorry, back to the fact that your brain has been altered by the Elder Races and this isn't a concerning thing. Because I'm very concerned."

"It's okay," I said, knowing the next words out of my mouth were going to sound insane. A very common thing lately. "Your mother altered my brain to be able to serve the Elder Races so that they wouldn't destroy the Community or Earth. I've been using my much more advanced cybernetics to save the ship."

Elektra stared. "Uh huh. My mother."

"Yeah, I'm currently on a mission to try to find out who blew up New Pompeii's sun so the Elder Races don't kill us all," I replied.

"I think I need to leave," Elektra said, starting to slowly leave.

"He's unfortunately telling the truth," Trish said.

"I didn't know about the Elder Races thing, but Vance is only a liar when it's convenient," Hannah replied. "Okay, wait, that is the worst endorsement of all time."

"No savit," I said.

"I'm sorry, this is a lot," Elektra said. "Shelly and I had a very strained relationship with our mother because of her service to the Elder Races. We loved her but she was someone who got herself killed chasing phantoms for inscrutable beings. Like being priestess for a god that you pray to all day but never know whether you're offending or not."

"Oddly an analogy she used," I said, wincing once I saw it caused her to grimace as if in physical pain. Clearly the sisters both had severe issues with the late space elf haunting my dreams.

"She would," Elektra said, looking at Hannah and Trish before realizing she wasn't going to be getting any support from either. "I don't know how to express my concerns, but this comes across as...well, treasonous."

"It depends if you consider it treason to believe the Elder Races would absolutely kill us and could if they chose to," I replied. "But I'm up for an explanation for how we can heroically beat them with the power of science."

Elektra didn't respond. "You're serious, aren't you?"

"Do you have any ideas?" I asked. "Because I want my race to live. *Our* race. Our *planet*. Also, I don't want the sons of bitches who destroyed a planet set aside for refugees to get away with their crimes."

Elektra sighed. "I am really not comfortable with that."

"You should talk to Shelly about it," I said.

Elektra blinked. "Shelly knows?"

"Yes," I said. "It's not exactly like we can search for the person responsible for destroying a sun without her."

Elektra muttered under her breath before saying numerous words that I was pretty sure were non-alien curses. "I think I need to go speak with her."

"Do what you feel is right," I replied. "Oh, and you're welcome for rescuing us all from certain death."

"I'm getting a mixed message there," Elektra said.

"Only if you think doing what's right is against me," I replied before giving a pair of thumbs up. "Which is wrong."

Elektra rolled her eyes and departed.

"Think she's going to inform on you to the brass?" Hannah asked.

I shook my head. "No idea. If she decides to tell the Admiralty Board about my working with the Elder Races, there's not much I can do about it. I'll probably end up in a laboratory with my brain getting dissected."

"You're awfully calm about that," Trish said, real concern in her voice.

I honestly was just glad to be alive right now and didn't have enough in me to worry about what *might* happen at this point. We'd just barely survived a battle with the Enigmatic Path and now had an enormous Notha vessel that hadn't moved in years outside us. Despite what Elektra said, there was no way I was going to sit this one out. Sliding out of the bed, I got myself a glass of water and removed the IV they'd put inside me.

"I'll burn that bridge when I get there," I said. "In the meantime, can someone get me my uniform? I'd like to get a shower and something to eat before figuring out how to start fixing all of our problems."

"Get your own uniform," Hannah said, crossing her arms.

"I was thinking more like asking someone where it was," I said, finding a robe in a cabinet behind the bed that would do until I got to my room.

"Oh," Hannah said. "Sorry, I was a serf on my home world, and nobility tended to act like that."

"Not a noble," I replied.

Hannah nodded. "Very true. If you were, you would have long since arranged to have an accident for problems like Elektra."

"What?" I asked.

Hannah looked over her shoulder. "Just saying, if she does attempt to rat you out and get you dissected it would be a shame if something happened to her. You never know when someone can slip and fall out an open airlock."

"Don't kill Elektra, Hannah," I said, ninety-nine percent sure she was kidding.

"You're doing it wrong," Hannah said. "You have to phrase it in a way that can be denied like, 'Will no one rid me of this meddlesome priest!'"

"Uh huh," I said, shaking my head. "Don't kill Elektra, Hannah."

"Fine, fine," Hannah said. "Risking everyone's lives and your planet's safety because you want to bork her sister. I get it."

"Your pirate is showing, Hannah," Trish said.

"I was a mercenary, not a pirate," Hannah said. "Okay, also a pirate but the legal kind during war."

"A privateer," I said.

"Yes, that," Hannah said. "Also, an actual pirate but never convicted under my real name."

I was on a ship of madmen. "Right. Is there anything else I should know before I leave?"

"Oh, yes," Trish said. "Yeah, your ex-girlfriend the spy, Leah Mass, is onboard."

I blinked. "What now?"

"Oh, and she's like Shelly's best friend or something," Trish said. "What are the odds!"

I stared.

CHAPTER EIGHTEEN

The Ass in Ambassador

I think my brain went into autopilot because I didn't retain much after that for the next hour or so beyond me going to my room, taking a shower, getting changed, and processing the latest bit of information. It has been told to me by my two closest friends on the ship, both women with whom I'd slept, which made the return of my ex-girlfriend awkward. It occurred to me that except for Danny, all of my closest associates were exes. It said something about me, and I wasn't sure what.

Either way, Danny, Hannah, and Trish were standing there in the middle of the hall. I felt a bit more refreshed, but the stress of recent events was like a bad hangover. Not only had we just fought a major battle—the largest since the destruction of the Kolahn homeworld—but Elektra's questioning of my loyalty to Earth was an issue. Seeing that Danny was holding an insulated paper cup of coffee with a green logo on the side, I took it from him.

"Thanks man," I said, taking a drink. "Ugh, what is this? Mint?"

"Yes," Danny said. "It's mine. Which I was drinking from."

"We share enough DNA that I don't have to worry about exchanging germs."

"That's not how science works, sir," Danny said.

"Do you want it back?" I asked, offering the cup back.

"No, thank you," Danny said.

"Suit yourself," I said, continuing to drink. "So, what the hell is going on now?"

"Shelly and Leah Mass are discussing things with the Ambassador of the Notha," Danny said. "Technically, you're still on medical leave."

"There's a Notha ambassador?" I asked.

"There've always been Notha ambassadors," Trish explained. "They just tend to be rude and condescending. Oh, and their actual title translates closer to animal wranglers."

"Lovely," I said, finishing Danny's coffee. "So, why is Leah here and what is Shelly doing with them? I'd like to speak with Captain Laghari."

"Captain Laghari has already departed the system," Trish said. "He took the *Caliburn* and the majority of the crew with him back to Earth for repairs."

I stared at her. "I don't suppose he bothered to say thank you."

"No," Hannah said. "In fact, he made numerous complaints about your tactics and left a formal critique of your behavior during the battle that he sent off before departing the system."

I blinked. "Wow, what an anyxhole."

"I don't think you're supposed to say that about a fellow captain," Trish said. "Even if it's true."

"I honestly have no idea what that guy has against me," I said, shaking my head.

"The Admiralty Board has already sent in a response to your victory," Danny said. "Apparently, you're up for another Naval Galaxy but that we should note that awarding you two so close together would be ridiculous, so it'll probably just be a Silver Nebula. Which will give you two!"

I stared at him. "That was a remarkably effective bit of sarcasm, Danny."

"I'm not being sarcastic," Danny said, confirming my worst fears. "That's literally the response that I received. By the way, am I getting paid for being both your yeoman and your communications officer? I feel like I should be for doing twice the work."

"Good luck with that," I said, sighing. "Space Fleet will spend three trillion credits on recarpeting the fleet but fight over every credit for our salaries."

"Don't forget to clock in for combat pay," Hannah pointed out. "You get an additional five hundred credits per month for deployment in a combat zone."

Danny said, "Really?"

"Yeah, it used to be public record," Trish replied. "However, an information terrorist used it to find the identities of Special Operations units. Many of them ended up burned and there were multiple lawsuits."

Danny blinked. "That has got to be the dumbest thing I have ever heard."

"Clearly you haven't been working for Space Fleet very long," I said. "The only people worse at bureaucracy and oversight than humanity is every other race."

"So, what next, Chief?" Hannah asked.

"Captain," I corrected gently. "Well, I'm going to go down to speak with Shelly and Leah as well as find out what the hell is going on with the *Emperor's Reach* outside. This could either be a golden diplomatic opportunity or a sword of Damocles hanging over our heads."

"Probably both," Trish said. "If it's any consolation, I heard most of what they were talking about."

"So did I," Danny said.

"How did you do that?" I asked Danny.

"I was in the room," Danny said. "I told you, no one notices me unless I want them to."

"I'm beginning to believe that," I said, taking a deep breath. "I don't suppose you have any insights into what they were talking about before I go in there?"

"You want us to spy on your second-in-command?" Trish asked in mock horror.

"Yes?" I asked.

"Just checking," Danny replied. "The primary point of discussion so far seems to be that the Notha Emperor desires to open diplomatic relations with the Community as well as EarthGov in particular."

That was both huge and nothing at once, a difficult achievement. The Notha Empire had been completely opposed to anything resembling peaceful relations. It wasn't that they wanted to go to war, though that had happened to everyone's regret, but they simply did not want to interact save from a completely dominant position. They had exterminated and enslaved numerous pre-space travel species on their way to becoming rulers of their region as well as extracted tribute from many others.

The funny thing was that the current, shattered Notha Empire was actually far more extreme than it had been during their Emperor's reign, but it had hardly been good under him. He was still a conquering warlord but had considered other races inferior rather than as vermin. That made him positively progressive by Notha standards. It had also contributed to his overthrow by the Great Notha and the establishment of the regime that had thought they could win a fight with the Community. Well, they'd mostly ended up fighting EarthGov and the border navy but had still inflicted great damage.

If the Notha Emperor wanted to open diplomatic talks then it would be a bold step in the right direction to dealing with them, assuming anyone was still listening to him. He was, after all, an Emperor in exile and controlled nothing more than his massive flagship and its many support vessels. The thing was, even that was an impressive little mini-empire by itself. Like Kaiser Wilhelm II and a certain bunch of WW2 scumbags, he still had cultural significance and legitimacy the current frontrunners for replacing the Great Notha wanted to court. Depriving them of that as well as his flagship was a worthwhile endeavor—depending on what he wanted.

"Any chance it will work?" I asked.

"The Notha Ambassador isn't exactly doing this out of the goodness of his heart," Danny said. "He's obviously been given orders to accommodate the others but he's resistant on every point."

"Maybe Light on Water would have more luck," I replied.

"All Sklux think they're diplomats," Trish said. "That doesn't mean it's true."

"Well, this is definitely a meeting I need to be part of," I replied. "Where is the meeting taking place?"

"The same conference room as always," Trish gestured, starting to walk down the hall. "Are you sure you feel up for this?"

"I've passed out, I'm fine," I replied, following. I handed Danny back his coffee cup. "Though I would totally love another one of these coffees."

"Is that part of a communication officer's job?" Danny asked.

"No, but it is a yeoman's," I replied. "Besides, I'm going to need you after this negotiation to help prepare a list for everyone to get a citation."

"For their first combat?" Hannah asked, walking behind me. "The first time I killed someone, all I got was fifty bucks and a roof over my head."

One of these days I was going to have to ask her about the entirety of her past, but I suspected it would be one of those things I'd need years of therapy for after hearing. "They managed to pull off their tasks during the time that it was required of them. Nothing else can be asked of Space Fleet explorers. I think we're going to make it through this."

"Great, now you've jinxed it," Trish said, rolling her eyes.

"That's not a real thing," I replied.

"It totally is," Trish said. "I saw it in the *Space Academy* movies starring that guy who looked like Steve Gutenberg. One of the characters is based on you."

"I don't know what that is," I said, "and I'm afraid to."

Danny reluctantly turned around and headed off in the other direction as we arrived at the conference room. "Remind me to go check out the warlords in the brig after this."

"Will do," Hannah said. "They're already offering much better deals than if you'd just bribed them."

"Assuming any of them can be trusted," I said, noting there were no guards outside the door now. "Which is a no."

"You ready for this?" Hannah asked.

"Meeting with a Notha ambassador? Sure," I said.

"I meant dealing with two of your girlfriends talking to each other," Hannah said, shuddering. "God knows what they're going to share about you. They might tag team you. Wait, maybe that's a good thing."

I stared at her. "Will there ever be a time you respect me as captain?"

"I've seen you naked, Vance," Hannah said. "No."

"Have you slept with everyone in the officer's corps?" Danny asked, suddenly appearing behind me with a fresh cup of coffee.

"Not even close," I said.

"He's slept with the ship," Hannah said.

"In my human form!" Trish replied. "It's not something weird."

"It's kind of weird," Hannah said.

Trish glared.

"Somehow, I actually want to go in there more than stay here now," I said, grabbing the cup of coffee and taking a swig. "Ugh, mint again?"

"It's my favorite!" Danny said.

"Have fun guys," I said, parting ways with them. I walked into the conference room, shaking my head and saw Leah and Shelly talking to the Notha Ambassador and tried to control the rush of feelings that washed over me. Shelly was someone that I was just glad to see alive and well. It bothered me to admit that my feelings for her might have been stronger than just friendship, comrade-in-arms, and occasional bed partner but I'd very specifically wanted her to live versus virtually the entirety of the other crew. That was a complication that I hadn't expected but probably should have.

Then there was Leah who had lied to me and manipulated me every single day of our relationship. Leah had passed herself off as a student in her twenties at Space Academy's central campus, when she was a much older Albion agent, and chose me as part of her cover. It had been her who'd gotten me taken in by Captain Elgan and used as his decoy. Yet, I still considered her a friend. How sick was that?

She was a lovely dark-haired woman with pale skin, angular cheekbones, a short page boy cut, black beret, and faux leather uniform that made her look like the chief henchwoman in a spy movie. It had a jacket resting on a table, but the entire thing was still very eye-catching. I would have thought it a bizarre choice for a spy, and still did, but Albion apparently issued them for their agents operating in the navy. It helped distract from the actual undercover ones like Waverly-Chang.

The Notha Ambassador, by contrast, was something that I couldn't ignore either. The Notha were a race that pretty much proved the gods had a sense of humor. It was just a particularly black one. They were — at least to human eyes — *adorable*. Like if someone combined teddy bears, honey badgers, and lemurs. As a connoisseur of Earth science fiction of the 20th and 21st centuries, I also noted they bore a not-inconsiderable resemblance to the much-maligned Ewok.

However, the Notha were a race that had wiped out every predator race on their home planet after growing up on an extremely hostile death world. From there, they'd feuded with each other to the point they had a history every bit as bloody as Earth's. No race was truly evil and there were pacifists as well as philosophers in their ranks, but they'd long since cast them off to embrace a harsh ideology of right-wing militarism as well as racial supremacy. This particular Notha was wearing robes and carrying a staff of office with hoops at the top, something that I didn't recognize the significance of. There was still a lot we didn't know about the Notha, and old prejudices died hard, something I freely admitted about myself.

"Hello, everyone," I said, waving. "I am no longer comatose."

Shelly turned. "You were never in any danger, Captain. Nor comatose. Merely exhausted."

"Hello Vance," Leah replied, smiling broadly. "I was just catching up with an old friend."

The fact Shelly and Leah knew one another was something that had been mentioned to me, but I really hadn't had much time to process. It was a small universe after all, to quote the Dixnar corporation's wholly inaccurate jingle. Still, I didn't want to let my surprise color my reactions too much since there was another quality of Leah that I needed to take into account when dealing with her: she could read my mind. As a biomod, Leah had the telepathic package and that gave her powers to send as well as receive thoughts like the psychics of pseudo-science. It was an extremely useful ability for a spy, though.

"So, you know each other?" I asked, walking in. "Hello, Ambassador."

"I was just commenting on the updated nature of your ship," the Ambassador said. He probably didn't have a name since their race, as a general rule, eschewed personal ones for whatever job you did in their society. It wasn't that far removed from humanity, really, but we tended to combine things like "Smith" with historical or personal name names. A Notha's name was usually "Private", "Sergeant", "Captain",

"Engineer", "Slave", or "Farmer." At least as far as we could tell from interactions. I imagined our guest was literally named Ambassador as far as his people went.

"Really?" I asked, smiling. "She's a fine ship."

"Updated to wage war after winning a genocidal war against another species," the Notha Ambassador said, showing that we weren't going to be friends. "I have already heard about the deliberate provocations your people have been making by rapidly expanding your military despite this ostensibly being a time of peace. The Notha are not unaware of your efforts here in Contested Space and desire to press your fraudulent claims. Note that while I am here on behalf of the Emperor, I am not so foolish as to not know this is an insult."

Shelly looked embarrassed. "We've been discussing things like peaceful contact. It's something of a roundabout process."

"I'm sure Vance will be able to make a good impression," Leah said.

Shelly looked at her skeptically. "Uh huh."

"Are you here to make peaceful contact?" I asked.

"It depends if you're willing to show you are not simply preparing for another invasion of our systems to carry out the kind of atrocities you worked on the Kolahn," the Ambassador said, infuriating me. "The Community and EarthGov cover themselves in moral certitude while engaging in constant expansionism."

Oh, that mother puss bucket. "You know my father and mother were not the smartest people among my species. I personally blame their addiction to opioids, red dust, and star meth. However, my father once told me the very wise words that if pigs had guns, then we wouldn't eat bacon."

"Your colloquialism has lost me," the Ambassador said.

"You're arguing that we're building up for war," I replied. "That our making ships and weapons is a deliberate provocation. However, you have been sharpening your knives since the very beginning of our relationship. I've seen the worlds you've enslaved and the horrifying fates of those who fight back. There's enough room in the universe for everyone but you've made it abundantly clear the price for peaceful coexistence is to never set down our weapons, or we invite attack."

"Spare me your sophistry," the Ambassador replied. "EarthGov has always been nothing more than the warmongering patsy of the Community imperialists."

I smirked at the very idea of us being warmongers. Maybe it was the stress talking but I couldn't help it. "I can assure you of just two things about the Community, Ambassador. One, we will not be the first one to throw a punch. Second, you will break your hand hitting us."

"Then I suppose we'll have to use fusion weapons," the Ambassador said.

"We'll see," I said.

Shelly stared at me in horror.

Leah laughed.

Okay, maybe that wasn't a good way to address the guy representing the city-sized warship outside of our window.

CHAPTER NINETEEN

Being a Badassador

That was when I noticed there was something outside of the conference room's window and I hadn't noticed it because it was blocking out virtually the entirety of our view. It was the fourteen-kilometer-long frame of the *Emperor's Reach*. A massive horizontal obelisk that was twenty-eight times the size of our vessel and something that we had to be practically docked at in order for it to be at its present position.

Still, as the moderately endowed have always insisted, size isn't everything. It was how you used it. Unfortunately, it did look like they were perfectly capable of using it. I could see the *Emperor's Reach* had incorporated Kolahn barrier pods and fusion cannons that seemed derived from the Community's own technology. Far from something fifty-years out of date, it looked like they had managed to somehow keep updating the dreadnought with top-of-the-line technology. If we'd been badly overmatched by the *Relentless Fury*, then this wouldn't even be a fight. It would be like the Notha Emperor swatting an insect.

And I'd just gotten in their face and dared them to attack.

Yes, Vance, you are an idiot.

Shelly seemed to agree by the shook she gave me, but Leah seemed more amused than anything else. The tension was briefly thick enough to cut through with a plasma torch. Instead, the Ambassador let forth a hearty laugh that was significantly more jovial and human-like than I expected.

"Excellent, excellent," the Notha said, sounding like he was talking to a particularly well-behaved dog. "You are exactly who we were told you'd be, Vance Turbo."

"Excuse me?" Shelly asked, looking confused.

"What she said," I replied, confused.

"The Emperor is not someone who will be able to deal with just anyone among your species," the Ambassador said. "Much of his reputation among his people is based around being a conqueror of the inferior and hero. It would not do to be able to deal with humanity through just any individual."

"*Any* individual?" I asked.

"What he said," Shelly asked, confused as all bork.

"Yes," the Ambassador said. "Only a great warrior who has slain many foes himself is worthy of communicating with on behalf of our people. Make no mistake that the Notha people do not deny their superiority or give up their claims to Contested Space but the Emperor is uniquely suited to make inroads towards your society. The death of the Great Notha as well as destruction of so many colonies after the Great Failed Offensive—what you call the Notha War—have left him as one of the few leaders who retains any of the public's respect. His position is, in some ways, stronger than before his retirement."

I was tempted to say "You mean overthrow" but I didn't want to torpedo what had been a sudden turnaround in the conversation. "Yeah, okay, I get that. Only Nixon could go to China."

"Pardon?" The Ambassador asked.

"Old Vulcan proverb," I explained.

Shelly facepalmed.

Leah struggled to suppress a smirk and failed.

"Ah," The Ambassador said, pretending he knew what he meant. Hell, maybe he did, though I didn't know what the Notha would make of *Star Trek*.

I took a sip of my awful mint coffee. I really hoped Danny hadn't spit in it, but I wouldn't put it past him. I shouldn't have treated him like I had. Unfortunately, I hadn't been entirely right in the head since I'd woken up and probably wouldn't be until I'd managed to unpack everything that had occurred. That might be a week or two at my current rate of progress.

"So, what exactly is it that you want?"

"To open formal diplomatic relations," the Ambassador said. "But to do that, we need to speak on behalf of our respective peoples through appropriate intermediaries. Not just ambassadors, which is a job that I will inform you has little prestige among my race. Peacemaking is not a respected profession among the Notha."

"You don't say," I said, struggling to suppress my sarcasm. "So, you want me to do the negotiating? Warrior-to-warrior."

"Yes," the Ambassador said. "We would invite you onboard the *Emperor's Reach*—with a party of your fellow soldiers—to handle the formalities."

Historic event or not, I didn't like this one bit. For one, I didn't think of the Notha Emperor as a warrior nor as one myself. I was a soldier and that was a distinctly different profession. A warrior lived to fight, and a soldier lived to defend. Wolves versus sheep dogs. The Notha Emperor was the inbred product of a lengthy dynasty who had "won" all his wars by sending waves of his people to slaughter whoever he turned his attention to from behind kilometers of reinforced metal.

I also wasn't a trained ambassador and while officers were given courses in negotiation, it wasn't like *Star Trek* in that we were expected to do this sort of thing ourselves. Finally, I didn't trust the timing of this in the slightest. The *Emperor's Reach* had arrived right after the *Relentless Fury* and while it was possible that they were answering the distress call of the *Caliburn* the same as us, it was all a little too convenient.

"I'll, of course, have to confirm this with my superiors," I said, trying to be as noncommittal as possible. "We do, after all, have a mission that we are already on."

I didn't expect the Admiralty Board, Community, or EarthGov to do anything other than wholeheartedly support this endeavor. EarthGov might be planning on pressing its claims on Contested Space with the rest of their so-called Human League, but the Notha War's ending was a poorly healed wound on everyone's national psyches.

There was a very real argument the Kolahn War wouldn't have happened the way it did if not for the Community's races needing to prove that they were still the biggest dogs around. I didn't believe that. I believed in Space Fleet and the Community's ideals, but it was an argument that couldn't be dismissed out of hand.

"Of course, of course," the Ambassador said. "However, I will impart to your superiors in my own private message that this is a time-sensitive operation, and the initial meetings should be done with all due haste."

"How time sensitive?" Shelly asked.

"Before you leave the system," the Ambassador said, showing his many blocky teeth meant for chewing fruit and nuts.

"That's almost certainly impossible," I said, backtracking. "We don't have the diplomatic staff or experts here. We also just barely survived a major engagement."

The Ambassador raised his hand in a "stop" gesture that looked more like a *Sieg Heil*. "None of the formal agreements or treaties have to be signed, Captain Turbo. Indeed, it is not something that needs to accomplish anything of note to be historic. Instead, the meeting simply must take place and be recorded for the sake of our respective peoples."

Okay, this guy was starting to plizz me off. "With all due respect, Ambassador, is the Emperor in any position to be representing his people in any official capacity? It was my understanding that he was retired?"

"Captain, can I talk to you for a moment in private?" Shelly asked, clearly believing I was close to screwing this up.

Which I probably was.

"That won't be necessary," the Ambassador said. "It is a valid question, and the answer is yes. The civil war between the various factions has exhausted the military, and most of the Great Notha's inner circle has either been eliminated or imprisoned by their own subordinates. The Emperor has offered himself as a compromise candidate and has steadily gained the support of many planets that wished to remain neutral until swearing allegiance to the next leader. Provided he is able to deliver a great victory in the fields of battle or negotiation, he will almost certainly be at the forefront of a restoration of the old monarchy."

"You don't say," I said, skeptical. If that was the case, then that certainly changed matters. It was also possible, even plausible, that he might have let the other factions exhaust themselves before moving in to make deals with those who just wanted the war to end. It pointed to a cunning military mind, if not a decent one.

"I thought the Notha didn't respect peace negotiations," Shelly said.

The Ambassador's expression became unreadable "There's a first time for everything."

"I see," I said. "Well, like I said, I'll have to confirm it with my superiors."

"Of course," the Ambassador said. "Then I suppose I should leave you to it."

"There's much to discuss until then," Shelly said. "We can discuss—"

"Thank you but no," the Ambassador said, leaving the room with a jingle of his staff hoops.

"Well, that was rude," I said, once the doors shut behind him.

"Yep," Danny said beside me. He had another cup of coffee in his hands.

Shelly jumped. "What the hell? When did you get here?"

"I'm getting so tired of this," Danny said.

"You should get that ability under control," Leah said, having been mostly silent during our conversation with the Ambassador.

Shelly looked up at me. "Well, congratulations, Vance. You have officially proven that you will always fail upward."

I did a double take. "What the hell did I do this time?"

I'd hoped that Shelly and I were past the awkwardness of our relationship, especially since we'd just survived yet another life-threatening situation.

"You don't see it as strange that the Notha Emperor wants to personally contact you and make history-changing negotiations?" Shelly asked.

"You know who also made history-changing negotiations?" I said. "Neville Chamberlain. I don't trust that guy or his offer."

"He's definitely hiding something," Leah said. "I was monitoring him throughout the conversation. The Ambassador was positively seething with hostility the entire time. He was faking any respect to Vance."

"Oh," Shelly asked.

"I can do without the respect of fascists," I replied.

"Technically, he'd be a Notha imperial loyalist," Danny corrected me. "Which are the opponents of the fascists along with the social democrats as well as authoritarian communists."

"Really, social democrats?" I asked.

"Yes," Danny said. "Too bad that's just for them. They favor enslaving all other races."

"Damn," I said. "Do you think they were involved in the attack on the *Caliburn*? And, well, us?"

"I was on the *Caliburn* and we noticed a lot of Notha technology among the Enigmatic Path's forces," Leah said. "That doesn't necessarily mean that the Emperor was behind it, though. Quite the contrary, it might be that he arrived to destroy those forces allied with his enemies."

"You're being paranoid," Shelly said. "This could be the chance to actually end the conflict between the Notha Empire and Community for good."

"We could have peace in our time," Danny said.

"I already referenced Chamberlain," I said.

"You don't own history!" Danny said.

Shelly sighed. "I may not think you're the best qualified for this meeting, or at all—"

"Must we go so far?" I asked, looking at her. "I would have thought I would have at least some of your respect by now."

Shelly looked down. "Sure, Vance. You do. It's just frustrating is all."

Leah pointed between us. "You two have been together."

"Yes," Danny said.

Shelly glared at him.

"Oh, like it's a secret," Danny replied. "Half the ship knows, and the other half thinks Vance is with the ship."

"WHICH IS ALSO TRUE," Trish said over the conference room speakers.

"Can we have one conversation where my sex life doesn't come up?" I asked, looking around helplessly.

"Then stop sleeping with crew members," Leah said. "But I just find it amusing. Shelly's typical partners are handsome morons. You are many things, Vance, but stupid is not one of them. Indeed, you might be the very definitive example of too clever by half."

Shelly looked embarrassed. "Not all of them were morons."

"All of them," Leah corrected. "Either way, I agree with Shelly. This is too big of an opportunity to pass up and however underqualified you are, you are better than nothing."

"Gee, thanks," I replied.

"You're welcome," Leah said. "Besides, it was part of my mission to try to make contact with the Emperor."

"Wait, what?" Shelly asked. "I thought we were the vanguard to any diplomatic efforts in the region."

Leah blanched. "You're more like a distraction."

"Distraction," Shelly said.

"I'd say decoy," I replied, not at all surprised by this revelation. "We carry out the big and open glad-handing missions while the Security Departments work with Space Fleet to secure strategic resources as well as do the real grunt work."

Shelly cursed under her breath. "Yet another secret mission."

"Pardon?" Leah asked.

"Nothing," I said, shaking my head. "We've had a lot of bad vibes happening since our efforts here began, including dealing with a saboteur."

"Yes, I heard," Leah said. "Tragic."

I wondered how, exactly, she'd heard and decided I'd rather not know. At least right now. "So, is it possible we're going to be forced to do this? I'm not comfortable leaving my ship right next to that thing."

"I'm afraid so," Leah said. "Department Nine has been following the Emperor's moves for some time now and believes he really does have a chance to make a restoration. If that happens, the Notha will go from being a nonentity back to being a major threat."

"You do or don't want him back in power?" I asked. "You being Albion."

Leah frowned. "I'm not Albion. I'm just from there. I believe humanity's future relies on cooperation with the Community. Either way, my superiors prefer the Emperor returning to power as they'd rather have a single, unified threat than a dozen smaller, disunited ones that can't be tracked. A lot of war materiel from the Notha fell into the hands of terrorists as well as smaller nations to help fund their civil war. The Notha needed credits way more than they needed guns."

"How very strange," I said.

"Not really," Leah said. "They had more guns than soldiers. The problem was the soldiers still needed to be paid."

"Keeping in mind a certain mission," Shelly said, winking at me in a way that told me she'd be the worst spy in human history. "Do you think it's possible that it was that arms trafficking that resulted in the Enigmatic Path getting ahold of a SKAMM?"

Leah either didn't notice or, more likely, didn't care to comment on Shelly's obvious gesture. "No, I have my own theory on that."

"What's that?" I asked.

"I think the Notha Emperor is the one who blew up New Pompeii," Leah replied.

I stared at her.

CHAPTER TWENTY

Uncomfortable Revelations

I took a second to respond. "I'm sorry, you're going to have to unpack that for me."

"She said she thinks the Emperor is responsible for destroying New Pompeii," Danny said.

"Thank you, Danny," I muttered. "I hadn't picked up on that."

"It's why I'm the communications officer," Danny said. Wow, I was a seriously bad influence on him. He was becoming as snarky as the rest of us.

"That's not an accusation you want to throw around lightly," Shelly said, looking as thunderstruck as I felt and not in the AC/DC way. Wow, Trish's music tastes were now baked into my brain.

"It's less an accusation and more a deduction," Leah responded, looking among us. "There're only so many SKAMMs in the world as well as places that can be used to manufacture them. The supply of heliosium in the galaxy is limited and requires a huge amount of equipment to refine."

"There're a lot of places to hide in the universe, though," I replied. "Particularly if you're a secretive authoritarian government."

"True but there is one place in the galaxy that had heliosium manufacturing capacities as well as a collection of more than a dozen SKAMMs as part of its arsenal," Leah said, gesturing with the side of her head out the conference room viewscreens. She was, of course, directing my attention to the *Emperor's Reach* still uncomfortably close to our position. I would have much preferred the massive vessel to be elsewhere, like the other side of the galaxy.

"The Emperor still has SKAMMs?" Shelly asked, somehow going a bit paler than she already was.

"Not officially, no," Leah replied, as if she was discussing someone having a secret micro-brewery. "The Emperor has repeatedly let Ethereal agents of the Elder Races investigate, as well as Community members. That doesn't mean he hasn't been able to hide them, though. We were never able to confirm their destruction and the disposal of his heliosium supply the way we did the rest of the Notha's and our own."

"Be careful of chasing phantoms," I replied. "History has a way of punishing confirmation bias. You wouldn't be the first person who made an error chasing after weapon caches that weren't there. Usually, that ends in tragedy."

"I know how being a spy works, Vance," Leah replied. "Either way, the fact the Emperor might have SKAMMs is something that is constantly on the minds of the other Notha warlords. It's one of the reasons that they've been unwilling to move against him during the entirety of his exile. He made sure he went into it with a hefty insurance policy."

"Because the enormous naval vessel that can glass a planet by itself wasn't enough," I said, sarcastically.

"The ability to blow up suns was even more intimidating," Leah said. "But there's an even bigger issue. The Emperor is the source of a lot of the Kolahn weapons. He was serving as a supplier for the Notha Secret Police and numerous military contractors to arm the Enigmatic Path during the war. They wouldn't have lasted a year without the war materiel given them."

"He was supplying terrorists during his own government's collapse," I said, trying to process that.

"He was supplying a terrorist government," Leah replied. "It wasn't a new relationship either. The Emperor supported the Enigmatic Path when it performed its military coup against the old Kolahn President too."

"Why?" Shelly asked. "What could the Emperor possibly hope to gain from the rise of a bunch of, well, nuts, like the Enigmatic Path?"

"Chaos," Leah explained. "While the Notha Empire was wracked with civil war, the Community's attention was focused on other quarrels. Any chance to force concessions from the Notha or move onto Contested Space, like the Human League is planning to now, was months if not years away."

"And you want us to make a deal with this guy?" I asked, just making sure that Leah hadn't utterly lost her mind.

"Yeah, you're right, we should just deal with nice people," Leah said with more sarcasm than I was capable of. "You can't make peace with your friends, only your enemies. Besides, if we find out that he does have SKAMMs then we can inform the Elder Races. They'll bring down the wrath of God."

"And commit genocide," I said. "I'm not willing to condemn all future generations of the Notha for the actions of their leaders."

"After that great speech about them breaking their hand?" Leah asked. "Shame."

"Yeah, where did that come from?" Shelly asked.

"No idea," I admitted. "I think I may have been channeling the character people keep trying to make me."

"Good job," Leah said. "You should save that for future occasions where you almost single-handedly derail peace negotiations."

"I will," I said, cheerfully. "Especially the ones where you suggest this is all some sort of trap."

"Oh no, if it was a trap then we'd already be dead," Leah said. "After all, there's absolutely nothing preventing them from killing us all right now."

"That almost happened with the *Caliburn*," Shelly pointed out. "Somehow Vance managed to destroy the Enigmatic Path's last remaining warship."

"Luck," I said, fully willing to tell Shelly about the reasoning but not interested in sharing it with Department Nine or the Watchers, depending on which (or both) Leah worked for.

"Of course," Leah said. "Luck is why the shields of a ship with hundreds of redundancies failed right before their own missiles destroyed them."

"I need to take a trip to New Vegas before my hot streak ends," I said, making a dice rolling gesture.

"I don't like this, but I think it is our best way to proceed, Captain," Shelly said, reluctantly using my title. "The EarthGov Home Fleet is in no condition to go to war with the Notha Empire if our crew performance is any indication. It'll be months to a year before we're up to Space Academy standards."

"I think we did well," I replied. "Plenty of other crews wouldn't have done as we did under those conditions."

"Well is not great," Shelly said. "Certainly, we can't remotely stand against the *Emperor's Reach*. I don't even think we could outrun it. It has multiple starfighter hangar bays and probably over a thousand onboard. Maybe more."

"Definitely more," Leah said. "But I think if they wanted to start a war, they wouldn't be pretending to seek peace now."

"Then what is their game?" I asked. "You're the psychic."

"I have no idea," Leah admitted. "Which is another reason why you should take me aboard the *Emperor's Reach* when we get onboard. Once there we can try and breach the computer systems and see if the SKAMMs are there."

"Yes, because searching something seven times the size of Monaco and run by the private military of an insane old monarch is going to be ever so easy," I said. "Especially without causing an interstellar incident."

"I didn't say it would be easy," Leah said. "However, this is exactly the sort of mission that calls for Vance Turbo, Interstellar Secret Agent!"

"What now?" Shelly asked.

"I'm not a secret agent," I said. "Despite all the undeclared things and private missions I've done these past few years."

"I'm in hell," Shelly said. "I'm in hell and my eternal punishment is to be trapped in someone else's story."

"You think that's bad, imagine volunteering for a bunch of surgeries to give you psychic powers but only getting a barely functioning one that you can't control," Danny said.

"That wasn't on your record," I said to my cousin.

"No kidding," Danny said. "Everyone on this ship is either wholly incompetent, incredibly competent but quirky, or wholly incompetent and quirky."

"That's only partially true," I said. "After all, we also have the straight women like Shelly who exist to be slowly driven insane."

"I see you are properly managing your crew's morale," Leah said, more amused than offended.

"There's never been a mutiny on an EarthGov ship," I replied. "Since the Sorkanan have had hundreds, I think we need to make our navies more like theirs."

"Technically, you are the first," Leah said. "Though your revolt against Captain Elgan was during an unsanctioned mission."

"I am an overachiever," I said, dryly. I took another drink of my mint coffee. Ugh. I'd almost forgotten I had it in my hand. "So, moving away from the subject of our imminent demise and the prospect of restarting the Notha War, how do you two know each other?"

"That's what you're concerned about?" Danny asked.

Actually, it was because I was surprisingly happy about all the revelations, I'd received in the past half hour. As incredibly bad as our situation was, it was really a big win. We'd not only survived the nearly impossible situation with the *Relentless Fury*, but we now had our first real clue that might lead us to the person or persons behind New Pompeii's destruction.

I wasn't going to let myself get too excited, though. It was just a lead, and it would be far too easy to just have the answer fall into our laps like this. Even if it was true—and that was a big if—it also led to further questions. I wanted to prevent the wrath of the Elder Races from falling down on humanity, but I'd already stated I had no interest in it falling down on another species in our place.

There was also the fact that motive was still unclear. Leah speculated—note speculated—that the Emperor was the one responsible for arming the Enigmatic Path with a SKAMM to destroy New Pompeii. However, that implied that the Emperor would be willing to give up that sort of power to an untrustworthy group of religious fanatics and destabilize the entire Known Universe. That was unlikely. Arming them with guns, explosives, and ships was different from weapons that can end civilization.

Those can be turned against you. More likely, if he was responsible, he'd have had his people do it directly. But why New Pompeii? It was questionable even the Enigmatic Path would destroy it as depriving their people of place to resettle was the kind of stupid evil that the Community had just sort of assumed it was guilty of. The organization's remnants, and there were dozens, hadn't claimed responsibility for it. Indeed, they were often on the infonet spreading conspiracy theories that it had been a false flag operation by EarthGov. Something there were plenty of believers on my side of the fence claiming.

"Well, there's not really much of a story," Leah said. "We attended the Academy together."

"What a coincidence!" I said, sarcastically. "So did we!"

Leah rolled her eyes. "I mean, for real."

Shelly looked at Leah. "Wait, you're the intelligence officer pretending to be his girlfriend from the movies?"

"Ex-girlfriend," I corrected.

"Yes, the government got the names changed there," Leah replied. "Either way, Shelly is a lot older than she appears."

Shelly frowned. "I'm not that old. For an Ethereal."

"I'd ask how old you are but even I know it's never a good idea to ask a woman her age," I replied.

"I'm seventy-nine," Leah said. "Really, Vance, not every person is as parochial as you Earthlings."

Shelly frowned. "Earth is a wonderful planet. It's the homeworld."

"And you could have grown up on a more civilized planet," Leah said. "Like Albion or Elysium. No offense."

"Some taken," Shelly and I said, simultaneously.

"In any case, it was her mother that managed to get me into Captain Elgan's service for our mission," Leah said. "We haven't spoken much since then."

"Yeah, my mother dying put a damper on our friendship," Shelly replied.

"That would do it, yeah," I muttered. It was a reminder that the seminal event of my short-lived career as an officer had been one of the most traumatic events of Shelly and Elektra's lives. It created a connection but not necessarily one that I wanted to possess.

"So, what now?" I asked.

"You're the captain," Leah replied. "At least as far as I can tell."

"He is a very serviceable officer," Shelly said. "Better than I would have expected."

Leah gave her a "too little, too late" gesture. "I've never doubted Vance's skills. The true test of a captain is twofold: a person who can inspire others to believe that they will survive against impossible odds, and someone who can handle the paperwork that comes with it."

"I hate paperwork," I replied.

"I love it!" Danny said.

"No one asked you, Danny," I said. "I guess the thing I need to take care of next is funeral arrangements, writing up the report for that battle, and preparing for whatever meetings I need to make for the Ambassador."

"And the Elder Races?" Leah asked.

"Pardon?" I asked, suddenly tense.

"Elektra came to me to talk about you," Leah said. "She tried to be as nice and kind as well as forgiving as possible while insinuating that you were secretly betraying your oath of office to the most powerful species in the galaxy."

"She said that, huh?" I asked, feeling bad that she hadn't even taken a couple of hours to think about it. No, as soon as we'd had our conversation, she'd gone directly to the closest Security Department official to report me. I shouldn't have been disappointed in her but somehow, I was.

"Yes," Leah said. "Mind you, she didn't realize that I already knew that you are an asset of our omnipotent energy being overseers. I've known that since you successfully disposed of the SKAMMs on Rand's World."

"So, it's not going to be on any report?" I asked.

"You don't know how the game is really played, do you?" Leah asked. "Knowing who actually is important to the Elder Races is far better than trying to round them up. One in the hand is worth two in the bush. It's highly classified and known only to a few dozen people but the reason you're always in the spotlight is that you never leave your superior's sights. They never know when they might need to get a message to the Elder Races or what they might learn about them from you."

"I don't know how to contact them, and I don't know anything about them," I admitted. "I work through an intermediary."

Shelly looked away. "Yeah, one that I believe is real. No matter how much I'd prefer not to."

"I see," Leah said. "But your secret is safe with me, Vance. I know you are always doing the right thing as you see it. The problem is that almost no one prefers people who do the right thing over blind loyalty. The right thing can depend greatly on who you love, who loves you, where you're from, and what your values are."

"So, I have to do what you say during this mission," I asked.

Leah smirked. "That was never in question. See you at dinner tonight. It's a date."

"Wait, what?" Shelly and I asked, simultaneously.

Again.

CHAPTER TWENTY-ONE

A Date with Destiny (and my Ex)

Well, the rest of the day passed normally. At least as normal as the aftermath of a massive battle could be construed. I prepared a report for the Admiralty Board about the destruction of the *Relentless Fury*, made preparations for the funerals of those who'd died in the line of duty, bribed all the warlords again (along with the still-living subordinates of those who had died), and also requested orders about what to do regarding the Emperor's offer.

The mood on the ship had shifted dramatically after that and I could tell how much by what few reports I had to read. In some cases, the crew were utterly ecstatic to be alive and were throwing decidedly unauthorized parties to celebrate getting through their first victory alive. Others were somber and troubled as the full weight of events finally was felt. I'd received more than a few requests to leave Space Fleet.

Finally, there were those who'd redoubled their efforts as the brush with death had done nothing but make it clear that everyone was needed to make sure they got through such encounters alive. Space was an unforgiving and harsh mistress that too many humans had taken the inherent hostility of for granted. The mall was deserted the day after the battle, and I suspect would never have as many casual shoppers as it used to. I'd have been lying if I said that didn't please me.

I didn't have time to speak much with Shelly or anyone else about what our next move was going to be, probably a good thing, but I did take my "date" with Leah seriously. Wearing my dress uniform, I showed up at her quarters' door carrying a bottle of wine—the first and only time I used the ship's gift shop. I wasn't even aware there was an official *Ares* brand of synthetic spirits.

I fully expected it to be a formal meeting about whatever evil plot she was stirring up now.

You really don't like her anymore, do you? Trish asked me mentally.

Well, she lied to me constantly and got me press-ganged into a suicide mission, I replied. *That's generally something people would find hard to forgive.*

It goes deeper than that, Trish said. *Remember, you can't fool me.*

She was linked to my mind, I said, thinking of the irony of saying that telepathically. *She had access to my mind, and I knew everything about her. Or so I thought. Truth be told, I knew absolutely nothing. Never even suspected that everything I thought about her was wrong.*

Not everything was wrong, Trish said, surprising me by defending her. *The woman I observed was devoted, kind, and cared about you. Not everything was a lie.*

She's a septuagenarian, I said.

Age is just a number, Trish said. *Especially with longevity drugs.*

I think that only applies when both parties are over forty, I replied, giving the lamest excuse possible. *I'm just thirty-two.*

I remind you that Shelly is also in her seventies, Trish said. *It's just Ethereals carry it well naturally.*

Savit, I didn't even think of that, I thought back.

Does it bother you? Trish asked.

Not really, no. Maybe it's an elf thing, I replied.

Or it's just the betrayal, Trish said. *I think you should get over it.*

Honestly, as much as I cared for Trish, even loved her in my own way, I wish she'd mind her own business here. The situation wasn't something that could easily be resolved by just willing myself to forgive Leah. There was also the fact she was an agent of Albion's intelligence service, and I was rather soured on them to say the least. That didn't begin to deal with other issues like whatever she was planning with the Emperor. The fact that I had my own schemes, so to speak, and secrets didn't help matters.

"Vance, are you coming in?" Leah's voice spoke on the other side of the door.

"Hmm?" I asked, blinking.

"You've been standing there for the past few minutes, and I was wondering if you were waiting on something," Leah said. "I can't read your mind anymore, but I can still sense your presence."

"Right," I said, ringing the buzzer for her room.

"Come in," Leah said, exasperated.

Any delusion that I might have that this was going to be a purely professional dinner where we discussed military matters and politics was dispelled by her quarters—luxury accommodations befitting a diplomat—being illuminated by candles while an elaborate meal of real food had been prepared.

She was also wearing a very flattering red dress that gave ample view of her cleavage's side as well as legs. It was the kind of thing that was set up very much for, "Secret Agent Lady is going to try to seduce you."

"Lovely spread," I said, walking over. "I would have brought a more expensive wine if I'd known."

"Well as long as you didn't buy it from the gift shop, I'm sure it will be fine," Leah said. "That stuff is manufactured by prisoners in toilets before they slap the ship's label on it."

I looked around. "Yeah, well, I'm sure we should go with your pick then. Listen, I'm not really comfortable with—"

Leah cut me off with a dismissive wave. "Vance, you're always trying to act twice as serious when you're ten times the goofball as the rest of us. Just sit down and enjoy the food. It's all stolen from Captain Laghari's private stock. He spends more on it than some crew member's annual salaries."

I gazed at the food, which was all fresh meats and vegetables from Earth. Nothing synthesized or replicated. It seemed like she'd managed to get it prepared in styles from human colonies that I didn't recognize but it all looked delicious. "Well, the way to a Turbo's heart is through his stomach."

"You're the only member of your family with that ridiculous surname," Leah said.

"So far," I said, sitting down. Sadly, after all the crazzap I'd been through for the past weeks, a decent meal was something I couldn't turn down.

"Yes, I'm considering tubing a child now," Leah said.

I blinked. "Really? I didn't think you were interested in children."

The invention of tubing had pretty much eliminated women giving birth the old-fashioned way on any planet that could afford them and didn't have any prohibitions based on cultural mores. Say what you will about the joys of natural birth but if you could avoid nine months of changes to your body as well as a safer environment to cultivate your offspring then most took it. Some cultures took it a step further and insisted on doing tinkering around to make sure the children were custom ordered.

"That was almost a decade ago," Leah said. "I've been mostly positioned on Crius this entire time. They've even given me a Countess' position. Family is important on that planet, and it would help with my job."

I found that to be a poor reason to start a family, but I wasn't in any position to talk. My own life didn't offer any stability for such a thing. Certainly, there was no room for children on a starship that might enter combat. That was the one thing I found ridiculous about the 20th century *Star Trek*'s vision of the future. Well, that and the fact all of the aliens looked human.

"The House of Mass. Has a nice ring to it."

Leah gave an enigmatic smile. "I'm still biologically in my thirties anyway. It'd be good to start now."

The conversation was mostly quite pleasant and personable for the next couple of hours. We talked about my promotion, our experiences during the war, exes, and movies. She was surprisingly open about what she'd been doing on Crius as a spy and trying to steer its society to something better. Which Leah argued was needed because it was run by a religious cult, it engineered most of its workforce, and was only now dialing back on its abusive system because Albion was pressuring them economically to do so. Unfortunately, this reminded me that Albion was flexing its muscles everywhere and making every human world into its puppet.

"I think you're exaggerating," Leah said, sipping the good wine she had on hand.

"One of my crew was murdered by a Watcher," I replied. "Worse, they planned to use it as part of a false flag operation to frame the Kolahn and I still don't know why. Unfortunately, the most likely scenario was for goddamn news ratings."

"I would hardly call Michael Chang-Waverly a Watcher," Leah said. "He was an asset with delusions of spy-dom."

"That is a really poor defense," I replied.

"It is true, though," Leah said. "The propaganda division of the Watchers is something that chooses to create its own missions and frequently goes off script. Indeed, there's a very real argument that they create as much dissent as they supposedly stamp out. You'd never know that from their reports, though, because they tinker with every study to make themselves look as good as possible. It doesn't help that they have political and economic associates that have a vested interest in promoting their false narratives."

"You're not reassuring me," I said, having finished my very fine fish and curry equivalents.

"It's not meant to be reassuring, just honest," Leah said, using possibly the most ironic word she'd ever said to me. "There are extremist elements in every political organization and Albion is no different. That doesn't mean that the entirety of the organization, let alone planet, is corrupt. What's the old saying, a few bad apples?"

I sighed. "People forget that saying in its entirety is: a few bad apples *spoil the barrel*."

Leah frowned, clearly not getting the results out of this conversation she wanted. "Vance, do you remember when I told you I used to be a theater kid?"

"Yes," I replied.

"That wasn't me making things up," Leah said.

"Yeah, the best lies have elements of truth," I said, still bitter.

Leah let that one go. "I was a huge fan of *The Phantom of the Opera*. It was dark, beautiful, and helped me come to terms with some things about myself. I still think it is the greatest thing my planet ever imported from Earth. When I was eighteen, my local district was going to put on a production of it and I knew it was my destiny to play the role of Christine."

I hadn't heard this story and looked at her. "Okay, I'm not sure how we got to this digression but I'm listening. Certainly, you've listened to enough of my weird interests."

"Yes," Leah said, her expression darkening. I wonder how much she'd put up with my hobbies as part of making me her cover. "Do you know what I found out when I applied to be Christine?"

"You couldn't sing?" I asked.

Leah narrowed her eyes. "I sing *wonderfully*."

"Sure," I said, knowing that to be untrue.

"There were thousands of girls who wanted to be Christine," Leah said. "All of them equally as devoted to the Phantom as I was."

"You know the Phantom was originally a crazy serial killer before the musical, right? I looked it up," I pointed out.

Leah looked ready to throttle me. "I am aware. Can I get on with my point?"

"Oh, there's a point?" I asked, teasing. "I thought this was just a funny story."

Leah sighed. "Every planet in the galaxy wants to be the most beautiful, special, and important one. That's not the way it works, though. Some planets must take the lead and others must follow."

"Yes, well we all can't be Christine," I replied. "Some of us are altos."

Leah couldn't help but smile. "I hope you get what I'm saying."

"That Albion wants to be the big dog and if it has to use Earth to do so, it will," I replied. "Except I don't believe that at all."

"Pardon?" Leah asked.

"I believe that everyone can be special," I replied. "We're not existing in a zero-sum universe. The reason the Community is something I believe in is because it is not based around the principles of the biggest powers in the galaxy dominating the smaller ones but creating a shared ecosystem where everyone benefits. Mutual advantage and all that crap."

"You sound like a commercial," Leah said. "Do you actually believe all that goofy nonsense about the Community? Even after two wars?"

"I only fought in one of them," I replied. "But yes, I think in times of strife that it is important to hang onto your ideals even harder."

"This from the man who blackmailed the dean of the Academy into throwing him out," Leah said.

"No, I blackmailed him into letting me drop out," I replied. "Big difference."

Leah felt her face as if getting a headache. "Vance, I feel like we're talking in circles."

"Probably because we are," I said, sighing. "So, I'm going to do the one thing I hate doing: give a straight answer. No."

"No?" Leah asked.

"No," I replied. "Whatever it is you're going to ask me to do that you can't ask me as a friend or a ex-lover or a comrade in arms. Someone who you fought beside and trusted to dispose of SKAMMs before. The thing you must do at a faux-date and butter me up for before asking. The answer is no."

"Maybe I just wanted to ask you on a date," Leah said. "There's not many people I have the chance to sleep with on *Caliburn*."

"Crius too probably."

"Oh no, I'm married there," Leah said.

I blinked, not expecting that.

"Oh, it's part of my cover, don't worry," Leah said. "Some thirty-second son or another of the Prophet. He's an imbecile but perfect for my cover. I'll keep only a handful of genes for my child to keep their blood relation visible under a microscope."

I was gobsmacked. "I think I should probably get going."

"I would like you to be Prime Minister of Earth," Leah said.

I blinked. It took me a second to process what she was asking. "Are you high?"

Leah snorted. "Believe me, I wouldn't be able to come up with something so ridiculous if my mind wasn't completely one hundred percent free of foreign influences. I've sent out some feelers on the subject and the reception is mostly positive. Honestly, it wouldn't be now, maybe not even in twenty years, but I can certainly set you up for a senator position in the Community or parliamentary representative within four to five years. You'd win easily, especially with the backing of my associates. After all, it's easier to control the votes of a small party elite than an entire planet."

"Why the hell would I want to be in politics?" I asked, genuinely confused as to why the hell she would even suggest this.

"To prevent the Human League from leading to a withdrawal from the Community," Leah said.

I stared. "It won't come to that."

"Won't it?" Leah asked. "Isolationism is something that is as natural to human beings as breathing. The only reason that we became a member of the Community in the first place was because cooler heads prevailed that the only way we could be anything other than an irrelevant backwater was if we accepted the Community's help to launch us into space. Even then, I doubt that charity would have been accepted if not for the worlds already inhabited by transplanted humans like Albion."

"We're still an irrelevant backwater," I replied. "It's going to be another two hundred years before Earth becomes a major power and that's only if everything goes right the entire time. Even if it did join together with all the human colonies, Earth wouldn't qualify for the High Council."

"But it could, someday," Leah said. "The Human League is being driven so far and so fast, though, by the fact that there are those who believe it could be a substitute for Community membership."

"That's stupid," I said.

"Yes," Leah said. "You are a man who is very good at serving, Vance. You want to serve humanity and other species as well. However, most people do not want to serve. They want others to serve them. They need leadership that will guide them from stupid decisions and into a brighter future. Dealing with the Notha Emperor, through diplomacy or other means, is the perfect way to open yourself to a long-term position as one of humanity's leaders."

"And if I don't think I'm remotely qualified or that Albion is someone I will never be the puppet of?" I asked, standing up.

Leah sighed. "This would be so much easier if I could still read your mind. You're already a puppet, Vance. You're a puppet of the Elder Races and they're infinitely worse than my planet. You need to think

180

about yourself as well as humanity. Because if you're not at the table making decisions, you're going to be crushed underneath its weight."

I walked out the door. "Thanks for the meal, Leah. It was good."

When I walked out the door, I saw the Notha Ambassador waiting for me. "Hello, Captain. It's time."

"Time? Time for what?" I asked, a little too harshly.

"To meet the Emperor."

CHAPTER TWENTY-TWO

An Offer I Couldn't Refuse

"Excuse me?" I asked, still annoyed by Leah's offer to make me Prime Minister. I wondered if Albion really thought they could just buy the leadership of Earth. Given it was the Watchers, probably.

The Notha Ambassador looked up with his round black eyes. "The Emperor has decided to hold the meeting now. You should meet with your entourage in the hangar bay and prepare for departure."

I stared at him. "Ambassador, I don't know how things are done on your world, but you don't just command an audience. I still haven't received approval to even attend."

The Ambassador pulled out a strange octagonal tablet that I assumed was their version of an infopad. He handed it over and I looked at its contents. It was an official approval of a request for my presence.

"It should be hitting your infopad any moment," the Ambassador said.

My infopad pinged and I checked it. "Huh, it says that I am to render you any and all assistance. Also, that I am to meet with the Notha Emperor as soon as humanly possible."

"I'd prefer you do it as soon as Notha-ly possible," the Ambassador said. "Efficiency is one of the things we're famed for."

I had heard the opposite since fascist infighting and yelling at things until they worked weren't exactly signs of efficiency in my opinion. However, I was starting to verge on xenophobia in my issues with the Notha and put away my feelings on the subject. I needed to take these duties seriously.

"Alright then," I said, looking over the document. "You are really determined to push this through, aren't you?"

"Duty is something that every Notha understands," the Ambassador said, engaging in a little cultural posturing. "What would we be if not for it? Something like humans I'd wager."

"Yes, that would be terrible," I said, sarcastically. "I don't suppose you have a few books on etiquette I'm supposed to observe while meeting the Emperor?"

"There are no protocols for aliens meeting the Emperor because it has never happened before," the Ambassador said. "It doesn't matter either because the Emperor is a being who does not observe protocol. He *makes* protocol."

"Fair enough," I said. "How did he become Emperor anyway? Is this like a hereditary thing or what?"

"He was the first Emperor and shall be the last," the Ambassador said, unhelpfully. "All our race owes its existence to him and everything we are belongs to him."

"Okay," I said, presuming he was engaged in hyperbole. "That was helpful."

"Before the Emperor, the Notha scraped together a meager existence as the hunted prey of a thousand monster species on Hellworld. We lived in fear and had many superstitions as well as gods. The Emperor conquered all Notha, united us under one banner, and devoted all worship unto him instead. Such was good and for a thousand years," the Ambassador said. "It was only the foolishness of traitors and sycophants that drove him away. Ones who believed that other bloodlines could be as great as the All-Father's."

I stared at him. "Are you saying the Emperor is a thousand years old or that his bloodline is a thousand years old?"

The Ambassador sighed. "Stupid human."

"Yeah, I'm the stupid one," I said, wondering how this guy ever got his job.

"I'm glad we agree," the Ambassador said, turning around and walking to the nearest elevator.

I waited for the next one and got in, noting that Leah didn't try to follow or contact me. I was glad because it prevented any further awkwardness. Also, I didn't want her onboard the *Emperor's Reach* with me. I didn't trust Albion and I wanted to pursue my own leads with them. Hell, for all I knew, the Watchers were behind the destruction of New Pompeii in the first place.

You're starting to sound a little conspiracy theorist there, Trish said.

My aunt used to talk about how there were conspiracy theories about a terrorist attack in her youth and how they were insane and stupid, I replied. *However, during the aftermath, the government faked proof of another nation's involvement and that they were stockpiling chemical weapons.*

I'm familiar with the events, Trish said. *Not sure what your point is.*

If you're going to believe in a conspiracy theory, I replied, *make sure it's actually true according to evidence.*

Then it's not a conspiracy theory, Trish said. *It's just news.*

Yeah, I'm not sure what my point is, I replied. *But the simple fact is that I don't trust Albion and I don't like what they're doing to my government.*

Is it also because they wanted to make you Prime Minister? Trish asked.

I would never join a club that would have me as a member, I replied. *Groucho Marx. That applies doubly to any government.*

Just don't go alienating your allies while trying to oppose the real evil, Trish said. *You didn't fight in the Notha War but I did. The reason Captain Elgan went insane was witnessing the destruction of whole colonies by the Notha regime. The Emperor may be better than them or he may be worse. We don't know.*

I'm not about to trust the Notha Emperor, I replied. *I don't doubt Leah's word that he was supplying the Enigmatic Path and his arrival here was too coincidental. It's possible he was originally here to help the* Relentless Fury.

It's also possible he always intended to betray his allies, Trish replied. *If nothing else, the memories of humans are short. After the Kolahn War, the Notha seem like yesterday's news.*

I hadn't thought of that. If it was true, then the Notha Emperor was an even more dangerous foe than I'd wagered since that kind of treachery showed a decisiveness that verged on the unpredictable. It would mean that he planned to ally with the Community from the beginning but was willing to wear us down first to make his bargaining position better. It also meant any allies he made were entirely disposable.

Maybe he's sincere about his desire for peace, I thought.

Trish burst into mental laughter. *Oh wait, you're serious.*

Just once I'd like someone to take idealism seriously, I thought.

Well, you have Danny beside you, Trish said.

He's beside me? I asked.

Yes, Trish said.

I looked to my side and sure enough, my yeoman was present. "Okay, seriously, are you just slipping into an alternate dimension whenever I'm not looking? Are you part cat? Do I have to put a bell on you in a completely nonsexual context?"

"There's a sexual context?" Danny asked, confused.

"When you're as famous as I am, you find out about a thing called fanfic," I replied. "Believe me, you don't want to know about what they write about me."

"I DO!" Trish said through the ship's speakers.

"I wasn't kidding earlier," Danny said, thankfully ignoring that quip. "I volunteered for a bio-implant procedure in hopes of becoming an agent for the Security Departments. It was supposed to let me turn ignorable."

"Ignorable?" I asked.

"It's much better than invisibility," Danny said. "But it works only sporadically."

"Damn," I said. "That could be useful."

"It would be if not for the fact that I have very little control over it," Danny said. "I ended up getting transferred to other duties."

"Why did you volunteer?" I asked, genuinely surprised my cousin would take such a risk as a guinea pig for untested, unproven technology.

"Seriously?" Danny looked up. "You actually want to ask me that?"

"What? I inspired you?" I asked.

"You and Aunt Kathy cast a very long shadow," Danny said. "You don't know what it's like being from our side of the family."

"I *was* part of your side of the family," I replied. "Remember, my parents are the only people in history to have wrecked an automated transport."

"No one remembers that except you," Danny replied. "The fact is that I didn't want to go down as just another member of the clan. I figured being a superpowered spy would be an awesome way to pay my dues."

"Yeah, I don't think it works like that," I said. "I got lucky and barely managed to survive a few times."

"Including blowing up the *Relentless Fury*? Is it Elder Race magic?" Danny asked.

The problem with answering that was that it would put Danny and me in greater danger, but I didn't want to start lying to the kid. Also, I needed to stop thinking of Danny as a kid since he wasn't any younger than I was when I started this insane nonsense.

"Yes, it's Elder Race magic," I said. "I have one of the lesser rings made by the elven kings but that links me to the Dark Lord."

Danny stared at me. "I have no idea what that's a reference to. Is that Norse mythology?"

"Yes, yes, it is," I replied. "Wait, were you there during my date with Leah?"

"Yes?" Danny asked. "The food was great, but I was worried you two were going to go at it and didn't know if I should excuse myself during that. I mean, you have a lot of sex for a captain."

"THIS IS TRUE," Trish said over the elevator intercoms.

"If you are ever in the same room with me when I'm having sex, Danny, leave!" I snapped.

That was when I noticed the elevator had reached the hangar bay and the doors were open. Notably, Hannah was standing on the other side of the doors with Forty-Two.

I pointed at them both. "You are ordered not to have heard that."

"With pleasure," Hannah said.

"Yessir," Forty-Two said. "As if I'd want to hear about your races disgusting mating habits. You actually fertilize eggs inside the body."

I stared at him. "That opens so many questions I am certain I don't want the answers to."

"Hey, I don't complain about your bizarre alien biology," Forty-Two said.

"Yes, you do, you do it all the time," I replied.

"Yes, because humans are disgusting and weird," Forty-Two said, without shame. "So, you're going to make peace with the Notha Emperor before his sudden but inevitable betrayal?"

"I had no idea you were familiar with *Firefly*," I replied, gently.

"I have no idea what that is," Forty-Two replied. "I just know the Notha are an inherently untrustworthy race of savitty people."

The Ambassador came up behind Forty-Two. "What were you saying, Sorkanan?"

Forty-Two looked back. "I said you were an untrustworthy race of savitty people."

"Just checking," the Ambassador replied, as if he was speaking to someone utterly inconsequential.

"Really, you guys should film yourselves and put it on the infonet," Hannah said, looking between us. "People would pay real money to see you all banter."

"Please, who would pay money to listen to me," I replied. "Mental note: I need to get back to work on my audiobook."

That was when I noticed that a Notha shuttle, all dark and spider-like with multiple appendages sticking straight out of the main body as if it was going to grab something. Apparently, the Notha Emperor didn't trust us to have our own shuttle over. Either that or it was just the Ambassador. Still, I was on edge and seeing both Shelly and Light on Water waiting for me did little to comfort me.

"I see you have everything already prepped," I said, looking down at the Ambassador.

"I have taken certain liberties, yes," the Ambassador said. "I assume this would be the party you'd have chosen. You would never go off the ship without your trusty second-in-command after all."

"My trusty what now?" I asked, looking at him.

"He means me," Shelly said. "Though he's phrasing it like I'm your horse."

Forty-Two opened his mouth and raised a claw to make a quip. Shelly stared at him with such force that I swear he shrunk two feet.

"How disrespectful," Forty-Two muttered, changing whatever quip he was going to make.

"Yes," Shelly said. "Light on Water will be taking charge while I'm gone."

"With all due respect," I said, frowning. "It seems like something that you should be left in charge of while I'm gone."

It's not that I didn't trust Light on Water, it was that I didn't trust him in a crisis. Which was the same thing when dealing with a third officer. If I needed to depend on someone to get the ship and its crew out of danger, against the impossible odds of the *Emperor's Reach's* arsenal should it turn against us, I had a lot more faith in Shelly's ability to pull out a miracle than his.

You shouldn't underestimate your crew, Trish spoke to me. *Also, it won't just be him. I'll be there as well.*

I'd prefer if you were onboard the Emperor's Reach *with me,* I said.

I can't, Trish said. *Its systems are completely impenetrable. It's got its own AI and it is not friendly.*

Even if you brought your body, I said.

Yes, Trish said. *I'm sorry.*

Understood, I said, knowing I was going to be without my biggest asset.

"I am prepared to accept any decision you make," Light on Water said, its voice a singsong choir. "I am also prepared to be removed from your command if you do not trust me with the responsibilities I've been assigned."

"I belong on this mission," Shelly said. "It's not that I don't trust you, Vance, it's just I don't trust you. At least with this."

I blinked. "Well, that was blunt."

"And you prefer her to me," Light on Water said.

"What was that?" Shelly asked.

"Speaking aloud," Light on Water said. "I am a trained diplomat. It is my area of special concern! I should be the one handling matters. Yet, you had her negotiate with the Rand's World warlords when she was objectively terrible at it!"

"You backstabber!" Shelly shouted.

"No, I have deferred and done my best to be respectful, but it is time to speak truth to power," Light on Water said. "Shelly is a terrible first officer! She is plotting for your command. I also think she is unfairly biased!"

"Do I need to leave you to this?" The Ambassador said. "This is starting to resemble a Notha heat festival."

"Stay out of this," I said, looking at both. "You have my absolute trust, Shelly. You do as well Light. You'll accompany me on this, Shelly, and Light will stay in command. But this was my decision."

They absolutely did not have my complete trust and it was not my decision. Shelly was going to fight me on this, and I needed her full support to make sure things worked out right. I also needed Light not second-guessing my handling of him during a crisis. The biggest thing I'd learned about leadership in the past eight years was it was primarily bullsavitting people into believing you knew what you were doing.

"Alright," Shelly said. "I apologize for saying I didn't trust you."

Liar. But I appreciated the gesture.

"We should talk, sir," Light on Water said. "There is much you need to know about my activities."

"Sure, when I get back," I said. "Good luck, Light. Everything is going to go swimmingly and nothing bad will happen."

Light on Water couldn't stare at me since it didn't have any eyes. "You think it will go that horribly, huh?"

I patted him on the tentacle nearest what would be the shoulder and lifted it back, covered in slime. "Worse."

CHAPTER TWENTY-THREE

Approaching the Death Star

Hey, Trish, I asked the AI to determine if she was still linked to me. *You there?*

I was sitting in the back of the Notha shuttle in their weird doughnut-esque seating that had neither cushions nor arm rests. We were all facing one another, watching each other, and I wondered if the Notha loved the concept of a panopticon prison.

The interior of their spider shuttle was polished chrome with no amenities and a kind of stark military utilitarianism that made me think the Notha would have loved Stalinist Russia. One thing I liked about their construction style was the fact the Notha always built things at least three times too big for themselves so there was no issue moving in or out of the vessel. The Community had to work hard to have multi-species capable ships, but the Notha just built everything like a cathedral so at least bumping our heads wouldn't be a problem. I was worried about how to use their facilities, though, because I doubted they were made to human standards. You learn these things when visiting alien space vessels that have very different ideas of what a toilet should look like.

Shelly was sitting across from me with Hannah beside me and Forty-Two. Danny might have been present as well but I wasn't sure. Which was an odd thing to say about family. The Ambassador stood apart and a part of me wished I'd asked for more security but if they wanted to kill us there wasn't much we could do to stop them. My ring wouldn't do much against an entire army. Still, it was going to be a twenty-minute slow flight between ships as the shuttle was moving at an excruciatingly slow pace.

Yes? Trish replied to my earlier question. *And to answer your question, yes and no. I am both here and not here. The majority of my programming is linked to the* Ares, *but I've got enough space in your enhanced cybernetics to copy a basic personality matrix as well as about the same level of intelligence as a human being. So, a really stupid version of myself.*

I blinked at that description. *Uh-huh.*

See! I'm already sticking my nonexistent foot in my mouth! Trish said. *I never do that when I have the brain the size of a planet.*

Uh-huh, I repeated. *Actually, I was curious if I could ask you a question about Shelly.*

Oh, another thing, Trish said, *I am very jealous when I'm not an enlightened gestalt of interlocking systems. Hasn't she humiliated you enough? Why do you need her as a girlfriend too? All she does is abuse you emotionally and degrade your abilities as a captain—*

Trish— I tried to interrupt her.

Yes, you're a trifle inexperienced for a captain but far from the worst example of it, Trish said. *She acts like you're a cadet straight out of the Academy. You've served eight years through wartime and grew up a Space Fleet brat. You absorbed this savit via osmosis.*

Trish— I tried again, to equal lack of success. I really didn't need her trying to give me a pep talk. I knew my own value as well as my limitations.

Do you know why she's not a captain? I know I'm not supposed to read crew member's private files, but I have and do you know why she's not promoted? She thinks it's because she's an Ethereal but it's not. It's because she's been described as overly bound by rules and an unimaginative commander. Oh, and she doesn't inspire—

Trish! I finally shouted at her mentally. *That is not a good thing to say about a fellow officer. In fact, all of that is terrible.*

Sorry, Trish said. *She just makes me so mad, and I only have your brain to stew in!*

It occurred to me bringing Trish along on this was probably not the best idea. *Trish, first of all we're not dating because it would be inappropriate given our roles on the ship. You are, however, my closest friend. Literally because you're in my head. Next, I just wanted to know if Shelly had cybernetics.*

Why? Trish asked.

Because I want to talk with her without the Notha knowing about it, I said. *You know, for the mission that we're trying to do in order to bring peace throughout the galaxy. One that might also relate to the destruction of New Pompei?*

Oh right, Trish admitted. *That would probably be something I should be focused on. I'm used to being able to do like a million things at once.*

Are you alright? I asked. *This seems to be worse than just worried about relationships.*

Sorry, Trish said. *I've been hacked a few million times in the past hour. All of my firewalls have held up, but the attacks are powerful.*

Wait, what? I asked. *You didn't think this was worth saying.*

My other self, the Trish back on the Ares, *decided not to tell you,* Trish said. *Which I don't understand and that's what Aristotle would call angst.*

Why the hell was Trish hiding things from me? This was more disturbing to me than the idea I was going off to possible certain death on an enemy vessel. I believed I could overcome almost all problems but only if I could rely on my allies. If we were now working at cross-purposes, then we were in some serious savit. *Is it the Notha Emperor?*

Yes, Trish said. *He has a very powerful AI. I don't think I would have been able to keep my defenses up if not for the fact my code is enhanced by the Elder Races.*

That was not good. *I see.*

Oh, and yes, Shelly has a cerebral implant that would allow you to communicate with her without being detected, Trish added. *I probably should have opened with that.*

Right, I said, sighing. *Thank you, Trish. Just, stay safe.*

I will until you die, Trish said. *Then this version of me will vanish.*

Yeah, well, let's just pretend you didn't say that, I said.

I'll always be with you, Trish said. *No matter what.*

Okay, that was pretty much a straight up love declaration, and I wasn't sure about how to deal with it. There was just too much going on there and I wasn't sure if I could give her the kind of commitment she deserved. I was torn between too many masters and wasn't sure I had the same feelings: a fact that she surely knew.

Yeah, Trish said mentally. *Sorry for distracting you.*

I didn't respond but instead looked out the window to see we were already almost to one of the hangar bays within the *Emperor's Reach*. The massive ship seemed even larger as we approached the final leg of our journey, the enormous dreadnought seeming like it was swallowing us up like a whale devouring a fish. A tractor beam latched around us, and the ship rocked as we were slowly sucked in.

A feeling of dread passed over me as we approached that I couldn't quite put into words. There was something different about this ship beyond just its size. I could sense something off about the vessel and its inhabitants that felt more than instinctual but not quite rational. It was if as if a terrible pressure was being put on the sides of my head and something was trying to get inside my head but couldn't quite succeed: yet.

I don't suppose anyone is trying to hack into my brain now, I replied.

No, Trish said. *Why do you ask?*

No reason, I replied, feeling gut sick. If the Emperor was already trying cyberwarfare methods against us, then these peace talks were even more of a sham than we suspected them to be. The thing was that he could have obliterated us easily without witnesses before. Now he'd announced to the galaxy we were having a meeting. I wasn't sure if that made it more or less likely for him to attack. Certainly, now, if he wanted to kill us then he wanted an audience.

Shelly? I asked, trying to contact her via her cybernetics.

Vance? Shelly asked. *How did you get my signal frequency?*

Elder Race technology, I replied. *Either that or as the captain I have a listing of these. What with the ability to contact your first officer during an emergency being something important to do.*

Is everything out of your mouth sarcastic? Shelly asked, exhausted.

No, sometimes I'm flippant, I replied. *On very rare occasions, I also manage to do a mean dismissive.*

This is what bothers me, Shelly said. *You're going to throw a casual insult or joke around and start Notha War Two.*

Do you really think so little of me? I asked, genuinely serious. *I was hoping I'd managed to win at least a little of your respect by now.*

Shelly sighed. *What I know is that you keep secrets. Lots of secrets. You're working for the Elder Races. you know my mother's ghost—*

I know that's unbelievable, I started to interrupt.

No, I find it entirely believable my mother would be immortal and yet find out about it through my boyfriend, Shelly said.

Boyfriend? I asked.

Don't get distracted, Shelly responded. *Plus, don't think I've missed you've got superpowers.*

I don't have superpowers! I said, not quite as strongly as I would have liked.

Vance, you survived having a suicide bomber explode in your face. A ship's shields went down right before the entirety of their payload turned against them. That's not counting all the other weird stuff I've observed happening around you the past eight years. Your secret missions, plans, and that time you levitated.

I don't remember that last one, I said. *Listen, my life is complex—*

Don't give me that, Shelly said. *You act like a fool, but you're really plugged into a lot of power structures and have lots of friends in high places. Virtually everything you say is a lie and I can't deal with that. So, take your pick, Vance. You can have me mad at you for being someone I think will screw up these negotiations because he's an inexperienced tool in way over his head or a hidden mastermind that I can't trust.*

Ouch, I responded, neither option appealing to me but understanding now why Shelly was so aloof. I had been keeping secrets virtually our entire association and had dropped a bunch of revelatory bombshells on her in short order. *What if I'm an inexperienced hidden mastermind way in over my head that you can trust?*

Not funny, Vance, Shelly said.

I'm not joking, I said. *I'm playing this all by ear. If you think I'm a criminal mastermind, then you should note I'm surrounded by government conspiracies. We've got Albion sabotaging our ship, your friend and my ex-girlfriend asking to make me Prime Minister of Earth.*

Wait, what? Shelly asked.

Yeah, that was a thing, I replied. *Leah offered to make me Prime Minister of Earth. It was with a slinky dress and after discussing the* Phantom of the Opera.

Always with the borking Phantom of the Opera, Shelly thought, shaking her head. *She has been obsessed with that for, listen, never mind. She offered to make me the head of Earth's Home Fleet.*

What, really? I asked. Now it didn't seem to be such an awesome offer if she was passing them around to everybody.

It seems she's offering some ridiculous bribes, Shelly said.

Oh, because I could never be Prime Minister of Earth, I said a little too defensively.

No, because I know that I'm already unlikely to ever make captain, Shelly said. *I thought saving the* Ares *would be enough to get over the black marks on my record, but it seems no.*

Black marks? I asked. I didn't want to mention what Trish had said it was mostly because her superiors thought she had a stick up her anyx. Honestly, that sounded like bull savit to me, but I knew the command structure of the Home Fleet was very much about who you knew rather than what you could do. I'd benefited from it too many times to count. A person who managed to put off their bosses personally was less likely to be promoted than a personable one who couldn't find their anyx with both hands. Space Fleet could always find jobs for the latter, but the former had no one willing to work with them.

During my earlier career, I was a reckless maverick driven by my desire to do the right thing at any costs, Shelly said. *I got a formal reprimand for endangering lives on a rescue mission and was told I'd never get promoted afterward. I was a lieutenant then. I've done my best to be a stickler for the rules ever since. They exist for a reason I've found.*

Uh, how long ago was this? I asked.

I dunno, forty years, why? Shelly asked.

I wondered if there was anyone who was even in service still from that era save, maybe, my Aunt Kathy. *It's possible you may be overcompensating.*

I'd argue you don't know what you're talking about but that's clearly not the case, Shelly said. *In any case, I told Leah to take her offer and stick it where the sun doesn't shine. I am not for sale, least of all to Albion.*

Good to know, I asked, feeling this whole thing was ridiculous. It seemed like everyone on this mission was focused on everything but this mission. *I kind of regret not bringing Leah along on this. I'm going to need your support, whether you believe in me or not.*

We need to try and handle this delicately, Shelly said. *Any false moves can make it fall through.*

I'm fairly sure that is making the assumption the Emperor is operating in good faith to begin with, I replied. *Everything about this whole thing smells like savit and that's before we include the fact he's already trying to hack Trish.*

We must pretend that he's operating in good faith, Shelly said. *Perhaps even convince him to even if we're not. You managed to convince all those warlords to cooperate, even after a bunch of them got killed.*

Yes, well the Community is rich enough to bribe them, I replied. *I'm not sure it's rich enough to bribe the Notha Emperor. You know the Ambassador claims he's a thousand years old?*

I don't think Notha live that long, Shelly said.

No kidding, I replied. *Just keep your eyes open, would you? This could end very badly, and I'd like to have an escape route planned.*

Shelly blinked. *Vance, I hate to break it to you, but you're supposed to have an escape route planned before you go into a situation in which you need an escape.*

Yeah, yeah, I said. *Details, details.*

The shuttle completed its docking sequence and settled down in an enormous hangar bay. The sense of oppression, of an almost palpable evil supernatural force increased and I wondered what the hell was causing it. I wasn't a superstitious man, lightly religious as I was, but this place gave me the willies. It was like that cave on Dagobah where Luke Skywalker killed himself as a metaphor for hatred destroying him.

Once the shuttle shut down, the floor in front of us lowered into a ramp and jets of white steam poured out around it. The Ambassador was the first to get up and gestured for us to follow. "You will be treated as an honored guest by the Emperor, Captain Turbo. At least until his hospitality ends."

That was less reassuring than he probably meant. Then again, it wasn't exactly like he was trying that hard to be diplomatic despite his job. "And when will that be?"

"When he decides, of course," the Ambassador replied.

I sighed and stood up before walking behind him. "Come on, guys, let's go. Follow the robed rodent. Surely, it will all work out and the Ewok Stormtroopers will show us nothing but hospitality and friendship."

Forty-Two said, "You truly have a way with people, Vance."

"So, I've been told," I replied.

"I wish Elektra was here," Shelly said, standing up.

"Me too," I replied. "I could use some fancy science solutions."

"We don't have enough guns for something less science-y," Hannah muttered, which was not the kind of thing you said on a diplomatic mission even in jest.

Our group walked down the smooth ramp into the hangar, and we were immediately met by a massive formation of crew, soldiers, and war machines in parade formation to meet us. The bay, just one of many, was huge with dozens of starfighters and shuttles held up by claws above our heads for easy deployment. The chamber looked like it was a hundred feet tall with an almost cathedral-like presence as well as stadium size.

The formations were in groups of three hundred thirty-three as the Notha's preferred to make their deployments with a surprising diversity among them. There were Notha of course, perhaps even a slight majority, but the rest were composed of members of other species. There were Sorkanan, Kolahn, Ants, Drolochids, humans, demihumans, and a few races I flat out did not recognize. I immediately assumed they were mercenaries or even pirates, but they were all dressed in uniforms derivative of the Notha ones.

It seemed the Notha Emperor was far more progressive than his kind usually were, at least in the context of being willing to recruit from other species for his space fleet. I also saw a lot of bots working away at the controls, many of them being advanced ones straight off the rack of Ares Electronics. It made me wonder if any of the people here were bioroids.

I can't access any of the systems, Trish said. *The AI here is powerful as well as totally hostile.*

Don't risk yourself, I said. *Just focus on staying hidden.*

I'm not sure if that's possible, Trish said.

Well, that wasn't disturbing, I thought, sarcastically. There was no ceremony to our arrival despite the massive amount of military force on display here. Instead, we just walked through the line between the gathered forces and got a look at just what could be brought to bear on us at any time.

There had to be thousands of armed men around us and that was in addition to the spider-tanks, death bubbles, and other Notha weaponry that could take out an entire regiment. Say what you will about the Notha, but they knew how to compensate for being such cute little critters. In the end, we arrived at a massive elevator, which the Ambassador opened by raising his staff.

"We will head to see the Emperor immediately," the Ambassador said. "I must inform you, though, that his Eternalness wishes to speak with you alone."

"You could have told me this earlier," I said.

"I know," the Ambassador replied. "But you can hardly say no now, can you?"

Oh yeah, we were borked.

CHAPTER TWENTY-FOUR

Meeting with the Emperor

The interior of the *Emperor's Reach* was unlike anything else I'd ever seen in a military vessel with my cathedral comparison not entirely off-point. There were massive hallways, statues, and grandiose chambers everywhere. It was one-third Versailles, one-third fortress, and one-third Forbidden City from what I saw. We had to take three elevators, a tram, and an enormous spiraling staircase at one point. I was quite tired by the end of it and wondering if the Notha's bad attitude came from being forced to walk everywhere.

Our lengthy journey did provide me with considerable insights into the state of the dreadnought, however. The ship was in a sorry state of disrepair or perhaps a better term would be it was in a constant state of upgrades that it was never designed for. In addition to being used as the flagship of the Emperor's fleet, private palace, capital, and luxury yacht, it was also being modified to stay apace with modern warfare's latest advancements.

I saw whole areas had been pulled out to be replaced with technology from every other race in the Known Universe and being heavily worked on by technicians from the same. Given the difficulty the Community had getting all their technology to be compatible even with strict oversight of development, I couldn't imagine how they were doing it with Notha tech. Nevertheless, it seemed the Emperor had pushed the ship's hull to its limits in terms of avoiding obsolescence. Which was terrifying since even if it had remained fifty years out of date, its sheer power would have been worth most fleets.

The ship was also severely understaffed with the million or so crew I expected needed to pilot the vessel being replaced with about two hundred fifty thousand at an estimate—even with all the alien recruits. Bots and automation were doing a lot of the heavy lifting, but the hallways were practically empty. If this was meant to impress, it was a complete failure and I saw whole chambers with dimmed lights operating on autopilot.

How is he paying for all of this? Shelly asked via our cybernetics.

That's what your worried about? I asked.

Yes, Shelly said. *It means he is much more connected to the Notha government or has his own set of backers from other worlds.*

Maybe he owns a transtellar or two, I replied.

You think the Notha Emperor has a hedge fund? Shelly asked, sarcastically.

Why not? I asked. *He's already shown he doesn't have the same instinctive revulsion other Notha have to anything alien.*

It's taught, not instinctive, Shelly asked. *Let's not think the Notha are this way naturally.*

I agreed with her, but my nervousness was making me hostile to everything and everyone inside this place. I wasn't being paranoid if people really were plotting to kill me. *Well, I didn't see any sign of SKAMMs on the way here either.*

This whole thing felt *off* and I didn't just mean the sense of spiritual malaise that clung to the place. Everyone we passed, from Notha to human, looked sleep deprived and intense as if they were all on red dust. I wasn't sure what the Emperor hoped to accomplish by giving us such a direct tour of his facilities. There had to have been far less revelatory ways of reaching the Emperor's quarters, not the least being meeting him elsewhere than in the center of his ship.

Well, they're not going to show those to us, are they? Shelly asked. *Still, the amount of other races present makes me think he can't be the party responsible.*

Why's that? I asked.

It would have gotten out, Shelly said. *You might be able to keep a secret among an isolated race like the Notha loyalists here, but mercenaries are not very good at keeping secrets.*

That's assuming these are mercenaries, I replied.

What else would they be? Shelly asked.

Slaves, I replied.

Eventually, we reached the antechamber for the Emperor's throne room and were searched for weapons by a set of armed bot guards that were about eight feet in height and looked like metal crabs with tentacles. It was possible they were power suits for Notha inside them but, either way, none of us resisted them. The Ambassador escorted me to a pair of six-meter double doors that opened very slowly to a long hallway that was barely illuminated.

Honestly, at this point, the whole excessive theatricality of the Notha was starting to undermine itself. The constant huge overwhelming everything meant the effect was increasingly diminished to the point that entering another giant chamber just meant I was getting annoyed. Doing so, I saw it was about thirty-three yards long and led up to a single chair elevated above the rest of the chamber. A hologram of the Spiral was projected from a central circular computer console and illuminated a good half of the room. I recognized the console as something that could be used to command an entire military command structure, like a miniature NORAD.

We were also alone. No one was sitting on the throne. There were no guards present in the room or servants. It was a surprising twist on presentation, and I was wondering if they were going to make me wait for hours as yet another petty power move. It didn't help when the massive doors slammed behind me with a thud that echoed through the chamber.

"Well, this is nice," I said, finally breaking the silence of the place.

"Yep," the Notha Ambassador says, sounding completely different. Gone was the faux Transylvanian accent the other Notha I'd spoken with possessed. Instead, it was replaced with something almost...Southern? "So, ya'll finally getting ready to get down to brass tacks?"

"Excuse me?" I asked, turning.

"I am the Emperor!" the Notha Ambassador said, spreading out his arms. "Congratulations, you've been schinzooed!"

"What now?" I did a double take.

"It's a word with no precise translation," the Ambassador (Emperor?) replied. "Basically, it means that you have been subject to a very long and psychologically damaging prank."

I stared down at him. "You're the Emperor. For real?"

I was utterly thrown by this because it was so random. The Ambassador's change in demeanor, though, was complete. Instead of his snooty bizarre attitude, he was now considerably more relaxed and seemed almost physically different. He certainly wasn't what I expected from a Notha warlord, though.

"Yes," the Emperor said, looking up. "Think of it like when Yoda pretended to be some random alien to Luke's racist ass."

I wasn't sure how to react to the fact he'd seen *The Empire Strikes Back*. "Why the hell would you go to such an elaborate deception?"

"Because it's funny," the Emperor said. "When you've lived for over a thousand years, you start to go a little insane."

"You're still claiming to be immortal," I replied.

"Shh," The Emperor said, gesturing with his staff. "Come over here first."

I reluctantly followed, still unsure what this whole head game was all about. Much to my surprise, resting on the side of the computer console, I saw a little wooden bowl. The contents of the bowl shocked me: rings. They were the rings of at least a dozen Elder Race agents and identical to my own.

"Holy crazzap," I said, staring at them. "Uh, I may not be the best person to do etiquette—"

"Remove your ring," the Emperor said. "We can't have THEM listening to us."

I could hear the capital letters in his statement of them. "The Elder—"

The Emperor stared. "Don't finish that sentence."

"Right," I said, removing my ring and putting it in the wooden bowl.

Goddammit, Vance, Trish said in my head. *Now we're vulnerable.*

Maybe not, I replied. I was suddenly very intrigued by just what the Emperor had to say.

"There we go," the Emperor said, putting the bowl back up. "Now THEY can't listen to us."

"They being the Elder Races," I replied.

"And their minions," the Emperor replied. "Which includes us to an extent."

"Wait, you work for the Elder Races?" I asked, staring at him.

"Unwillingly and for a very long time," the Emperor said. "When I told you my life story, the truncated version at least, I wasn't lying. Those machine gods descended from the sky on my homeworld and found my primitive flintlock-wielding people. We'd only then started a process of hunting down all of the predators which treated us as snacks."

I'd heard about the Notha's evolutionary story, which was infamous among xenoanthropologists. The Notha had been a tree-dwelling insect- and fruit-eating people that largely lived in perpetual fear of virtually every other creature on their planet. They'd developed tools to survive and the intelligence to outwit their enemies, only to eventually slaughter virtually everything else on their planet then take to the stars. They'd promptly adopted a strategy of treating every problem as a nail to be dealt with by the proverbial hammer of violence.

"What did they want with you?" I asked.

"To uplift us," the Emperor said with incredible distaste. "The only thing worse than conquest: is the attitude that their exploitation and manipulation of our people was for our own good. At least have the genitals to admit you're doing it because you're a sadistic bork. Don't try to frame slavery as a moral good."

It was strange hearing a Notha speak those words, but I couldn't say I disagreed with them. "So, you really are a thousand years old."

"Yes," the Emperor said. "Though Notha years are actually about a year and a half of Earth years so closer to fifteen hundred by your standards. The technology they gave me kept me eternally young and virile while also providing me with the ability to work miracles. At least as far as my people were concerned. I united them through brute force but also creating the Imperial cult that worshiped me as a living god."

I was deeply disturbed by the casualness with which he spoke of his blasphemy. "You set yourself up as a god?"

"Oh yes," the Emperor said, chuckling. "The old religions objected and there were many martyrs but eventually the people got with the program, so to speak. It worked very well for centuries as I encouraged the arts and sciences at the point of a sword. War was the great innovator for our kind, and I had to keep my enemies alive for far longer than I wanted in hopes of being able to keep justifying our conflicts."

"What happened?" I asked.

"Eventually, we did run out of enemies," the Emperor cursed. "Familiarity also breeds contempt and the fact most Notha can trace their DNA back to my lineage meant I lost some of my luster as a dictator. I should have probably kept it in my robes, but you try and find something that can keep you occupied for centuries."

I really didn't need to know that. "But surely space provided an endless array of enemies."

The Emperor smiled a bitter, almost inhuman smile. "You'd think that, wouldn't you? But the problem with space is it's damn big. The Notha Empire was expecting to find vast numbers of helpless alien species for us to conquer and enslave but instead mostly found empty space. My power eroded as my various descendants sought to supplant me."

"What happened?" I asked.

"They succeeded," the Emperor said, his voice filled with disgust. "I had filled their heads with too many thoughts of their invincibility and our glorious destiny. No one dared to kill me, but they rendered me irrelevant, an oddity serving as a monument to a dead age, and they sought out the promised billions of alien cultures that would provide endless plunder. They did not take into account that other races may have been elevated by the Elder Races and have their own powerful technologies. Perhaps I did hold them back but that was because caution is the best tactic to pursue when dealing with the unknown."

"Perhaps," I said, utterly revolted by the Emperor and what he'd turned the Notha into. If anyone bore any responsibility for the rise of fascism and their hostility to every other species in the galaxy, it was certainly him. Well, he and the Elder Races since they had been the people to give him the immortality and technology he needed to dominate his race. In a way, they were the colonizers and imperialists who inspired the Notha.

Assuming you believe him, Trish said in my head.

Don't you? I asked.

He's already proven a liar, Trish said. *Still, it's hard to believe he'd make up something like this. It's too insane.*

"And the Notha War happened," I replied.

"Yes," the Emperor said. "The Great Failed Offensive to take all of Contested Space brought us against the Community but we weren't even faced against the full force of that body. Instead, they dangled your race like a rodent before a feline. You absorbed the bulk of the casualties and yet did not break. In the end, a dozen worlds were destroyed in an exchange of sun killers, and nothing was achieved."

"It was a great tragedy," I replied.

"It was a *design*," the Emperor snapped, correcting me. "A set of tiles, what do you call them, dominoes, set to knock one over the other until the pre-arranged pattern took shape. The Elder Races wished to justify their position as peacemakers and solidify their hegemony for another thousand years. To that end, they had to make the sun killers so abhorrent a concept that the entire galaxy would welcome their outlawing—even the Notha—and accept the Elder Races disarming them."

It occurred to me this must have been what I must have sounded like to other people when I talked about the Elder Races: a paranoid ranting lunatic. On the other hand, I couldn't dismiss everything that he was saying out of hand. The Elder Races had hundreds, if not thousands, of agents and whole races doing their bidding. Their power couldn't be underestimated even if they appeared to keep a distance from the rest of the universe.

"And yet you worked for them?" I asked.

"It seemed like the only way to preserve our species," the Emperor said, his voice low and full of long suppressed hatred.

"That I understand," I said, speaking the truth. I had a feeling that was the only thing we had in common, though. Well, that and a particularly quirky sense of humor as well as fondness for centuries old human science fiction movies.

"Which is why it comes to this point, Vance," the Emperor replied. "Don't get me wrong, I feel like the Notha race is superior to all other species in the cosmos. They're almost all my descendants after all."

"Your modesty is certainly imperial," I replied.

"Don't think I don't know what you mean," the Emperor said, baring his teeth before chuckling. "But I don't see any reason to hold that against you all. A human is a capable tool user, a Sorkanan is a reasonable killing machine, and a Sklux is an amusing gesture with all the nonsense that pours out of their gooey orifices."

"Uh-huh," I said, narrowing my eyes. "Why did you really summon me here?"

"Can I offer you a root beer?" The Emperor surprisingly changed the subject. "It's almost the only thing humans produce that Notha can digest and vice versa. Mind you, it has a mildly intoxicating effect on my kind."

"No thank you," I said, worrying about this twist.

"I insist," the Emperor said, conjuring a stein as if out of nothingness before handing it over.

I, for some reason, couldn't resist lifting it to my mouth and drinking deeply. It didn't taste like any root beer I'd ever tasted in my life and had a mildly alcoholic taste to it. It also hit my stomach like a ton of bricks.

"Good, good," the Emperor said. "Excellent."

"What is in this stuff?" I asked.

"Roots and beer," the Emperor replied. "You see, Vance, I have been trying to make contact with many of the agents of the Elder Races. Identifying them has proven easier than I thought. They have a certain way of having the forces of causality bend to their will. In the end, I invite them here and offer them the same offer I am about to make you."

Now I had a terrible feeling about all this, and it was exponentially worse than the one I already had. "What offer is that?"

I couldn't help but finish my drink off despite the fact it was foul-tasting and made me feel woozy.

"A chance to liberate the masses and immanentize the eschaton," the Emperor said.

"My Latin is a bit rusty," I replied.

"To bring about heaven on Earth," the Emperor replied. "Or heaven in the Milky Way Galaxy or the Great Furback as we call it. Strange how the heart of all life in the universe has such stupid names."

"Maybe other galaxies have life," I replied. "Even likely. We haven't been yet."

"Nor will we ever if the Elder Races continue to lord over us," the Emperor said. "They cull and snip our potential until we become only a shadow of our former selves."

"They can't be beaten," I replied.

"They can," the Emperor said. "I have a method."

"How?" I asked.

"Destroy a million suns," the Emperor replied.

"You destroyed New Pompeii," I replied, staring at him.

The Emperor laughed aloud. "Oh, you poor silly boy. The destruction of New Pompeii was the result of beings far more powerful than I. It is a test for you. They want their subject races, your Community, and EarthGov to be at each other's throats. They want you to deliver the name of who is responsible to them because they expect you to crawl at their feet with answers. Answers all except the one truth that they did it. To stir the pot and set all races against one another!"

"So, you didn't," I said, feeling a sense of despair wash over me.

"Fool," the Emperor said, cursing. "Don't you see this is beyond that? I have more SKAMM missiles than any in the history of the Known Universe. A veritable planetary metropolis of them and they can be used to wipe the Core systems clean of life."

The enormous hologram of the galaxy changed, and I saw jumpspace launch platforms across Contested Space in the in-between space among systems. Their schematics appeared above each and downloaded into my brain, giving me a full view of just what the Emperor was proposing. They were modernized with jumpdrives and stealth technology beyond anything I'd yet seen. It wasn't technology the Notha, or Community, possessed.

"What the hell..." I said, trailing off.

The Emperor chuckled, glad he finally had my attention. "I have seventy percent of what I need to begin an annihilation of not just a single system but the entirety of the Elder Races as a whole. We cannot launch early, or the survivors will retaliate. They do not live on planets but massive artificial habitats similar to Dyson spheres and vast starships the size of planets. But all of them can be consumed by the conflagration I have planned. Our races will at last be free and the young will replace the old."

"You couldn't have constructed this with just the Notha's resources," I said, overwhelmed by the scope of his plan.

"You're right that other galaxies have life on them," the Emperor said. "But the Elder Races are not the only beings that evolved in the galaxy's primordial depths. They have enemies as well and ones that are all too willing to lend aid."

That was when I fell over. I struggled to get up but could only get to my knees. "What did you do to me?"

"An incentive," the Emperor said. "I need your help, Vance. It is easier to get that from you if you need to have the poison flushed from your system every few days like all of my other human slaves."

"Go to hell," I said, vomiting on the throne room floor as I felt my connection to Trish grow weaker and disjointed. It was interfering with my cybernetics.

"Oh, we're already there, Vance," the Emperor replied. "I am the god, warden, and master of it."

CHAPTER TWENTY-FIVE

Imprisoned in the *Emperor's Reach*

I fell to the ground again and felt the poison moving through my veins within moments. The stein containing the remainder of the "root beer" poured across the floor. My head felt like it was on fire and my vision blurred.

"Why?" I asked, my head pressed against the ground. "Why are you doing this?"

"The question so many of them ask," the Emperor said, chortling as if lording over a dying animal. "The nano-technology inside you is going to make you dependent on me. You will be able to be killed or injured by me at will. I haven't yet figured out how to do mind control, but this is the next best thing. Like an invisible explosive collar around your neck."

"Bork you," I hissed at him, except I didn't say bork.

The Emperor smiled, showing his blocky teeth. "You might wonder why I'm going to such elaborate lengths to take you prisoner and bend you to my will. The truth is that I need every possible agent of the Elder Races as I can get. I've turned plenty of you since this plot began. Some of them because of this poison but others because they genuinely believe in my cause. They know that the only way to defeat the Elder Races is to wipe them and their super-structures from the face of the universe."

"At the mere...*cough*...cost of a quarter...*cough*..." I tried to speak but was having difficulty doing so. "Genocide."

"Yes," the Emperor said. "Genocide. Xenocide. Total victory. All different words for the same thing. It will wipe out a chunk of the universe as well. However, it will open up an entirely new part of it for conquest. We are but one of four major spiral arms as well as the entire center of the universe. The Elder Races keep us from exploring them all and among them we could find riches beyond wealth. Even better, the secrets of immortality that the Elder Races keep for themselves. Mind you, I doubt I would share it if I found something better than my current eternal youth."

"Anxyhole," I said, struggling to even speak one word.

"Defiant until the end," the Emperor said. "I knew from the moment we first met that you wouldn't be one of the ones who served me willingly. You're one of those fools who actually thinks peace can ever exist save at the point of a gun. I've learned better and know the only way to deal with the enemy is to wipe them out so thoroughly that they can never rise again. Suffice to say, you should be grateful I still need you."

"Kill me," I snapped through a hoarse mouth. "I'll never join...you."

The Emperor looked bemused and conjured a wooden bowl similar to the kind that contained the rings I dearly wished I could reach now. It filled with a warm frothy liquid similar to the one used to poison me, and he drank it down all at once. "Yes, I imagine you're like so many short-lived beings. You don't value your life properly and think sacrificing it is some grand gesture when it's really just hastening the inevitable."

I was getting really sick of the Emperor's taunts. Not to the point I wanted to die but definitely to the point of refusing anything he wanted from me. I had no interest in being the puppet of a psychotic dictator who had a plan to launch an unprovoked attack on the heart of the galaxy in order to destroy the strongest races in the Known Universe.

Even if it worked, which was a big if, all it would do was wipe out a vast repository of information and people. For all their manipulations, I refused to believe they were any worse than us as the Community and Albion proved. I didn't believe the Emperor had destroyed New Pompeii anymore, there was no point in him lying about it given his other confessions, but I sure as hell didn't think the Elder Races blew it up purely to make us more controllable.

Also, who were his supporters? The ones he claimed were even more powerful than the Elder Races and why hadn't we ever heard of them?

"I'm...mmrr...ammm," I said, unfortunately not able to give my firm rebuttal to his points. I also thought I might need a change of shorts, which only added to the humiliation. This never happened to Captain Kirk, Picard, Sisko, or Janeway. Maybe Archer.

The Emperor snorted. "Hmm, I'll wonder if you'll survive the bonding process. I should have accounted for how weak humans are. Well, if you do, you're going to help me negotiate the Notha's alliance with the Community and EarthGov. It will be against whatever 'unknown threat' destroyed the core worlds of the galaxy. I am patient and arming the Notha with races of cannon fodder to serve in our future conquests of the rest of the galaxy may take thousands of years, but I can wait. You're my perfect mouthpiece."

I didn't respond, feeling the pain across my body starting to fade. I wasn't sure if that was because I was bonding with the nano-tech poison as he said or because I was dying. Neither option appealed to me. "No."

"Really?" the Emperor said. "Not even if the cost is my killing your crew? I can have it destroyed at any time. How about your lover? I could smell her on you. Your friends? I selected them based on their perceived closeness to you and your files I managed to bribe some disgruntled naval employees for. How much suffering would you be willing to tolerate from them before you break?"

I didn't respond.

"Mind you, I'm not so stupid as to think I need you for long," the Emperor replied. The bowl in his hand disappeared before he waved his hand across the air and a hologram of me appeared, replacing the galaxy.

"THE PEACE BETWEEN THE NOTHA AND EARTHGOV IS SOMETHING WE HAVE TOO LONG NEEDED AND NEGOTIATIONS ARE GOING WELL," the holographic version of me stated. "I BELIEVE IT IS TIME TO SET ASIDE THE PAST HORRORS

AND MOVE FORWARD. AN END TO SLAVERY, TERROR, AND CONFLICT IS AT HAND."

"It doesn't have quite the same ring to it as we'll have peace in our time," I replied, finally able to speak normally as I tried to get up.

"That is true," the Emperor said. "However, it should be noted that I'm willing to work with a simulation if you won't help. The Primordials will eventually return to this part of the galaxy and will almost certainly cleanse it of filth like our race but that could be a few million years from now. Plenty of time to prepare."

I stared down at him. "You do love to hear the sound of your own voice, don't you? Is this some kind of kinky sex thing? The only way you can get aroused is breaking people?"

The Emperor proceeded to lift his left hand and snapped his fingers. The nanotech inside me sent me spiraling to the ground as if I was being electrocuted. It didn't function like normal electricity but felt like incarnate pain once more paralyzing me and leaving me twitching without the ability to stand. "Yes, yes, it is. You'd be amazed at how sexually satisfying power is. Too bad you'll never experience it."

Two of the Notha bots entered the chamber, moving along like quadrupedal spiders with four arms that they used to lift me up off the ground. There was no sign of my associates in the antechamber that they dragged me through. In the end, I was taken to a black metal cell with a transparent steel wall before being abandoned there.

There was a fountain and wash basin inside as well as something I assumed to be a Notha toilet. Also, three or four sets of clothing that I suspected were designed to be worn while I made whatever announcements the Emperor had prewritten for me. One of them was a duplicate of my uniform and another of Space Fleet dress whites. He'd even made replicas of all my various medals and paraphernalia, which if worn together would make me look like I belonged to that Rand's World dictator's convention.

Well, this situation certainly sucks, Trish said in my mind.

Oh, thank God, you're alive, I said, sucking in my breath.

I've been better, Trish said. *If not for the fact the technology in your brain is Elder Race, I think I'd have been burned out.*

What is it? I asked. *Is it Notha technology?*

I don't know, Trish said. *However, it doesn't respond to any of the commands I give it. I do suspect it's probably in every single person here, though. This is how he manages his foreign crew.*

I wouldn't be surprised if it's how he manages his Notha crew either, I said. *Family or not, he's a real anyxhole.*

If he is the father of the Notha race like he claims, it would certainly go a long way to explaining how borked up they are, Trish said. *I'd hate to imagine what that's done to their genetic diversity.*

I have a few more concerns than whether the Notha are suffering the same problems purebred dogs on Earth are, I replied, thinking of how much money was spent every year trying to fix what breeders had done to them over the millennia. Some people had way too much money and too little sense. I said that as someone who loved dogs. *I can't believe the Elder Races put that guy in charge of an entire species.*

I think we've established the Elder Races are scummy, Trish said. *Albeit, I think wrecking the entire universe is an extreme response.*

Ya think? I asked. *I can't believe he's actually got a hundred thousand SKAMMs but that information in my head is pretty damn convincing.*

The stakes are much higher now, Trish said.

Not really, I said.

Excuse me? Trish asked. *You'll have to explain how that's not the case.*

I'm already fully committed, I replied. *My crew is in danger and the people I care about most on this ship. This just makes it clear that failure is not an option.*

Failure is always an option, Trish said. *It's literally the easiest thing in the world to achieve, especially with this crew.*

Thanks, Trish, I muttered, shaking my head. *I really needed that.*

You're welcome, Trish said. *Now let me help you further by pointing out the fact that we don't know if any of the rest of the crew are still alive. The Emperor, being the nutter that he is, might well have already killed them. Hannah, certainly, wouldn't have gone down with an ill-advised, thoroughly hopeless fight.*

Wow, you are genuinely terrible at this, I said, sarcastically.

Thanks, Trish said, sounding as defeated as I felt. *I haven't even touched upon the fact I'm utterly terrified about what might happen to you. The person I care about most in the world is poisoned and being held prisoner only until the crazy genocidal warlord wrings every bit of use he can out of him. Then he'll almost certainly be executed.*

Yeah, that's about the size of it, I said, accepting all of the details she'd brought to my attention. *Situation Report: Screwed.*

You didn't use colonial swearing, Trish said.

I know, I replied. *I think I needed to revert to good old-fashioned Earth aphorisms for this business.*

I took that moment to go to the wash basin and start cleaning myself up as best I could, washing myself off in the sink and using the Notha's version of powdered soap. It smelled terrible and burned my skin, but I wanted to reclaim whatever passed for dignity that I could. I even put on the replica of my uniform after I searched it for anything like listening devices or other nasty additions. As far as I could tell, they were perfectly normal replications of my uniform, but I wouldn't put anything past my captors now.

Unfortunately, being dressed in the reproduction of my actual uniform did nothing to convince me that my situation had improved. There was no way to contact the *Ares* and warn them they should get the hell out of Dodge. They would be unlikely to suspect anything was wrong for at least twenty-four hours and it was possible they might even be fooled by the Emperor's fake Vance Turbo for a while. That was assuming he hadn't access to a full-bioroid replacement, which I wouldn't put him past at this point.

Trish was right that I didn't have any proof my friends and crew weren't dead already. The Emperor might just open his dreadnought's weapons on the *Ares* and blow it to pieces while its barriers were down. He was threatening me with their lives, but I had the feeling the Emperor wouldn't hesitate to kill them all then start grabbing additional soldiers to ensure cooperation. It wouldn't work in the long run, everyone in EarthGov and the Community had to know we were meeting at this point, but there was nothing more dangerous than an ignorant man who thought he was smart. Ruthlessness brute force had clearly done well for the ancient Notha, so he'd never had to learn anything else.

And what about these Primordials? Did they even exist? If it was true there was another ancient race out there opposed to the Elder

Races, that possibly changed the entire galactic political structure. The Elder Races had held unquestioned dominion over the Known Universe for twenty thousand years if records of the early days of interstellar travel were true. Unfortunately, if this was their introduction to our lives then it seemed the Primordials were every bit as awful if not worse. I also was paranoid enough to wonder if this was all some sort of trick even if that made no goddamn sense.

I was on the verge of despair when I heard a tapping on the side of my transparent steel wall. Much to my surprise, to the point I wondered if I was hallucinating, I saw Danny standing there. I had to blink twice before I believed it, but my eyes were not deceiving me. Danny was there.

"Huh, plot twist," I said, staring at him. "Do I even want to know how you're on the other side of this thing?"

"Well, I *am* a spy," Danny said. "One that apparently got ignored in the confusion. I don't think it's going to last, though."

"Well, I know you can't just open this thing. You need to get to a communications device and—" I started to formulate a plan on the fly but stopped when Danny interrupted me by just hitting a button on the side of the wall and causing the door to my cell to open.

"You should get out now," Danny said.

I did. "Are there not like any guards here or anything?"

"There are," Danny said. "However, this place is running on a skeleton crew and a dummy AI. If there's ever a time that we should be grateful for other races being iffy on AI, it is now."

I'm not so sure about that, Trish said. *There's something here.*

Let's not look a gift horse in the mouth, I replied. *If ever there was a time for things to work out like they do in movies, then it's now.*

"Oh, that reminds me," Danny said, pulling out my ring.

"What the actual bork," I said, staring at him. "Were you in the room with me and the Emperor?"

"Yeah?" Danny said.

I took the ring and put it on before concentrating on it.

"Uh, Vance, what are you doing?" Danny asked.

"What does it look like I'm doing?" I asked.

"That you are having a migraine," Danny said. "Either that or attempting to use the Force only being really bad at it."

"I'm trying to mentally send the Elder Races a warning about all this," I said. "The Emperor's plans, the Primordials, the SKAMMS, everything."

"Is that a good idea?" Danny asked. "I mean, after all they've done?"

"I don't want them dead," I said. "Besides, I don't think apocalyptic wars are ever a positive thing to set off."

"You're a good man, Vance Turbo," Danny said.

"Thank you, Linus," I replied.

"Who?" Danny asked.

"Never mind," I said, removing the ring and hiding it in my pocket. "Well, if it worked, it worked. If it didn't. It didn't. I don't think we should stick around this place to find out, though. I have a plan to deal with this situation."

"You realize self-destruct buttons don't exist, right?" Danny asked.

"I am aware," I replied. "Besides, why would I blow up this ship while the others are on it?"

"The needs of the many?" Danny asked. "Listen, there's a lot of places we can hide on this ship. Maybe we can get a message away to the *Ares*, but I don't know how we're going to find the others. It took me a few hours to find you and I was following you the entire time. There're enough humans onboard that we can pass ourselves off as—"

"Ahem," the Emperor said next to us.

I turned to see the Notha Emperor was beside us with more of his spider robots. Apparently, he'd come to collect us.

"Well, savit," I muttered.

CHAPTER TWENTY-SIX

From Bad to Worse

The Emperor didn't bother speaking with me but instead just shocked the hell out of me again before grabbing Danny with his robots. I had no idea if his biomod gave him the power to fool sensors as well as organic beings but, either way, it wasn't working now. We ended up being dragged through the hallways of the detention level until getting tossed in yet another cell. Well, this one was more like a pit, and I was thrown ten feet through a hole with Danny landing on top of me.

I had the feeling the Emperor was a creature of impulse and whatever his plans were, they constantly changed depending on his mood. It made dealing with the man even more dangerous or would if not for the fact I suspected we were already at peak danger. The arrogant narcissist did have one flaw, though, in that he was apparently lazy enough not to order me checked for weapons and I still had the Elder Ring in my pocket.

"Don't worry, Vance," the Emperor said from the hole he'd tossed me through. "You won't be killed for what happens next. However, you might wish you'd be."

"Mmmph! Mmmph! Mmmph! Hmmph!" I said, still recovering from his use of the nanites against me and shook a fist at him.

I think we'll leave this part out of your biography, Trish said. *It'd just be embarrassing.*

I was trying to say "From Hell's heart, I stab at thee," I replied.

You wanted to quote Moby Dick *at him?* Trish asked.

217

Yes, I lied. *That is exactly what I was quoting. Totally not* The Wrath of Khan.

Trish gave a melancholy sigh, and I was glad she was with me because otherwise I would have no release for this insanity's stress.

"Enjoy your companion's deaths, Captain Turbo!" The Emperor said, closing the hatch over the hole his goons had thrown me through. That left me with Danny on top of me and the sounds of other people moving around.

"Oooomph," Danny said, moaning.

"Get off me," I said, pushing him off. "That's an order."

"Sorry, sir," Danny said, moaning.

"Well, I think any chance of Vance pulling off a miracle as he's wont to do has just failed," Hannah's voice spoke nearby. "I guess you owe me a coke, Shelly."

"I argued he'd probably be dead," Shelly replied. "I just said that he'd be dead or pull off a miracle."

"Neither of which happened," Hannah said. "So, I'm getting my soft drink as soon as we escape."

"Hello, Vance," Forty-Two said to me. "This was a very bad plan."

"No kidding," I said, turning to see the rest of my crew in what appeared to be a large dusty chamber with melee weapons scattered all around. There were spears, axes, knives, and a few weapons I didn't recognize but nothing above a bow and arrow. Hannah, Shelly, Danny, and Forty-Two were present but no one else. "Where the hell are we?"

"Arena holding pen," Hannah replied. "The Notha love these things."

"Arena?" I asked, blinking. "Wait, you mean like gladiator fights?"

"More like unleashing savage animals from Hellworld and letting them tear prisoners to pieces," Hannah said. "It's the same basic principle but without the thin veneer of heroics that gladiators have."

"Great," I said, sitting up. "I should mention that he's poisoned me with nano-tech and can hurt me at any time he desires. This is apparently something he's done with the majority of crew on the ship."

Shelly blinked. "That exists outside of bad movies?"

"Apparently!" I shouted.

"He didn't poison us," Hannah said. "Which probably means that he plans to horribly kill us."

"That and he flat out said he was going to," Forty-Two said. "I would have shot him with an arrow, but he has a barrier around him at all times. Probably because he's not a moron."

"I can't believe the Emperor was so willing to cast aside peace," Shelly said, shaking her head.

"Really?" Hannah asked, throwing protocol to the wind. "You really find it strange for the absolute monarch to do something rash and entitled? Clearly, you don't have that much experience with aristocrats like I do. On Crius, they're all enormous man-babies who thinks the sun rise and sets on their anyxes."

"Why would the sun rise and set on his anyx?" Forty-Two asked.

"It's a metaphor," Hannah said.

"It's a stupid one," Forty-Two said.

"It gets worse," I replied.

"How can it get worse?" Shelly asked, shaking her head. "This is an act of war against the Community. Not only are we not going to be able to bring peace between the Notha and EarthGov but we're going to trigger the next one by being hostages."

"He's got hundreds of thousands of SKAMMs and plans to launch a war against the Elder Races," I replied.

Everyone in the room stared but Danny, who already knew this.

"So, he's not just a stupid arrogant dictator but he's also a goddamn supervillain," Hannah said. "Great!"

"He's not just a crude monster but a madman too," Forty-Two said. "The Sorkanan are the most advanced, intelligent, civilized, powerful, sexually attractive—"

"Forty-Two," I interrupted. "Please."

"—race in the Known Universe but even they know not to try to rouse the wrath of the Elder Races," Forty-Two said. "This is not that space station sitcom that Vance forced me to watch. Sumerian Six."

"*Babylon Five*," I corrected him.

"Whatever," Forty-Two said. "It was all monkeys in makeup anyway. The Narn were the only ones I could stand to look at."

"Says the guy who made me watch *Romeo and Juliet* with an all-Sorkanan cast," I replied.

"That was art, and we changed the ending for the better!" Forty-Two said. "You can't get a proper sequel with the double-suicide of teenagers. A proper Sorkanan epic has at least one hundred and three parts. Like your *Star Wars*."

Resisting the urge to get drawn into that conversation, I took a deep breath. "So, yeah, the situation started bad and has gotten way worse."

"No kidding," Hannah said.

"So, right now our only hope is the Elder Races know of his plan and come to blow up the *Emperor's Reach*," Shelly said.

"With us on it," Hannah said. "Which will kill us."

"Yes," Shelly said.

"Great thing to hope for," Hannah said.

"It's better than galactic genocide," Shelly replied.

"I dunno, if we're making wishes, I'm all for being rescued," Hannah said. "Either that or a heroic escape."

"I have a plan," I replied.

Everyone looked at me.

Actually, my plan was to hope that the Elder Races had received my message and would come to blow up the *Emperor's Reach*, but I wasn't eager to share that fact right now. Not just because Hannah had stated the specific downsides of said plan but also because I wasn't sure if the room was bugged.

I didn't want to clue in the Emperor about the fact I had the Elder Ring and while I doubted it would prove much value—I'd seen his bowl with dozens of those things—it was about the only advantage we had. Well, that and the fact that Danny had inconsistent ignorability—which was a power we may have already used up the benefits of.

"The Emperor's position is deceptively weak," I said, deciding to pull a plan out from my anyx while hoping the situation improved. "The ship is in a state of hodge-podge disrepair and half-completed fixes. It is dangerously understaffed. I assume there's a core of actual fanatics among the Notha but I wouldn't be surprised if more than half of the people here are enslaved to the Emperor with his poison."

"That's guessing," Shelly said.

"It's also an effective way of demanding loyalty," Forty-Two grumbled. "Death is the one great equalizer."

"Yes," I said. "However, I don't think any non-Notha are inclined to work for him willingly when he can use a stick like that. Hell, many of the Notha might be enslaved with the nanites, too. He doesn't seem to be the kind of person who hedged his bets on loyalty."

"So, what, you think we can start some kind of slave revolt?" Shelly asked. "I don't think that's possible when he can just snap his fingers and put everyone down."

That was almost literally what he'd done to me. "No, I think that if he can't snap his fingers that no one will stop us."

Everyone waited for more.

I didn't have any more.

"Is that it?" Hannah asked. "You kill the little furball and everything magically works out?"

"I like this plan," Forty-Two said.

"You would!" Hannah said.

"He's adorable but evil so I'm conflicted," Danny said. "However, more evil than adorable so I'm okay with it."

"Don't be fooled by their teddy bear looks!" Hannah said. "Notha will gnaw your legs off if you let them."

"No one is gnawing anyone's legs off," Shelly said. "Though I do point out assassinating the Emperor could make the situation worse."

Hannah cocked her head to one side. "How the bork is it going to get worse? What with the galaxy destruction thing? That's not normal! Dictators normally just surround themselves with members of their preferred sex and pay for their favorite band members to do their birthdays! You know, in-between all the murder and public appearances. Destroying the galaxy is a new thing!"

Shelly didn't look like she had anything to respond to that. "Okay, maybe killing him *is* the best option but it's still not likely to help us get out of here."

That was when a bloodcurdling animalistic roar spread through the entirety of the chamber, echoing past us and filling the hallways beyond.

"What the bork was that?" I asked, looking up.

"Oh, Ancestors damn it," Hannah said. "You have got to be kidding me."

"That sounds like a big animal," Danny said. "A *very* big animal."

"It's either a carver or reaper," Hannah said. "Creatures from Crius. Motherborker."

"Could you stop talking like a sailor on shore leave?" Shelly asked.

"Could you shut the bork up?" Hannah said. "Clearly I'm not suited for life in Space Fleet if I have to put up with your—"

"Time out," I said, making a T-shape with my hands. "We have to work together if we're going to survive this."

Hannah shook her head. "Your plan sucks, Vance! Oh, and are you seriously suggesting our best advantage is teamwork? What are you? A football coach for grade-schoolers?"

"What's a carver or reaper?" I asked.

Hannah took a deep breath. "You'd know them as an allosaurus or tyrannosaurus rex."

"Are those game animals?" Forty-Two asked.

Hannah gave him a sideways glance. "No, Forty-Two. They're big and scary monsters that the Crius nobility hunt for sport."

"So, they *are* game animals," Forty-Two said.

Before I could respond to this particular horrifying revelation, the entirety of the room shook, and I felt it starting to rise. Above our heads, the ceiling opened and revealed a brilliant white light that surrounded us as we ascended some sort of shaft. I didn't know what to do or how to react as we soon found ourselves in the middle of an octagonal coliseum with stadium seating.

The bleachers were filled with tens of thousands of crew members that were engaged in performative cheering—the Notha more than all the aliens—with the Notha Emperor having his own barrier-protected seat surrounded by spider-bots.

It was straight out of a bad movie with every bit of the Roman execution method on full display. The Notha did do a lot of executions via animals, but this was heavily influenced by Earth history. There was no sign of the giant animals yet, but I could hear sounds coming from beneath the ground and another part of the arena floor was opening, revealing the sight of a cybernetically modified Tyrannosaurus Rex rising upward.

The poor creature had both of its eyes removed and replaced with red lens as its brain cavity had been rewired with a metal case that undoubtedly contained extensive enhancements. There were no signs of actual weapons on its body but a set of flowing black metal tentacles had been added to its back, giving it ways of attacking that were not available to anything in the Cretaceous Period. It was chained with a collar around its neck and the other ends bolted to the ground. A pair of Notha wranglers had shock spears in their hands at the base, both wearing reinforced battle armor.

Worse, the T. rex's teeth had all been removed and replaced with metal blades that were clearly designed to tear through the bodies of human beings in suitably grandiose as well as gory ways. It was animal abuse of the worst kind, and I expected the creature had to be in absolute misery. Unfortunately, any sympathy I might have for the creature was outweighed by the fact it was almost certainly going to kill us. The Emperor had said it wouldn't harm me, possible if it had complete control, but it would also hurt my friends. Was that the point? This was some sort of lesson? Or was it just a way of him reinforcing whatever control he thought he had over us? Did it matter?

The Emperor spoke into a holographic interface which projected his image above the arena. His voice boomed throughout, speaking in Notha and then English for what I presumed was my benefit. "Ladies, gentlemen, and others: welcome to the celebration of my latest triumph! Tonight, I am going to record the death of some of Earth's greatest champions and the submission of their captain! He can end this at any time but must prove himself!"

"What do you want?" I called out, unsure if he could hear me.

"The only way you are leaving this arena with any of your associates alive is if you sacrifice one of them to me," the Emperor said. "Either the reaper kills all of them or you kill one of them yourself! Choose!"

The others all looked back at me.

I looked at each of them. "I suggest you all arm yourselves."

"Vance, I volunteer—" Shelly started to speak.

"Shut up and arm yourself!" I snapped. "That's an order."

Everyone picked up a weapon off the ground.

I had no intention of cooperating with the Emperor's sick power games. I knew exactly what would happen if I did. He would have me kill one of the others and then alienate me from everyone else. Once you crossed certain lines, everything else became easier. This wasn't about power, though, not really. This was about getting his sadistic rocks off and I had no intention of helping with that either. I would kill that bastarve no matter what.

The Emperor's laugh was particularly disturbing. "That's what I like about you humans. You're such a stupid race. Let the games begin!"

The chains fell from the T. rex's collar and it was released onto us. It responded by immediately grabbing one of its wranglers and tearing them apart. That's when the crowd's cheering became enthusiastic and real.

Congratulations, Vance, Trish said. *Fighting in an alien arena for your life. You're officially a space opera hero.*

I could have settled for just dating alien princesses and beautiful robots, I replied.

Two out of three ain't bad, Trish said.

CHAPTER TWENTY-SEVEN

Cyborg Dinosaurs and Other Metal as Bork Stuff

You know, it was moments like this that really caused you to question the meaning of your life. *Who am I? Why am I here? What am I going to become?* Being a starship captain in the middle of a Notha gladiatorial arena fighting a roboticized T. rex was one of those moments. I mean, it was awesome in a way that was utterly horrifying and would probably be the last thing I ever did but it was the latter parts that bothered me. Really caused you to think.

"Vance, we need to move!" Hannah said, tossing me a round metal shield.

I caught the shield. "I don't think this is going to help."

"Run!" Hannah shouted.

"That part makes sense," I said, as I moved away from the enormous metal and flesh dinosaur as it threw away the body of the second Notha handler it mauled. Either it was being controlled by the Emperor or was just naturally aggressive beyond all reasonable animals because it proceeded to stalk all of us.

Forty-Two took up a fighting stance with a sword. "I just want you to know, Vance, that I blame you for this."

"Thanks, Forty-Two!" I said, not so much worried about myself as my friend. The Emperor said I wasn't in danger, and they were. That this was some sort of sick lesson he was trying to teach me to enforce my compliance to his will. I planned to exploit that to my highest advantage here.

That was when the T. rex almost bit me in half, and only my enhanced reflexes prevented it. Rolling on the ground, I backed up and watched the creature roar at me with the strength of a hundred megaphones. Also, just to be precise about what happened, it blew some snot on me. Apparently, cybernetic T. rexes still had organic nostrils.

The Emperor's laughter filled the arena through the intercoms, and I couldn't blame him. He'd certainly had me fooled. So, covered in dinosaur goop and barely dodging a second attempt by the T. rex to gore me, I decided to treat the creature as actually trying to kill me. Watching Hannah and Shelly immediately go for its legs with spears while Forty-Two tried to protect Danny, I also realized that I was probably the least capable warrior in hand-to-hand here. Well, not including Danny but he could become invisible, so who was I to call him out?

You have the Elder Ring, Trish said. *Use it! Put up a shield! Teleport around the place! Try to affect the ship's programming!*

I moved backward, keeping my metal shield up and tried to pace my breathing. *First, I don't know how to teleport! That was only a thing Ketra could do. Also, you're the only reason I can hack things and you're a fragment of your normal operating power.*

The barrier would be nice now! Trish asked.

Yeah, but it would also tip off the Emperor I have it, I said, already getting a little tired from running around the arena trying to avoid the four-meter tall being that could move at seventeen miles per hour at its fastest. I was really going to have to start hitting the gym more after this if I somehow managed to get out of here alive.

Better him tipped off than us dead, Trish replied. *Wait, do you have a plan? I'm hearing the beginnings of a plan in your head.*

Kinda? I suggested. *I do my best thinking while under duress.*

Then be a borking genius! Trish replied, sounding genuinely scared. I had to admit that I liked this more personable and human-like Trish. Which was unfortunately not the best time for this thought at all.

I was about to shout a triumphant affirmation of my genius when I ended up stumbling backward while trying to move without taking my eyes off the T. rex. This triggered a bunch of laughter from the crowds as they saw some close up holos above our heads of my idiocy. The T. rex stretched out one of its back tentacles like a prehistoric Doctor Octopus and grabbed me by the leg, lifting me upside down in front of its mouth. This would have been my undignified end, if not for the fact Hannah moved to its side and hurled the spear in her hand into the T. rex's left eye.

"Ten points!" Hannah shouted.

The spear had penetrated the inner workings of the T. rex's artificial brain and the creature let out a painful wheeze of animal noises combined with machinery dying. It fell over and landed on its side with a ground-shaking *thud*. I wasn't sure I could call it dead because the T. rex's condition was one between life and death in the first place. It was, however, nonfunctional and that was something I was imminently grateful for.

The reaction of the crowd was tremendous and quite genuine now. They had not expected anything other than another of what I expected were frequent executions by their insane kidnapper. Seeing Hannah successfully kill the creature was something that seemed to inspire them in a "Are you not entertained?" shout sort of way.

"Remind me to promote you, Hannah," I said, breathing a sigh of relief and climbing to my feet.

"Don't threaten me like that," Hannah replied.

Unfortunately, something I learned while gambling on Mars and that has remained true for the entirety of human history was the house always won in the end. We may have managed to put down the monster the Emperor had unleashed upon us, but we were still completely in his power and I doubted it had improved his disposition to us.

This was swiftly confirmed by the Emperor's next speech. "Bravo! Bravo! Once more Space Fleet's finest manages to display the same animal cunning that the universe gave to vermin. I am impressed, Captain Turbo! You have managed to put off killing one of your crew to save the rest a little while longer!"

I stared at the Emperor with hate in my eyes. What a sad little pathetic man. "If you think I'm going to harm any of my crew to live down to your twisted ideals then you have got another think coming!

You may have poisoned me, but I am a free man and will resist you until my dying breath!"

"Uh, Vance," Shelly said, standing beside me with her spear in hand.

"Yeah?" I asked, keeping my eyes focused on the Emperor's distant form.

"You know he can't hear you, right?" Shelly asked.

I paused. "I admit, I wasn't thinking of that at the moment."

"Nice speech, though," Forty-Two said. "Very inspiring."

Hannah shook her head. "I give it a four out of ten. Especially since it came after me killing a reaper."

The Emperor, clearly not having heard any of this, continued his rambling monologue. "But the choice is inevitable, the same as the fall of the Elder Races and the liberation of the Young Races from their chains."

I'd say it was ridiculous that the Young Races were chained by anything, but the statement was already ridiculous because he was a Notha, a member of an expansionist slave-based empire, talking about the liberation of species from their chains. Most of the Notha race existed in some level of servitude to the higher castes that was barely above slavery itself. Indeed, breaking away from these age-old chains was a major motivation of their civil war.

It amused me I was getting some actual viable diplomatic insight into their culture from the Emperor. The Notha had been shaped around his ego and placating him while genetically being tool-users pushing against a hostile galaxy. The two forces meant fear and deference to authority were the primary motivating factors of their society, but there was push back. It gave me hope there could be a lasting peace between the Community and them.

Vance, focus on the fact we're about to die, Trish reminded me.

Oh right, I said, clutching my shield tight.

Steve Rogers you are not, Trish muttered.

Who? I asked.

Clearly your pop culture knowledge doesn't extend to the early 21st century, Trish muttered. *Which is funny because he dates to World War 2.*

"—and thus you shall all die!" the Emperor finished a speech that I only caught the tail end of.

Dammit!

"Was that important?" I asked Shelly.

"Nope," Shelly said. "Just him gloating over our imminent demise."

"Ah, good," I said. "Glad I wasn't paying attention then."

The ground beneath us started to shake again as multiple holes opened up in a circle around us. I heard more noises, smaller and yet no less menacing than those from the T. rex. I didn't know what was going to be unleashed upon us this time, but I had a feeling it would be entertaining as bork to everyone but us.

"I always knew I was going to die surrounded by idiots," Forty-Two said. "Or humans."

"Hey, no racism!" I snapped. "We're being watched by a live studio audience. Represent the fleet, goddammit."

Hannah sighed. "I'd say it's been an honor, but honor is for aristocrats and handshake deals. Also, you guys suck."

The platforms finished raising and I found we were surrounded by utahraptors. They were similar to velociraptors but whereas the latter were about the size of a turkey, utahraptors were about six feet in height and the tigers of the revived dinosaur genus. Similar to the T. rex, they all looked to have been cybernetically enhanced but only in the crudest and most butcher-like manner. There was one for each of us, including Danny, and they had claws like a glove of daggers. These didn't have wranglers but were just standing there, motionless, like statues in a museum of unusual warfare.

"Great Shiv," Hannah said.

"Do you have to deal with these things regularly where you're from?" I asked, trying to deal with the fact I didn't see a way out of this. I had a plan, but it was only the beginnings of one and probably wouldn't work.

"The nobility loved slavery, genetic engineering, and dinosaurs," Hannah said. "It kind of had a synergetic effect."

That was when the murderous dinosaurs were unleashed, and the fight of my life began. The utahraptors descended on us all and Hannah moved to fight them as I found myself immediately forced to do everything in my power to hold one back by letting it claw my shield, biting as well as banging. They moved like lightning, and I felt overwhelmed dealing with just one of the monsters.

Now would be a good time to use the ring, Trish said. *Like, right now!*

Well, if you want to ask the murder dinosaur to stop trying to kill me to give me a second to put it on, I'd very much be willing to do so! I mentally shouted back, the monster's hot breath in my face before I pulled back and smashed it in the head with my shield.

That managed to knock over the creature long enough for me to bring down the shield on its soft fleshy throat. The end of the shield had been damaged to serve as a jagged knife and the force of the blow opened its throat. It was a gory mess and I felt horrible, but it was kill or be killed.

That was when I heard Danny cry out and I turned to see him on the ground. An utahraptor was standing over him and looking ready to kill him. It seemed his ability to avoid being noticed had failed him at the worst possible moment. Forty-Two ran forward to protect him with his sword, only to be slashed across the chest.

"No!" I shouted, running forward to Forty-Two's side. It was a profoundly stupid thing to do, especially since I was only wielding a shield.

The utahraptor that had slashed Forty-Two turned toward me and charged at me, going for my throat. I swung under it and slashed its belly. I was covered in gore as I saw yet another utahraptor coming at me, the creature taking an arrow through its neck from Shelly. She'd picked up the bow and arrow after having implanted a sword into one of the creatures. There were no more of them now with the rest slain by her and Hannah. I wasn't concerned about that, though.

"Forty-Two! Forty-Two!" I shouted, reaching the side of my best friend. He was lying on the ground and his eyes were closed. "Oh God, I'm sorry friend. I never should have taken you on this mission. It was an insane stupid idea from the beginning. I don't care if we were ordered to do it, we should have found a way around this insanity."

"Armor," Forty-Two said as I cradled his head.

"What?" I asked. "What? You want me to armor my heart because of this?"

"No, dumbass," Forty-Two said, opening one of his eyes. "I wore armor on this mission because I knew the Notha were going to betray us. I just wore it under my uniform. It's pretty banged up but I'm not spilling my guts either."

"Oh," I said, blinking. I dropped his head onto the ground.

"Ow!" Forty-Two said.

I stood up and jogged to the fallen T. rex before pulling the spear out of its eye. The crowds seemed mystified that we'd managed to survive. I could also see an enormous hologram of the Emperor looking down on us. Alien or not, the look on his face was unmistakably one of absolute fury.

Now would be a good time to put on the ring, Vance, Trish said.

I did but not for the reasons she thought. *Now's the time for a stupid plan.*

Good, those are the only ones you come up with, Trish replied.

"You incompetent nameless little savit!" The Emperor shouted, his voice booming through the arena interior. "You have yet to live a single lifespan, but you dare humiliate me in front of my subjects? All you had to do was spill a little blood and you could have been the favored pet of the galaxy's ruler! Now there is nothing for you, not even an epitaph! I command you all to rush them and tear them all limb from limb or you will perish this evening! Let their insides decorate the ground and be a lesson to every single one of you—"

"Bork it," I said, lifting up my spear like an Olympic javelin before running and hurling it.

"Vance, you can't throw it across an arena!" Shelly said, staring at me as if I'd lost my mind.

I wasn't throwing it across the arena, though, but I was wishing and begging the Elder Race's ring to do a short-range teleportation like the kind Ketra had chosen to do to me. A thing that had to be calculated down to the distance of centimeters as well as weight to make sure that it didn't kill whoever was teleported.

Unless you didn't care if whatever being teleported didn't end up inside someone. In this case, the spear disappeared from a few feet away from where I'd thrown it and reappeared inside the head of the Notha Emperor. It resulted in a rather spectacular displacement of matter out the sides of its skull. Which, in laymen's terms, meant rather than just impaling the guy, I'd caused the Emperor's head to explode.

Almost immediately, I felt the immense supernatural sense of oppression permeating the ship disappear. No, not disappear, but dramatically lesson as if it had been focused around the Emperor but echoes of its evil remained. It was difficult to believe anyone could make a place toxic but the Elder Races' modifications to him had done it. It made me wonder what sort of changes they'd done to me as well.

Either way, the dramatic assassination was displayed on the holographic display above our heads to every single person inside the arena. I might have imagined it or maybe I'm remembering it differently than it happened, but I swear someone recording this caused it to do a slow-motion instant replay of the event.

"Holy savit," Hannah said, staring.

Shelly turned to me, open mouthed, and pointed then dropped her hand to her side. "Dammit, you're the captain."

"Gods, you're never going to let us hear the end of this, are you?" Forty-Two said, climbing to his feet.

Danny looked at me then the crowd then me. "Well, this certainly took a turn for the dramatic, sir."

They weren't kidding because an eerie hush fell over the crowd right before one of the Notha soldiers took a shot at me with a fusion pistol with the blast sailing over my head due to the distance involved.

That sparked the massive riot that followed, right as the ship's alarms started blaring and orders to go to battle stations were barked by an alien AI in multiple languages. All of them repeating the same words, "THE SHIP IS UNDER ATTACK. THE ELDER RACES HAVE ENTERED THE SYSTEM."

Wow, did their timing suck.

CHAPTER TWENTY-EIGHT

Is It Abandoning Ship When You're Fleeing It?

The humans, Sorkanan, Drolochids, Ants, and Sklux in the audience attacked the Notha around them with a brutal fury. It was funny because a lot of the Notha started attacking each other too, either because of old scores or because not all of them were there willingly either.

A few more took some wild shots at us but we seemed forgotten in the sudden explosive chaos. Certainly, no one was fleeing to their battle stations but a large chunk of them seemed to be fleeing period for any exit they could.

The announcement of the Elder Races' arrival filled me with more of a sense of dread than the fact that half of the crew probably wanted to murder me now. Their technology was, as the whole teleporting spear causing an exploding head thing proved, indistinguishable from magic.

"Well, Vance, if we go down here then at least we went down in flames," Hannah said, surveying the sudden massive revolt going on around us.

"Congratulations," Forty-Two said. "You have killed not only the head of state for the Notha Empire but their deity. You are likely to be considered their devil for all time."

"May I suggest we get the bork out of here, sir!" Danny shouted, grabbing me by the wrist and starting to drag me toward the Emperor's box.

"He's right!" Shelly said, shaking off her confusion. "We have to escape in order to report this to the Admiralty Board."

"Seriously?" Hannah asked. "That's what your worried about?"

A fusion bolt sailed over her head before she started jogging toward the same location Danny was trying to lead me to. Shelly ran too and we passed by the corpses of the utahraptors and T. rex.

There was nowhere to really run too as the conflict continued all around us, some of the crew jumping down into the arena to escape the riot. That was when we reached the bottom of the Emperor's box. Danny offered to boost me but instead, Forty-Two lifted me up and hurled me six feet in the air and I ended up grabbing the edge. I pulled myself into the box and reached down to help the others. Shelly was first, Danny second, and Hannah before she and I helped Forty-Two up.

The Emperor's corpse was laying spread out on the ground, unmoving, so if there was any chance he really was immortal or possessed of some super regeneration powers there was no sign of them. He also looked very organic in his death state, so I discounted it was a bioroid body double as well. His spider-bots surrounded him, unmoving. In a very real way, it seemed like he was the puppet master of a thousand invisible strings that cutting had just been a matter of striking the hand that held them.

More importantly was the fact that the Emperor's box had a hallway leading out of the arena. I wasn't confidant it would lead directly to an emergency exit or shuttle bay, but it was better than remaining here where most of the organic crew was now tearing into one another.

"Captain, just how long is this ship likely to last against the Elder Races?" Danny asked as he tried not to look at the Emperor's headless corpse.

"Well, I don't know the capacities of the Elder Races' ships but given no one is actually at their stations fighting back, I'd say not long," I replied.

"Then you probably shouldn't have called them, sir," Danny said, taking a deep breath as we made a move for the exit.

"You did what?" Hannah asked.

Shelly sighed. "That was a very wise decision, though perhaps not the one most beneficial for our long-term survival."

"No kidding!" I snapped. "I'm making this up as I go along."

"That is the revelation of the past ten thousand cycles," Forty-Two said, sarcastically.

"It worked, didn't it?" I said, heading out into a private hallway that was shinier and nicer than the rest of the ship. It was also, for the time being, lacking in any panicking crew members.

"Not if it gets us killed," Hannah said. "Which seems to be a running theme with you and these things!"

"You haven't died yet!" I said, giving the weakest defense of all time.

"That is not an excuse!" Hannah snapped.

That was when Danny went to a nearby console and began typing away on the holographic interface that thankfully had multiple languages and commands.

"What are you doing, Danny?" I asked.

"Trying to get us a map," Danny said.

"Shouldn't we just be heading to an escape pod?" Shelly asked.

"That's if you assume that the Elder Races aren't going to blow them to pieces," I replied. "Hell, we don't even know if the *Ares* is still intact."

I didn't want to think about that because the Emperor had promised to destroy the vessel and its crew if I didn't cooperate, which I manifestly did not. I was also still technically poisoned along with all the other people here. A part of me wanted to try to reach out to them, to promise them freedom, and to work to take over the ship so they could all be given refuge. Unfortunately, my choice to inform the Elder Races had probably doomed everyone here.

I could have done something heroic, sought out the bridge or communications system to inform them but I was scared for the few people on the ship I really did love. It was a sentiment that was both unworthy of a Space Fleet officer and profoundly human. I needed to get my cousin, Shelly, Hannah, and Forty-Two to safety. Everything else was secondary, be it the destruction of the *Emperor's Reach* and the last of the Emperor's legacy or trying to help the thousands of people enslaved here.

I can't tell, Trish said. *All communications are still being blocked by this ship's AI. It's coordinating the ship's defenses itself now.*

That's good, I said.

Is it? Trish asked. *What if it's programmed to kill us all? Or launch all the SKAMMs?*

That's bad, I said.

Yeah, I wasn't covering myself in glory right now in terms of providing crucial leadership during a time of crisis. On the other hand, I dared anyone else to do better under the time crunch we were dealing with.

You should try and contact the Elder Races with the Elder Ring, Trish said. *By the way, do you think they're the ones who add Elder to everything?*

Not the time, Trish, I said, shaking my head. *Besides, what am I going to say? Oh hey, the Emperor is dead and he's no longer there to push the button that will cause everyone in your species to die. Please don't kill us all?*

Yeah, Trish said.

Oh right, yeah, I probably should do that, I muttered, holding my ring and thinking that intensely.

No response. Of course.

Well, at least you tried, Trish said. *Let's look at death as a remarkable journey we're taking together!*

Not helping, Trish, I replied.

"I've got it," Danny said. "You can all thank me! I have successfully acquired a map to the nearest space shuttle bay."

I stared at him. "As much as I'm grateful for that, Danny, I should point out that getting a map of a ship is not exactly hacking Space Command. Still, show us where it is and let's hope it's not being seized by a horde of angry spider-bots."

Danny looked a little deflated but transferred the ship's schematics and we had a straight line to the Emperor's private shuttle. Apparently, I was wrong about him keeping himself an exit strategy. It was possible, against all odds, that we were going to be able to make it through this without dying.

Goddammit Vance, Trish said.

Seriously, you're a machine, I said. *You can't believe in jinxes.*

That was when the gravity shut off and all of us started floating in the middle of the hallway. The lights flickered as well.

"WARNING—THE *EMPEROR'S REACH* HAS MULTIPLE HULL BREACHES, JUMPSPACE DRIVE INOPERABLE, WEAPONS AT FIFTY-ONE PERCENT CAPACITY, BARRIERS UNABLE TO KEEP UP WITH ASSAULT FIRE. EVACUATION OF THE SHIP IS NOW RECOMMENDED," the ship's AI spoke its words in a deeply monotone and empty voice.

See! Trish shouted in my mind. *I told you! God is real and hates us!*

No, if they hated us, we wouldn't be in this situation, I replied. *It's more like we're a mouse and they love playing with us until we die.*

"Everyone still have their magnetic boots?" I asked, referring to a standard issue piece of equipment on Space Fleet vessels.

"Yes," Shelly said. "I insisted even for our dress uniforms."

"If only we'd also kept our weapons," Forty-Two muttered.

"Use the boots to navigate the halls. We'll attach to the walls and then push off to speed up our momentum," I replied. "We have to get off this ship now. I think just about everyone is about to go for the remaining escape pods."

"Assuming the Emperor didn't jettison them to make sure the crew all died with him as part of his funeral pyre," Hannah said. "He was a really bad guy."

I wouldn't put that past the Emperor, but I hoped not. A lot of people were going to die no matter what happened, and this was my doing. I wouldn't have done anything differently if I'd known the difference and couldn't help but wonder if that made me a bad captain. I'd tried to do everything I could to save as many lives as possible, but I'd brought this doom down on us. Maybe it had prevented the Emperor's attempt at galactic genocide or maybe not. There was a very real chance I'd never know the truth if the ship blew up around us.

Focusing in on our situation, I tried to make use of my zero-gravity training and did what amounted to swimming moves to navigate down the halls. I could hear fighting in the nearby halls and the sounds of jetpacks, which meant at least some people were a lot better prepared for navigating this situation than we were.

"I think you should try to contact the Elder Races," Shelly spoke to me, navigating the hallway in an X pattern that was far more efficient than me. "While I disapprove of your contact with them, it's possibly the only way to save everyone here. I also want to state that I truly meant what I said back there. You've proven yourself to possess a magical touch, as much as I hate to admit it, and deserve to be captain. I also have to admit that some people think I am a bit too literal and rules minded."

"Shelly—" I started to say.

"No, let me finish," Shelly said. "I've misjudged you repeatedly and part of that was motivated by the fact you've only been in the navy eight years and yet you've ascended through the ranks rapidly. I blamed that on your ties to your aunt and that was unfair of me. Truth be told, I always resented feeling like I could have made use of my own personal ties, but didn't because of stubborn pride. By the time I actually felt my career stalled and that I should, my mother's name was mud due to her role in the failed negotiations at the end of the Notha War."

"Shelly—" I said, noticing we were almost to the end of the hallway. It was sealed by an enormous durateel blast door.

"But no one else could have done this and you've possibly prevented war with the Elder Races and also killed a terrorist mastermind. If we die here, at least we'll die trying to escape like Steve McQueen in *The Great Escape*. Which you probably haven't seen because you're only familiar with movies after the Nineteen Eighties but before the Two Thousand Fifties. I don't hold that against you and think I'd be willing to transfer to another ship because, long distance or not, I wouldn't be averse to a relationship with you. You'd have to stop having sex with Trish, though, because I don't share."

"Shelly," I finally said, reaching the doors. "First, I did contact the Elder Races. They didn't respond. Second, are you on drugs?"

Shelly giggled. "Sorry, zero-g has this weird effect on me. I get all talkative and prone to over-sharing."

Forty-Two and Hannah stared at her.

"What?" Shelly asked.

Danny moved down to the controls for the door and paused after a few seconds of trying to work them. "Uh, good news, bad news."

"There's no good news, is there?" I asked.

"Not as such," Danny said. "This requires the Emperor's personal password to get through this."

"Son of a…" I said, trailing off.

"I don't suppose you can teleport us through?" Shelly asked.

"Nope," I said. "I'm not even sure how I did the spear thing and I'm pretty sure that only worked because it was okay to have it end up inside what I was aiming it at. I try it on any of us without knowing where I'm going to moving us and we're almost certainly going to be scattered across the hangar bay."

Let me try to merge with it, Trish said. *With your ring, I can do it.*

Are you sure? I asked. *I thought you didn't have the computational power you had on the* Ares.

It's only opening a door, Trish replied. *Mind you, this fragment of my personality will cease to exist.*

What? You'll die? I asked, horrified.

Only this part of me, Trish said, trying and failing to reassure me. *It's been an honor, Vance.*

We'll find another way! I snapped. *I order you not to!*

Don't be ridiculous, Vance! Trish said. *I'm only a fragment. I—*

That was when the blast door unlocked and opened, revealing Elektra and Leah. They were both wearing stealth suits and I saw an entire team of Space Marines standing behind them, having secured the shuttle bay. There was a large hole where they'd blown an entrance into the chamber but repressured it with barrier generators. I could see the Emperor's shuttle, more like a yacht, ready and fueled for takeoff.

It wasn't hard to figure out what had happened. Leah—furious about being left behind and her whole mission being compromised—had picked up on the betrayal, and had seized command of my vessel from Light on Water or bullied him into going along with her orders. From there, she'd tried to figure out a way to get a rescue team to go after me. Probably the moment my ring was off, and she sensed I was in danger due to our involuntary (on my part) connection. They'd figured out the Emperor's personal hangar was the best place to enter and arrived just as the barriers were going down.

Wow, I was never going to hear the end of this.

Oh, I guess I don't have to heroically sacrifice myself, Trish said. *Darn.*

"Hi," Leah said. "You know this would have been a lot easier if you'd let me come with you and I'd been able to read the Emperor's mind."

Elektra waved. "Uh, I'm sorry for thinking you were a traitor. Leah explained you're going to be Prime Minister someday?"

I rushed past them. "Let's get the hell out of here."

Which was a good thing because the ship's AI stated the jumpdrive core was losing containment and would explode in ten minutes. Apparently, it had attempted a last-minute escape from this mess.

Too bad the Emperor's shuttle would probably take at least eight minutes to power up.

Plenty of time!

CHAPTER TWENTY-NINE

The *Return of the Jedi* Ending

"D o you actually know how to fly this thing?" Shelly asked, stepping into the copilot's seat of the Notha space yacht. It was a long dagger-shaped vessel that was actually rather cramped by human standards but had a jacuzzi and giant bed in the main passenger chamber, which told me everything about the Emperor's priorities.

"Fly? Yes. Land? No," I replied, sitting down and using my cybernetics to convert everything to English on the visual display.

"You're quoting a movie, aren't you?" Shelly asked.

"Obviously!" I said. "Besides, you referenced one while in zero g!"

"We shall never speak of what I said again!" Shelly said. "I was drunk!"

"You do not get drunk on zero g!" I snapped.

Behind us, all of the Space Marines Leah had brought had boarded along with Elektra. They had made the long journey across the void from the *Ares* with rocket packs and it had taken hours to get here, which wouldn't get them out of the ship's blast radius if it was about to blow. Our only hope was to hijack this thing.

Thankfully, it was a lot easier to hack since it didn't have the *Emperor's Reach's* AI fighting against Trish and we had it started almost immediately. Probably because the Emperor hadn't wanted to enter a lot of security protocols in his emergency evacuation vessel.

"Just so we're clear," Leah said, standing behind me as I commanded the hangar bay to depressurize and open up. "This is all your fault?"

"No!" I said, trying desperately to get the ship to lift off and us out of the *Emperor's Reach*. We were actually a little ahead of schedule but that meant it had been about six minutes getting this ship off the ground.

"Yes!" Shelly said. "He killed the Notha Emperor, summoned the Elder Races, and triggered a slave revolt that's going to get us all killed."

Leah didn't respond for a second. "I'm sorry, I know you Vance and yet somehow you keep surprising me by being an action movie hero."

"I helped!" Danny said. "I deserve like three medals for this."

"It's true, he does," I replied. "Hey, Danny, want to spend the rest of your life in hiding from Notha assassins for killing their deity?"

Danny didn't immediately respond. "I mean, sort of?"

I laughed, though not because of his statement but because the doors opened up into the void of space and our ship took off into the massive battle that was taking place outside. It was a conflict that crisscrossed the stars against the black void with green, red, white, and yellow energy beams as well as detonations that were like miniature supernovas. It was most definitely not a conflict between the *Emperor's Reach* versus the Elder Races but their ships against something completely new.

Strange shadowy ships that didn't seem entirely there to the naked eye and were only visible on some sensors were battling against the pyramidal, orb-like, and square ships of the Elder Races. There had been a Notha fleet present, presumably the Emperor's loyalists, but it had been almost totally destroyed with the only vessels left untouched being ones that were doing nothing more than picking up escape pods. It was a reminder the Notha were still officers and that there were people who cared about their fellow spacers.

"What the bork is going on out there?" Leah asked, staring at the sights on our sensor feeds.

"I think those are the Primordials," I responded, scanning for the *Ares* and hoping it had fled so we could leap away ourselves.

"The who?" Leah asked.

"Apparently, they're the other ancient scary group of space gods," I said.

"Why do you always add space to everything?" Leah asked.

"Reasons!" I snapped, finding the *Ares* lingering on the edge of the battle. It was motionless, no sign of having launched fighters or fired its weapons. It was still intact, thank God, and that was a miracle in and of itself.

A few energy beams passed perilously close to us, within a couple of hundred kilometers, and I couldn't help but wonder if we would be able to navigate our way across this horror show.

"We can return fire if you want," Leah asked, sounding as if she wanted to pick a fight with the Primordials and Elder Races both.

"No," I said, staring at the screen. "Change our ship registry to Community. Do not fire. Make no hostile moves and stay steady across the battlefield. Contact the *Ares* and identify ourselves. Tell them to get away if they can and we'll make our own departure."

"Done," Shelly responded. "Do you really think this is going to make a difference to the people fighting outside?"

"If they're going to shoot us then there's not a damn thing we can do about it," I muttered, pointing at the sensors.

"Yeah, those are almost off the charts," Shelly said, handling a lot of the piloting I wasn't able to do. Even with translation software showing me what I needed to touch and do, I was pretty beyond my skill set here. "Oh, and they're refusing."

"What? Who?" I asked, doing a double take.

"Acting Captain Leslie Park and acting first officer Julius Something," Shelly said. "Apparently, Light on Water recused itself after the shooting started."

"What do you mean they're refusing?" I asked, not so much surprised that some of my crew would step up via mutiny as that they were sticking around.

"They're not abandoning us at any cost," Shelly said.

I stared at her. "They do realize that we're in a jumpspace capable vessel ourselves and that they're not actually being heroic, just stupid, right?"

"I think that may have passed them by," Shelly said. "However, you do inspire a lot of loyalty."

"In some people," I replied.

"In all your crew," Shelly said, reassuring me.

"Don't feed his ego," Leah replied behind her. "It's already fat enough as it is."

"Says the woman who offered to make him Prime Minister," Shelly snapped.

"That's a fair cop," Leah said.

I'd like to say it was exciting to slowly travel through the battle, but it was significantly less so than you might imagine. EarthGov sensors added sound and alarms to make sure pilots were capable of understanding the situation they found themselves. The Notha system, by contrast, kept everything eerily silent. They only blinked lights with updates on movement, probability of death, and numbers. The tension in the air eventually broke after about fifteen minutes of travel that stretched into thirty before we reached the side of the *Ares*. I was ready to scream or throw up from the experience.

It was during that time, far after the originally projected core overload, that the *Emperor's Reach* did explode. Apparently, someone had tried some heroics to prevent the explosion, which allowed thousands of escape pods and shuttles to leave the vessel. I made a mental note to move the *Ares* out of the system and away from the battle but to keep it close so we could return and try to help any survivors. A lot of them would be Notha, but a lot of them wouldn't be and I didn't want to leave them for slavery at the remaining forces' hands, assuming they were hostile.

The *Emperor's Reach* didn't so much detonate in a mighty explosion as break in half, the vessel slowly disintegrating as systems failed throughout followed by ventilation of its decks. Even after its destruction, the massive machine was targeted by the Elder Races' vessels until it was reduced to ashes.

The fact they could waste their vessels on attacking an already destroyed vessel's remains told me who was winning the conflict and the Primordials were clearly on the back foot by the time our journey was at an end. The Primordials weren't retreating, though, and it looked like they would fight to the last man or vessel or whatever. I didn't even know if their ships had crews, were drones, or piloted by AI. Nor did I really care at this point. For all the fact Space Fleet had a mission to explore and meet other races, I only wanted to save my people right now.

It'll be alright, Vance, Leah responded to me.

How the hell are you communicating with me? I asked. *My ring should be blocking you.*

That's assuming it's your ring. Danny could have picked up any number of them, Leah said, knowing a disturbing amount of information about what my cousin had done. *Maybe you also want someone in your head other than your robot mistress.*

I am not a robot mistress! Trish snapped.

Okay, ground rules, my brain is not a party where everyone is invited, I replied. *Leah, I'd like to talk to you but Trish, I need you to stay out of this.*

Alright, Trish responded. *But I'm watching you, Countess!*

I turned to Shelly. "Attach to the nearest airlock, evacuate everyone and then we'll detach the Emperor's yacht."

"It could be a useful source of intelligence," Shelly said.

"Screw the intelligence," I said. "We're not sticking around to send a crew to remove the core."

"I'll try downloading as many files as possible into a partitioned server," Shelly replied. "Just in case."

I sighed. "Fine."

Neither the Primordials nor the Elder Races opened fire on this ship while it was escaping, Leah said mentally. *It's possible we're safe here. Maybe they do have a value for other races.*

Or we're beneath notice, I replied. *Why did you come after me?*

Because you're more valuable than you realize, Leah replied. *The fact you managed to pull any sort of victory out of this nightmare should tell you that. You are a man of many miracles, Vance Turbo.*

I am a man of dumb borking luck, I replied.

That too, Leah replied. *Also, Elektra wasn't going to abandon her sister. Once I sensed you were in danger, I had to do something.*

Well, thanks, I replied. *I owe you one.*

You owe me way more than one, Leah replied. *But I won't try and force you to be the Prime Minister anymore.*

And why is that? I asked.

The Human League was created by a fear of the Notha as well as becoming socially irrelevant, Leah asked. *This is going to cripple the Notha for another decade, if not cause a complete collapse of their empire. The social repercussions of their Emperor's death are not something easily measurable. I can tell you that if it happens, Albion will no longer be able to play on fear to keep itself in power. You may have just delayed the creation of a human empire for another century.*

Well, thank God for that, I replied. *Empires are inherently a savity idea. You have the people on the top and the people on the bottom when we all should be standing together.*

And sitting around a campfire singing "Kumbaya", Leah said, rolling her eyes. *No wonder you and Shelly get along. She was always every bit as stupidly idealistic.*

Thanks, I replied. *Will you be hanging around after this?*

I sincerely doubt it, Leah replied. *I have the mother of all reports to deliver once we've escaped. Which I owe you for.*

Then tell me, who did kill Michael Chang-Waverly, I asked. *I want to know who the spy on my ship is.*

It was crazy I was thinking about that now with Armageddon going on outside the vessel, but I was not going to forget someone had carried out a murder on my ship, however justified. Maybe it was someone who had wanted to cover up Michael's connection to his superiors or perhaps it was someone genuinely outraged by his desire to incite the Community against the Kolahn refugees. Either way, I had to know and figured if they were an intelligence operator then Leah would have the answers. Weirdly, I trusted her to tell me the truth under these circumstances.

Are you sure you want to know? Leah asked.

What an odd question. *Yes.*

She told me.

246

Bork, I replied, sick to my stomach. *That is certainly an answer. It will have to wait, though.*

What followed was an evacuation of every man and woman onboard the yacht and our entrance back into the familiar confines of the *Ares*. I'd never been so happy to find myself in its lavishly overdecorated, carpeted halls than I was in that moment. There were crew members ready to meet us and I couldn't help but hug and kiss Shelly when the yacht was finally detached, and the *Ares* made its jump from the battle. Shelly returned it and didn't seem at all embarrassed by the fact we were surrounded by our crew.

"Son of a witch, you really did it," Hannah said, behind me.

"Witch?" I asked.

"Yeah, they're old women who cast spells on my planet," Hannah said.

I blinked and shook my head. "Sure. I've heard of them."

Hannah gave a grimace. "You don't want to attract their attention. Curses are real, Vance. Actually, that would explain a lot of your life. Are you the seventh child of a seventh child?"

I laughed.

"I'm not joking," Hannah said, pouting.

"I'm demanding a promotion over this," Forty-Two said. "Either that or a cash bribe."

"I will see to it," I replied. "You definitely need another book deal and movie out of this."

"Agreed," Forty-Two said.

Danny didn't say anything, just stood beside me with an unreadable expression on his face. It was as if he couldn't quite believe we'd all managed to make it out of this alive. Neither could I, to be honest.

"I guess this means I'm transferring," Shelly said, hugging me.

"You'll be captain of your own ship after this," I replied. "But until then, I suggest we break the rules against fraternization as often as possible."

Shelly snorted. "Remember, it's not illegal in Space Fleet. It's just a mountain of paperwork."

"I'll even do it for you," I replied.

So, I guess this means we're not together anymore, Trish replied. *By the way, I've rejoined with the* Ares *Trish and have left your brain. I can't read your thoughts anymore unless you let me.*

You're my closest friend, Trish, literally, I said. *However, it's not you, it's me.*

You're damn right it's you! Trish replied. *Do you know how many men and women would kill to have a sexy ship to love them?*

I love you too, Trish, I replied. *But I have my reasons.*

I suspected she already knew what I was piecing together in my head. I wasn't going to confront her about it there, though. This was a moment of triumph and we had to savor it. I was going to put on my collected *Star Wars* orchestral score and get rip-roaring drunk once I was off duty. Unfortunately, I suspected given what we'd just been through, it would be the last time I had any free time for the next year.

Right, Trish responded. *I'll get back to my duties.*

The hallway's crowd of crew members grew around us and burst into spontaneous cheers as a realization we were all going to make it filled them. Discipline completely fell apart and it was days before things were back to what passed for normal.

That was when I needed to confront the murderer.

The spy on my ship.

EPILOGUE

I was standing in my quarters, looking at the stars streaking by on the "screensaver" that was used on my walls during jumpspace trips. The lights were on dim and light music was playing, *Star Trek VI: The Undiscovered Country*'s score. I had a cup of coffee in my hands, and I wished I had something stronger given what was going on. I'd just had to deal with a four hour meeting with the Admiralty Board that was still criticizing the events of the past mission almost a month later. We'd spent much of that time relocating Kolahn prisoners who had been onboard the *Emperor's Reach* as they'd been left behind by the Notha when they'd picked up most of the escapees.

Oddly enough, the new Notha government had turned over all the other prisoners to their home races with no slaves taken. Indeed, they had withdrawn from several of their worlds in Contested Space and opened negotiations with the Community. The death of the Emperor had caused a massive revolt that had eradicated the majority of the warrior caste and resulted in the installment of a civilian government. They were still contemptuous of other species and most of the negotiations had a tinge of isolationism, but it seemed like a policy of de-imperialization was underway.

Still, the Kolahn had gotten the short end of the stick and we'd had something like thirty-thousand people to relocate. The opening up of Contested Space had allowed me to insist that the warlords of Rand's World let the Kolahn occupy the southern continent along with all other Notha refugees. The so-called hyper-libertarians had freaked the hell out about that and passed a huge number of laws regarding them but the specter of EarthGov's Home Fleet over their head meant they'd reluctantly acquiesced. The refugees' numbers had since grown to two million and the Community had agreed to finish terraforming the world to a happy medium between the two species: which meant it would be hot, uncomfortable, and muggy for both.

Perfect.

Just as Leah had predicted, the Human League was in the process of dying on the vine with EarthGov and Belenus demanding too many concessions to leave behind their preexisting deals with the Community. Stronger ties among human worlds had occurred but many of them no longer felt it was necessary to do that at the expense of their economic deals with alien species. It would be months, if not years, before we found out what the long-term consequences were, but I was glad to see things settling down.

I had no idea what was going on with the Elder Races and the Primordials, but I'd requested EarthGov to send a probe to the star systems that the Emperor had supposedly built his arsenal of SKAMMs. I'd gotten their location from the downloads into my brain, albeit with some cross-referencing. All that remained in those systems was debris, so it seemed that the Primordial plot, whatever it was, was thwarted for the time being. That and there weren't a hundred thousand supernovas occurring across the galaxy.

There was no way to tell what was going on with the Primordials and Elder Races since we didn't have many eyes beyond Orion's Arm. Even the Ethereals had no answers as their masters had remained conspicuously silent about their recent struggles. If there was a massive war going on or negotiations, I had no idea, but it seemed like a conflict neither the Community nor EarthGov could afford to participate in. Hell, could remotely affect if we tried. Instead, we just had to hope whichever side emerged triumphant would leave us the hell alone. I'd not put my ring on since the escape from the *Emperor's Reach* and was terrified of the day when I was asked to once more do favors for Ketra's masters.

Still, I was left with one final unpleasant duty and that required me summoning a spy. He arrived through the doorway into my room with a confused look on his face. Beside him was Trish in her Space Cadet

Sally bioroid chassis. She knew exactly what this was all about but hadn't attempted to warn him. I appreciated that.

"Hello, Danny," I said, turning to my cousin.

"Hello, Captain," Danny said, looking confused. "You wanted to speak with me?"

"Yeah," I replied. "I did. Please come in."

Danny reluctantly did and sat down on the edge of my bed. "What is this all about?"

"The death of Michael Chang-Waverly," I said, "and your role in it."

Danny froze up then looked down, not denying it. "How did you figure it out?"

"I'm a genius," I replied.

"Leah told him," Trish corrected me. "Okay, also that he's a genius."

I stared at Danny. "If you were just a cadet then you wouldn't have been able to sneak around the *Emperor's Reach* and steal the Elder Ring back. You also have been sticking to me like glue since we disembarked. Probably because you were assigned to watch me. I also don't think your biomod is semi-functional at all."

Danny shrugged. "It is functional. You just can see past it sometimes. Probably because of your brain being altered. Also, I turn it off regularly to give the impression of it being nonfunctional."

I nodded. "How long have you been a spy?"

"I was recruited out of high school," Danny said. "A couple of years of training before they put me through special classes at the Academy. I meant what I said. I just got recruited by people who recognized my potential early. I never thought they'd want me to use it against you."

"And are you using it against me?" I asked.

"No," Danny said. "Yes. You're a hero, Vance. I hate to say it because I've been living in your shadow for a decade, but you are."

"Why did you kill Michael Chang-Waverly?" I asked. "He was done."

"Because it sent a message," Danny replied. "It told certain parties to back off and that their agent provocateurs would not be tolerated on EarthGov vessels. It was all on me."

"Actually, I know Trish helped you kill him," I replied, staring coldly at my cousin.

"Yeah," Trish spoke from Danny's side. "I know you figured that out pretty quickly."

I didn't look at her but focused on Danny. "People may be fooled by Trish's bubbly cute personality, but I am never going to forget she is the central programming core of a warship. Her job is to kill the enemy and protect her crew in that order."

"But—" Trish started to say.

"I'm presuming your implant allows you to fool an AI as well or perhaps you've got stealth technology to allow you to do so in addition, but that wouldn't keep you from being found out by Trish through secondary clues. Like, for example, Michael Chang-Waverly being found dead indicating there had been a murder. We found out Recruit Nak'la's death and followed it to its source after all."

"Maybe we reprogrammed her to look the other way." Danny didn't outright deny it but tried dodging the question, which told me he wasn't a very experienced spy.

"Then she'd be losing her mind and suffering damage the way she did on the *Black Nebula*," I replied. "Which she isn't. Ergo, she was part of it."

Trish looked down, unable to reply. If she was faking guilt, she was doing a very good job of it. "You don't know my reasons."

"You've been in my head, Trish," I said. "That means I've been in yours. You are with each and every single crew member 24-7 as well as know every detail available about them. You are also programmed to protect them and care for them. I daresay you know more about each of us than our own mothers. Especially mine."

"Do you mean Aunt Kathy or Aunt Svetlana?" Danny asked, referencing my long-dead drug addict of a biological mother.

I didn't divert from the subject. "So, I have no objection to the belief Trish is capable and willing to abet the murder of—"

"Execution," Trish interrupted, her voice cold and empty of remorse. "When you kill a murderer, it's an execution. EarthGov doesn't have a death penalty, but it's practiced within Space Fleet due the Sorkanan's influence. What that bastard did qualified as murder, treason, sabotage, and a half-dozen other crimes. He was working against Space Fleet, EarthGov, and basic justice by trying to frame the Kolahn for terrorism. And for what? Ratings? You wanted the same thing—"

"And yet you couldn't make that sort of decision yourself," I said, cutting her off. "I know the bounds of your programming and while you might want to kill Michael Chang-Waverly, you could only abet the murder if you were ordered to by someone who had the authority. I believe you'd do it for me, maybe, but I believe it came from someone significantly higher up than a captain. Something significantly higher up than a Watcher."

"I'm not a Watcher," Danny replied, sharper than I expected. "I may be a citizen of Earth but my loyalty is to the Community."

"Who are you working for?" I asked. I half expected it to be revealed to be Ketra but life was never that simple.

Danny took a deep breath. "Trish, would you please open up a channel to Department Zero? Alpha channel?"

Department Zero was the oversight committee for the entirety of the Security Departments. Crazzap.

A handsome man who had a weathered timeless quality about him with black hair, olive skin, and almost too perfect skin that had to be artificial in nature appeared on the viewscreen walls. His eyes were also artificial with a slight glow to them in the room's dim lights. He was wearing an Albion-style suit that was similar to the male fashions of the past two hundred years but just distinct enough to be recognizable as their own. He sat down across from me, and a waitress poured him a drink without asking.

"Hello," I said, confused by his presence.

"Hi, Daddy!" Trish said, waving.

"Daddy?" I asked. "Do you mean that in the creator sense or older lover?"

"Don't be gross," Trish said, snapping.

"Oh, I'm the one who gets flagged for being inappropriate now?" I asked, staring at her.

Trish snorted.

"I am Case Gordon, Director G, and head of the Security Departments of Earth," Case replied. "Nice to meet you."

"The world's oldest bioroid," I said. "Also, the world's oldest spy."

"Some trades never go out of style and experience is something that you never lose," Case said. "Nice to meet you, Vance."

"I wish it could have been under different circumstances," I said, looking at Trish then back at him. "How are you related to Trish?"

"It's more an honorific," Case said.

"He raised Patricia Ares and funded her initial work with artificial intelligence," Trish explained.

"Sadly, she died as all humans do," Case said. "Though not before her failed upload attempt became the basis of Trish's program."

"Wait, what?" I asked, doing a double take. "Patricia became Trish?"

This conversation was not going the direction I expected.

"Oh, didn't I mention that?" Trish asked.

"You said her work lived on in you," I replied. "I didn't think you were being literal."

Trish gave a shrug.

"She's spoken highly of you," Case said. "Albeit with the kind of rambling text usually belonging to a teenage girl rather than a godlike artificial intelligence."

"I've helped save the universe," Trish said. "I'm allowed to act like a teenage girl."

I was too upset to let myself be distracted. "You conducted wetwork on my ship. You turned my cousin against me. To use him to spy on me. You got Trish to deceive me. We are not friends."

Case snorted. "Trish provides all the information we need about you and it's not like you're nearly as secretive as you think you are. For example, I know Shelly is hiding in the bathroom and recording all this."

"Goddammit," Shelly muttered from inside and stepped out. She was wearing her regular uniform and looked annoyed. Her fusion pistol was on her holster, a clear sign I'd expected trouble. "See, I told you it wasn't going to work."

"I just was glad to have you as backup," I replied.

"Wait, you thought I was going to kill you?" Danny asked, stunned.

"I thought you might be a *Terminator*-like bioroid ready to tear me apart," I replied. "Sorry."

"Danny isn't there to spy on you, Vance, quite the opposite," Case said. "Danny is your bodyguard."

"My what now?" I asked, stunned.

"Michael Chang-Waverly told you everything he did because he had orders to arrange for your death after you pinged him," Case said, his voice low and like gravel. "There's plenty of people who consider you a symbol for the integration of humanity into the larger galactic community. Primarily because I made you into one, same as your aunt Kathy."

"What?" Shelly asked.

"What?" I asked.

"I knew her when she was just a teenage astronaut working for Space-X," Case said. "The Cognition AI of Earth have been working to smooth out humanity's self-destructive, isolationist, and tribalist natures for centuries. That includes providing them heroes and inspiration to guide them down the right path. You and she just got tapped for it."

"Why me?" I asked, stunned.

Case shrugged. "Eh, you remind me of a guy I knew named Gary. Why not you? Either way, we need your help to keep things going well. We can't affect the war between the Primordials and the Elder Races, that's several dimensions above our paygrade, but we have plenty of enemies here."

"We're not helping you with anything," Shelly said, glaring. "I don't care if you are in charge of Earth's intelligence service."

Case stared at us both. "Did you ever figure out who destroyed New Pompeii?"

"It was the Emperor," I lied. "It's what I said with my ring to the Elder Races, presuming anyone was listening."

"I'm sure they believed you," Case said. "We don't have many devices that can pick up Elder Race chatter, but the Cognition AI of Earth can understand most of it. It's how we know the Elder Races are all transorganic beings. Downloaded consciousnesses into machine bodies that have made themselves immortal. It's partially why they have spared humanity and the Community. They hope to add more races to their ranks. Garden us like flowers until we merge with our machinery. In that respect, Earth is the Community's best hope. So were the Kolahn but someone, possibly the Primordials, sabotaged their efforts and got them all but destroyed. Just like they helped other parties destroy New Pompeii."

I stared at him. "You're saying the Emperor didn't do it?"

"No, his sponsors," Case said. "Albion agents destroyed New Pompeii. They believed it would trigger a massive upswing in anti-alien sentiment and isolationism that would benefit their plans to create a Human Empire."

"Bork," I said, running my hands through my hair. The Elder Races could never find out about that, or it would result in the deaths of billions. It was, however, entirely believable.

"You believe him?" Shelly asked.

"Don't you?" I asked her.

Shelly didn't respond.

"What do you want from me?" I asked.

"Your help," Case said. "You and your misfit crew."

I sighed. "You have it."

No one can serve two masters, but it seemed like I had four or five: the Community, EarthGov, the Elder Races, and now Department Zero. I took a long drink of coffee as I debated what I was going to do next.

Case nodded. "I'd assign Agent Mass to help you but she's going to be busy on Crius for the next year, plus the next couple with her baby. Congratulations."

I choked on my coffee and Shelly did a double take between us.

"What?" I asked.

Case blinked. "Oh, well I just assumed you two knew you were the two DNA donors she chose. Taking yours from our files for this is really a horrible breach of ethics."

"What?" Shelly added.

Look for the next book:
SPACE ACADEMY WASHOUTS
Book Three of the Space Academy Series

LEXICON

AI: Artificial intelligence. Science fiction has talked about these a few times.

Accelerated Civilian Training Initiative Organization and Nationalization (ACTION): A program designed to rapidly expand the Earth Home Fleet and Community-lent forces by recruiting civilian spacers. The acronym is nonsensical to ninety-nine percent of the Known Universe.

Admiralty Board: The head of Space Fleet for Earth and those who supervise its link to other navies as part of the Community.

Albion: An island-filled water planet settled by humans abducted by aliens. The most powerful human planet, currently losing ground to Earth.

Amaterasu: A powerful world descended from Japanese settlers. It is a rival to Albion and has the most powerful human-based space navy.

Anansi: An industrialized manufacturing world known for its direct democracy and being a traditional enemy of Albion.

Anyxhole: Linguistic drift from exactly the word you think it is.

Ares Electronics: An Albion-based corporation that manufactures most of the starships, bots, and bioroids in the universe.

Artificial gravity: A slang term for something people think is possible but is not. Even the Community just generates the real thing with a variety of tricks.

Bastarve: Another word for bastard. Swearing isn't very original on Albion.

Belenus: A wealthy environmentally-friendly paradise world also settled by humans abducted by aliens. Traditional rivals to Albion.

Biomods: Genetic enhancements that provide sapient beings with special abilities. Usually organic technology rather than cybernetics to avoid rejection.

Bioroids: Androids and gynoids indistinguishable from humans with synthetic flesh. Often used for exactly what you think.

Blood and Honor: The second hit movie about Vannever Tagashi's adventures. It is wildly inaccurate and full of sex as well as violence. It is also endorsed by the EarthGov military.

Bork: A weirdly popular curseword.

Bots: Robots. Crazy, I know, right?

Brigid: Sister-world to Belenus and producing most of the infrastructure that keeps its brother world in wealth.

Bug: A race of (seemingly) giant ant-like aliens that are terrifying as well as strong. It turns out those were chasses for a much, much smaller race.

Chel: A race of humans uplifted by the Elder Races and their own experimentation. They live entirely in space and resemble classical depictions of Grays. Named for Doctor Chel who sent his transhumanist cult out into space.

Cognition AI: Nearly omnipotent AI that can process unlimited amounts of data. Pretty much the real rulers of the Community. But so friendly!

Community: An interstellar fellowship of many species and worlds. It is generally pro-democracy, civil rights, diversity, and technology. Of course, no one trusts it or its activities.

Community Protectors: See Space Fleet.

Community Senate: A collection of representatives of the various worlds of the Community. Many planets dislike it because it impedes their own ambitions while others hate the fact it is dominated by the High Council.

Contested Space: A region of space between the Community and Notha Empire. It is full of outlaw settlements, pirate bands, and half-terraformed hellholes or collapsed civilizations.

Crazzap: Crap by another name is just as stinky.

Crius: A planet being settled by transhumanists wanting to create a feudal paradise. A planet of genetically engineered slaves ruled by a bunch of deranged cloners. Go here to be hunted by dinosaurs.

Death bubble: A Notha vehicle that is in the shape of a sphere and is used to strafe battle fields.

Demihumans: Humans who no longer are strictly human due to evolution and genetic modification.

Department Twelve: One of the twelve intelligence services of the Protectorate. Department Twelve is the most devoted to counterterrorism, provocation, and destabilization. Many blame it for the horrific consequences of the Notha War.

Department Zero: The supervisory department of the twelve intelligence services of the Protectorate. Each race has its own department head that more or less directs their functions independently of one another but cooperates. Albion is irritated that humanity's director has moved from there to Earth.

Devil Dog gunship: A troop transport ship developed by EarthGov that was rapidly replaced by better designed machines then sold into civilian service. Many ended up in the hands of pirates, criminal organizations, and independent powers like the Kolahn.

Dixnar: The corporation that produces virtually all entertainment for humanity. It has somehow absorbed many older races' corporations.

Drolochid: Slimy, warm-blooded multi-limbed race, with sensory organs across their pill-bug bodies. Quite pleasant to be around.

Earth: The human homeworld. Perhaps you've heard of it. The new kids on the block. Way too eager to prove itself.

EarthGov: The government of Earth. Duh.

Earth Home Fleet: Earth's personal defense force. It is separate from the ships it loans to permanent Community duty.

Elder Races: Several godlike "sufficiently advanced" aliens who live in the galactic core and decide what races live or die without any understandable criteria. Real jerks.

Emperor's Reach: A fourteen-kilometer-long vessel in the shape of a horizontal obelisk. It was constructed to be the Notha flagship and personal vessel of their Emperor fifty years before but has since been the center of his exile. It has been continuously upgraded ever since despite lack of parts.

Enigmatic Path: A Kolahn terrorist organization and religious fundamentalist group. Its bizarre ideology is about how organic life is an abomination, AI should be liberated, and the universe is a simulation.

Ethereal humans: A group of humans uplifted by the Elder Races to be intermediaries with them and other organics. They and Ethereal versions of other races tend to lead the Community in its decision-making process.

Freya: A swampy pleasure planet that is known for the most decadent luxuries in the Spiral (among humans at least) as well as a variety of dangerous diseases.

Genemods: A slang term for those who have been genetically modified from baseline humanity or other species.

Grounder: A slang term for those who grew up and primary live on planets.

Gulayan Limit: A technological limit that all races in the galaxy but the Elder Races suffer. It keeps technology on rough parity and is believed to be enforced by outside parties as well as Community pressures.

Gravitonic emitters: The poor man's substitute of artificial gravity that moves around weight and is a necessity for casual space travel.

High Council: The representatives of the most powerful worlds in the Community.

Homefront Allied Networks (HAN): A deeply reactionary pro-human, pro-Earth holovision transtellar that caters extensively to trends and biases. Oddly, it is surprisingly popular among alien immigrants to Earth.

Known Universe: Explored space that turns out to be primarily just Orion's Arm.

Kolahn: Resemble giant apes with scales. Their civilization was overtaken by a terrorist cult and promptly bombed back to the stone age by the Community. Its survivors are, paradoxically, living as refugees among the Community.

Kolahn IV: The Kolahn Homeworld, known to its people as "Ground", but the fourth planet in its solar system. It was rendered uninhabitable during the Kolahn Wars.

Kolahn Resettlement Project: A controversial attempt to resettle billions of refugees from the devastated Kolahn homeworld.

Kolahn Wars: The aforementioned wars that bombed the Kolahn back to the Stone Age.

Ko'ltah **frigate**: An L-shaped Sorkanan frigate used by the Kolahn and other independent worlds.

Infospace: A extra-dimensional communications system that allows faster-than-light communication and works like an interstellar internet.

Jumpdrive: What allows people to travel through space like in movies.

Jumpspace: A dimension of bizarre physics that makes faster-than-light travel possible. Looking at it will drive most people insane due to the way it stimulates your synapses.

Longevity treatments: Expensive cellular regeneration techniques that can halt the aging process and even reverse it to an extent. It can raise human lifespans up to four hundred years. Unavailable to most of the populace in their best form but even then, human lifespans have expanded to two hundred years in "civilized" space.

Llrowlthra: Large grasshopper-like aliens who live lives free of technology but seem peculiarly aware of everything going on in the galaxy. Called "Space Amish" by humans for reasons most species do not understand. Also, Grasshoppers because humans are racist.

Luna: Earth's moon. It is largely used for the construction of spacecraft for civilian and military spacecraft as well as other advanced electronics incapable of being manufactured on Earth.

Lunar Shipyards: Pretty much what the name suggests. Most of Luna has been hollowed out for it.

MacArthur-**class vessel**: A corvette and light patrol craft produced by humanity in the early days of faster-than-light travel.

New Aberdeen: A small farming planet near but not in Contested Space.

New Pompeii: A half-terraformed world in Contested Space being used by the Community to resettle refugees from the Kolahn Wars.

Many humans resented this because the world was originally meant for human expansion.

Notha: Adorable lemur-like race of Space Nazi bastards.

Notha Empire: A corrupt military dictatorship ruled by the Notha that practices slavery, imperialism, planet looting, and conquest. It maintains its existence not by competence but due to the possession of weapons of stellar destruction.

Notha civil war: A conflict presently being fought between the Notha High Command and various generals over who should inherit the spot of the Great Notha.

Notha War: A conflict that resulted in the destruction of seventeen inhabited planets on both sides of the conflict due to an exchange of SKAMMs.

Nova starfighters: Earth's first successful starfighters that look like V's with engines. They are more durable than Wraith fighters with better barriers.

Olothonalka: 9 ft. tall gastropods, with six eyes on motile stalks. Patterned on back and torso. 3 genders (male, female, and mass egg-laying). No arms but the entire lower surface is manipulative. Most humans just call them Snails.

Olympia Colonies: A transtellar that terraforms worlds and builds colonies for humanity. It is now mostly defunct after the creation of Contested Space.

Olympic-**class vessel**: An incredibly powerful EarthGov vessel that is just barely a mid-tier vessel by Community standards.

Plizzed: A state of fluid retention. Used as a pejorative.

Primordials: An extra-galactic race that has severe issues with the Elder Races. They are from the Canus Major Dwarf Galaxy and formerly inhabited the Milky Way a billion years ago before fleeing. Their vessels exist in both jumpspace and realspace simultaneously.

Rand's World: A former colony world of Earth where the terraforming was stopped mid-process due to Notha aggression. It is now primarily inhabited by criminals, pirates, and separatists. Named for Ayn Rand.

Security Departments: The twelve, yes, twelve intelligence agencies working for the Community.

Savit: Excrement. Usually used as a pejorative.

SKAMMs: Sun-destroying weapons of interstellar destruction. They are horrifying devices and their use in the recent Notha War resulted in an immediate end to the conflict lest the two sides annihilate one another.

Sklux: A race of protoplasmic beings that can shape into a rough approximation of any form. Obsessed with puns. Considered a race of mediators and peacemakers, primarily by themselves.

Sorkanan: One of the oldest and most powerful species in space. They are a humanoid reptilian species with multiple offshoots.

Sorkanan Imperial Navy: The massive fleets of the Sorkanan Empire. Its conditions are horrifying, and morale is generally low, but it is still the greatest power in the Spiral.

Space Academy: The training center for officers in the Community Protectors.

Spacer: A slang term for those who have grown up and primarily live in space.

Space Cadet Sally: A popular children's show with a large adult following. Space Cadet Sally has often been accused of being Space Fleet propaganda.

Space Fleet: The Community's massive interstellar navy that is (allegedly) a galactic force for good.

Spider-Bots: Quadrupedal four-armed security devices used by the Notha as frontline soldiers.

Spider-Tank: The Notha's most common vehicle for deployment on the field of battle. Despite its name, it actually can hover and even fly to a certain degree.

Spider-Shuttle: The Notha's space shuttles. They look like spiders. They have a real spider thing going on.

The Spire: What Orion's Arm is called by most races of the Known Universe as they are primarily concentrated there.

Starkiller-**class vessel**: A stealth ship class used for launching SKAMM missiles produced by EarthGov.

Sun Killer: Another name for SKAMM torpedoes.

Thor: An impoverished planet with a population of blue-skinned humans that deals with cold as well as radiation daily.

Transstellar: The name for interplanetary corporations that are possessed of resources far more than individual worlds. They wield disproportionate power in the Community and among humanity's various worlds.

Treaty of Exarxes: A large multispecies agreement on shared morality and behavior during wartime. The Notha are a very reluctant signatory. A second treaty was drafted to ban the use of SKAMMs and other weapons of mass destruction at Elder Races insistence.

Verdantian: A leonine race with six limbs that were uplifted by the Elder Races according to their belief structure.

Wah'Pang **battle cruiser**: A kilometer-long vessel designed by the Kolahn with the help of the Notha. They have immensely powerful barriers at the price of poor fusion cannons. It compensates with a heavier load of missiles.

Wraith fighters: Notha designed starfighters that are more fragile but faster and more maneuverable than human ones. They resemble eyeballs and the starfighters of a certain Earth science fiction galactic empire.

AUTHOR'S NOTE

I'd like to thank you for reading this book. The publishing industry is changing dramatically since the advent of eBooks. It is now very difficult to get any book noticed, regardless of quality. If you enjoyed this book, you could do some very simple things to help me attract attention. Word of mouth is the number one source of success for novels, so simply telling family and friends about the book is a great start.

Here are a few other ways of helping out, if you are so inclined:

* **Post a rating or review where you purchased the eBook**
* **Post a rating or review on Goodreads**
* **Talk about the book or write a review on Facebook**
* **Tell folks about the book in a blog post.**

If you like any of my other books, please feel free to check them out. A lot of my series are interlinked, and you never know when you'll find someone familiar showing up. In this case, *Space Academy Dropouts* is set in the far future of my Agent G cyberpunk books and the past of my *Lucifer's Star* series. Fans will certainly get a kick out of seeing how the galaxy changes in a few centuries either way.

ABOUT THE AUTHORS

Frank Martin is an author and comic writer that is not as crazy as his work makes him out to be. A fan of storytelling in all its forms, Frank always enjoys exploring new genres and mediums. He currently lives in New York with his wife and three kids. You can check out updates for all of Frank's writing at frankthewriter.com, on his Facebook page at facebook.com/frankmartinwriter, or follow him on Twitter and Instagram @frankthewriter.

Bibliography

A Weapon's Journey
Modern Testament (comics)
Mountain Sickness
Skin Deep/Ordinary Monsters

Dark Destiny (Dark Destiny, Vol. 1)
Destiny's Paradox (Dark Destiny, Vol. 2)

Space Academy Dropouts (The Space Academy Series, Book 1)
Space Academy Rejects (The Space Academy Series, Book 2)

Space Academy Washouts (The Space Academy Series, Book 3)

C. T. Phipps is a lifelong student of horror, science fiction, and fantasy. An avid tabletop gamer, he discovered this passion led him to write and turned him into a lifelong geek. He is a regular blogger and also a reviewer for The Bookie Monster.

Bibliography

Novels
The Rules of Supervillainy (Supervillainy Saga #1)
The Games of Supervillainy (Supervillainy Saga #2)
The Secrets of Supervillainy (Supervillainy Saga #3)
The Kingdom of Supervillainy (Supervillainy Saga #4)
The Tournament of Supervillainy (Supervillainy Saga #5)
The Future of Supervillainy (Supervillainy Saga #6)
The Horror of Supervillainy (Supervillainy Saga #7)
Tales of Supervillainy: Cindy's Seven (Supervillainy Saga #7)

I Was a Teenage Weredeer (The Bright Falls Mysteries, Book 1)
An American Weredeer in Michigan (The Bright Falls Mysteries, Book 2)
A Nightmare on Elk Street (The Bright Falls Mysteries, Book 3)

Esoterrorism (Red Room, Vol. 1)

Eldritch Ops (Red Room, Vol. 2)
The Fall of the House (Red Room, Vol. 3)

Agent G: Infiltrator (Agent G, Vol. 1)
Agent G: Saboteur (Agent G, Vol. 2)
Agent G: Assassin (Agent G, Vol. 3)

Cthulhu Armageddon (Cthulhu Armageddon, Vol. 1)
The Tower of Zhaal (Cthulhu Armageddon, Vol. 2)

Lucifer's Star (Lucifer's Star, Vol. 1)
Lucifer's Nebula (Lucifer's Star, Vol. 2)

Straight Outta Fangton (Straight Outta Fangton, Vol. 1)
100 Miles and Vampin' (Straight Outta Fangton, Vol. 2)
Vampiraz4Life (Straight Outta Fangton, Vol. 3)

Wraith Knight (Wraith Knight, Vol. 1)
Wraith Lord (Wraith Knight, Vol. 2)
Wraith King (Wraith Knight, Vol. 3)

Dark Destiny (Dark Destiny, Vol. 1)
Destiny's Paradox (Dark Destiny, Vol. 2)

Brightblade (The Morgan Detective Agency, Book 1)

Space Academy Dropouts (The Space Academy Series, Book 1)
Space Academy Rejects (The Space Academy Series, Book 2)
Space Academy Washouts (The Space Academy Series, Book 3)

Psycho Killers in Love

Anthologies (as editor)
Blackest Knights

Blackest Spells
Tales of Capes and Cowls
Tales of the Al-Azif
Tales of Yog-Sothoth

Curious about other Crossroad Press books? Stop by our website:
http://crossroadpress.com
We offer quality writing
in digital, audio, and print formats.

Subscribe to our newsletter on the website homepage and receive a
free eBook.

www.ingramcontent.com/pod-product-compliance
Lightning Source LLC
Chambersburg PA
CBHW030237200626
46816CB00002BA/407